Why?

"Why did my father leave me?"

Kiersten Lewis

Chapter 1

"Nina"

Hi, my name is Nina! Yes, this book is about me, but not just about me. This is more about my life. I'm 15 years old and growing up I've always been a rather curious child; Curious about this, curious about that, you know? Have *you* ever just wanted to know **WHY**? Well…. maybe you'll find out. I sure am hoping to find out **WHY my father left me.**

Chapter 2

"Father"

There's four of us… Well, there <u>was</u> four of us. There used to be me, Josie, Mama, and Father. Now there's just me, Mama, and Josie. Josie is my little sister. I was told Josie was named after my Father, Joey. Mama's name is Carol. Father used to be around a lot until he left. Every other Thursday he'd let me skip school. Then we would go out for dinner at the best restaurant in town, "Harmon's Palace". You know, Mama never told me why he left. Sometimes, I like to think maybe my father was curious. Maybe he wanted to explore parts of the world with a new family. But "WHY"? Father has a family…. Well, at least <u>had</u>. Now, it just feels like he doesn't exist. Why would he leave me and mama? Why would he leave me and Josie? Why?

Chapter 3

"Mama"

I believe my Mama feels like she has to be the superhero of the family. Probably because she thinks she needs to be there for me and Josie. Sometimes she overworks herself. I...I just wish she would slow down sometimes. I don't tell her because, maybe it keeps her mind off Father leaving. She acts like it's okay, but I see the pain and frustration she suffers from. I think she acts this way because she doesn't want me and Josie to worry. She refers to Father a lot, whether we're out eating or inside playing. She always says stuff like, "*This is something Joey would've liked to do.*" If it really hurts her that he's gone, why does she act like it's okay? Why doesn't she just tell me what happened? Why can't she see I'm here for her? Why?

Chapter 4

"Josie"

Josie is eight. She's the sweetest little girl you could ever meet with a side of sass. Overall, she's pretty cool. Honestly, Josie has never met Father. I was seven when he left. Mama was just pregnant with Josie during the time. She didn't get to experience what I felt when he left. Josie loves hearing stories about me and Father. She always goes to school and tells everyone how great Father is, even though she never met him. I don't think Josie cares about our father leaving. I just think she's eager to meet him. That's if he comes back. But why would he leave with Mama being pregnant with Josie? Why?

Chapter 5

"Harmon's Place"

I used to love coming here every Thursday with my Father. Mainly because I got to skip school, but also because I loved the food. Mama used to work here at Harmon's Palace before she became a doctor. Father was a therapist. The man who owns the place was Father's best buddy. That's one of the reasons why Father took me here to hang out with me and Mr. Harmon. Mr. Harmon comes around the house a lot to check up on Mama. He and Father used to watch the football game a lot when Father was here. Mr. Harmon and Father were both jokesters. Father was always funnier. Mr. Harmons is a nice man. I guess I didn't think he would still come around now that Father is gone, but he's mama's friend too. So that explains it. When Mr. Harmon comes around, he doesn't stay for long. He usually comes to bring food from the restaurant. He chats with us for a while then leaves. Josie seems to love him. She always asks questions like, "*Is he anything like Father?*" I tell her, "*Yes, he is!*" I get the feeling that he may know something about Father leaving. I get this feeling because when Mama refers to Father, Mr. Harmon looks as if he didn't mean for him to leave. If he knows, why can't he just tell me and Josie? Why can't he just tell me? Why?

Chapter 6

"School"

I go to Milo High. I love my school. When I was younger, I went to Milo Academy, which is where Josie goes. I have a friend group, which consists of Hannah, Jadah, and I. They're pretty cool. I've known them my whole life. Hannah is Mr. Harmon's daughter. She helps her Father out at the restaurant sometimes. Jadah is Hannah's cousin. We're all pretty close. When Father left it, was pretty hard on me, but they were there to lift me up. We all take French together with our favorite teacher Mrs. Shai. Mrs. Shai was there for me too when Father left. She and Father were pretty close. I remember the day Father took me, Jadah, and Hannah out for ice cream. Father told me that they were good girls. Jadah's father died when she was three. Jadah once said, "Mr. Joey is like a father to me," which was not hard to believe because my father was like a father to many people. He made people feel like family. That was the kind of man he was. School has never been a problem for me. I am a straight A student and so are my friends. Sometimes, it is hard to focus though because I'm always thinking about my father. That's when Hannah comes in. We take the most classes together. She has a very bright personality. But if Mr. Harmon is her dad, and he knows something about Father leaving, she must know too. But why not tell me? I mean, after all, I am her best friend. So why?

Chapter 7

"Clueless"

Nothing interesting has happened in my life since Father left. I mean, even if something exciting comes up, it's just so hard to even try to have fun. You know, I try every day to figure it out. Why would Father leave? If only I knew. If only <u>they</u> knew how it felt to have your father leave and not know anything about it. People don't just leave, or do they? Growing up my father would always tell me, "Nina, the more you dig, the more you'll find." I feel like that's not true anymore. I've tried for **eight years** to figure out why he left, and why not one person would tell me about it. I just wish there was a sign that would lead to his disappearance, because right now I'm clueless.

Chapter 8

"Church"

I feel like going to church puts me closer to Father, mainly because he was a big church guy. We didn't go to church every Sunday, but we went. Father loved the Lord, which made me love the Lord. Sometimes, I may be sitting in church and start to think about my father. Then I wonder why God allowed him to leave. I don't fault God for my father leaving because Father once said that God does things for a reason. So maybe that's it, I just have to figure out the reason; but maybe there's more to it. Josie always falls asleep in church, like she did today. Mama usually wakes her up. My Mama's the reason we kept going to church after Father left. She said, "*Joey would have liked us to get closer to the Lord.*" Mama and Father were super close, so I don't understand why he would leave. Why would Father leave? Again, why?

Chapter 9

"Home"

Home has been pretty quiet without Father here. Mama was trying to tell us about her day while she cooked, but I could only think about what Father's day was like. Josie couldn't stop staring at the TV long enough to listen. I wish Josie could have met him before he left. She could have seen how awesome he was. Mr. Harmon came by today and ate with us. Josie sat in his lap and laughed at his jokes, while I just smiled at them. Mama said it sounded like something Joey would've said, and then left the dinner table. Mr. Harmon followed, so I did too. I figured maybe they would say something about Father. Turns out I was right. Mama was crying, which was weird because she usually kept a smile on her face. I found some stuff out that made me question Mr. Harmon and Mama for a second.

His name was Joe, which I thought was strange because he was always referred to as Mr. Harmon. I didn't think much of it because I couldn't stop thinking about what Mama said. She said, "*I can't keep doing this Joe, Nina needs to know the truth.*" Why would Mama lie?

Chapter 10

"The Reason"

When Mama came out of the room, she and Mr. Harmon stared in disbelief and asked what all I had heard. I stood up with tears in my eyes because I had finally figured out why my father left. I would have left too. I asked them both what was the reason Father left, even though I figured it out and went to my room. Mama called my name as I ran up the stairs. I didn't care because I finally knew the reason.

Chapter 11

"The Truth"

It hurt so much to know what happened to Father. I didn't hate Mama for not telling me, but I didn't favor her either. Guess this is what she meant when she said that Josie is named after her Father. Guess this is why Father left when Mama got pregnant. Guess this is why Mr. Harmon didn't tell me why Father left. I have my answers. The only question now is who Josie's father is. Joe or Joey? But now I know the truth.

Meet the Author

Kiersten Lewis, born and raised in Mississippi, is a naturally talented gymnast, singer, and author.

"Why?" is her debut book as a teen author.

Zoë Life Publishing

Zoë Life Publishing is a publishing imprint that releases titles committed to offering encouragement and that are life transforming. We desire for our titles to impact readers in a way that is beyond entertainment; a way that will bring healing, restoration, or even productivity to one's life. Our catalogue includes now children's titles, notebooks, and journals.

Scan the QR code below to visit our website today view our catalogue and services.

Waltz on the Big Meadow

by

Dorothy A. Bell

Waltz on the Big Meadow

Cover Art by *Tina Lynn Stout*

The Wild Rose Press, Inc.
PO Box 708
Adams Basin, NY 14410-0708
Visit us at www.thewildrosepress.com

Publishing History
First Edition, 2024
Trade Paperback ISBN 978-1-5092-5262-6
Digital ISBN 978-1-5092-5263-3

Published in the United States of America

"You don't care for socials, Mrs. Obenchain? We are bringing in a new century tonight. This should be a joyous occasion—a once-in-a-lifetime occasion. Surely you don't want to miss out."

"I…I think socials are very nice," she said, avoiding his gaze. Stammering, she continued, "I…I can't believe it's the twentieth century…but…but you see…"

"Ah, but I think I do see. You don't care to come to the social and listen to all the welcome speeches on my behalf," he said, one eyebrow raised. If she'd look him in the eye, she'd know he was teasing. "I have a very fragile ego, Mrs. Obenchain. I find it very lowering to my self-esteem. You, my own landlady, don't want to attend a party that, in part, is being given in my honor. How would it look, Mrs. Obenchain? No…I don't think it's to be allowed. You have a duty to perform, Mrs. Obenchain, as do I. We'll go together."

Picking up his spoon, he said, "Good, now that's settled. I would be honored to carry your delicious pies. In return you will lend me your support. I will be meeting a room full of strangers and curiosity seekers. Mrs. Laidlaw has made it clear I am to be made the main attraction. I will need you there to help when I wish to escape."

He watched her shrink back into her chair. He could almost feel sorry for her, but he didn't intend to leave her behind to play the martyr. No.

Chapter One

Central Oregon 1897

Head down, Irene Obenchain scurried across the road and entered the narrow path between the saloon and the blacksmith. At the end of the path, she rushed up the dry, rutted lane to Meda-Belle Lamphere's brothel, also known for miles around simply as the boarding house. Coming to a halt on the stone walkway before the wide steps of the grand veranda, she mustered her courage. *Odessa needs shoes. We need food for the table. I have to do this. I must speak with Mrs. Lamphere—today.*

Cool lips pressed tightly together, she reached for the bell to the side of the door. She paused with her hand suspended above her head, staring at the ominous words burnt into the wooden sign on the porch wall.

RING BELL BEFORE NOON AT YOUR PERIL!

Irene shut her eyes and gave the leather thong a hard yank. The sound of the bell echoed in the cool morning air. In response, coming from the opened window above the veranda, a woman's shrill voice shouted, "Go 'way. Can't you read?"

Irene waited, indecisive. Her stomach growled and cramped. She stared at the closed door, gathered her courage, and yanked on the cord.

From overhead, cursing, the woman's voice responded. "Read the sign, numbskull."

Defiant, Irene gave the bell cord another tug. She nodded with satisfaction when she heard from within the house women swearing and the slamming of more than one door.

Braced, she stood her ground.

"I don't give a tinker's damn who does what to who," Irene heard a woman say.

The woman with the stronger voice volleyed back, "Grace, you look like a sun-dried cowpat, smell like one, too. Go soak your stinkin' head. Paulette, go back to bed. I'll take care of this peckerwood."

Irene heard someone clomping down stairs. "Hold your water," a woman's voice said behind the closed door.

Red-faced and hopping mad, Mrs. Lamphere, whom Irene had seen many times from afar, jerked open the door. She glanced down the alley before she turned her ocean-blue eyes back to Irene. Relaxing her shoulders, the spectacle appeared to shed her rage, her mouth letting go of its grimace. She leaned her supple body against the doorjamb and folded her arms across her snowy white bosom.

Irene didn't care for the speculative gleam in those calculating blue eyes. They shifted from the top of her head down to her scruffy old shoes. A smirk twisted her lipstick-stained mouth into a grotesque bow, and it took everything Irene had not to turn tail and run. Holding her sign to her chest like a shield, she heard the little whimpering voice in her head, *Shoot, terrible idea. Stupid, stupid. Shouldn't be here?*

The black satin sleeping mask plastered across Mrs. Lamphere's forehead accentuated the unnatural reddish-pink color of her hair and creamy-white complexion.

Cowed, mouth pasty dry, Irene lowered her gaze and discovered a pair of adorable pink mules, each one sporting a fluffy, feathery white pompom on the toe. The sight of the ridiculous and completely impractical women's footwear rendered Irene unexpectedly envious.

Tipping her head slightly to the side, Irene let her gaze travel up to make another startling discovery—the woman was naked beneath the gossamer kimono. The garment, falling off the woman's creamy, slightly plump shoulders barely concealed her voluptuous feminine assets. The kimono was a lovely thing, shot with gold threads that outlined an oriental theme of white cockatiels and jade bamboo. Irene thought it a shame the hem of the lovely fabric now pooled on the floor of the dirty porch. Coming face to face with the infamous Meda-Belle Lamphere was like seeing a tornado or tidal wave—fascinating, awesome, and frightening.

The disaster spoke, effectively bringing Irene out of her stunned state. "So you gonna stand there and gape? I been wonderin' how long it'd be before you come around. Your scalawag of a husband been gone, what, near a year, ain't it? Well, come on in—let's see what you got. Can't see nothin' with the getup you got on your head."

Before Irene could protest, the woman took her by the arm and hauled her into a front parlor. Petrified yet curious, Irene's gaze traveled and took note of the piano in the corner. Fringed scarves, like discarded undergarments, decorated the backs of chairs, tufted stools, and small, ornate tables in a deceivingly careless fashion. Beaded lamps dripping with crystal prisms catching the morning sun cast rainbows on the red-and-gold-embossed walls.

"My old mother used to wear one of these," the woman said and yanked Irene's brown prairie bonnet off her head, not bothering to wait for Irene to untie the ribbons. "She wore it on her head—it seemed to me—night and day. Bet she screwed with her old bonnet on her head—the bonnet and her apron."

Erupting into a good-natured belly-laugh, Mrs. Lamphere, to Irene's everlasting discomfort, expounded on her theme. "You know I never saw her without her apron on. I know she screwed. She must've. She birthed ten brats. Sure as hell didn't find 'em in no pumpkin patch."

Feeling as if she'd been dropped down the rabbit-hole like Alice in Wonderland, and in a haze of frangipani, stale whiskey, and cigar smoke, Irene came to and reached out to retrieve her headgear.

Mrs. Lamphere snatched it out of her grasp. "Ah, ah, ahhh, now you come over here where the light is better. You got me outta bed. I know you can read, so you must'a wanted to see me bad. You ignored my sign, so we're gonna do this. You come over here, and I'm gonna give you an interview. You don't say much. Ain't no bad thing for a woman in this line of work. Men like to do the talkin'."

Cocking her head, closing one eye, sighting in on Irene, the woman asked, "You sing or play the piano?"

Irene could play the piano, and she didn't have a bad voice, but it had been a while since she'd played or sung. In shock, the gears in her head slow to mesh, she nodded before she realized the ramifications of the question. It was clear there was a definite misunderstanding going on, and Irene at last shook her head in protest. "No, please, excuse me...but..."

Her interjection going unheeded, Mrs. Lamphere circled her, pinched at her hips, which weren't wide, but Irene didn't consider herself bony either. Mrs. Lamphere nodded and mumbled her approval. She pulled at the bodice of Irene's brown, high-neck cotton dress and tweaked the stray brown curls at her ear lobes.

"You got nice big eyes, a good bust. You're healthy enough, not too old, but old enough—I like that. Don't worry. I won't ask to see your teeth."

The woman continued her inspection. She laughed a rumbling sort of snort Irene found particularly infectious and caught herself about to giggle. "Your hair—I think, could use some henna, or maybe we could lighten it up with some peroxide. You need color. You shouldn't wear brown, dear. No, I think green, dark green…maybe a shade of moss green. We'll see. And I bet you'd be somethin' in blue…sapphire. If you wear red, it should be on the plummy side.

"You got a kid, don't you? I have a kid…a boy. He's back east to school. Good kid. Never done him no harm his mama bein' a businesswoman. And it won't do your girl any harm, either. Why, who knows? She might want to join the sisterhood after a couple years. You and her could share trade secrets. By then, you'll be an expert, eh?

"You did the right thing comin' here. I'll see you get treated right. I ain't one of them hard old biddies who would as soon cheat a girl as spit. No, sir, I've always been fair. You work hard, keep your nose clean, and I'll protect you and see you get your fair share of the take. Now, I do charge fifteen percent I got upkeep on this place. You get your food and a roof over your head. And, like I said, I give all my girls my protection."

Irene stood open-mouthed, glassy-eyed—blinking.

Mrs. Lamphere continued, "I know, I know, you ain't got no experience, but you had a man. And if you had one, you've had 'em all, honey; take my word on it. Oh, sure, they all got their little quirks. Some is mean, but most want some attention for an hour or so. In no time at all, you'll start to enjoy yourself. You'll have some coin in your stocking. I guess what I'm saying is, this is the beginning, not the end—a new life for you."

Despite her tongue being as dry as an old sock and feeling as if it had doubled in size, Irene heard herself shout, "Mrs. Lamphere."

To calm herself, Irene closed her eyes and in what she hoped was a rational tone, said, "It's true, Mrs. Lamphere, I have come looking for work." She opened her eyes to say, "However, you have leaped to an erroneous conclusion. I...I have come to offer you and your...your...*boarders*...a laundry service." Irene turned her sign around so it could be read more easily.

Mrs. Lamphere looked dumbstruck, then shook her head. Red lips pursed, eyes narrowed, she said, "*Erroneous conclusion?* Well, ain't you all fancy-pantsy."

To Irene's utter relief and bafflement, Mrs. Lamphere, after a thoughtful pause, burst out laughing, apparently finding the situation highly amusing.

Desperate, believing herself close to getting tossed out the door, Irene rushed to explain her mission. "I can do mending and sewing. I'm very handy with needles and thread. I worked for a milliner, a dressmaker in Oregon City from the age of nine until I married. I could make gowns for all of you...pretty gowns."

It was no use. The woman was laughing too hard to

hear. Irene gathered her bonnet, tucked her sign under her arm—resigned to leave willingly rather than wait to get kicked out.

Mrs. Lamphere, visibly struggling to stifle her mirth, shook her head, reached out, and grabbed her arm. "Here…here now, you took me by surprise, is all. I didn't mean to hurt your feelin's. There's been some…speculation, you see…and the boys, and me too, was wonderin' how long it would be until you got starved down far enough to come 'round lookin' for work." She shook her head. The woman's red hair tumbled over her right ear and down between her breasts.

Mrs. Lamphere's eyes mocked her. It was a mistake—she should've known better. Irene tried to break free, but Mrs. Lamphere had a strong grip, and short of prying the woman's fingers from her arm, Irene had no recourse but to endure her humiliation.

Mrs. Lamphere thunked the sign with her middle finger and said, "Good idea, a laundry service—give the girls and me more time with customers. Now you come back here and tell me your rates, and we'll work out a deal. You got guts, woman. I admire guts."

To Irene's surprise, Mrs. Lamphere sounded sincere. Lips still twitching, obviously working hard to swallow down her mirth, she drew Irene down beside her on the love seat near the parlor window.

They sat side by side for the better part of half an hour and worked out the details of the arrangement. Once the deal was struck, Irene made an attempt to make her escape as quickly as possible. However, Mrs. Lamphere, her hand gripping Irene's wrist, wasn't about to let her go without voicing her opinion. "You'll soon be tired of chilblains and an achin' back. Whole town's been waitin'. The boys been worried about you. Plenty of them think they'd be pleased to have you here as one of my girls. You'd make more money. Be a damned sight warmer and more comfortable. I know you could make a fine livin' for yourself and your girl."

Irene choked down her outrage, but she dared not risk giving offense. "You...you're most kind, Mrs. Lamphere."

It was one thing to suspect she was the talk of the town, but to have it confirmed made Irene's stomach turn like soured milk. She managed a thin smile and looked Mrs. Lamphere directly in the eye. "I...I don't think...I would be very good at...well...*it*. I have more...aptitude for sewing and scrubbing. My talents, I believe, lie in the application of a needle and thread."

Irene gathered her composure and her bonnet and started to leave.

The woman followed her to the door and called after her as she rushed down the steps. "Make more money on your back, Mrs. Obenchain. Now we got to know each other a little, you'd be a welcome partner. We would work well together, make this place famous."

Irene's feet couldn't move fast enough. She didn't want to run. That would be undignified. And she didn't want to offend; after all, Mrs. Lamphere had been all things kind. But the woman's voice carried so, Irene was certain the whole town could hear.

Chapter Two

After her mortifying experience at the boarding house yesterday, Irene's confidence level had taken a tumble down the well. Certainly word had spread, and she supposed speculation now ran wild. Feeling guilty for no good reason she could think of, she suspected some would deem her ambition foolish and unladylike. But, surely, no one could fault her for seeking honest work to support herself and her daughter.

The swish, swish of a broom alerted Irene to the presence of Rupert Laidlaw, the owner of the Cascade Emporium/Grocery & Feed. Shifting her painted cedar shake sign to her other side to keep it out of sight, she squared her shoulders, put up her nose, and stepped a little farther away from the wooden sidewalk. Looking straight ahead, she prayed she and Odessa would be able to get by with a brief, polite salutation.

Mr. Laidlaw called to her from the doorway of his store, "Good morning, Mrs. Obenchain."

Irene waved Odessa to keep moving. "Good Morning, Mr. Laidlaw."

"We've had inquiries about your sign," he said and came forward to the edge of the boardwalk, looking both ways, making it obvious he didn't want anyone to overhear their conversation.

Irene pressed her lips together, stifled a groan, and came to a halt.

Mr. Laidlaw glanced over his shoulder to the dark interior of his store, then back, and in a hushed voice, said, "You didn't tell us yesterday you'd come from the boarding house when we agreed to post your advertisement in our window. I heard about it from one of my customers, and then over the supper table last night, Sarah told me what she'd heard."

Stepping closer to the edge of the sidewalk, he leaned on his broom, bent down, and whispered, "You didn't need to go to those ladies at the boarding house, Mrs. Obenchain. You should've come to me first. We could've come to an understanding. I could let you have a line of credit here. We'd keep it an arrangement between the two of us."

He winked at her. Blinking, Irene fought her impulse to laugh in his face but stopped herself. *Ridiculous, repulsive…no, no, no.*

Rupert Laidlaw wasn't a bad-looking man, black hair, tidy, but he was too soft for Irene's tastes. Catching herself considering the idea of becoming Rupert's…*charity case,* she sputtered a bit before making a response. "Mr. Laidlaw, if you know I went to the boarding house, then you know *why* I went to the boarding house. I will be doing custom mending, sewing, and washing, and that…*is all.* As for accepting any kind of credit arrangement, I'm certain you would be uncomfortable keeping secrets from your wife. There is nothing I could ever do to repay you."

Their gazes clashed. She prayed she'd made her position loud and clear.

A sharp voice called from the doorway of the store, "Good morning, Mrs. Obenchain." Sarah, her demeanor territorial and possessive, came out of the store and took up a position beside her husband. Lips tight, delicate brows raised over her blue eyes, she folded her arms across her chest and looked down at Irene over her nose.

Now branded an abandoned woman, that particular glare had been directed Irene's way a lot over the past year and a half. She'd done nothing to deserve the catty sneer of disdain. On the contrary, Irene took great pains to make herself appear as drab as possible—which wasn't hard when one had only two dresses to one's name.

Irene shaded her eyes against the sun's glare and glanced over Sarah's shoulder to see the sign she'd made positioned in the corner of the store window—it could be read from the street: *Mrs. Obenchain will take in laundry, 10 cents a pound. Mending, 3 cents an inch. Custom sewing: shirts $2, dresses $3, trousers $5, ladies' undergarments $1. Fabric not included in pricing.*

Following Irene's gaze, Sarah said in a snide tone, "When I put your sign in our window, I was unaware you'd been to the boarding house. You should've told us. I take it you still haven't had any news of your husband?"

Lifting her chin on the defensive, Irene said, "No, I haven't had any news from my husband. I would imagine you would be the first to know, as you handle all the mail coming and going. As for my visit to the boarding house, Mr. Laidlaw and I were talking about that."

Irene cast Rupert a sideways glance. He lowered his head and directed his attention to attacking some mud on the boardwalk in front of the store, and took a couple of swipes at it.

To Mrs. Laidlaw, Irene said, "I'm certain you've already heard, but so there is no misunderstanding, I

11

assure you I'll be doing laundry and mending for Mrs. Lamphere and her boarders. I also hope to make dresses as well, and that is all."

Mrs. Laidlaw put up her nose. "Do you think it's wise? Associating with women like that? Think of Odessa. Young girls can be very impressionable. After all, you're a woman alone without a man to protect your daughter or you. Do you really think it proper?"

"Sarah...Mrs. Laidlaw," Irene said, feeling the sting of criticism and resenting the need to go on the defensive, "the ladies from the boarding house come to your store for their dry-goods and groceries—do they not?"

Sarah blinked and conceded with a slight nod.

"I don't see how my business with them will be so different from yours."

Sarah huffed. "The difference is, I have a husband to protect me, and I don't have to go down to that...that house of ill repute to do my business, Irene Obenchain."

Dumbfounded, about to make a sharp retort, Irene reminded herself of her mission for the day and pressed her lips together.

Sarah's focus shifted to the twelve-year-old little girl skipping up the street. Her gimlet gaze returned to Irene. Her body language veritably screamed, *Move on. Stop tempting my husband.*

"Odessa," Irene called out to bring her daughter to a halt. "Wait up for Mama." The girl stopped short and kicked at the pink cinder dust with her bare feet by way of protest.

Very near to tears, Irene nodded her head. Offering Sarah Laidlaw a weak smile, she uttered a pathetic response. "Well, good day to you both. Thank you for putting my sign in your store window."

Sarah sniffed.

Irene sighed and shrugged her shoulders. The woman was pretty and had everything a woman could want—four lovely children, a husband who adored her and made a good living for her. It seemed heavy work to have to defend her motives when it should be obvious why she needed to earn some money and do so in as honorable a fashion as possible.

Irene took a step, then stopped to say, "I am on my way up to the logging camp this morning to post a sign."

Turning her back on Sarah and her husband, suppressing the urge to stick her tongue out at them, she said, "That should make it easier for you two to spread the word—now you won't have to speculate as to what I'm up to." Behind her, she heard Sarah harrumph over the swish, swish of Rupert's broom.

Abel had left a year ago last March to find gold in the wilds of the Yukon. He'd given her a hundred dollars, along with his promise to return before the New Year. The New Year had come and gone, spring had passed, and so had the summer, and now it was fall. Irene was fast losing hope of his ever returning, and the money was gone. In hindsight, she realized she should've used the money to pack herself and Odessa up and go home to Virginia instead of trying to hold onto their home in Meadow View.

Ahead of her, Odessa gathered the big, prickly pine cones among the long needles beneath the stand of giant Ponderosa Pines that fringed the town. "Look, lots more have come down. We can use them to start our fire."

"You're getting pitch on your dress," Irene said as she, too, began to gather up the cones. Odessa bobbed around from find to find, the skirt of her dress pulled up into a handy basket, revealing patched and mended bloomers.

"I want to go to the logging camp with you. I don't want to go to school. It's too hot. I want to come with you."

September could be warm, at least during the day. The nights could be clear and frosty, bringing mornings of frozen fog, but so far, the summer weather had held.

"You'll go to school," Irene told her.

"Daddy took me to the logging camp. If Daddy was home, he'd let me come," Odessa said. Pouting, Odessa stacked her cache of pine cones behind a log.

Irene straightened her spine. In the thirteen years she'd been married, she'd given birth to three babies. Odessa was the firstborn. After that, she'd lost two babies in less than four years, one a son, born dead, the other a girl who'd lived only six months before succumbing to pneumonia.

Irene took Odessa by the shoulders, tilted her head to one side and smiled into the girl's pink face, trying to see the future in her daughter's hazel-green eyes. She brushed the dust off Odessa's short, stubby nose. Gently, she pushed back the wispy, fine curls of strawberry blonde at Odessa's temples and tried to tuck the hair back into the French braids that followed the perfect oval of her face.

"You will go to school, Odessa. Look there...." Odessa looked in the direction Irene pointed. Two boys had stepped out from under the trees near the creek. "There's Silas and Trenton."

"Oh. Oh. Hurry. We have to hurry. Silas said he'd bring his arrowheads to school. I want to see them first."

"Well, hold still, and let me brush the dirt off your dress."

Odessa pulled away and ran out from under the trees, giving no regard to the gouges and pokes assaulting her bare feet. Irene winced at the sight and renewed her resolve. Her daughter would have shoes for winter. She'd tried to patch Odessa's old boots, but they were busted out at the toe, and the soles were gone. The girl was almost as tall as she was now, but that wasn't saying much. She was barely five feet tall.

"Bye, Mama," Odessa said, and skipped to keep up with Silas and Trenton. The two Davis boys ran forward from the small, grassless play area before the school to greet the Trask boys.

Irene waved to her, and Odessa waved without looking back. "Have a good day," Irene called out, knowing full well her words fell on deaf ears. She raised her voice to remind the girl, "If I'm not here when you get out, you come straight home. I'll try to get here."

She stood for a moment and watched Odessa, Junie Davis and her big sister Anna, and Susan Laidlaw, who was only six and new to school this year, crowd around Silas and Trenton. Probably looking at Silas's arrowheads, Irene thought.

Silas had to be almost fourteen, Trenton twelve. They wouldn't be able to go to school many more years. Irene realized it was going to be difficult to get Odessa to go to school without Silas and Trenton there.

This line of thinking brought Irene's wandering thoughts back to her current mission and the cold fact that a boy had more chance of earning a few honest dollars than a grown woman. Boys could fire-watch, muck stalls, groom horses, shear sheep...herd cattle. The choices weren't as numerous or nearly so adventurous for girls...or a woman on her own.

Although Irene considered, as she walked away from town, some might consider being a prostitute an adventurous occupation for a girl...or a woman—and lucrative.

****

Odessa heard her mother, but her mother was always there after school, so she didn't feel obliged to respond. Besides, Benny and Carl Davis were bursting with news of a new colt at their farm. The Davises were rich, Trenton said. Their papa had a freight hauling business that ran from Meadow View north to Madras and over to the railroad at Shanico.

Odessa didn't play much with girls, especially girls her age. The boys were more interesting, more exciting. They didn't mind her tagging along—Trenton and Silas liked her. They even went out of their way to include her in their adventures, like the time they'd dyed Laidlaw's chick hatchlings with bluing. And once, Silas had peppered Mr. Pederson's snuff with chili powder. The poor man sneezed and sneezed until his nose bled. They let Odessa be the lookout. Silas said she was a good distraction—cute—kind of innocent looking.

Yes, the boys were much more to her liking. But Odessa kept that secret. Her mama wouldn't like it, her playing with the boys so much. Sometimes she lied, telling her mama she was going to meet Junie Davis to play with her paper dolls. But she didn't meet Junie, who was fourteen and a big know-it-all. She met Silas and Trenton, and they played down at the creek or out near the caves. Those were fun days, exciting days. And all the more savory because her mama never knew, never suspected.

Chapter Three

Leaving town, Irene set her mind to the task ahead, certain after yesterday's experience at the boarding house, going to the logging camp would be, yes, easier possibly, but no less humiliating. Humiliation, she knew, from this point on, would be a permanent side-effect of the course she'd set for herself. She'd have to toughen up—get a thicker hide.

Barclay Russell, the owner of the Suncrest Logging Company, had proven to be very kind to her—a bit too kind. Irene's instincts warned her Mr. Russell's interest could quickly develop into something more if she gave him a little encouragement. As lovely as it would be to turn over all her problems to a big, kind, strong man, Irene couldn't think of herself as a wife to anyone but Abel. That is, assuming matrimony was what Mr. Russell had in mind. She wanted to believe his intentions were honorable, but after her startling exchange with Rupert Laidlaw, she no longer trusted her judgment.

The far-off scream of the punk-whistle of the donkey-hauler, as it dragged the fir and pine logs up the side of the steep slope of the Three Sisters Mountain Wilderness, alerted her she was close to her destination. The sound of noisy cable rigging and creaky, heavy wagons grew louder and louder with each curve of the road. The air, thick with the mingling smells of fresh pitch and cinder, formed dust-devils that swirled down the road and over the banks into the logged-off draws.

The donkey whistle screamed, and suddenly a team of big, brawny draft horses lurched up over the bank onto the track only yards from where Irene was walking. Her cedar shake under her arm, she scrambled up the bank on the far side into the trees. The beautiful bay horses, their powerful necks lathered and bowed against their task, passed her by only a few feet. Behind the horses, Abner Bodeman, holding the reins, straddled two long pine logs.

Irene recognized him and felt a small bit of relief. He was a kindly, benign man, good to his family, and hard working. She knew his wife, Ida, and their daughters, Laura and Helen. Those girls were in their twenties—so much to look forward to. A depressing thought crossed Irene's mind. She was the same age as Mr. Bodeman's girls, but she thought herself much older...*ancient*...*past her prime*.

Bringing his team to a halt, Abner called out to her, "Mrs. Obenchain, what you doin' up this way? You best be on the lookout ma'am, we're cuttin' timber below there."

Irene wiped the perspiration from her brow, and quickly grasped a low hanging branch to keep from sliding down into the road. "Mr. Bodeman, I thought I *was* watching out. But I guess I didn't realize how close I was to camp."

"We moved it down over the weekend," he said, grinning. "Always movin' is this outfit."

A rumble of skids moving over rough ground and the jangle of harness alerted them that a sled of logs was coming down the hill. "Sorry, ma'am, I got to get this team up to the landing. You have a care. Young Bill is comin' with a load. You stay up outta the way till he gets by. The camp is up the draw a little past the cut."

"Thank you, Mr. Bodeman. I need to speak to Mr. Russell."

Abner tipped his hat, giving her a glimpse of his bald head. He said, "Good day, ma'am."

Heeding his advice, Irene made her way, staying up and under the trees, above the road. Soon another team of thick-muscled, sweaty draft horses hauling a sled full of logs driven by Bill Laidlaw, one of Mr. Laidlaw's sons, by his first wife, appeared on the way to the sawmill. Bill waved to her and passed her in a swirl of dust.

The logging camp was less than half a mile up the road. Irene quickly covered the distance, eyes and ears open. Hearing the crash and whump of a tree falling in the draw behind and below her made her pick up her pace. The sounds of the loggers hollering to each other and the screech of strained cables, steam-donkeys, and pulleys rang through the air.

The Suncrest Logging camp was nothing more than a row of pup tents lined up with their backs to a stand of tall pines. The tent faces opened to a rutted, dusty, and gouged wagon track. Having visited the logging camp to deliver Abel his lunch on more than one occasion, Irene knew the approximate layout no matter the actual location. At the far end of the camp, there were two larger tents. One was the mess, and the other belonged to Mr. Barclay Russell. It was his home and office.

Looking between the open flaps of the tent, Irene saw Mr. Russell seated on a camp stool studying an open ledger book. He scratched his coarse, black beard. Irene had, so far, met all Mr. Russell's overtures with quiet refusal and a sweet smile. She knew him for a practical man, a man used to ordering men and making decisions. She thumped on the tent post. He came to his feet and tipped over his wooden camp stool. Consequently, the contents of the cup in his hand spilled down the front of his shirt and onto the dirt floor.

The smell of unwashed bedding, sawdust, tobacco, and something sour, maybe strong coffee, maybe whiskey, maybe both, assailed Irene's nostrils. Startling the man, seeing him stumble and spill his coffee, she didn't know what to do—help him with the mess or stand back and ignore his dilemma.

Irene found Barclay Russell a bit forbidding with his dense, black brows shelved above his wonderfully sharp, piercing, opaque, gray eyes. He was built to climb mountain sides like a billy goat—short, powerful legs, a thick chest, and a thick, strong neck. She was sorry, but the cold reality was she could feel nothing more than plain friendship toward the man.

Dressed in the uniform of the day for those in the logging profession, Mr. Russell, as did most of the men of his crew, wore a bright red flannel shirt, now stained with black coffee. His shirt, open at the throat, exposed the faded red long johns he wore beneath his clothes for extra insulation—a thatch of black, curly hair formed a ruff around the edge of the neck. Brightly colored shirts were the order of the day, making the men more visible in the woods. The woodsmen wore black canvas trousers cut short to the top of their spiked boots to avoid getting pant-legs caked with heavy, wet mud and snagged on branches or tangled among cables and chains. Irene noticed Mr. Russell's trouser legs were dry and relatively clean.

"Good morning, Mr. Russell," she said. Pausing a moment, she gave the man time to regain his composure.

"Mrs. Obenchain, ah, you…you took me by surprise," he said, his ruddy cheeks bright with high color.

"Here, allow me to give you a seat." Picking up the stool, he set it down near her at the table. "Would you care for some coffee? You're in luck. I've got a fresh pot goin' this mornin'," he said, shaking the spilled coffee off his papers.

"No, thank you. Maybe some water?" she asked, seating herself, grateful for the momentary rest. The walk was a longer one than she'd thought—more uphill.

Mr. Russell ripped out a back page from his ledger and proceeded to scrub out a coffee mug for her as if it were a matter of course. He dipped out a cup of water from the wooden bucket that sat on the plank-board counter behind him. He set the cup down before her and pulled up an empty wooden cask to sit across from her.

"Well now, you've come a piece this mornin'. What can I do for you? You heard from that man of yours?"

He pulled in his chin and shook his head. Pulling back, he looked everywhere but into her eyes. "Damn, I'm sorry, ma'am, I shouldn't have asked. I'm a clumsy clod."

Facing her again, he tried to muddle his way through. Irene felt sorry for him.

"Of all the things I could've said, I'm sorry I asked you about your erstwhile husband. I should've said how pretty you look this morning. Your eyes sparkle like dew on the fern. Your cheeks are rosy, and your smile puts the sun to shame. And I'm pleased as punch you come to visit."

Seeing his blush making his face turn almost purple, Irene became alarmed, afraid he might have a stroke. Puffing like a steam engine, the man came to his feet and scrubbed his face. "Sorry, sorry." He repositioned the keg and sat. "I'll shut up. I been thinkin' about you all mornin', and now here you are. Sorry, sorry."

Irene sat helpless to save him.

"Damn, there I go again, sayin' too much and scarin' you off. I'm a fool, I guess. I sure hope you can forgive me."

Blushing, she tipped her head and offered him a sympathetic smile. "Far be it for me to chastise you for complimenting me on my looks, even though I'm sure you're being much too generous. I look a fright. But that is neither here nor there."

This man really did deserve someone, someone special—but not her. Irene lowered her gaze to her hands trying to think of a way to keep from hurting his feelings.

The truth, she was getting tired of people asking about her absent husband. She didn't want to think about Abel. It was time, past time, to move on and get on with the business of life. When she looked up, she made herself meet Mr. Russel's lovesick gaze. Leaning forward a little, she decided to come to the point of her visit. After all, she wasn't here to waste his time or to make small talk. That would be precisely the wrong impression. This was not a social visit.

"I haven't heard from Abel," she answered with a little shake of her head and, surprisingly, without the usual tears that naturally came to her eyes at the thought of her husband's fate. "And that's precisely why I've come to you this morning. I would like to post this sign up here in camp." She passed the cedar shake she'd been

23

holding under her arm across the table and remained quiet while Mr. Russel read the words she had so carefully printed in black paint on the whitewash.

Clearing his throat, squirming, frowning as if the cask under him was too small, Mr. Russell put his tongue in his cheek and nodded his head. "I can put this up where the boys'll see it."

The disapproval plain to see on his big open face—the silence yawned between them.

Finally, he heaved a big sigh and asked, "You sure about this? Doin' laundry is hard work. My mother took in laundry. After a couple years, she was bent like a rusty horseshoe. I sure would hate to see you get that way, especially if you don't have to, you know."

Irene tightened her resolve, set her jaw, and squared her shoulders.

His gaze never leaving her face, he sat back. "I can see by the set of your jaw there's nothing I can say to change your mind. I may not know much about women, but I know enough not to argue. I'll put this right in front of the mess tent. Yeah, I think that would be the place. You'll get business, ma'am. Yes, indeed. More than you want, I reckon. Ah…this may not be the right time. I know you don't know what's become of Abel…and…you…"

This was the moment she'd been dreading. This man, for all of his strength and good intentions, could be hurt, and Irene didn't want to give him any room to hope. "No…" Irene interrupted, anticipating where he was going, "No…I don't know what has become of my husband. It's because I don't, I must do what I can to take care of my child…provide for us as best I can until Abel returns. And…if, if, he doesn't return…then it would be best, you must see, to have a way to make our way without him."

"But…there must be something, something more I can do for you to ease your burden. You have to know I'll do anything."

Irene closed her eyes and shook her head. When she opened her eyes, her gaze locked with his. He looked like a kicked hound. His eyes dark and soulful, she nearly relented. She bit her lip, sorry to see him so defeated, but it was for the best. She decided it was time to tell him the rest of her plan. "I'm not looking for cash money. I'd be glad to trade, you know, laundry for cordwood or venison. We need sawdust for the floor this winter."

"Ah, yes, I see," he said.

She sincerely hoped he did. She held his gaze without blinking for a very long moment.

He shrugged his big shoulders, smiled at her, a twinkle in his eye. "So what you're saying is you don't want me. You want cordwood, and sawdust. Well then, so be it. I think it's a right fine idea. You bet, Mrs. Obenchain. I'm sure the boys will agree." He held out his thick, callused paw, and they shook hands.

"If you change your mind. All you have to do is say the word. I'd be honored to relieve you of all your burdens, Mrs. Obenchain."

Irene finished her water. She started to leave. He stopped her with a word of caution, placing his hand on her arm. "You be careful. Boys ain't lookin' for a little girl on the road or up in the trees, all right?"

"I'll be careful, and thank you again, Mr. Russell. I appreciate your support more than I can say."

"Don't thank me. You're gonna get a lot of washin', I'm thinkin', and that's gonna be mighty hard work for a little bit of a thing like you. If and when Abel shows himself around here, I'm gonna wring his paltry neck. Yes, sir."

Irene smiled up at him, and on impulse, she kissed his cheek and left the way she'd come.

Chapter Four

Taking stock of her larder, Irene sat at the table with Odessa in near darkness, lamps unlit, daylight fading fast. The notion of taking Mr. Laidlaw up on his offer of a line of credit at the mercantile tempted her. However, the idea of being in his debt was decidedly unappealing and repugnant.

Tomorrow, she'd pick up the first laundry and mending from the boarding house. She felt fairly confident there'd be steady work for her there. But it would be a week before she'd see a return on her labors.

Once summer ended and fall set in, the evenings had started to get cold. The firewood supply had dwindled to sticks and whatever dry limbs Irene could scrounge. Unable to heat all three bedrooms, she and Odessa set up their cots in the sitting room before the hearth. By candlelight, Odessa read to her from her bed while Irene churned the butter at the table

****

Irene, up before dawn, milked Dilly, the cow. Odessa's blue dress wasn't quite dry from the washing of the night before. They might be starving and cold, but Odessa would not go to school tattered or dirty. Irene warmed her iron over the fire-plate and began to press the dampness and wrinkles out of the fabric, which was wearing thin. She'd let down the hem more than once. She hoped the dress would hold together a little longer.

The jangling sounds of an approaching wagon interrupted her thoughts, and she put her iron back on its plate at the hearth. Usually wagons, freight or otherwise, didn't come past their house but went north and west, heading to the lava fields and through the high passes of the Cascades.

Glancing out the window in the kitchen, she could see the cold blue dawn arriving, as well as a freight wagon coming down the short lane to the house. Before leaving the window to go to the door, she heard the driver shout to his team, "Whoa, Dolly, you old hay burner... Whoa, Rex."

From the opened doorway, she watched Barclay Russell climb down from the wagon, then reach under the wooden seat to retrieve two bales of muddy, dingy clothes. "Mornin', Mrs. Obenchain. Well, here it is. I advise you to leave it out here in the open air until you douse it in your wash-water. The stink of it purt'near makes my eyes water. I got another bale here on the other side.

"George. Where'd you go?" Mr. Russell looked back at his wagon, but Irene didn't see anyone else. Then big George Krauss appeared from around the team of horses, a bale of dirty laundry upon one wide shoulder and a wooden box filled to overflowing with food tucked under his other arm.

George Krauss was a big, open-faced young Swede, probably not more than sixteen or seventeen years old. He was handsome, with a beautiful head of yellow hair and eyes as blue as the sky. He was always grinning, it seemed to Irene, and this made him appear slightly idiotic, but she had long since realized George was not at all simple. He was happy. She thought it strange

George's happy outlook and the fact he was foreign and had an accent made him seem stupid. It wasn't right. How lovely it would be if everyone could be as content with life as George Krauss.

Irene greeted him, "Good morning, George." He grinned, showing the dimples in his strong cheeks and a mouth full of straight, white teeth.

"Mornin', ma'am. Da vood, vhere you vant it should go, ma'am?"

Irene looked to the wagonload of cut wood, afraid she'd never be able to pay for more than a stick or two. She had nothing to give, but...*Oh God, how wonderful it would be to have the whole wagonload.* "Mr. Russell...Mr. Russell...I don't think..."

Barclay read her mind. "What...ma'am?" he said, a gleam of amusement shining in his dark eyes. "Yup, it's all yours. And before you say another word, I assure you, you will earn every splinter of wood, ma'am. Earlier in the summer, George and the Laidlaw boys cut up this load from a slash pile near the old camp. It should be good and dry. You know the Laidlaw boys got to do for themselves. Sarah's got her hands full with the young'uns, so the boys were plumb tickled to turn their laundry over to you. And George, he's grateful. He does like to be clean, does George.

"We have a surplus of beans—as *always*—and before you object, believe me, none of my crew, or myself, is sorry to see them beans gone The winter squash is from Mrs. Bodeman—she'd appreciate you washin' Abner's trousers, as her girls don't like beatin' the mud off 'em. There's mendin' to do in these bundles. And, I got to say, I'm right ashamed to hand 'em over to you, 'cause in my opinion, the lot of it should be burnt.

But clothes what they are out here, we got to wear 'em until our butts...excuse me, ma'am...ah...until there ain't nothin' but a string holdin' 'em together."

Irene barely heard any of what he'd said. She couldn't take her eyes off the box of food George placed inside her door. At a glance, she spied two bags of beans, a bag of rice, a bag of coffee beans, and a bag of lentils that had slid off the top and landed at her feet. A slab of fatback stood up at the end of the box with a jar of honey and a tin of sultanas stacked against it. Tucked in tight into the remaining space in the box, she thought she could see a large bag of dried apples, a bag of flour, and bags of sugar and salt. George grinned at her before heading back to the wagon, and when she finally looked up, he was already coming back with a burlap bag full of potatoes slung over his shoulder and two huge yellow squash under his arm.

Irene couldn't speak—she wanted to get down on her knees and cry. Instead, trembling, she put her hand over her mouth to keep from bawling.

"Close to da door dis vood I'll yust trow over here. A hind of venison for you I got," George said in a tentative voice, concern on his big face and in his kind eyes.

Irene put out her hand to hold Mr. Russell back from going to help. "It's too much...too much," she managed to say while sobbing, horrified she was falling apart.

"Now...it ain't," he assured her, and patted her hand while holding it against his chest.

Irene, feeling his big heart beating beneath her fingers, realized the impropriety of the gesture and slowly pulled her hand free.

Dropping his arms down to his side, Mr. Russell's

tone, when he spoke, was brusque. "We want all this stuff done up right clean, pressed, and mended. This here's Tuesday. I'll be by to pick up freight Saturday. Reckon that'll give you enough time to take care of this load? And it'll give me an excuse to come see you, maybe do a little courtin'. I ain't discouraged, Mrs. Obenchain. I'm a patient man. You'll find out."

"Yes, yes…I'll have everything ready by Saturday," Irene said, although assailed by huge, dark doubts and fears of hidden strings, having caught the wily gleam in Mr. Russell's eye.

"And we can get you some sawdust. God knows we got lots," he told her before he disappeared around the end of the wagon to help George.

"Mama? What is it…who is it?" Odessa asked, rubbing the sleep from her eyes.

"We're going to have griddle cakes for breakfast," Irene said, giggling through the tears in spite of the lump in her throat. She snatched up the bag of lentils off the floor, shoved the box inside with her foot, then scooted the heavy box closer to the kitchen table. Odessa followed, dragging the bag of potatoes, going back for the squash.

"There might be a half cup of sourdough starter," Irene muttered to Odessa over her shoulder. "I think it's still all right. We can add flour now." Her fingers lovingly touched all the bags within the box. She called out each and every treasure as she set them up on the table. "We have beans, rice, flour, and sugar. We're going to be all right, honey, we're going to be all right."

Odessa, in her flannel nightgown, rubbed her eyes. "Where did it come from?" Then, hazel eyes blinking as if finally coming awake, she repeated, "*All right?* What

31

do you mean...*all right?* Why is Mr. Russell delivering food to people?"

Still in a daze, Irene talked to herself. She didn't really hear what Odessa had asked. "Mr. Russell brought us wood, lots of wood. And we're going to get fresh sawdust to put under the rugs for winter. We're gonna be warm, sweetheart, nice and warm."

"Why? Why, Mama?"

Finally, Irene stopped to look into her daughter's sleepy eyes. "I'll be doing laundry...lots of laundry for lots of people...and mending. The men at the logging camp don't have anyone to do their wash or sew their clothes. I'm going to do it. Sometimes we'll get cash—sometimes we'll get wood or food, or maybe a line of credit at the Emporium. We'll see. But today we have this lovely food and lots of wood. I'm going to put the hind of venison in the root cellar and see if I can help with the wood. You get the sourdough going for the griddle cakes. We'll put sugar on 'em, real sugar."

Odessa, looked at the food and wrinkled her nose. "It doesn't make sense. Why would anyone want to wash anybody else's clothes, and why would anyone pay anybody with beans?" Irene simply giggled and handed Odessa the sourdough crock off the shelf before she went outside to help unload the firewood.

Mr. Russell refused for himself and for George, Irene's invitation to join them for a cup of coffee and a stack of hotcakes. After saying thank you one more time and waving George and Mr. Russell farewell, Irene went back inside and found herself rendered speechless at the sight of the banquet Odessa had created in her absence. "You can take some of this to school for your lunch. You've made enough for a week of breakfasts. It's getting late," she said between bites, trying to enjoy Odessa's feast. "I won't be walking you to school anymore or coming to walk home with you. I'm going to start all of this washing.

"Listen to me," Irene said, watching Odessa fold a couple of sugar-coated griddle cakes around some bacon and wrap them in a hanky to put in her lunch pail. "You'll be thirteen in a week, Odessa, and I expect you to help. Yesterday you lost track of time after school. You have to come *straight* home today and every day. It's time to grow up, Odessa. Trenton and Silas have chores, and now you have chores. I'm depending on you."

****

It was noon, the sky overcast with high clouds, the air still. Irene hung up the second bundle of washed clothes on the line. She didn't know if she was supposed to keep the bundles separate, but she had anyway. She looked to the mountains. Clouds were coming over from the west, creeping up around the shoulders of the Three Sisters. She prayed her wash would have time to dry before it rained. The last bundle of clothes sat soaking in the rinse water from the two loads before.

Inside the house, she dried her hands on the skirt of her dress and brushed aside her hair from her brow. Humming "Oh, Susanna," she mixed up some bread dough, then set it aside on the hearth to rise. It was time to get the laundry from the boarding house. The sun was overhead. She hoped it was past noon—she didn't want to disrupt Mrs. Lamphere's sleep again.

She had no time to sit and eat, so she grabbed some of the bacon and cakes and a pocket full of dried apples to eat on the way. No time to waste in business now. She intended to make it successful, even if it killed her.

Before ringing the boarding house bell, she braced herself for Meda-Belle's coarse demeanor and flamboyant appearance—however, the woman who answered the door was one of Mrs. Lamphere's boarders. And once again, all rational thought left Irene. The girl was wearing, or barely wearing, a see-through, bright pink dressing gown with pink feathers around the neck and sleeves and very little else. Irene blinked and blushed. The woman—*no, beneath all the paint and powder, she's a girl, not more than sixteen.* The girl nodded and waved her across the threshold without so much as a smile or greeting.

Irene could almost find humor in the situation but for the presence of the woman who stood with her back against the wall at the bottom of the stairs. She looked to be Indian—coal black hair and sharp features, but her eyes were a strange color of green, opaque like green marbles. She was wearing a short, white leather robe covered in multicolored beads. The robe did nothing to hide the black satin chemise or her bare legs. She stood glaring, making Irene feel about two feet tall and as ugly as a boil. Her strange-colored eyes bored a hole in Irene's head.

The green-eyed woman sidled up to her. "We all miss the Abel man." The woman's husky voice and hot breath too close to Irene's ear. The woman stood so close Irene could feel the heat of her body. The smells of gin and musk, flesh and lust, surrounded her. Irene's pancakes and bacon sloshed and rolled up one side then the other of her stomach like bars of soap in a pan of water.

"He's one a woman can't forget. Abel's the only man I ever knew what could screw you and spout poetry at the same time. Sing too—make me melt. Bet you get all wet thinkin' about him, know I do." The woman laughed too loud and slapped Irene on the back. "Then, maybe you dried up a long time ago. Yeah, that would explain a lot."

The flesh on Irene's arms and neck crawled. Nauseous, she felt her breakfast bubble up into her throat and stay there. Her instinct said run, but Mrs. Lamphere was coming down the hall with the laundry. Irene ordered herself to stand at attention.

Meda-Belle, carrying a bundle of soiled sheets and underwear, instructed her how she wanted her sheets ironed. Holding back her mortification, her pride in tatters, Irene listened and nodded, knees trembling.

"We all want new dresses. It's been a while."

The green-eyed woman, over Irene's shoulder, voiced her second to Meda-Belle's plans, her breath hot, filling Irene's nostrils with the smell of her nasty venom. Gleefully, the woman helped to load Irene up, rolling the pack of wash over Irene's shoulder and tucking the smaller bundle of mending under her arm.

Meda-Belle stood back and cocked her head. "We're going over to the Emporium today to select fabric and patterns. You got until next Tuesday on all this. You gonna be able to deliver?"

Ignoring the woman with the mean eyes, Irene looked Meda-Belle in the eye and found the strength to reply as truthfully as she could, "I'm sure going to try."

Meda-Belle nodded her head in understanding.

Irene made her way down the alley. Tears blurred her vision and streamed down her cheeks. Her fingers were so tight they cramped from trying to hold on to the bundle of whorehouse linen. In her head, the picture of

Abel, handsome, laughing, in the arms of the green-eyed harlot mocked her. In that moment, Irene experienced a loathing she'd never known before. And, for some strange reason, the green-eyed slut, Irene knew, returned the sentiment.

Chapter Five

December 1899

The chilblains caused her fingers to bleed from under her fingernails. After two years of doing laundry and mending, Irene had learned to salve her hands with bag-balm every night and wear her old Sunday gloves to bed. Tonight the gloves and the pain made it difficult to hold the pen. She dipped the nib in the inkwell, adjusted her grip, and took a deep breath, determined to impart only positive news in her letter to her father.

The men at the logging camp are faithful customers, and Mrs. Lamphere, at the boarding house, is most kind. I upholstered a sofa for Mr. Laidlaw, a birthday gift for his wife. The Laidlaws own the Emporium. I received a twenty-dollar line of credit in payment. With that and the wood we get from the men at the logging camp, Odessa and I are comfortable.

She paused and thought of the new sign she'd posted at the Emporium and the post office: *Mrs. Obenchain has room to let, meals included: $10.00 a month.*

The posting had been up for three months with not a single nibble. Sarah Laidlaw complained the sign prevented passing customers from seeing the enticements of her displays in her front window. Irene realized she wouldn't be allowed to leave it up at the Emporium much longer.

Deciding to change the subject in her letter—and in

her head—Irene freshened her nib with another quick dip in the ink pot.

Our little town is growing. We now have a church, Congregational, and a regular minister who comes every second Sunday. One of the loggers, Mr. Bodeman, gives a good service on the alternating Sundays.

She paused, blotted her paper, and turned it over to write on the back side.

We are to have our own doctor. We had hoped he would be in residence before winter set in, but we were told he and his wife were delayed in Boise, caught in the big blizzard. We expect them to arrive any day now. Mr. Laidlaw, the owner of the Emporium, is now our mayor. The Suncrest Logging Company has created a Forest Service station, and we have a post office. You may now send your letters to me at our new address: 21 West Cascade St., Meadow View, Oregon. We have a grange hall, built last summer, and our New Year's celebration will be held there.

Please write soon. It took almost two months for your last letter to reach me. I pine for news from you all. I pray you are all well.

With all my love, your daughter, Irene.

She read her letter over. She didn't mention the frightening hailstorm that tossed a huge tree limb onto the roof of the house, which made a big hole in the roof and stripped the clothesline from the shed. She'd sprained her ankle and received a knock on the head from one of the tree limbs during the storm while rescuing her laundry. Without Mr. Russell's and George's help, she never would've been able to make the repair to the roof.

She didn't tell them Odessa was a constant worry. At first, the girl had helped some with the laundry, but the wash soap burned her hands. She tried to sew, but Irene had to do her stitches over so often it wasn't practical. Odessa did cook for them, but she was terrible at cleaning up after herself and dirtied too many dishes. It had become easier to do the work and get it done rather than ride roughshod over the girl.

Secretly, Irene didn't want to *make* Odessa help. She wanted her daughter to *want* to help. She wanted her daughter to love her enough to try to ease her burdens. But instead, as the only parent, and the only one trying to enforce discipline on the girl, Irene had become the target of Odessa's bitterness.

This evening Odessa's anger erupted into a fiery blast of irrational blame. She accused Irene of purposefully driving her father away with what Odessa termed as her constant harping, frowns, and disapproving scowls. And to top it off, Odessa had called her ugly, plain, and drab.

Compounding her daughter's vile accusations, there lurked the certain knowledge—*no matter how hard Irene tried to push it out of her mind*—Abel had visited the boarding house, visited the green-eyed Grace Wolfe, and possibly, the young and pretty Paulette, and maybe even the flamboyant Meda-Belle.

Realizing she wasn't going to add anything more to her letter, Irene blotted her paper and blew out the flame of the kerosene lamp on the table. Odessa's lamp still burned, light coming from under her door. Now they had enough wood to stay reasonably warm, they each had taken a bedroom on the living-room end of the house.

Before going to her own bed, Irene knocked on Odessa's door. "Odessa." No answer, "Odessa," Irene called out a little louder, and cautiously, she opened the door expecting to find her daughter prostrate and weeping. Instead, Odessa sat on the edge of her bed, hairbrush, hairpins, and hair combs strewn about the coverlet around her, attempting to do something with her hair. But it was clear she was failing. Her hair slid down over one ear and flopped on her shoulder in a heavy tangle.

Irene sat down on the side of the bed, too late to halt the avalanche. Quietly, she brushed out the tangles and began to coil Odessa's locks and place combs, and before long Odessa's lovely, silky, strawberry blonde tresses were styled in a Grecian knot on the crown of her head, with a couple of ringlets over one shoulder.

The spark that had lit the fuse and sent Odessa off like a Roman candle was Odessa's insistence she have a store-bought dress for the New Year celebration, or she would die. Irene didn't have time to make a dress for her, and the cost of a new dress wasn't in the budget. Now, after a little time for the girl to simmer down, Irene offered Odessa a compromise, a compromise she'd only this moment thought of. "I'm really behind in the ironing. If you would take care of the sheets, I think you could have five dollars to buy a dress and maybe have enough for some new ribbons to wear to the social."

Turning and throwing her arms around her, Odessa pledged, "Oh, oh, yes, Mama." Her willingness warmed Irene's heart, easing the sting of her daughter's hurtful outburst. "I'll iron. I'll do it."

"You know Mrs. Lamphere expects her laundry back the day after tomorrow. She's fussy about her linens. They're satin, and you have to be very careful not to get your iron too hot. You can't scorch them, or only iron the edges. I've shown you how she likes them."

"Oh, yes, yes, I know, I know. I'll be very careful. I'll do as you say. You'll see, I will "

All the next morning, Odessa ironed. Irene put up with her moans and groans of: *"My feet hurt. My back, right between my shoulders, hurts. It really, really hurts."*

After lunch, Irene finished the wash from the logging camp and mended a half dozen pairs of long johns. It was snowing lightly. Bright bursts of sunlight popped out to blind and dazzle. The world outside, held in a dry freeze, caused the tree limbs to pop off in random and unexpected amputations as pockets of moisture within the wood expanded and froze solid.

Whacking ice off her wash, Irene removed stiff, frozen trousers from her clothesline and laid them across the wicker basket at her feet. Fingers cold and stiff, she pried the shirts, arms flat as a board, frozen solid, off the line.

Poking her head out the back door, shivering, Odessa called out, "I'm going to see Susan for a little while. I have two more sheets to do, and I'll do them when I get home."

"Odessa, those sheets better be done by tomorrow," Irene called out, but to a closing door.

Sighing in exasperation, nose running, fingers burning with cold, Irene removed the last shirt from the line and carried the basket of board-stiff clothes into the kitchen. She hurried to the fireplace, rubbed her hands together to bring life back to her fingers.

By the time Odessa returned two hours later, Irene had the clothes from the line thoroughly dried, ironed, and folded. While she silently put supper on the table, Odessa finished the sheets. That evening, Irene mended while Odessa read to her from the book by Charles Dickens that Odessa had borrowed from Anna Davis. Before going on to another chapter, Odessa quietly mentioned, "We looked at dresses today."

Without looking up from her mending, Irene smiled and, a bit sarcastically, muttered, "I thought as much."

Odessa went to bed, and Irene, about to put out the lamp in the kitchen, saw the stack of wrinkled, clean sheets. They hadn't been in the basket with the others but in a pile on a little stool beside the basket. Unmistakably Meda-Belle's sheets, but Odessa obviously, had overlooked them or simply ignored them. There were five sheets that needed ironing before tomorrow morning. Irene erected the wooden board and set the iron and the warming plate on the hearth, resigned to stay up until they were finished. But, she had to wonder, would she forever be picking up her daughter's tag ends.

****

"I'm very sorry your wife—Marie, is it?—decided to turn back," the elderly Doctor Carter said.

Elias had wondered when his mentor would come around to the topic of his missing spouse. Hearing her name, he winced. He felt guilty certainly, embarrassment probably, but he felt regret more than anything else. He didn't completely understand what had happened—why she'd turned back—except to admit it was his fault. The reasons were too painful to analyze, although getting the question out of his mind was like trying to stop his heart from beating by wishing it.

They'd traveled by rail to the Great Salt Lake, then by coach to Boise, Idaho. Bad weather, broken axles, and delays hindered their progress. A blizzard of monumental proportions followed them into town. The storm stranded not only the passengers on the stage but flocks and flocks of sheep and their drovers.

The drovers, more than pleased to take advantage of the weather and live it up for a few days, gave the town no rest. Night and day, the wind wailed and whistled, and the snow, crystalline sharp and abrasive, flew sideways past their hotel window. The drovers fought, drank, and whored. It simply was more color than Marie could accept, and she refused to go any farther.

Elias tried to reason with her, beg her, cajole her, and finally, he threatened her. But Marie was adamant— *she wanted to go home.* "If you love me, truly love me, Elias, you won't ask me to live out here. I can't. Think of our children. I couldn't have children and bring them into this desolate country. I won't. We should be home right now, getting ready to celebrate Christmas with my family. I hate this place. I hate it."

He begged her. "Please, come to Farewell Bend. It's beautiful. You've seen the photographs of the mountains, the trees. Remember? It won't be anything like this place. Come with me, we're almost there, another two weeks, maybe less if we're able to travel by train, and we'll be in Farewell Bend. We've come this far, don't turn back, please."

Stubborn, shaking her head, she flatly told him, "No. I've read Doctor Carter's letters over and over. The loneliness is there. You'd be off doctoring, away from home for days…weeks, maybe months, and I would be alone in a wilderness. And God help me if anything should happen to you. Then I really would be stranded. I don't want to be alone. I was prepared to be a doctor's wife in Chicago. There I could attend garden clubs and ladies' aid societies, but who knows what women do in…in Mountain…where ever. No. I've made a terrible mistake. I'm sorry, but I'm going home."

"Marie, you're my wife."

"Yes…yes, I know. We cannot get a divorce, not within the Catholic Church. I'm willing to be alone the rest of my days, but don't expect me to live out here in this ungodly country. It's dirty and savage, and…and…uncouth. Come home with me, Elias. Come home and resume your practice with Father. You'll see, we'll be happy…have children. We'll simply call this our honeymoon, an adventure before settling down."

"Marie, I promised Doctor Carter I'd come. He helped me find this practice. He helped me through school. He's helped me in so many ways—I've explained all of that. I was supposed to be in Meadow View before the end of October. We're late. It's the end of December now. With the wedding and the planning, we were delayed. I sent him a wire and explained all of that. But I won't make him wait any longer. All of my supplies and equipment, even our furnishings, are on the way out here. I won't let Doctor Carter down. He helped me through medical school."

"Then go. I'll wait for you at home. Get this lunacy out of your system. Stay out here for a year or two—however long it takes. But I won't stay. I won't stay here with you—I can't."

The clock ticked away on the mantel. Silent, Elias stared into the fire. Outside, the snow had stopped, and the parlor lamps shone a shaft of pale, pink light across the yard and onto the icy cold waters of the Deschutes River only yards from the doctor's back door.

Doctor Carter brought Elias out of his musings, commenting, "I remember the first time I met you. It was what, about six years ago? I was lecturing medical students in Chicago on the joys and pitfalls of being a country doctor. At the time, I thought you showed promise, so full of questions. I remember you were too thin. I'm pleased to see you've filled out over the years. Matured—a man now, almost as tall as I am—you must be around six-foot-two?"

Elias nodded. "I remember every word of your lecture. I was starving, putting myself through medical school, working two jobs, but I was enthralled with the life you described. You made everything sound adventurous and challenging. I've thought of little else but becoming a country doctor since then. Coming out here is what I've longed to do, what I feel I was called to do."

Dr. Carter chuckled, a rumbling sort of laugh, like the sound of distant thunder. "I remember thinking, here's another soul who longs to be a frontier doctor. No city will ever hold young Rayburn for long, that's what I thought back then, and I still believe it's true. There's something in both of us driving us to be men of medicine in our hearts, but in our blood, we're men with a craving for exploration and adventure, and I'm sorry you've come west at a cost. I apologize for butting in, your personal affairs are none of my business, but I am sorry to hear your bride returned to Chicago."

Coming out of his funk, Elias shook his head and gave his mentor a lopsided smile. "There's no reason for you to apologize. I'm the one who should be apologizing to you. I...we...meant to be here all set up and settled before winter set in, and now it's nearly New Year's Eve."

Gathering his thoughts, Elias decided it might help

him if he opened the wound and allowed his hurt to drain—talk about it. He might even discover the truth, and yet, maybe that was the reason why he didn't want to get everything out in the open—maybe he didn't want to admit the truth.

"I'd like to give you an explanation for my late arrival, but I'm not certain what, exactly, happened. Marie and I were married at the end of September. Marie is young…eighteen, but her father is a physician, and she, I presumed, understood what a doctor's life is like. I don't know what she expected. We talked of my plan to come west, leave my practice in Chicago. Her parents were concerned but rather envied us, I think. At least her father did—he'd taken me into his practice. He even told me once if he were my age, he would go west, maybe to California, somewhere fresh and new.

"I read your letters to Marie, and I showed her the brochures you sent. She'd never been any farther west than Des Moines and never a day away from her parents. I could see, as we traveled farther west, the more frightened she became. The weather was really horrible all the way. But I thought…*I*…would be enough for her—together we would be…*enough*. But, when it came down to it, she wanted to be with her family and home more than she wanted to be with me."

Twirling the ends of his salt-and-pepper, handlebar mustache, Doctor Carter stayed quiet a moment. He cleared his throat, then offered Elias a rum-soaked cigar, offering to light it for him. Ceremoniously, he proceeded to light his own. After a few draws and puffs of white smoke, the old gent revealed a bit of his own history.

"My wife, Pearl, beautiful woman inside and out, died in childbirth, bled to death, right there on the couch behind you. She was young, too. Everything had been going along fine, the pregnancy, the labor. There wasn't anything I could do. She gave birth to a daughter. Abigail is twenty-seven, has a family of her own now. She lives in the valley in Eugene."

The doctor shifted forward in his chair and set his cigar aside. "We have a fella…Glen Percy…he packs the mail from Eugene by burro. He comes over the pass through blizzards, sleet, hail and high wind. Glen gets the mail through. We write to each other, Abigail and I.

"I see her and her husband and my grandchildren about once a year. She doesn't care for it over here. She likes city life. She says it's too big, empty, here…lonely. Me, I get lonely in the city." He chuckled and offered Elias a refill of the brandy.

Elias declined.

"I need my friends, the wide open spaces, the junipers, the snow-covered mountains, and the clear, fast-moving streams about me. Those are my good friends," said the doctor.

He tossed the remains of his brandy to the back of his throat and swallowed. Sitting up straight in his chair, he turned all business. "We'll get you on the stage in the morning to Meadow View. I think you're going to like it there. Pretty place. They've got this big, wide-open meadow with the most spectacular view of the mountains. It takes your breath away. Well, you've got to see it to believe it—good folks.

"Oregon is growing, this part of the state especially. Once people discovered you could fatten cattle and sheep better and faster on bunchgrass than on valley grass, it didn't take long to start a boom. We've doubled our population in the last ten years. Used to I could cover the whole Deschutes Basin by myself, but now there's too many people. I'm very happy you've come, son.

"You take the territory from MeadowView to Redmond and north to the reservation at Warm Springs and work in Prineville. That's a lot, but it's got to get covered. I'll cover Tumalo, Farewell Bend, and south down to Silver Lake country."

Elias listened intently. "I want to get to work. I've been sitting around for nearly two long months in Boise, of all places—uncertain if I would ever get here. There was a moment back there when I had resigned myself to going back to Chicago. I almost had myself convinced. But when it came down to it, I couldn't go with Marie.

"I put her on the train. She looked fine and beautiful, like always. Marie has beautiful hair, thick and dark. She likes clothes and is very…dainty. She was crying. I wanted to make her happy, but something held me back. A voice inside my head kept telling me even if I did what she wanted, eventually, I'd disappoint her, make her unhappy.

"Yesterday, when the stage headed down into the gorge to cross the Crooked River, I looked out to those mountains and watched the sunset, then I looked to the east and saw a wall of jagged rock reaching up to the sky, the sun turning it a burnt red, and I knew I was coming home. It felt like home—it amazed me, almost made me weep. It was so strong. I believe I've waited my entire life for this, but at long last, I am home. Unfortunately, I guess Marie didn't feel the same—her home is in Chicago."

Chapter Six

Meda-Belle always weighed the clothes on her kitchen scale before handing them over to Irene, so she knew down to the penny what she owed as far as the wash was concerned. Irene had learned early on to count her inches carefully on the mending because Meda-Belle measured those too.

The men at the logging camp didn't care how many inches or how many pounds. They paid her what they had, and they were very generous, so Irene gave up weighing and measuring their laundry and mending. There was an rusty old steelyard in the cowshed—she'd cleaned it up to use, but so far, she hadn't needed it.

Meda-Belle counted out twelve dollars and forty-six cents on the bill for the week—that was three cents more than Irene had estimated. She kept still—it did no good to argue with Mrs. Lamphere.

"You got a dress made up for yourself for the social, Mrs. Obenchain?" Meda-Belle asked. Head down, she tucked her little beaded green coin purse back into the garter on her thigh.

Irene politely looked away.

Head up, Meda-Belle pressed on. "I see you made a coat from the blankets. Looks right fetchin'. Fur's a nice touch. Saw your girl's got a new coat. Lined it with the blue satin, did you?"

Irene smiled and nodded and started to make a

comment, but Meda-Belle cut her off. "I gave you the blue satin to make *yourself* a dress, not line a coat. When you gonna give yourself somethin' pretty? Somethin' pretty that don't have no other use 'ceptin' to be pretty? The blue-lavender stuff was nice, soft, had a warm feel to it. I forget what the Laidlaw woman called it. *Crêpe de chine*, I think it was."

Meda-Belle continued, giving Irene no opportunity to defend herself. "You done a nice job on the blue dress you made for me. I ain't gonna wear it to the social, so if you was to make somethin' out of the same fabric and wear it New Years, it would be fine."

Meda-Belle held up her hand against Irene's attempt to get in a word. "No buts. I want to see some color on you New Year's Eve. We're startin' a new century. Who knows what it will bring? We got people talkin' on wires. We got horseless carriages. It's new times comin', Mrs. Obenchain—new times. You got to be ready. Get them colors on your back. You're a young chicken yet. Strut them feathers."

Cheeks burning, Irene escaped and crossed the street to the Emporium, where she planned to meet Odessa. She might surprise Meda-Belle, Irene decided—she might indeed. Meda-Belle was her friend, Irene had come to realize—she was generous and loyal. It felt good having Meda-Belle for her friend. It certainly made it easier to withstand Meda-Belle's business associate Grace Wolfe's snide remarks and nasty looks.

With the bundle of dirty linen under her arm, Irene stepped inside the Laidlaw Emporium. She recognized Odessa's squeal of delight coming from behind a curtain in the back room. Anna Davis and Junie stepped through the curtain, then thrust it aside, and Odessa made her entrance. She dazzled, sparkled—she looked radiant. Technically, Odessa hadn't earned the dress she so proudly wore, but that fact was momentarily shunted to the back of Irene's mind.

The dress, made of a white, polka-dot Swiss over an underskirt of emerald green satin, had a wide green sash that circled Odessa's tiny waist and accentuated her budding bosom. The color complimented her strawberry-blond curls, her peachy complexion, and highlighted her green eyes. It suited her to a T. The realization her daughter had become a young beauty did not set Irene's mind at ease…not a bit.

"Mama, isn't it gorgeous? Don't you love it?" Giggling, Odessa twirled around the store in her stocking feet.

"It is lovely," Irene said.

Sarah Laidlaw followed the girls. A smug look on her face, she sidled up to Irene and leaned in to say, "Doesn't she look a treat?"

This was disconcerting too, Sarah Laidlaw speaking to her as if they were bosom-bows

"The dress is a little dear, I'm afraid, but one pays for quality. I believe white stockings are called for," Sarah said. "They grow up so fast, don't they?" she said, her lips pursed in a mother-to-mother-hen way Irene had, heretofore, never been privileged to receive.

Irene nodded and watched Odessa preen and prance before her friends. "How dear is it?" she asked. Mouth dry, the question scratched her throat.

Sarah, aware her husband had given Irene a twenty-dollar line of credit as payment for upholstering her husband's gift of a refurbished sofa, had little underhanded ways of letting Irene know she disapproved. The reupholstering of the sofa had been a challenge—Irene had never done anything like it before. She'd been pleased with the results and, at first, delighted to have the credit.

Drawn to it, Irene reached for the price tag dangling at Odessa's elbow. She turned the tag over in her hand, six dollars and seventy-five cents. She closed her eyes and gulped. That was enough money to supply her and Odessa with food for at least a month—it was payment for two loads of sheets for the boarding house to pay for a dress. And of course, there would be new stockings and ribbons to pay for.

When she opened her eyes, she met the sly gaze of Sarah Laidlaw. She wore a smile like a cat that had cornered a mouse.

"Oh, Mama, you do love it, don't you?"

"Yes, yes, it's lovely. I wonder, will it be warm enough? It doesn't seem to be a dress for winter. It's more for summer socials."

"Hardly," Mrs. Laidlaw promptly said, "the green in the sash and the underskirt more a mistletoe green really, don't you agree, speaks of the holidays—very festive."

Irene could see the dress would be Odessa's—she'd been routed right and proper. On her way over to the Emporium, she'd decided to spend some of the remaining credit on a new pair of shoes for herself. Hers were cold, the soles patched with card and leather from an old feedbag she'd unearthed from the cow shed. Those shoes were out of the question now.

Big innocent eyes wide, Odessa said, "I know it's not...I know it costs more. But I'll do more. I'll help Really I will. Please, may I have the dress?"

All eyes were trained on her. Anna and Junie...and

Sarah Laidlaw, all of them waited. The store had gone very quiet. Outside, Irene heard the jangle of harness, a man shouted to his team, and the rolling rumble announced the stagecoach was pulling into town. Irene's gaze locked with Sarah's, and she saw the gleam of victory there and knew it was useless to struggle.

Setting her jaw, Irene surrendered—so be it, but she wasn't about to spend the hard-earned cash Meda-Belle had paid her to purchase this bit of foolishness. Instinct told her to keep the fact of the cash she had in her pocket to herself. There was probably enough credit left on the account to buy the dress.

Irene left Sarah to her petty triumph, happy to be away from silly, giggling girls, glad to be outside where she could breathe. She had work to do at home. Wash was slow coming from the logging camp this winter. Heavy snow and a month of temperatures never reaching above freezing had halted work.

Deep in thought, head down, Irene conceded her daughter was growing up, as were the Trask boys. On Christmas Day, she'd inadvertently eavesdropped on a conversation between Trenton and Odessa—he'd sounded upset he'd have less time to spend with her. Odessa brushed him off, taking his news as a matter of course.

Her daughter hadn't reacted the same way the summer before when Silas had quit school to take on a full-time job at the livery. After Silas told her he didn't have time to play with her anymore, that he was a man now and didn't have time to play games, Odessa sank into a blue funk—petulant and moody for weeks and weeks. This fall, with Silas no longer attending school, Odessa's schoolwork had suffered, as Irene had feared it would.

The stage had pulled up before the post office. Silas ran to the horses' heads, then helped a passenger disembark. He began to unload luggage and the mailbags. He waved to her as he dashed around, Johnny-on-the-spot.

Irene waved back but kept walking. The awkward bundle of boarding house laundry under her arm threw her off balance as she pushed against the wind. Concentrating on staying on her feet, she negotiated the wagon ruts packed with ice and the deeper drifts to the side and in the middle of the road. Her feet burned with cold, the wind blew up her cloak, and snow caked on the hem of her brown dress.

"Mrs. Obenchain, Mrs. Obenchain," Silas called out. Turning to glance over her shoulder, she stopped and waited for him to hand the only passenger—a gentleman—his valise and black bag.

Silas leaped over the ruts and skidded down the road, making his way across the street to catch up with her.

Shivering with cold, Irene hugged the bundle to her chest in an attempt to capture her body heat.

"Mrs. Obenchain," Silas said above the howl of the wind, clapping his gloved hands together. "Sorry, ma'am, I won't keep you out here in this weather. The thing is, Pa says Trent and me can have the boat on New Year's Eve."

Irene didn't know if the cold had numbed her brain, but she couldn't make the connection between a boat and New Year's Eve.

A smirk on his good-looking face, Silas started again. "We're gonna' hitch up the plow-horse—use the boat as a sleigh. Well, ma'am, Trent and me, I mean Trent and I was wonderin', can Dessie, I mean Miss Odessa, can she come out with us? We'd pick her up around seven or so, after supper, and get her to the Grange—we'll see to it she gets home all right too."

Irene didn't know what to say. She thought Odessa too young to be included in such an enterprise. The question gave her pause.

Her hesitation offered Silas the opportunity to put forward further argument. "Anna, Junie, Carl, and Benny are all comin' along."

Irene laughed. "Sounds like you'll need more than one boat unless you have a yacht."

Silas grinned. "Yes, ma'am, Trent and I will ride Toby."

"I see," Irene said but couldn't hide her smile. "It does sound like fun. I think Odessa would probably hang herself if I didn't let her go. So, yes, I guess it would be all right. But I'm going to hold you responsible for her safety, Silas Trask. She's all I have, so you take care."

The boy, who was now nearly a foot taller than Irene, beamed from ear to ear. "Yes, ma'am, I'll do that all right. Me and Trent will take real good care of Miss Odessa. Like a sister to us," he said over his shoulder and dashed off to get back to work.

Head bowed against the wind, Irene almost forgot her near-to-frozen feet. It did sound like fun. She wanted to ride in a boat behind a horse on a starry, snowy winter's night, laugh and sing and squeal with joy. She smiled to herself all the way home, vowing to send a blanket along with Odessa. Young people didn't seem to mind the cold, but she couldn't afford to have Odessa come down with a chill.

Once she arrived home, instead of picking up the mending where she'd left off, Irene got out the lovely fabric Meda-Belle had given her—it was a fine, velvety, frosted plum color. She thought she'd some black lace somewhere. She'd bought some to dress up one of Paulette's skimpy chemises.

****

Elias, satchel and black medical bag in hand, looked around at the little town Doctor Carter had described as a magical hamlet tucked in under a fine stand of stately ponderosa pine. He pulled the collar of his long, brown cashmere coat up around his neck and adjusted the wool, tweed muffler so it covered more of his chin and jowls and set his black fedora more firmly on his head.

He watched the boy unload his two traveling trunks and saw them safely inside the post office. One of them, he regretted to say, contained his lined winter boots, wool stocking cap, and fur-lined gloves. He shivered. He didn't know what he'd been thinking not to have taken them out on a day like today. He was frozen to the quick.

Doctor Carter had recommended going directly to the Cascade Emporium and Grocery and speaking to Mayor Rupert Laidlaw, who had offered to give him a room. Elias didn't want to dispute these arrangements, but he was not well disposed toward living with a family of six, four of which, Doctor Carter informed him, were children. Elias figured he'd no doubt be seeing enough of them without having to actually live in the same house. It was with this thought at the front of his mind that caused him to inquire of the stagecoach driver if he knew if they had a boarding house in Meadow View.

The stage driver, whose face was almost completely obscured by a full beard of gray, grinned large, revealing two missing front teeth on the top row. After spitting a stream of black tobacco juice into a snowdrift, he said, "Damn, we got us as fine a boarding house as you could want. Meda-Belle's is famous around these parts. Good cook too."

Elias took mental notes as to directions and set his feet to go past the livery and down the alley, headed toward a promising whitewashed, two-story house behind the saloon. It was late in the afternoon, the snowstorm bringing a rapid end to the day.

He raised his hand to ring the bell, then read the sign on the side of the building and glanced at his watch. It was getting dark. He felt safe to take the chance, smiled, shook his head and tugged the leather thong that dangled from the cowbell.

It all happened very fast. One moment he was standing on the porch with an icy wind breathing down his neck, and the next moment he was being hauled by his lapels over the threshold by a scantily dressed woman with red war paint on her face, dressed in a white leather tunic that barely covered her torso.

"Lookit what just blew in," said his captor, kicking the door shut behind him. "Well, look at you. Not from around here, I'll wager. You're pretty as can be," the female said. Circling him, eyeing him up and down, her slender fingers slithered across his chest, to his arm, to his back, and around to his chest again. Tugging him by his arm, the woman turned him to the stairwell. "You come with Grace. I'll take real good care of you," she said as she pulled him up the stairs. "Come on, I bet you're cold."

Stopping on the step above him, she wrapped her arms around his neck and one leg around his hip like a snake wrapping itself around its prey to squeeze it to death. "Come on, honey, let Grace warm you up. I've got a big ol' fire goin' in my room upstairs. I got some nice, warm brandy waitin' for us. I'll rub your feet for you, honey, and once we're between the sheets, you'll think it's the Fourth of July."

Elias at last came to his senses and took a moment to study his captor. She was an Indian, he decided—despite the color of her eyes—a strange color of green, too clear to be hazel and too light green to be emerald. There were yellow sparks like in a cat's eyes. He stumbled up two of the stairs to keep from going down on his nose.

Colorful beads decorated the woman's elaborately braided black hair. She had a red streak of war paint across her forehead, blood-red lips, bronzed cheeks colored with pink rouge. Her leather tunic was of soft white kid, fringed from her ankles up to mid-thigh, the garment barely held together by a silver coin belt around her waist.

"Are you the owner of this boarding house?" Elias asked, neatly turning his body out of her grasp and stepping down to the first floor.

Behind him, the woman snarled. She actually hissed like a snake. "Oh, hell," he heard his would-be captor say in a not-so-ladylike voice. Following him down the steps, she resumed her coiling, seductive tone. "No need to see her. She's not what you need. You look like a man with a cravin' for adventure. You won't find it with that bloated bag-a-bones."

"Bloated bag-a-bones, is it?" came a voice from the back of the hall. The owner of the voice gave his captor a hard look and snarled, "Who you callin' bloated, Grace

Wolfe? You she-devil."

"Good afternoon, ma'am," Elias said and came forward, moving farther away from the seductress, at last realizing he'd stumbled into a brothel.

He felt like a greenhorn—a rube. The woman who'd come from the recesses of the house was attired in the distinctive uniform of a prostitute. He didn't have anything against prostitutes. They were potential patients like anyone else. It was simply that he was not the kind of man who, well, could derive satisfaction from what they had to offer.

"I was looking for a room to rent," he said by way of explanation and offered his hand in greeting. "It appears I was misinformed."

The madam went very still, an unnerving gleam shining in her all-seeing and knowing blue eyes. He had the feeling he was being sized up, undressed, and graded. Coming to the end of her assessment, she nodded and smiled, wiped her hands on her little white Chantilly-lace apron, winked, and took his hand to shake. "Pardon the apron. I was cookin' our supper."

Elias caught himself before he burst out laughing. The woman was wearing very little else but an apron. She was, in fact, in her bloomers and a chemise.

"Mrs. Meda-Belle Lamphere, I'm the owner of this establishment. This here is one of my—ah—boarders, Grace Wolfe," she said.

Grace, her eyes shooting daggers straight at Mrs. Lamphere's bosom, bared her teeth in a frightening pretense of a smile.

"I didn't mean to cause friction, Miss Lamphere," Elias said, fully expecting a catfight to break out at any moment.

"*Mrs.* Lamphere," Meda-Belle corrected.

"Mrs. Lamphere," Elias repeated. "My name is Elias Rayburn. I'm the new doctor."

"Well, bless my soul. Don't give Grace no mind; she's a little disappointed, is all." Meda-Belle beamed a radiant smile that lit up her painted face. She held out her hand once again. "Welcome, Doc. We've been waitin' for you." She shook his hand with vigor this time. "Never expected you'd be...well...that you'd be such a fine example of male pulchritude. It's gonna be a real pleasure to take sick, yes, sir."

Elias began to experience a bit of panic. As bad as the weather was, he needed to get out of here. "I need a room," he said, and started to button up his coat, prepared to brave the elements.

"Well, I'm not gonna let this one get away?" Coming down the steps, Grace grabbed Elias by the arm.

Mrs. Lamphere moved to the bottom of the stairs and wedged herself between Elias and the she-devil. "You can't drag this poor man up to your room 'cause you got an itch, Grace. It's clear he don't want to go. Now let go of his arm."

The two women stared one another down. Mrs. Lamphere dug her red-painted fingernails into the she-devil's upper arm. The she-cat hissed and set Elias free.

He shook out the sleeve of his coat and straightened his collar. The Madame apologized and went on to explain in a very congenial way, a tense smile on her painted lips, "We got rooms here, honey, but we can only rent them out by the hour, and they come with a roommate, if you get my drift."

Elias could feel the predator behind him standing on the first step of the stairwell and prayed he could escape in one piece.

"Grace," the madam said, or rather barked, "you're scaring the man. Can't you see? Leave him alone, or he'll never step over our threshold again."

To Elias, the madam said in a sweet, genteel voice, "You'll have to excuse Grace. She's a bit overeager. A lot of our customers enjoy that sort of thing."

Behind him, Elias heard the she-devil...*Grace*...snort.

Meda-Belle ignored her and continued, "I can see you're a man of taste by the cut of your coat. If it's room and board you're after, there's a place owned by a nice woman on her own with a daughter. She takes in laundry and mending. She's got a nice place—big. She's a fine cook and an upstanding woman."

Elias felt trapped, he was sweating, and he didn't think he should take this woman's word for anything. "I don't know... Doctor Carter wanted me to go see the mayor, Rupert Laidlaw, I believe was the name, about a room. He said he would have a place for me in his home."

"Yup, if you like livin' in a zoo," said Mrs. Lamphere.

Elias grinned at her then. "Yes, I understand they have a large brood. That's why I asked the stage driver if there was a boarding house in town."

"Good ol' Puffer Clark, that's the stage driver. Bet he's havin' a good laugh at your expense right this minute. No. You take my advice and go back the way you come. When you come to the post office, cross the street and go west about four blocks, then turn south onto a lane, and you'll see her lights at the end. It's a fine big log house. She's got a big room on one end that ain't bein' used. Her and her daughter have the other end of the place. Kitchen and living is in the middle. You'd have privacy and quiet. You best get goin' if you don't want to get yourself lost in the dark."

Elias wasn't sure who to trust now, and it must have shown on his face because Mrs. Lamphere put her hand on his arm to reassure him. "Now, I'm pretty good at reading people," and with a sly gleam shining in her knowing eyes, she told him, "I wouldn't risk settin' the only doctor we got in town against me and my girls. The name's Obenchain, Mrs. Obenchain; she's quiet…clean—I wouldn't steer you wrong."

"Thank you, Mrs. Lamphere."

Elias adjusted his grip on his satchel and medical bag, turned to Grace, and tipped his hat. "A pleasure meeting you, Miss Wolfe. I apologize, but I must disappoint you this evening." And he was gone. A swirl of snow drifted inside the house before he closed the door behind him.

Walking away from the boarding house, Elias heard a woman's high-pitched curse. He thought it might have come from the predator Grace Wolfe. He didn't think he'd ever met any woman who frightened him as much as that hellcat. He shivered again, but not from cold.

Then he heard Mrs. Lamphere's definite screech. A series of volleyed curses rang through the crisp air. Elias heard words he'd never heard before, at least not strung together so imaginatively.

Chapter Seven

Through the falling snow, Elias could see Main Street and the pinkish glow of lamplight from the smoke-smudged window of the saloon at the end of the alley. He turned the corner and crossed in front of the open doors of the livery. The heat from the red and glowing forge within the doors beckoned, but he resisted, feeling an urgent need to find permanent shelter for the night.

He caught the eye of the postmaster, who was locking up for the day. "Best get indoors, mister. This ain't no night to be wandering around."

Elias could do no more than nod in agreement. His lips tight with cold, head down against the elements, he crossed the street.

****

Stepping off the boardwalk, Odessa realized she was in a lot of trouble. She didn't have far to go, but the snow was deep, shin-high in places. The wind in her face forced her to stop and tie her wool muffler across her cheeks and mouth and pull her stocking cap down over her eyebrows, leaving her eyes exposed to the elements. Head bowed, shoulders hunched, the brown paper parcel safely tucked under her arm, she set her feet for home.

"Ugh!" Her package went flying, her arms flailed, and she had to fight to stay upright. She'd collided with something very solid…and warm. She'd thought she was on the road, keeping the trees to her right. It was hard to see where she was going with the cuff of her cap pulled down over her half-closed eyes.

"Excuse me, I'm terribly sorry," the warm mass spoke in response to their impact.

"No. Excuse me," she managed to say, teeth chewing her scarf when she opened her mouth. It was a man—she couldn't see his face, probably no better than he could see hers. And for a few seconds, neither of them seemed to know what to say. "I couldn't see where I was going," she managed to squeak out. Looking down, she searched the snow around her for her parcel.

"I couldn't either. I'm not sure where I'm going. Terrible storm," the man said, his words also muffled by the collar pulled up about his ears.

Shifting out to the side, he dipped down and retrieved something from the snowdrift behind her. Handing it to her, he pulled his collar down to ask, "You wouldn't happen to know a woman by the name of Obenchain?"

"My name is Obenchain," she said without thinking, grateful to have her parcel back. A gust of wind dashed them about the head and shoulders with a bushel of snow.

"I'm looking for room and board," the man said over the howl of the storm. He coughed and spit the snow out of his mouth.

Some of the snow had flown into her eyes. The sharp crystals burned as they melted, and tears quickly followed the assault, blurring her vision, caking her eyelashes with ice. "A room?" She'd forgotten about her mother's plan to rent out the big bedroom. Odessa thought it a stupid idea, having a stranger in her house, but her mother had become obsessed with earning a dollar. "Follow me," she said and started to step around the stranger.

"Allow me to take your parcel," the man offered. He was tall like her papa, and it felt good to have his solid presence beside her to serve as a buffer against the weather. The wind pushed her back. She started to list to the side into a drift of snow.

The man quickly put his arm around her shoulder, and she heard him shout, "Hang on to me, and I'll hang on to you. How far is it?" he asked when she stumbled again, and he pulled her in closer to his body to steady her.

"Not very far. There's an old tree that was struck by lightning—has a big gash on its side—our lane is there, and our house is a ways beyond."

They found the tree, and they both stopped to catch their breath. Hanging on to each other, they waded through the drifts, fighting the wind, heading for the faint light coming from the window of the house.

****

Working on her dress, Irene hadn't noticed how late it was until she had to light another lamp to see her stitches. She opened the door and looked toward the big meadow, the snow coming down so heavy all she could see was a wall of white. Looking in the direction of the lane, hoping to see Odessa, Irene couldn't even make out the trees.

She went ahead and peeled the potatoes, scraped the carrots, and added them to the roast venison she had in the Dutch oven over the fire. The meat was falling off the bone. A half-hour went by. She checked the tenderness of the potatoes and went to the door again. Holding out the lamp, she strained to see or hear anything, but there was nothing but the howl of the storm.

What seemed like hours to her were minutes. At one point, she put on her coat, hat, gloves, and scarf, determined to go out and find her child. Then she took them off, only to put them on again a few minutes later. Lamp in hand, she opened the door and lifted the light to shine it out into the yard. At first, she wasn't sure if she'd seen movement or not, then she definitely could make out shapes—a tall and a short. The tall figure was dark and very tall, wearing a long coat and a hat, a hat like Abel's. Abel?

"Abel," she whispered. "Abel," she mewed. How like him to return in the middle of a blizzard—alive, bringing their daughter home safely to her. How like him to return tonight. Tonight she'd welcome him home, forgive him anything to know he was alive.

Shaking, she couldn't hold the lamp up a second longer. Taking a deep breath, she raised it again, her hand clapped over her mouth to hold back the joy, the relief. It was Abel. He was home.

****

Elias thought the light up ahead yawned wider and realized it was an opened door and thanked God. He didn't know about the girl, but his feet were frozen, as well as his hands and his face was numb. It was only a few more feet—they would be inside a house with a fire, just a few more steps.

"Mama," the girl called out and broke away from his embrace.

"Odessa. I was about to come looking for you." The woman at the door laughed a joyous greeting. They came closer. The woman reached out to the girl, then toward

Elias. Tears in her eyes, lips trembling, she attempted to embrace him as well.

The girl fell into the woman's arms, but the woman kept her tear-filled eyes on him, gazing at him with wonder and something else he would have to call love— it was as if she couldn't believe he was real.

"My toes." Breathless, the girl said, "I can't feel my toes."

Her words were slurred—probably her lips were numb with cold, like his, Elias figured.

"My fingers, I don't feel my fingers."

Elias couldn't feel his fingers either, but he was sure they weren't frostbit, but damn near it.

The woman reluctantly withdrew her gaze and hastily began stripping the girl of her mittens, then unwound the wool scarf from around the girl's face, all the while pushing the girl toward the fireplace.

Elias set his satchel and doctor's bag down, removed his coat and hat, and stomped his feet to shake off some of the snow from his shoes and pant legs while the woman tended to the girl. His vision was beginning to clear, and the first thing he noticed was the smell. The room smelled of soap and something savory, like beef stew, and he realized he was starving. His last meal had been breakfast with Doctor Carter.

The second thing he noticed was the laundry. It was everywhere he looked: coveralls, dungarees, long johns, stockings, shirts, and sheets hung all around on webs of cord that zigzagged across the expanse of the sitting room and the corners.

The third thing he noticed was how Spartan the room was. It was devoid of frills, no lace curtains at the windows, no cushions or doilies on the wooden furniture.

No, everything in this room was utilitarian, right down to the braided rugs on the floors. Which were, if he wasn't mistaken, made from old trousers and burlap bags. Taking another sniff, he decided there was probably sawdust under the rugs. He could smell it—it smelled of pitch and pine.

Setting the girl's parcel down on the oversized wooden trestle table in the middle of the room, he ducked under the clotheslines, wove in and out of the hanging laundry, looked around, and spied a shallow wash-pan on the kitchen counter. He filled it with tepid water from the water barrel and brought it back to the bench next to the girl. "Here's a pan of water. Put your feet in it. Don't worry, it's not hot. We'll warm you up slowly."

Bending down beside the woman, he gave the girl's toes a cursory examination. "I don't think there's any damage. There's no discoloration." Taking the girl's big toe between his thumb and finger he gave it a squeeze and watched it turn pink when he let up on it. "See, they're still pink."

****

Irene, holding onto Odessa's foot, stopped massaging Odessa's toes at the sound of the man's voice and looked up into a stranger's face—not Abel's, not her husband's face. Abel had gray-green eyes—the eyes that gazed into hers were brown. And it wasn't Abel's boyish face—this face was quite serious, no mockery in it. *So who the hell are you, and what the devil are you doing in my house?*

"Doctor Elias Rayburn," the man said in reply to her silent question. "I bumped into your daughter...literally, on her way home. I'm interested in the room to let."

Irene made a conscious effort to swallow. She

couldn't help it—her gaze went to the door. Abel wasn't there. He'd been there only moments before. He wasn't there, and there was a strange man next to—close enough—to her. His shoulder touched her own.

Needing a moment to compose herself, Irene stepped aside to observe the self-proclaimed doctor place Odessa's feet carefully into the pan of water while mentally tamping her disappointment down deep inside her heart where even she couldn't find it. She reasoned she should be grateful he wasn't Abel—instead, she might, perhaps, at last, have a boarder and the very real possibility of cash in her pocket.

Finding her voice, her fragile composure back in place, she apologized, "I'm…I'm very sorry. I…I mean, I'm glad to meet you." She held out her hand to the man, "My name is Irene Obenchain, and this is my daughter, Odessa. We are very grateful to you. I can't help but think if you hadn't been with her, she might not have made it home tonight."

The man looked up at her, and Irene became fascinated with his face. Watching his lips move, she noticed he had a dimple in his chin, and there were whiskers growing there. His Adam's apple jumped when he spoke. It took a moment or two before it registered that he was speaking to her, and she should respond.

"No need to apologize," she understood him to say, "or thank me. We helped each other."

"Well…" *gulp*, "I am sorry all the same."

It was hard not to stare. The man came up to his full height. She knew she wasn't very tall, but this man appeared to be something of a giant. Surely he was taller than Abel and broader of chest and shoulders—built nothing like Abel. She shook the image of Abel from her head, wondering how she could've mistaken this man for her beanpole of a husband.

It could have been simple fatigue from traveling, but he wore a weary smile on his face, and his eyes didn't smile. She saw sadness in his eyes. She scolded herself for her preoccupation with his looks—it was disconcerting, unseemly. To dislodge her mind from the subject of his face, she turned to Odessa. "It's very late, Odessa—very dark. I'm surprised the Laidlaws didn't insist you stay with them."

Odessa, she noticed by the slight shrug of her shoulders, had the grace to look contrite. "Well, they did suggest I stay over, but Mrs. Laidlaw kept asking me questions about you doing laundry for the boarding house and the lumber camp."

Mimicking Sarah, Odessa said, *"Does your mama have the men from the lumber camp to supper? Is she good friends with Mrs. Lamphere? Does she go over to the boarding house at night? S*illy questions like that."

Irene squared her shoulders and cautioned herself not to stare. She'd known she would most likely be renting the room to a man. She had no cause to get all fluttery now because of an Adam's apple and a dimple in a masculine chin. Oh, but the eyes, the warm brown, sorrowful eyes.

However, noticing now the fine wool of his suit coat and trousers and the fine linen of his white shirt, she questioned her sanity. How in the world could she ever have thought to rent a room out to anyone—a *man*? It was a large room but sparse. Her home, she knew, was rustic. She liked it that way. But it wasn't for someone as fine as this. This was a gentleman—an educated gentleman. He was handsome—much younger than she'd had in mind for a boarder. She'd thought possibly one of the loggers would want the room—an old bachelor or maybe a schoolteacher. Yes, a schoolteacher—a woman—now that would be very comfortable, but not a man—not *this* man. Then she remembered the doctor they were expecting had a wife. So where was the wife?

"I do have a room to let. It's ten dollars a month, meals included. As soon as you've warmed yourself by the fire, I'll show it to you. I think you should stay here tonight, whether you decide to take the room or not. You can't go back out there."

"I certainly hope not," he said, a little smile on his lips, his eyes crinkling up at the corners and showing a little sparkle in their brown depths.

A flush of chagrin rushed Irene's cheeks, embarrassed she knew she'd sounded less than enthused to take him in as a boarder or as a guest. The problem was—she decided, wanting to place blame anywhere but on herself—he'd taken her by surprise.

Abruptly she turned to a subject with fewer pitfalls. "I have coffee ready. And supper too," she said.

Getting busy, she poured coffee for three. Internally, she chided herself for her clumsy attempt at hospitality. She caught herself staring at his long manicured fingers as he took his cup and wondered what it would feel like to have those fingers touch her cheek. She shivered and scolded herself for thinking foolish thoughts, and consequently, when she spoke, her voice was clipped and borderline rude. "There's cream and sugar on the shelf." She thrust the cup of coffee under his nose. "I'll go light a fire in the other room," she said, hating herself for being a fool, and grateful to have something to do.

Escape—get your silly wits about you, girl.

She marched herself into the room she used to share with her husband.

You're a fool. You thought that man out there was Abel. Remember, you're through with men, especially good-looking, broad-shouldered men. Besides, he's married, and you are married too.

****

Elias followed Mrs. Obenchain with his gaze and sipped the potent restorative. She had to stand on tiptoe to hang up her coat and scarf on the peg by the door before she disappeared into what he assumed would be his room. She was trim, fragile in appearance. Mrs. Obenchain didn't look old enough to have a daughter who must be…now he could get a good look at the girl, on the verge of womanhood, maybe thirteen or fourteen. It was the woman's diminutive size, he decided. It obscured the fact of her true age.

The thought did cross his mind he might stay the night, then tomorrow look for a more permanent residence. A woman alone, even with a daughter, perhaps wasn't the best place for him to settle. Gossip, in a small town, he knew, could be brutal. He'd learned that lesson very early on in his practice in Chicago. Women, especially, made up illnesses to get him into their bedrooms. Most of the time, he found it amusing, but then other times, it was a damned pain in the butt to extricate himself from their coils.

Mrs. Obenchain, however, wasn't likely to try to take advantage of him. Far from it, she seemed as cold as ice—impervious to his charms. The thought of Mrs. Obenchain trying to seduce him made him smile, and he took another sip of the delicious cup of coffee to cover his amusement. He was hungry. Maybe he should sample her cooking. That would be a test, and then he could make up his mind.

****

Irene heard Odessa talking to the doctor as she lit the already laid fire in the grate of the big bedroom. She hoped it would burn. Snow had sifted down the flue on top of the kindling.

She heard Odessa say, "Thank you for helping me out there."

Her daughter's voice sounded sweet and sincere— Irene didn't trust Odessa when she was being sweet.

"I think it was providence I ran into you. Maybe you're my guardian angel."

Irene cringed. This sounded like flirting. Surely, Odessa wasn't flirting with the man?

"Likewise," the doctor replied. "I could say the same about you. You're far more angelic than I."

Irene could tell he was smiling, even without seeing his face.

God, he was flirting back.

That's all I need, a besotted teenage daughter in love with our boarder who is old enough to be her father.

Odessa giggled. "I may appear angelic, but if you ask Mama, she'll tell you there's little resemblance between myself and an angel."

Irene closed her eyes upon hearing her daughter's response.

"Well—tonight, you were a guardian angel for me. I never would've found this place. It was way too dark, and with the snow...I'm sure I would've, by now, been lost...probably frozen in some God-forsaken snowdrift."

Irene didn't like it—she didn't like this at all.

Odessa was becoming too friendly, too fast. This was a stranger, and if he decided to take the room, he would be their boarder. She would have to discourage Odessa from elevating the doctor to an honorary uncle. They needed the money. This was business, and Odessa needed to understand that.

Irene took a deep breath, smoothed her skirts down from the hip, and gave one last glance at the room. Bright, warm light from the kerosene lamp on the bedside table illuminated the bed fashioned from lodge-pole pine. A white, yellow, and blue patchwork wedding-ring quilt, made by her great aunt, over two wool blankets and the heavenly, soft goose-down mattress would make the bed warm. The quilt lay smooth, not a wrinkle on it.

She'd made love, born her babies, and watched them die from that bed. Scanning the room, she assured herself everything was clean and in place. She refused to look at the bed again. A solid, cold ache twisted up low in her abdomen. Hot, salty tears slid down her cold cheeks, and the big bed blurred into a shining pool of blue and gold. She swallowed down the knot of raw loneliness and longing—the longing she kept a secret to hold, caress, and protect.

Irene dashed tears from her cheeks with the back of her hand, *Stop it. This is what you wanted.*

Clenching her midriff, her fingers dug into her stomach. She told herself the room was just a room, *empty, unused, cold—like me.* Quickly, she crossed the room to the barrel table and the rocker on the other side of the hearth to light the other lamp. Smoothing down her skirts again, as if smoothing away the edges of her raw emotions, she returned to her kitchen.

Odessa and the doctor were laughing about something. Irene didn't ask what and proceeded to set the table. She warned herself she shouldn't overreact. It wasn't jealousy she felt at being left out or the room growing quiet with her presence. She told herself she didn't care if they didn't want to converse in front of her. She didn't need to be friends with the man—she needed his money.

"If you care to have a look at the room, bring your satchel and bag. It'll be your lodging, at least for tonight."

She bit her tongue, *why had she said that? Was she hoping he would go away?* No. She kept repeating in her head—we need the money.

****

Despite Mrs. Obenchain's stony demeanor, Elias found himself pleasantly surprised by the warmth and spaciousness of the room she had to let. It was Spartan, to be sure, but there was a big bed, which he was grateful for as he was a tall man, and most beds were too short for his length. The room also contained an armoire, a small table, an old oak barrel with a plank board on top, and a solid oak Morris-style rocking chair. There would be plenty of room for his desk and medicine cabinets, and he thought there would be room for an examination table as well. He might have to move the bed and the armoire, but the space would do nicely. He liked having his own fireplace. That was good, very good, and for ten dollars a month, the price was right.

In truth, it was so much more than he'd expected to find. He'd expected to be bivouacked in some square, little cubicle with barely enough room to turn around and forced to find another space for his office. But this was ideal. He could work here in the evenings and relax and wouldn't have to disturb the rest of the house.

Standing on the threshold of the room, her hands folded, held tight against her waist, Mrs. Obenchain's worry-filled brown eyes followed him as he examined the room.

****

"If you decide to stay, I have a kettle you may use. Fresh water is in the kitchen under the counter. Oh, yes, well, you already found that. The outhouse is out back behind the cowshed. I don't advise trying to go out there tonight—you'll find a thunder mug under the bed.

Irene couldn't tell what he thought of the room. She couldn't decide if she feared he would hate it and tell her no deal or if he'd loved it and wanted to stay. Either way, she knew she was going to be sorry.

"I serve breakfast and supper," she said, catching herself trying to bribe him. At the same time, she felt guilty for asking for so much rent—ten dollars a month seemed like a fortune for such a paltry space.

What about his wife? Sarah Laidlaw said the doctor had a wife. After all, his wife might not like the room— then what? A little desperate, Irene said, "You being a doctor, I would offer provisions when you go out on your rounds. I understand you have a wife. When do you expect her? Naturally, she'll want to see the room before you decide to take it permanently." Pressed to say something in the face of so much silence, she said, "Perhaps you'll want to wait before you decide," she said,

****

Good heavens.

Startled, Elias realized he hadn't thought of Marie

since he'd stepped off the stage. While giving the room a closer look, he knew Marie wouldn't have survived these last two hours, nor would this room impress her. The episode at the boarding house would've sent her over the edge for sure. He smiled, thinking about the hellcat. Oh, no, Marie wouldn't have seen the humor in that situation at all.

Taking a sideways glance at Mrs. Obenchain, he knew Marie would've looked upon the lady's lack of adornment and style as a definite flaw in her character. The stained and patched brown dress she wore like armor plate wouldn't have inspired Marie to be at all sympathetic. Maybe if Mrs. Obenchain would do something with her hair, Elias decided. But, as it was, pulled back and piled on top of her head, it looked like a helmet—as if she expected to go into battle at any moment.

She was plain, he decided, but then upon second glance, he thought no, she wasn't—it was the impression she wanted to project. Her eyes were fine, quick, alert, dark brown. Her complexion was smooth and slightly tan, probably from being out in the weather taking care of all that laundry. He had the feeling she was hiding behind her disguise of dowdiness, and he wondered why. She was all business—work-worn and no doubt tired beyond caring what the hell she wore, or how she looked, he decided, and instantly felt ashamed for judging her.

But Marie, he knew, wouldn't care for his new landlady. And for some reason, he didn't think Mrs. Obenchain would have much use for sweet, vain, and dainty Marie. Taking one more quick look around, his eyes landed on a small table to the side of the hearth. *I know Marie wouldn't like that table—too rough, too common.* After studying the object for a moment, considering its shape and simplicity, he definitely concluded he liked it fine. *Yes, I like that little barrel table a lot.*

Finally, he admitted aloud to himself and to his new landlady, "My wife won't be joining me."

****

Irene pressed her lips together to hold back the snide remark that came quickly to her lips. *So you've run out on your wife. Where did you leave her? Is she crying alone in some empty hotel room? I wonder, did you leave her with child—a gift to remember you by? Men, you're all selfish, unfeeling.*

It was none of her business. It was for damn sure she wasn't going to let a little thing like a weak character keep her from taking his money. For now, because necessity overruled her scruples, she would be charitable. After all, she was all too familiar with the uncertainties hidden within the marriage vows. Maybe doctors, as well as any other member of the human race, she supposed, had no special immunity from the vagaries of misfortune and misunderstanding within the institution of marriage.

She saw the doctor shiver and realized he probably wanted to shed his wet shoes and socks. What she didn't need was a sick tenant to care for, so they should get on with the deal. But how to prod him into making a commitment was the question.

"It's a fine, big room," he declared almost too quickly, making her doubt his sincerity. It was a big room, all right, but there was nothing *fine* about it. It had chinked log walls and a hard puncheon-log floor, with here and there a shabby rag rug, and as far as the furnishings went, they were old and scarred, handmade. No, there was nothing fine about it except the bed. The bed was truly a thing of beauty, big, soft, warm, and looking at it, she felt her heart bleed with need.

"Plenty of room for my things," he said. "If I take the room, I'll want to rearrange things. I'd move the bed over there to the far corner. And I'll want to examine patients here. I would use this room as my office. Do you object?"

Irene took a moment to consider this, then she nodded. Looking around her, her gaze fell on the bed, the comforter neat and cold, and her heart turned to stone. Her mourning was over—it was time to dismantle this shrine. She cleared her throat. "I have no objections. Do whatever you want to make it yours. This room gets a good deal of sunlight. Both of these windows face southwest and give a view of the big meadow. I've shuttered them against the blizzard. The sun and the view, God willing, we will see tomorrow if this storm lets up. Come spring, you could have a separate entrance put over there on the far wall or maybe here on the other side of the armoire. Put up some walls, whatever you think to give you and your patients more privacy."

"You wouldn't mind?"

"I don't give a da— Whatever you decide will be fine. Pay your rent on time, keep it clean, and we'll get along."

Money was money. She didn't have to like him, she told herself. She didn't have to approve. The way she felt right now, she could knock a hole in the goddamn wall herself. She wanted this room gone, and if it wouldn't go away, then yes, by damn, change it beyond all recognition.

****

Elias didn't understand why she looked as if she was about to spit on the wall, but the deal was right, and he was going to grab it. He smiled to himself. Besides, he wanted to stick around and find out if his landlady ever smiled or had she been born with a permanent scowl on her face.

"Fine, I think, Mrs. Obenchain. We should shake on it. I will take the room, and here's your first month's rent."

Chapter Eight

Two days after the doctor's arrival, Irene delivered a load of sheets to the boarding house. Meda-Belle couldn't wait to fill her in on the latest scuttlebutt. Sarah Laidlaw was miffed the doctor had taken up residence with Irene and not with Sarah and Rupert. Seems Sarah had received the news of the doctor's arrival not second-hand, not third or fourth-hand but way down on the grapevine. And Rupert was in the doghouse for not doing more to intervene. Meda-Belle laughed when she told Irene she'd received a scolding for her part in directing the doctor to Irene's house.

Which explained why Sarah had sent Rupert around the very next morning after the doctor's arrival to attend little Oren. Who, from the doctor's account, was not sick at all. Determined and deprived, Sarah had, no doubt, decided that at least she would be the first to make use of the new doctor's services. Which would allow her to be the oracle as to his demeanor, his qualifications, and character.

****

Walking alongside the young postmaster, Morris Melton, Elias found the world to be extraordinarily crisp—eye-blinding white, dazzling with sparkling snow. He didn't know why, but the snow appeared so much whiter here in this big country. The sky was the clearest, the purest of blues—he'd never seen a sky so clear. The snow wasn't melting. It was simply drying up and blowing away in the dry freeze. The drifts of snow had formed a hard crust on the top, but any path or roadway was almost clear of snow, and in places, the hard, dry ground was laid bare.

Young Morris had sought him out early in the afternoon. Morris's wife, Dora, was expecting their first child in a couple of months, and she was having a lot of lower back pain. Elias thought it to be the normal contractions of a young, healthy cervix, but he would call on Mrs. Melton every week between now and the time she delivered. In exchange for the examination fee, Elias bargained for the use of the telegraph. It was Sunday and New Year's Eve, but Morris was more than willing to comply.

As they walked down Main Street toward the post office, Elias revisited, in his mind, his first patient, Oren Laidlaw, and his introduction to his mother, Sarah Laidlaw. She'd shown him the room she was sure he would love rather than be holed up in that "Obenchain barn," The room, up two flights of stairs, above the store, contained a canopied bed, lace curtains on the one window and two fragile looking French chairs snugged up beneath a tippy little table.

Mrs. Laidlaw gave him her unsolicited opinion on a number of topics, but one in particular stuck in his head. "Irene Obenchain is all palsy-walsy with the Lamphere woman. There's something wrong there. You mark my words. It's not decent. I heard she cut George Krauss's hair. Bad enough she's washing unmentionables belonging to loggers and harlots."

After only three days in town, he found Sarah's assessment almost laughable. At first, he'd thought Mrs.

Obenchain didn't like him, but then he'd seen her with the storekeeper and Mr. Russell, and realized she was not discriminating—Irene Obenchain didn't like anyone. She was stiff and formal, always polite but remote. Unfortunately, her attitude spilled over to her interaction with her child. Miss Odessa was manipulative and charming—something of a caution, Elias thought, and shuddered to think what she'd be like at nineteen or twenty.

Mrs. Obenchain had a way of being surly and apologetic at once. The first morning after his arrival, she begged his pardon for the wash hanging across the living room when he'd returned from the Laidlaws'. She huffed and shoved her laundry out of his way as he made his way to her table. He tried to tell her he didn't mind her laundry at all.

This morning, she apologized for banging the baking tins while making biscuits for his breakfast. He assured her he was an early riser, and the sounds of her baking hadn't disturbed him as he'd slept until almost seven-thirty. And he told her once again the wash she had strung all over the place didn't bother him. But the more he tried to assure her he was fine with her occupation and her normal routine, the more she managed to twist his vows of tolerance into condescension.

He had to admit it had come as a bit of a surprise to learn how much laundry and mending she took in, but far from being put off, he rather liked the clean, steamy smell of it. As to her baking early in the morning, well, that reminded him of his childhood and his mother.

Elias had loved his quiet, stoic mother. She supported him in every way she could and sent him the money she saved from her household allowance. She made his clothes. She sent him food. She wrote him letters of encouragement. Yes, the smell of laundry on the line and biscuits before dawn, those were good memories of his deceased mother.

These thoughts led him to wonder—where was *Mr. Obenchain*?

Sarah Laidlaw had given him her unsolicited slant on the situation. "Abel Obenchain. Good-looking rascal," is what she'd said. "Ran off to find gold in the Yukon. It will be four, no five years come March, and nobody's seen or heard hide nor hair of him. He left Irene with nothing but her house and the few clothes she had on her back."

Elias was sure he'd find out from Sarah Laidlaw the history of every family in the Deschutes Basin in time. Small towns, they were something. He smiled to himself and began to whistle as he and Morris crossed the street to the post office.

Inside the office, he said, "I appreciate this, Morris," and removed his fur-lined gloves and set them on the countertop. "I want to send a telegram to Doctor Carter in Farewell Bend."

Green visor in place, seated in his official telegraph-sending chair, Morris handed him a freshly inked pen. "Write it out on this form. Will you be expecting a reply today?"

"Yes. Yes, I hope to have a reply as soon as possible." Then he amended, thinking aloud, "But, I suppose, if Doctor Carter is on a case, I shouldn't expect one."

"Well, let's send it out. Darrel Chilton, at Farewell Bend, will probably be able to tell us within a few minutes if Doctor Carter is in or out."

The message was rather long, as telegrams go. It read as follows: *Settled in—stop—Found room and board—stop—Send freight to Obenchain, 21 W. Cascade Ln—stop—Meeting all tonight—stop—You were right about Big Meadow—stop—Splendid—stop— PS. Please advise arrival of freight—stop*

Ten minutes later, a message came in return: *Tumalo road closed two days—stop—Freight out Wednesday— stop—Should arrive same—stop—Know Obenchain, good woman, clean, respectable, healthy—stop—Wish I could be there—stop—Social at St. Charles, big plan for new hospital—stop*

The message ended there, but as Elias headed toward the door, Morris began to jot down more code. "Wait, Doctor Rayburn, there's more for you." For the next few minutes, all Elias heard was the click of the wire, then Morris tore off the message and handed it over.

Received wire Mrs. Rayburn evening yesterday— stop. Arrived in good time Chicago—stop—Mother, father happy to have me home—stop—Believe this is best way—stop—Always, Marie—stop

Elias stood quietly for a moment, seeing Marie's face before him as he waved goodbye to her from the depot in Boise.

Morris stood quietly by and, after a second or two, asked, "You want to send another telegram?"

"No." He had nothing to say, but then changed his mind, "Yes, I think I will."

Morris gave him another form and passed him the pen. Elias deliberately used her maiden name on the form, *Marie Donnigan*—it was how he thought of her now. Marie had chosen not to be his wife…so be it.

"Send it to this address," he said to Morris, and wrote it out at the top of the form. *Marie—stop—Received news of your safe arrival—stop—You may reach me at 21 W. Cascade Ln, Mountain View, Oregon—stop—Found room and board—stop—Snowstorm waylaid freight—stop—Will return your furnishings—stop—All the best to you this New Year—stop—* Halting a moment to think, he added, *A new start for both of us—stop—Elias—stop*

God, he hated reminders of Marie—of his failure. He was tired of torturing himself, going over everything again and again, but he didn't think he would have done anything differently.

He salved his conscience by telling himself Marie didn't love him or trust him enough. That worked most of the time, but there were times, like now, when he hated himself for not doing more to make his marriage work—for failing to keep her at his side.

Leaving the post office, on his way back to his room, he shook himself out of his depression. He smiled in spite of himself, recalling a conversation the day before with young Miss Obenchain.

"Mr. Laidlaw said we might have a telephone at the Emporium someday…maybe next summer. Think of it, Doctor Rayburn, a telephone. You could call your wife in Chicago."

Yes, maybe that would help, he thought. But for now, there was more between Marie and himself than miles.

****

Irene had finished sewing the buttons on the shirt for Mr. Russell and the rest of the ironing. Finally, she had a few moments to herself to try on her new dress. Odessa was at the blacksmith shop with Silas and Trenton getting the boat harnessed up to the plow horse. She wouldn't be expected for a half hour or more. And the doctor called out earlier in the afternoon and was over to the Meltons.

Cocking her head to the side, she saw looking back at her in the long, narrow, cheval glass a younger version of how she imagined herself. The woman looking back at her was slim, but not too slim, a nice bosom and a small waist. The dress was a heavenly shade, not quite blue, not quite lavender, and it complemented her weathered complexion. The black lace fichu inserted into the low décolletage was a nice touch, she decided, bringing to the design of the dress a bit of gentility. She smiled in spite of herself.

She was glad now she'd accepted the dress pattern from Paulette and the fabric from Meda-Belle. At the time, she'd felt awkward and strange and accepted the offered cast-offs to appease the ladies in order to make a quick exit rather than out of anticipation of making anything for herself. At first, she'd thought to cut the pattern down for Odessa, but the color of the fabric was too somber for her daughter.

Irene stood at the mirror and started to experiment with her hair. At one point, it got away from her and fell down in a heavy, loose coil about her shoulders. She couldn't believe how long it had gotten. Accidentally, her gaze went to her reflection, and there in her mirror stood a sensual, sultry siren. The fabric of the dress clung to her hips and bust. Instantly, her reaction to her reflection was an accelerated heartbeat, nipples becoming erect, and butterflies fluttering in the pit of her stomach. Startled, struck by an unreasonable fear of anyone seeing her like—seeing this Irene, and discovering what she'd been keeping a secret, sent her into a panic. Fingers trembling, she scrambled out of the dress, ruthlessly wound her hair up tight on top of her head, and donned her old brown dress. For a few moments, she sat on her bed, arms folded tightly across her chest, eyes closed.

When she opened her eyes and caught her breath, she came to a ruthless decision—she would not wear the dress. She vowed never to look in the mirror again. The woman in the mirror must never be discovered. She must forget about young Irene, bury her. She had no time to mourn the loss of her other self.

Coming back down to earth, Irene rationalized two nights with very little sleep had left her jittery and testy. It was hard to sleep with a man in the house. She didn't know how to cook for a man anymore. She recalled Abel liked anything with gravy on it and potatoes—lots of potatoes. She was trying to cook that way again, but Doctor Rayburn didn't seem to have much of an appetite—there were a lot of leftovers. She had fried hash this morning from the leftover venison roast she'd prepared the first night he'd arrived. He'd eaten all of the hash plus two eggs.

It bothered her more than she could say. She felt compelled to please him. She asked herself why she should care. He wasn't her husband. He was some other woman's husband. She'd wasted a lot of her years worrying about how to keep Abel happy, and in the end, he'd left her—left his daughter. This man was no different. He was handsome, charming, but no different. He wasn't going to stay. He would leave someday, and he wouldn't give a thought to her.

She worried about her laundry being in the way, about the ironing board and the mending taking up all the room at the table. She worried he might need more blankets—she didn't have any more blankets. She worried Odessa would make a pest of herself with her chatter at the table. All of these worries, and a million more, crowded in upon her and made sleep impossible.

There were so many things she'd not thought of when she first advertised a room to let. The money was nice, very nice. She could almost relax and stop economizing. She thought she might even get a new pair of shoes. But, it was hard to justify the cost to her nerves against the easing of the budget.

Composed and calm, she closed her bedroom door, blocking the disconcerting image in her mirror from her mind. The front door opened—it was the doctor returning. Feeling caught out like a naughty child for playing dress-up, she felt her cheeks burn, and her words gushed out of her mouth. "Doctor Rayburn, didn't expect you back so soon. But...but you could have a light supper." Driven to please him, hating herself for contradicting everything she'd been thinking, she hustled to get food on the table. "I've soup on the hearth and fresh bread." Not waiting for a reply, she got down a bowl and began to ladle out the soup. "It'll be late before you get potluck at the Grange."

"Thank you," he said and hung up his hat and coat at the door. "Soup sounds good. I am hungry. The fresh air has improved my appetite, or maybe it's your fine cooking. I'm not used to so much gravy, though. I'm liable to put on weight."

****

He caught her looking at him as if he'd said something of great import, and couldn't for the life of him remember what they'd been talking about, so he said, "I smell apple pie and…I think, pumpkin pie."

She actually met his gaze, smiled, and set the bowl of soup down in front of him. "I baked two pies, one apple and one sweet potato for the potluck."

"Both my favorites," he said, pleased to think he'd brought a smile to her eyes. But, not wanting to make too much of it, he started to butter his bread.

Surprising him, she sat down at the table, and for a moment or two, she sat staring down at her empty bowl. She adjusted herself in her chair and raised her head. "I'll be staying home this evening. Would you mind very much taking the pies with you? I'll put them in a basket for you."

He stopped eating, laid his spoon beside his bowl, and folded his hands before his chin. Resting his elbows on the table, he looked into her brown eyes, so soft, so full of fear and uncertainty. "You don't care for socials, Mrs. Obenchain? We are bringing in a new century tonight. This should be a joyous occasion—a once-in-a-lifetime occasion. Surely you don't want to miss out."

"I…I think socials are very nice," she said, avoiding his gaze. Stammering, she continued, "I…I can't believe it's the twentieth century…but…but you see…"

"Ah, but I think I do see. You don't care to come to the social and listen to all the welcome speeches on my behalf," he said, one eyebrow raised. If she'd look him in the eye, she'd know he was teasing. "I have a very fragile ego, Mrs. Obenchain. I find it very lowering to my self-esteem that you, my own landlady, don't want to attend a party that, in part, is being given in my honor.

How would it look, Mrs. Obenchain? No...I don't think it's to be allowed. You have a duty to perform, Mrs. Obenchain...as do I—we'll go together."

Picking up his spoon, he said, "Good, now that's settled. I would be honored to carry your delicious pies. In return, you will lend me your support. I will be meeting a room full of strangers and curiosity seekers. Mrs. Laidlaw has made it clear I am to be made the main attraction. I will need you there to help when I wish to escape."

He watched her shrink back into her chair. He could almost feel sorry for her, but he didn't intend to leave her behind to play the martyr. No.

****

Irene recognized the look—he was studying her, trying to figure her out and if she wasn't careful, he might discover something.

Pompous—all men are pompous.

Chin up, she surrendered. "Very well, Doctor Rayburn, I'll go. But I don't think my absence would be remarked upon. As a matter of fact, I suspect it would be considered the correct thing for me to do."

Taking a moment to assess his reaction to her announcement and feeling outrageous, she said, "As for you, you are conceited, but no more and no less conceited than the rest of your gender."

He smiled large. "At last, a proper response." His laugh filled the room, and Irene blushed, and she felt something, something like warmth, heat. Blood surged through parts of her she'd forgotten.

"Ah, now we begin to understand one another," he said. A satisfied smile on his handsome face, he went back to his soup.

91

Irene put her head down to her food to prevent him from seeing her confusion. She'd deliberately insulted him, and she'd shamed herself. Drat the man for provoking her to such outlandish behavior. What was she to do? He inspired her to misbehave, grovel and serve. Damn the man. Maybe, if she were insulting enough, he would leave, but she didn't want him to leave. And anyway, he seemed impervious to her insults and snarls, so she held little hope of success—or rather her failure—again, she couldn't decide what she wanted.

****

Elias, distracted by her hands, wondered if he dared broach the subject. He'd noticed their raw, red roughness the very first evening when they'd shaken hands. He'd some herbal ointment that might be soothing. He hesitated to mention anything that would give her cause to retreat again. They seemed to have broken the ice somewhat. It was their first actual conversation, even if it had been more of a sparring match.

"You work very hard," he said by way of an opening. "In weather like this, your hands must suffer even more than usual."

He paused and noticed her bristle—chin up, jaw tight. She dropped her spoon and started to push herself away from the table. He wiped his mouth with his napkin and continued to sail into uncharted waters despite the storm warning. "I only bring it up because I'm a doctor, you know? I've noticed your poor hands, the chilblains? Must be very painful. I have some ointment in my bag, if you will allow me to give you some. As your doctor, I prescribe you apply this ointment to your hands right now and again before bed. You may use it on your cheeks, too. I do. In this cold, our skin can dry quickly under freezing conditions."

****

Mortified, Irene groaned and slid her hands off the table to her lap. "I know my hands are rough as tree bark." Cringing, she didn't know where to look or where to go. She wanted to run and hide—only her pride and a pair of weak knees kept her in her chair. She was well aware her face was peeling and cracked, her cheeks chapped. Facing facts, she realized she could probably go to the social tonight naked, and the only thing anyone would remark upon was her face looking like a baby's butt with diaper rash.

Bringing her head up, she met his wonderful tender gaze and felt even more of a stupid fool when he began to apologize, "I am sorry. I was only trying to give you aid."

Putting up her chin, she straightened her spine; after all, she'd earned her chapped hands and wind-burned cheeks. "The truth is, I don't have time to worry about my hands or my complexion when there is work to do."

After a few pregnant moments of silence, Irene relented, her voice cracking a little "I…would like some of that ointment. My fingers…the fingernails are split, and they do hurt. Sometimes they get infected. I've been using bag-balm."

He nodded. "Hmm, that's good, but I think we can heal them up altogether."

Working very hard not to get caught indulging in a bit of self-conscious, awkward silence, she hurried on to say, "Your things, will they be arriving soon?" To avoid his eyes, she picked up her bowl and put it in the dishpan at the kitchen counter. Without looking at him, she offered him a second helping of soup.

"They'll be here in a couple of days," he said, after a long pause, his eyes boring a hole in her head. "The road is closed at Tumalo, and yes, I'll have a refill on the soup."

Odessa came in, full of chatter and excitement about the evening, and for once, Irene was glad for the diversion. Odessa didn't want to sit down to eat, but Irene insisted. Since the doctor was still at the table, Odessa conceded she might be a little hungry. A lively exchange ensued about the kind of music they could expect. Irene set aside her misgivings and steeled herself to endure an uncomfortable social evening.

Chapter Nine

In her room, Irene brushed her hair and avoided looking in her mirror. Fingers shaking, she tucked her locks into a black lace chignon from ear to ear at the base of her neck. Her trembling fingers stroked the lovely soft fabric of the dress laid out on her bed and knew she would wear it and hoped none of the babies would throw up on her.

Dressed, she opened her door to Odessa's giggles as she skipped around the room, prancing like a show pony in her new dress. Irene wished the girl weren't so prone to exhibition, especially in front of the doctor.

"You keep a blanket over yourself in the boat, young lady. It's cold out there, even with a coat on. And you wear your scarf over your ears. If you come down with a cold, I'll have Doctor Rayburn fix you up with the most vile-smelling mustard-plaster he can think of."

Odessa stopped twirling, shook her head, green bow on top of her curls bouncing. "Oh, pooh, I won't get cold. I'll wear my mittens. I'll wear my scarf around my neck and one on my head. Anna, Junie, and I will bundle up together under the blanket. We'll be warm as toast."

Out of the corner of her eye, Irene caught Odessa staring at her. The doctor spoke before Odessa had a chance to comment. "You look very…charming," he said to her from his chair at the table. "That shade of blue becomes you. You smell nice too, you smell like the color of your dress—lilac?"

"Thank you. Yes…lilac and rose water." She scolded herself. She must stop her tendency to stammer and blush when faced with one of the doctor's compliments.

Odessa, thank heaven, stopped her from making a bigger fool of herself by offering a backhanded compliment. "I like the color of your dress. Not really a party dress though, is it? Reminds me of a funeral. But, oh, you do smell lovely. Can I put some on, too, please? I won't use very much. Just a little, please?"

"It's on my bureau, a little atomizer. Two squirts Odessa, two, no more. It came all the way from Virginia. My cousin Grace sent it to me as a Christmas gift last year. I intend to make it last."

Irene spared the doctor a brief glance. The provoking man sat smiling at her. His warm sable eyes danced with humor. Did he know she'd used four squirts? He couldn't, could he?

She averted her gaze, annoyed with herself for smiling back. He shouldn't be looking at her like that. He was married. She was married, and she certainly wasn't pretty or desirable, not by a long chalk.

Conscious of the silence stretching between them, now Odessa wasn't in the room, Irene said in a rush for the sake of distraction, "I don't know if Odessa's feet will even touch the ground tonight, she's so excited. She gets bored, says there isn't anything to do around here."

Irene chanced to look his way again and blushed. Meeting the twinkle in his eye, she wondered what was going on in that head of his. Surely he didn't believe she was fool enough to think he actually found her attractive? And he better not be thinking a little flirting and flattery would get more than the use of a room and some food for his ten dollars a month.

But he did look particularly handsome tonight, she had to admit. The ladies of the town would, no doubt, fall all over themselves to make him welcome. She didn't think he was as conceited as Abel, but the doctor knew he had charisma, all right—he knew it, and he used it to get his way. She was wise to him. Meda-Belle was right. If you knew one man, you knew them all.

This is awful. It's silly. In any event, here I am in my new, funereal-colored dress, not because I want anyone to look at me differently, but because, damn it all, it feels good to have a new dress. No one is going to care. The doctor noticed, but he's one of those, like Abel, who enjoys setting a woman all a-twitter, which is...provoking...and perverse.

Irene heard the sound of harnesses and laughing voices. It was dark outside and had been for an hour and a half, the full moon not yet up. "Odessa, I think they're here," Irene said.

Odessa erupted from Irene's bedroom and leaped like a spring fawn across the room to look out the window.

"Stop jumping around. Really, you must learn to behave as grown-up as you look."

Odessa waved her hand at her. "Oh, I'm going to have fun all night. And dance...I'm going to dance with all the boys...especially one boy—*Silas*. And he's going to think I'm the prettiest, the most clever girl for miles around. Where's my coat? They're here. The blanket...I need the blanket..."

"You're getting too big for your britches, young lady," Irene said, giving her daughter a little swat on the bottom for being so sassy and full of herself. "Now stand still, and get your coat on."

The doctor followed them outside, holding out a lantern to the party.

A little breathless, Irene helped Odessa into the long, low rowboat and saw her safely seated between Junie and Anna. Silas, with Trenton behind him, sat on the broad back of Toby, the shaggy-coated, chestnut Percheron. Puffs of warm, white breath emitted from the gelding's wide nostrils as he patiently waited, head relaxed and neck down, for his passengers to board.

"Pretty evenin', even prettier when the moon gets up," Silas said. "You're lookin' particularly fetchin' this evenin', Mrs. Obenchain," he added, a big smile lighting up his handsome face. It wasn't so much what he'd said. It was how he'd said it. Irene stifled a silly giggle. Ridiculous for a mature woman to get all giddy over a little flattery from a handsome young boy. Ridiculous—she dipped her head to hide her confusion. "Thank you, Silas, nice of you to notice. Are you going straight to the grange?"

"Thought we might take a turn or two around town—maybe see if some other folks need a ride," Trenton said.

Anna Davis spoke up to say, "It's too early to go to the dance. Hardly anyone is there yet."

Junie shared the wool blanket and tucked it in under her legs. Carl Davis, who was of an age with Silas, and his brother Benny, who was nine, sat fore and aft in the boat.

The boat rocked as everyone settled in. Toby, a little shy of the odd conveyance, shifted, which made the boat teeter even more. Irene foresaw disaster, the boat overturning, dragging the children underneath it over the frozen, rutted road. "You go easy, Silas. No, racing, you hear me? Odessa, don't you wiggle around too much—that's still a boat."

"Pa already said he'd have my hide if I upset this thing or kilt anybody," Silas said, his admission doing nothing to assuage her fears.

"He'll have to get in line behind me," Irene said without a hint of amusement in her voice.

They pulled away, and the sound of the hame-bells on the harness echoed in the still of the winter's night.

"They'll be fine," the doctor said. "I rather envy them. Maybe we could steal it after they go inside to dance, take a ride ourselves."

"I know," she said and sighed. Without thinking, Irene folded her arms across her chest to comfort the aching envy in her heart. Her eyes followed the unwieldy conveyance until it turned down the street at the end of the lane and passed out of sight. "I thought the same thing when Silas first told me what he was going to do. It does look like fun. I hope they don't get carried away with their fun."

The doctor shivered. "Here, you don't have on a coat. Come back inside. It's too cold to stand out here." And, without Irene even aware of it at first, because it seemed so natural, he put his arm about her shoulder. It was a simple gesture, but the sensations it evoked were not simple—not for Irene.

****

Irene, self-conscious, Doctor Rayburn's hand beneath her elbow providing support, quick-marched her way down the dark lane to Main Street and turned east to head for the Grange. The young people in their horse-drawn boat came up behind them. Of course, they were all in high spirits. Even their newest passenger, Mary Pritchard, the schoolmarm, a twinkle in her eyes and a tinge of color on her cheeks, looked especially animated…younger…this evening.

Ahead, traffic had gathered in front of the Grange. At the schoolhouse, a crowd of people stood around, talking and laughing. Highly aware his gloved hand wasn't simply bracing her, Irene registered the doctor was escorting her. She stopped in her tracks. Out in plain view now, both a little breathless, having reached the boardwalk at the brisk pace she'd set, they needed to put some distance between them. It was one thing for the doctor to walk alongside her. It was another thing altogether for him to have his hand on her. It would surely cause talk if anyone noticed.

Should anyone notice? What a funny thought— *everyone would notice*—you couldn't pass gas in this town without someone noticing. The doctor remained oblivious, unaware they were about to become the talk of the town. He prattled on about the stars in the sky being like diamonds and the moon a huge pearl.

He had her large wicker basket, the one she'd packed with the two pies, sausage rolls, and three place settings in hand. It was heavy, she knew, and felt guilty for making him carry it, but she meant to go the rest of the distance on her own steam. "I'll take the basket," she said and reached for it.

****

Huffing from the exertion of keeping up with her and in fear of losing his grip on the heavy basket of food, Elias fought to keep his balance while at the same time giving her his support. On reflex, he held the basket out of her reach and laughed at her attempt to take it away from him.

A moment ago, he'd thought he could cajole her out of her sour mood by pointing out the beauty around them, but after looking into her eyes, he could see she wasn't about to relent. His feelings of guilt only lasted a moment—now he simply looked at her as a challenge. Irene Obenchain might be stubborn and pigheaded, but he was equally so, as she would soon discover.

As if resenting its presence, her sad eyes gave the moon a brief glance. "I know that moon," she said. "It can be very powerful if you're not used to it." He wanted to ask what the heck she meant by that, but she immediately put her head down and tried to take the basket from him. He held it away from her. In a huff, she took off, arms swinging, chin up.

Catching up with her, he started to lock his arm with hers, but she pulled her cape closer about her middle, tugged her arm from his grasp, and tried once again to reach for the basket. Pulling back, he put both of them off balance. She listed, falling against his side. He caught her before they both went down.

Righting them both, he adjusted the basket in his grip and took her arm—which was stiff and unyielding. He deliberately placed her hand within the crook of his arm, leaned down, gazed into her eyes, and said very quietly, "I said I would carry the basket, and I am a man of my word. And unless you want to wrestle me for it, right here, right now, I intend to carry this basket all the way to the party."

****

Although Irene couldn't see his mouth because of the woolen muffler he had tucked up around his jaws, she could tell by the way his eyes were all crinkled up at the corners he was smiling—probably laughing at her. When he slipped his arm under hers and laid his hand on her wrist, drawing her into his body so they were now hip to hip, she thought she heard him chuckle. It wasn't dignified to argue, but she wanted to.

They had to dodge the traffic around the Grange. The Bodeman family had taken up most of the yard. Irene couldn't ignore them, not after Mr. Bodeman greeted them with a "Jolly good evening." Resigned, she performed introductions.

****

Elias hoped he wasn't expected to remember everyone's names tonight. He smiled and shook hands with Abner and Ida Bodeman, met their two daughters and their husbands, and admired the older daughter's six-month-old son John.

In the vestibule of the Grange, they encountered Mrs. Lamphere and Mr. Russell removing their coats. George Krause assisted a young woman Elias hadn't met before by the name of Paulette O'Day, who, obviously, by the amount of rouge on her cheeks and lips, was one of Mrs. Lamphere's girls. And then, of course, there was Miss Wolfe, whom Elias remembered all too well.

****

Irene blushed at the sight of Mrs. Lamphere, resplendent in her gown of burnt orange. She couldn't imagine where the woman got the nerve to wear that getup in public.

Paulette and Grace also wore their new gowns. Paulette wore a pink confection covered with tiny rose buds, a sweet dress but for the risqué neckline, which Irene had lowered three times to get it how the girl wanted it.

Grace looked magnificent in a gown of turquoise satin that clung to her svelte body like a glove. Irene had gone through torture sewing her dress, ripping seams, re-cutting fabric and enduring Grace's abuse. To proclaim her heritage, the woman wore layers of silver and turquoise jewelry around her neck and wrists and had her hair in two long braids, interwoven with a leather thong strung with seashells. Irene was certain Grace's aim was to appear wild and enticing. It was for certain she wouldn't go unnoticed.

Grace accidentally—on purpose—rubbed up against the doctor in the crowded cloakroom. "Sorry, Doc," she said, but her delivery was as seductive as a cat's purr.

Irene received a nasty sneer and a nod from the woman.

She'd sewn the creations these women were wearing, fitted them, and fussed over the details. It never occurred to Irene she'd ever see them modeled in public; she always assumed they'd be worn within the environs of the saloon or the boarding house. This was awful—embarrassing. She prayed no one would remark upon it being her handiwork—*please, God.*

Sarah Laidlaw, looking imperious and regal, stood next to her husband at the hall entrance, practicing politics. Irene watched the woman, her pasted-on, fake smile in place, as Sarah greeted Mrs. Lamphere and her party.

Irene had also sewn and fitted Sarah's high-neck gown of cream linen and lace. For Irene, it was a toss-up as to which woman was the more difficult client to please...Grace Wolfe or Sarah Laidlaw.

Rupert smiled and greeted Mrs. Lamphere and her girls. "You ladies are looking lovely this evening," he said in the same affable tone of voice he'd used to greet the Bodeman ladies. The look on Sarah's face was priceless, so sour it could have curdled cream, and nearly set Irene into a fit of giggles.

Everything would've been fine, but Meda-Belle couldn't let it pass. "Why, bless you, Rupert," she said, and winked at Irene. "We can thank Mrs. Obenchain's nimble fingers, aye…Sarah? I think I see her handiwork on you tonight, as well. She's turned us out in style, bless her."

Sputtering a bit, chin pulled in, Sarah reluctantly agreed. "Yes, very fine."

Wisely, Mr. Russell moved his party along, albeit with a grin on his face. Sarah directed the full force of her attention toward Doctor Rayburn, affording Irene the opportunity to slip the basket from his hand and make her escape.

Irene knew her place. Finding the buffet table, she began to set out the contents of her basket, then moved farther down, away from the gathering throng, to the bleacher bales where she knew the nursery would be. Sitting down, she removed her gloves and folded her hands in her lap, prepared to be entertained—watch the community surround the new doctor.

Sarah Laidlaw, in her element as hostess, performed posturing introductions as if she were a queen and this a grand ball or state occasion. Irene sneered while Sarah simpered and preened and flirted with the new doctor—it was sickening.

Oh, stop. You're getting as catty as she is. She's the mayor's wife. Why shouldn't she be the one to do the introductions? You're jealous. That's what you are, Irene Obenchain. You can't be getting possessive because you're renting a room to the man.

Giving a mental shake back to her senses, Irene's only real concern was Odessa. Everyone else could go hang. Which brought her around to asking herself, *Odessa, where are you?*

As if conjuring her daughter up out of thin air, Odessa, followed by Anna and Junie Davis, breezed into the hall. They were beautiful, New Year's nymphs, giggling, pink with cold. Anna, tall, almost Amazon, splendid in a dress the color of ripe cherries, the color perfect to set off her black hair and fair complexion. Her sister Junie, of the same color hair and complexion, although petite and dainty, was dressed all in blue. Odessa, her coloring creating quite a contrast with her strawberry-blonde hair, looked beautiful and all grown up in her new dress of white and green.

Silas and Trenton Trask, Benny and Carl Davis, and Tom and Bill Laidlaw, all dressed in their Sunday best dark suit coats and white shirts, came in directly after the girls, and immediately the volume of noise in the room went up almost one hundred percent. The room, full of young people—now felt crowded, everyone jostling for room and everyone talking at once.

Young Rob Morgan, fiddle in hand, Milo Pederson proudly carrying his banjo under his arm, and his wife Mary Jane, who played the piano, took the stage and began to warm up their instruments.

Milo Pederson, the blacksmith, a big man with a big, resonating voice, called the square dances. When he played the banjo, his big hands and sausage fingers and his physical aspect seemed inconsistent with the joy and the emotion he inspired through his instrument. Irene did enjoy the music at these gatherings, and she realized that yes, she would've hated to miss this. Despite her earlier reluctance to join in, she had to admit she was enjoying herself watching all the action and byplay.

A few of the gathered citizens, besides Irene, noticed the musicians had begun to warm up, starting the evening off with the "The Tom Bigbee Waltz." A few couples, Laura and her husband Tom and Helen and her husband Levi, took to the floor. Levi and Helen's baby, under the supervision of the grandparents, sat on the straw bales.

The musicians picked up the pace after a little fine-tuning and broke into "Seneca Square Dance," followed by "Footprints in the Snow."

Odessa danced every dance, twice with Silas, once with Trenton, once with George Krauss, and once with Doctor Rayburn. Odessa only wanted to dance with Silas. Irene knew that, but her daughter also knew it wasn't how these socials worked. At the socials, all the ladies, as well as the gentlemen, had to mix and mingle— no one was to be left out—with the exception of Irene.

Irene couldn't remember the last time she'd danced or laughed. The loss of her babies had dried up all the laughter and joy inside her. And with Abel's defection, she found little to celebrate.

An hour and a half later, Mr. Laidlaw called time out. "Time to put on the feed bag," he announced. Irene helped the Laidlaw children get seated on the straw bales with their plates of food. She didn't notice when Doctor Rayburn came up beside her.

"Where's their mother?" he asked, his gaze traveling around the room, looking for the Laidlaws.

"My goodness, you gave me a start," Irene said, teetering backward. She caught herself before tumbling off her perch. The doctor quickly steadied her, his hands encircling her waist.

"Sorry, I was wondering if you were allowed to eat," he said, his gaze still searching the crowd.

Irene slapped his hands from her waist. "Of course, I'm allowed to eat. What a ridiculous thing to say."

Dropping his arms to his sides, he drew his eyebrows together, then got the funniest look in his eyes. He looked hurt as if she'd insulted him—but that was impossible.

After another look around the room, he said, "So you're in charge of the nursery. Did you put yourself in charge, or was it assigned by peck order via the mayor's wife?" Pausing a moment, he narrowed his eyes and made another guess, this one purely silly but fun, "Or is this your way of sparing yourself from having your feet worn down to stumps."

Irene couldn't hold back the giggle. "Clever of me, isn't it?" Their gazes met—standing as she was on a bale of straw put her at his height. Self-consciously, she pushed a stray curl off her forehead, trying with little success to push it back into place into the chignon. He put up his hand to stop her. Then in a voice so low she barely heard him, he said, "Don't. I like that curl, it softens your face, and for a moment there, I think I saw the real you. You're much younger than you want anyone to know, and you're beautiful. What I don't understand is why that frightens you so."

Elizabeth Laidlaw spilled her cider in her lap. Irene was grateful to have something to do other than stand there and search for something to say.

Sarah Laidlaw popped up out of nowhere and elbowed Irene out of the way, very nearly toppling her off her perch. "Oh, dear, what's happened? You shouldn't be sitting way up here, sweetheart," Sarah said to her daughter over the child's wails of protest. Handing Irene the child's sopping wet plate of food and dripping cup, Sarah picked up her daughter by her underarms and brought the kicking and screaming child down to a lower bale.

"Irene Obenchain, whatever were you thinking to allow my baby to sit way up there?" Sarah said to Irene. "Never mind," she said. Catching the doctor's disapproving scowl, she amended, "Oh, well, I suppose you weren't thinking, so like you." And added a shrug of dismissal.

Taking advantage of the situation, the doctor took the opportunity to say, in a condescending, cheery voice, "Mrs. Laidlaw, you have everything well in hand, it seems." Before Sarah could think of a reasonable protest, he said, "Well, then, that's fine. Come, Mrs. Obenchain, before all of your delicious sausage rolls are gone."

None too gently, he guided Irene over to the buffet table, where they encountered Abner Bodeman and his wife Ida. Holding his plate and a plate for her, the doctor loaded up the goodies from the table for both of them.

"Evenin' Mrs. Obenchain," Abner said. "You're lookin' especially fine this evenin', ain't she, Ida?"

Ida Bodeman at first looked startled, as if surprised to find Irene right there, actually in line with her. She nodded and tried to smile, but Irene could see it was forced. The woman took a full fifteen seconds to study Irene's appearance. Irene could almost feel sorry for her, as the woman was obviously at a loss for words, but then she managed a half-hearted reply, "Yes, Mrs. Obenchain, you look very well this evening. A new dress? Very pretty color, very flattering."

"Thank you," Irene replied, uncomfortable at being the object of everyone's attention. Giving the doctor a dark look, she wondered why he couldn't have left her alone. She could've gotten herself something to eat, and no one would've given her any notice, but on his arm, she was as conspicuous as a buzzard among a flock of peacocks.

"Your dress is very nice, too, beautiful color," Irene said, compelled to return the compliment. It was a lovely dress, maroon crushed velvet with cream lace, very flattering to Mrs. Bodeman's mannish face and sallow complexion.

"Everyone looks nice this evening. It does feel good to get dressed up once in a while, doesn't it," Irene heard herself blather on, then wished she'd let the conversation die.

Thankfully, the need for further discourse with the Bodemans ended as Mr. Russell and Meda-Belle began to make their selections from the table. "Be careful there, Mrs. Obenchain," said Mr. Russell, a big grin showing a row of white teeth in the part of his black mustache and beard. "That chicken there is Santa Fe chicken, Meda-Belle's secret weapon. It'll put hair on your...a...beg pardon...ah...hot...hot as fire."

Meda-Belle laughed at his expense and nudged him in the ribs with her elbow.

"Fourth of July, I had some of Mrs. Lamphere's chicken," Mr. Bodeman confessed, "after the first couple swallows, it don't burn anymore."

"Lots of things happen like that," said Meda-Belle,

a wink directed toward Irene.

Irene noticed Mrs. Bodeman avoided the red-coated chicken and selected a slice of ham instead.

The doctor, however, found a nice plump breast and put it on her plate.

Irene couldn't resist saying, "I like your chicken, Mrs. Lamphere."

Funny, Irene thought, *it's easier to talk to Meda-Belle than anyone else here...and Mr. Russell...of course. He's having a good time. I'm glad.*

Irene shifted the chicken breast on her plate and said, "I, too, had some of your chicken at the Fourth of July picnic. Your chili, though. Now that's too much for me. Only the brave can eat whole green chilies, and you will not count me among their number."

"How 'bout you, Doctor Rayburn? You like your chicken spicy?" Mr. Russell asked.

Irene noticed Mr. Russell had been keeping his eye on the doctor all evening. The fact she hadn't given him any encouragement for quite some time was something of a sore spot with Mr. Russell, Irene knew. She suspected the challenge she heard in his words and the gleam she saw in his eyes was jealousy, but she couldn't be sure.

Meda-Belle, the minx, loved to put a ribald connotation on any conversation. She, of course, laughed at everyone's expense.

Doctor Rayburn surprised them all. Without hesitation, face devoid of expression, he selected a thigh and a leg and put them on his plate. "I'm a leg man myself, spicy or otherwise."

Meda-Belle, delighted, slapped him on the back and broke into whoops of laughter.

For a moment, Ida Bodeman looked to be in shock, then she, too, succumbed and burst out laughing. "You'd think the cider was spiked," she said under her breath, but they all heard what she'd said.

"It will be before the night is over," Irene heard Mr. Bodeman predict as he and his wife went off to find a place to sit and eat their meal.

Chapter Ten

Irene, seated with the children, hadn't been left without any adult company for all of the evening. Doctor Rayburn repeatedly asked her to dance. She had to admit she was tempted when he'd asked her to dance to her favorite waltz, "Midnight on the Water." Drat the man, he was hard to resist. He had accepted her refusal, but Irene could tell by the stormy expression on his face he wanted to challenge. It was his eyes—they scolded her.

Irene had, at first, after Abel had left, accepted invitations to dance, as she'd always done at these functions—dancing with whoever asked, thinking nothing had changed, she was still a married woman. But soon, she'd learned differently. For her presumption, she'd suffered the snubs, glowers, and glares of the wives and mothers of the males. Their accusing scowls and loud whispers suggested their men were being seduced, tempted to stray on the ruse of protecting, caring for an abandoned woman's needs.

It hurt. Humiliated—it was an awful punishment.

To protect herself, she'd learned to blend with the woodwork. For her cooperation in taking up her proper position as a non-person, the good people of Meadow View spared Odessa—allowed her to move freely among them, looked upon her daughter as—*almost*—one of their own.

Mr. Bodeman used the excuse he'd come to check

on his grandchildren, but he told her without embarrassment, "My dogs are killin' me. I don't work this hard haulin' logs. The doc seems like a good man," he said, after a bit of rest to catch his breath. At the time, the doctor was dancing with Sarah Laidlaw.

"I think he'll do very well here," Irene said. "He's going to have a lot of country to cover. He won't be here in town all that much."

"True, true," Abner agreed, "but it's good he's gonna put down roots here." He blushed and stammered. "I mean, ah, with an office and all."

Together, they watched the dancers take up the Virginia reel, and Abner was called upon to partner his wife.

No sooner did he leave than Mr. Russell sat down beside her. "So you got your boarder," he said and heaved a sigh. Their gazes followed Meda-belle, in the arms of George Krauss, twirling about the floor in her dress of lustrous burnt orange.

Irene didn't reply but nodded her head. Mr. Russell shifted his weight around so his body was turned toward her a little. Irene had never really understood before, but Barclay Russell was very protective of her. She could feel it. He wanted to know if she was all right, if having a new boarder was all right. He was a sweet man. She hoped he wasn't still attempting to woo her. That had been uncomfortable for too long. But, maybe now they could be very close friends.

His gaze never leaving the dance floor, Barclay said, "Haven't been able to give you much business, what with this weather and all. How you fixed for wood?"

"I have plenty of wood, thanks to you and George and all of the men at the logging camp. With the money from the room, I think Odessa and I will be fine. Maybe I won't worry so much."

"That would be good," he said and patted her hand. "Pretty little thing like you shouldn't have to worry. The doc's married, ain't he?"

"Yes," she said, uneasy with the topic.

"Wife ain't comin' is what I heard."

Irene, her gaze trained on the dancers, answered, "He hasn't said much about her. But that's what I understand too."

"Well, I'll be around once in a while—check on things. Man on his own—doctor—although—still a man—a stranger. You never know. You never know. If you need anything, you can count on me. Might be more work than you think, havin' a boarder. I can understand about the money—can't blame you there. You've done good keepin' yourself and your girl fed and clothed. Nobody can fault you. You've done it all on your own. Proud to know you—very proud of you."

Irene faced him, fighting back tears. A lump came to her throat. "You've always been very kind. Thank you, Mr. Russell."

"Can't you call me Barclay, just once?"

She swallowed hard and squeezed his hand. "Thank you, my friend. Thank you, Barclay."

George Krause took up the space next to Irene. Behind her, Sarah hovered over her brood, pretending to tend to them, but Irene knew she was listening in on her exchange with Barclay and now George.

"It's a fine evening. Music is good. Miss Odessa is having a fine time. She looks very grown-up tonight," said George.

"Yes," Irene said. " And to hear her tell it, she is all

grown-up now. I would feel easier in my mind if she would slow down a little."

Rupert took the stage a few minutes before midnight, and everyone gathered round. "I hope all of you have had a chance to welcome our new doctor, Elias Rayburn. Come on up here, Doctor Rayburn, and let everyone get a good look at you."

"Mr. Laidlaw, thank you for your warm welcome," Doctor Rayburn said, projecting his voice from the stage so all could hear. "My dream was to come west. The beauty of this place is so much more than I ever imagined. And now I've met some of its inhabitants, I am overwhelmed by my good fortune. You can find me at 21 West Cascade, at the Obenchain house. Very soon, I will have an office there. If I'm not there, Mrs. Obenchain will know where to find me, and I will keep her informed as to when I will be expected to return. I'm looking forward to many, many years as your doctor. Thank you again for giving me this big welcome."

Something more was said; Irene no longer paid any attention.

Going to keep me informed of his comings and goings. Presumptuous. That's what you are, Doctor Rayburn, presumptuous and…and…overbearing. Now I'm supposed to be your comptroller, as well as your cook, your laundry woman, and your landlady.

I need to find Odessa. Go home. I'm tired. I'm tired of being overlooked, taken advantage of—scorned. Tired of the struggle to remain invisible.

She moved up to the topmost bale to look around the room. George took her hand to keep her from falling. Odessa was missing, as were Silas and Trenton. She located Anna and Junie Davis—they were with their folks. People had been going in and out of the Grange all night. She knew there was hard cider and a gin jug getting passed around outside—there usually was. Pete Borseth supplied anyone looking to quench their thirst with his own home brew.

"Have you seen Odessa, George? I thought she was with the Davis girls. I don't see the Trasks—maybe she's with the Trasks."

"Over there," George said, pointing a finger toward the front door.

Irene spotted Ruby and Sam Trask, mother and father to Silas and Trenton. Sam, his silver blonde hair in a braid and a long, dusky beard down to his belt buckle, wasn't hard to spot. He always wore a white shirt and suspenders with his black canvas trousers. Ruby also stood out in the crowd—she liked to wear skirts of rainbow hues and blowzy blouses with lots of gold chains around her neck and usually a red bandanna on her head of dark hair. But, of Odessa, there was no sign.

"I vould go, if you vant...see if out back she is?"

"Oh, George, I don't know. I guess...if you wouldn't mind? I would like to go home."

"I don't mind; I could use a break. Fresh air, I tink, would be a good ting."

Rupert announced his intention to begin the countdown to midnight. Irene followed George's progress across the room. Head and shoulders above almost everyone else, he left by the back door to the side of the stage.

"20...19...18...17...16," the people called out, their voices mounting with their rising anticipation of the coming New Year and the twentieth century.

The doctor left the stage and made his way toward

her. Coming immediately to stand next to her, he put his hand on her elbow. "What are you doing up there? You're going to fall."

Irene couldn't talk. She wanted to cry. She wanted to go home. She could feel Sarah Laidlaw's eyes on her. She was closing in, no doubt annoyed she'd stolen the doctor's attention—*again*—when she'd done no such thing. In fact, she'd done everything she could think of to discourage him.

All a-twitter, Sarah sidled up to him and gave as her excuse, "I need to be near my sweet babies when this new century comes in."

Before Rupert could say "Ten," an ear-splitting scream rang through the hall.

Hands holding up the hem and the seat of her turquoise satin gown covered with a dark green substance, Grace Wolfe stumbled inside by way of the back door, screaming bloody murder, shouting death and destruction to the rooftop. Her war cry split the crowd in half as she made a beeline for the front of the hall and her wrap. The entire scene lasted for only a few brief seconds—everyone stunned into immobility.

"All of you, go to hell!" She screeched a few more parting oaths on her way to the exit and slammed the door behind her.

Irene, from her perch, looked for Odessa. Below her, Doctor Rayburn looked around the hall, as confused as everyone else. Sarah Laidlaw grabbed her children, holding Elizabeth's head under one protective wing and Oren's head under the other, no doubt to prevent their tender ears from hearing Grace's salty language.

Irene caught a movement at the rear door, and Odessa slipped in, moved to stand beside Anna and

Junie. She shed her coat, letting it fall behind her on a chair. She furtively scanned the room. Eventually, her furtive gaze locked with Irene's speculative gaze. Even from a distance, Irene took note her daughter's rosy cheeks drained of all color. The girl shivered and folded her arms across her chest, and quickly looked away. What Irene wanted to know, was the shiver the result of the weather? Or from trepidation, or maybe both? After all, it was cold out on the outhouse path.

Next to enter from the back door came Trenton, then George filed in, followed by a grinning Silas. Everyone started to talk at once, the new year forgotten. Meda-Belle emerged from the crowd and rushed toward the front of the hall. Barclay Russell followed on her heels.

George made his way over to the doctor and Irene.

"What was that about?" asked the doctor, "Does she need a doctor?"

"No, she don't need a doctor," George said, a snicker on his lips. "Vhat she needs is a can of kerosene." And that was all he said. The Pedersons and Rob, took the stage and without hesitation, began to play "Footprints in the Snow," and for the next hour, one lively tune followed another.

Meda-Belle and Barclay returned to the hall. Meda-Belle shook her head, waved her hands over her head in an attempt to dismiss the incident. Soon word passed around the room that some idiot had painted the ladies' outhouse seat with green paint. The paint, having been subjected to the cold, was sticky and wouldn't dry and would be the very devil to remove.

"Grace," Meda-Belle informed Paulette, within earshot of Irene and the doctor, "has a Bowie knife. She's hell-bent on castrating the little bastly who spread that stuff on the seat. And I don't doubt for a minute she could do it and not bat an eye. The woman's got blood in her eye. I only pray whoever done the deed is smart enough to keep it to himself.

"Auld Lang Syne" was played. Irene heaved a sigh of relief. The night was at last at an end. She helped bundle up the drowsy children for their parents.

Irene found Odessa, demure, all sweetness and light, seated beside Junie Davis—she hadn't moved since she'd returned from outside. Irene hoped her daughter's conscience pinched her a little. She wasn't sure of Odessa's role in all of this, but even a small part was too much to be borne.

Doctor Rayburn walked Irene to the cloakroom and, taking the much lighter basket from her, he helped her don her wrap. Odessa, barely stifling her giggles, joined them. Trenton helped her with her coat. There was no doubt left in Irene's mind her daughter had been in on the prank, and it made her sick with shame.

"We're going to take the Meltons home and come back for the Pedersons," Trenton informed her. Odessa looked everywhere but into Irene's eyes—another telltale sign of guilt. "Anna and Junie are going home with their folks," Trenton said. "So I guess we'll bring Dessie home, if that's okay?"

"Yes, Trenton," Irene said, jaw so tight it ached.

"I will be waiting for you," she warned her daughter.

****

Trenton took Toby's reins. He relegated Silas, a good three sheets to the wind, to ride behind him. They dropped the Meltons and the Pedersons at home, and Odessa remained the sole occupant of the horse-drawn boat as they made their final pass through town.

Everyone had left the Grange. The town lay quiet and dark but for the lights from the saloon spilling out into the street.

Silas demanded to get off. The sound of his shout echoed into the night like cannon fire. "Let me down. Gonna 'pologize to tha' lovely Injun," he said, and slid off Toby's rump, not waiting for Trenton to pull back on the reins to bring Toby to a stop.

Trenton grabbed for his coattails, catching nothing but air. "Ah, come on, Sy, you're stinkin' drunk. Don't be an idiot."

Silas fell to his knees, rose, and wobbled to his feet. He straightened his coat and adjusted his hat. "No. Idiot. Gen'elman, a gen'elman is what I mean to be." He staggered toward the alley and the boarding house. "Have to atone for my sins, Brother. Have to."

"Silas." Disentangling herself from the lap robe, Odessa scrambled ungracefully out of the boat. "Silas…please, Silas…" Running to catch up with him, she missed his arm and snagged him by his coat sleeve. "Silas, come home with me. Sleep it off at our house. She'll castrate you. Silas—she's got a knife."

Odessa wasn't sure what the act of castration entailed, but she sensed no man would deliberately choose to have it done. The way Mr. Pederson and Mr. Melton had reacted at the mention of the word made her think the procedure might even be deadly. And apparently, neither Mr. Pederson nor Mr. Melton doubted for a second Miss Wolfe capable of carrying out her threat and would delight in doing so.

"Nah, won't do that," Silas assured her. "Payin' customer, see. Got fif'y dollars here in my trousers. Gonna pay to get the stuff offin' her pretty little moooon.

You'll see, ol' Sy'll have himself a time. Tha's all, jus' a time, tha's wha' I'm gonna have. Man row, Dessie," he said and smiled down at her, gently wiping a tear off her cheek.

For a brief moment in time, they stood very close. Odessa waited for him to take her in his arms, but he didn't. Instead, he wobbled, tipped forward, and gave her a brief peck on the lips.

The kiss set her senses reeling, and before Odessa could respond, wrap her arms around his neck, he abandoned her. He left her shivering with cold. Tears blurring her vision, she watched him stagger down the dark alley and disappear into the night.

"Ah, let him get clipped," Trenton said, "drunk, he won't feel a thing. Come on, Dessie, I got to get you home. Told your mama I'd have you home in an hour. Come on. You're in trouble—she's on to us."

Odessa stood at the alley entrance and peered through the darkness. She heard the clang of the boarding house bell. "We can't let him go in there, Trenton. He's going to get hurt."

The boarding house door opened, and a shaft of light projected onto the porch and out to the yard gate. The sounds of female laughter and a piano escaped from the portal and floated out into the night. She caught a glimpse of Silas, a dark silhouette against the black of the night. The door closed, snuffed the light, and muffled the laughter and the music.

Silas's defection created a vacuum, an empty space. It was darker now, colder now, stark and lifeless. Odessa shivered and wrapped her arms about her chest. Trenton's voice, coming from behind her, brought her back from the brink of loneliness.

"He don't want to be stopped. Don't you get it, Dessie? I figure what happens now is his own lookout."

Huffing, infuriated, Odessa marched back to the boat. "Take me home, then you get your papa."

"Holy jump up, Christ, Dessie, no. Silas don't want Pa knowin' he's drunk. He's on his own. Pa ain't got nothin' to do with anythin'. And pretty soon, I'll be on my own. I ain't gonna pull Sy's balls outta the fire, and neither is Pa. Pa made that clear. Once we start making our own way, we don't have no one to depend on but ourselves. Now, stop wiggling around. I gotta get you home. We shoulda taken you home first. You shouldn't be out here this late."

Odessa pulled the blanket up around her, disgusted and confused by Trenton's cold-hearted indifference toward his brother. "What's the matter with you? Why are you being so mean? Are you mad at me? All I want to do is keep your brother from getting himself all cut up, for Pete's sake. I don't get it. What happened? We were having fun—we danced and laughed. The joke went as planned. Better, Silas said, 'cause Miss Wolfe gave a good show."

Trenton didn't answer her.

The taste of Silas's kiss lay on her lips, and the smell of stale cider lingered. Her fingers went to her mouth—he'd never kissed her before.

She'd wanted him to. She'd dreamed of Silas kissing her, holding her. Tonight she'd danced with him, and he'd kissed her, but it wasn't anything like she'd dreamed it would be. In her dreams, their first kiss didn't end like this—with Silas going off to the boarding house. This wasn't right. Odessa didn't understand where and why everything started to go so very wrong.

"Why did he kiss me, Trenton?" she asked, even though she realized Trenton either couldn't hear or had decided he wasn't talking to her anymore. However, his silence had never stopped her from talking before, nor would it tonight. "Why would Silas kiss me?" she repeated. Then raised her voice to ask, "Do you think Silas likes me? I...I mean, really likes me?"

****

New Year's Day, Doctor Rayburn departed to acquaint himself with the rest of his territory. He informed Irene he'd most likely be gone for the rest of the week. He expected his freight the middle of the week. He asked her to have it put in his room, and he'd sort it out when he got back.

"I'll send you a telegram as soon as I reach Redmond. I'll give you my location, where I can be reached should there be an emergency."

Tight-lipped, Irene accepted his orders and directions and wondered how it was she'd become his secretary by virtue of his being her boarder.

It was as well the doctor was leaving—she needed time alone with Odessa to bring the girl down a peg or two. She anticipated resistance, it was bound to get volatile, and it would no doubt get ugly—better to get it done in private.

New Year's Day, Odessa washed, ironed, and mended. Irene saw to it no sooner did she finish one chore than another awaited, and if each task did not meet Irene's rigorous standards, then it was done over again. By Tuesday, Odessa let it be known she was properly contrite—she'd even stopped whining and was now sullen and quiet.

"I'm going to the boarding house. You set the table

and have lunch ready when I get back, please." Irene hesitated before going out the door, almost challenging Odessa to rebel, but no rebellion was forthcoming.

It felt good to be out of the house—it was hard work keeping Odessa busy, checking her work, watching over her every move. Odessa hadn't confessed to anything, exactly, but she hadn't denied her participation in the outhouse prank.

Irene passed the livery. She looked for Silas, but he wasn't around. She turned down the alley and rang the bell at the boarding house. Paulette, in a canary yellow kimono and lace camisole, with thigh-length yellow hose and garters, answered the door, "Afternoon, Mrs. Obenchain. Meda-Belle's upstairs. I don't know what she's got for you today."

Irene heard a bump and looked up to the landing on the stairwell. There was Meda-Belle trying to stay upright, her kimono open, revealing her chemise and lace drawers, and Silas looking hung-over and sick, his arm around her shoulder. Irene could smell him as he got closer. He reeked of two nights and a day of debauchery.

Irene stood speechless.

"Mrs. Obenchain, got your next load right here under the stairs," Meda-Belle said, her usual sarcastic smile in place. "Got to send this young man on his way first. Can you stand, sweetie?"

At the mention of Irene's name, Silas blinked and came to his senses—a little. He actually peered at her, obviously having trouble focusing. "Wish I were dead," he said. "Remember some of it. Gotta get—money's gone."

He smiled sheepishly at Meda-Belle. She helped him on with his coat and hat and tucked his gloves into his coat pocket.

"G'day, Mrs. Obenchain," he managed to say. Without actually making eye contact, he staggered out the door.

"Reminds me of my own boy." Meda-Belle said and retrieved the bundle of laundry from under the stairs. "Came to apologize to Grace—did just fine for his first time," she said and handed Irene the laundry.

Chapter Eleven

June 17, 1900

Elias had been gone a lot throughout January, February, and March dealing with an outbreak of influenza. He'd missed the ice harvest at the end of February, and now it was June and time to harvest the ice again.

The ice caves were southwest into the lava fields in the mountains. He regretted he couldn't join the party this time, either. He would've enjoyed exploring, spelunking, and camping, but the younger Bodeman girl, Laura Kelsey, was due to give birth—twins, he was certain. He thought he should stay close by.

He insisted Irene stay home too. He needed her more than Mrs. Laidlaw needed a nursemaid to watch over her children and all the other children who would also be on the outing.

In the five months since his arrival, he'd acquired an enormous respect for Irene. When he moved west, he hadn't thought to find an assistant, but Irene had become invaluable in his office as well as helpful with his patients. She had a steady hand when faced with a crisis and could administer ether as well as any nurse he'd ever seen. They worked together, lived under the same roof. He saw her almost every day. She had his confidence, and yet she remained...distant and unapproachable.

She was his third hand when it came to dealing with

open wounds, and there had been several—axes gone astray, saw gashes, the occasional wound from a kicking mule, a boiler explosion at the mill. She instinctively knew how to calm and soothe small children and assure panicky parents. He wished she were free to go with him on his rounds, but that was out of the question.

His growing regard for her haunted his every waking thought and his dreams. Elias wanted marriage, a wife. Irene was there all the time, with him, beside him, helping him, so he told himself, it was logical for him to fantasize about her. But secretly, he knew it was more than that. Over time, he'd studied her face, her expressive eyes, the way her hair escaped and formed curls around her forehead and behind her ears, the way her body moved, nimble and quick, strong and soft. More than anything, he wanted to make her smile—bring some life to her. It had become his quest, his dream, to have her in his arms, laughing, smiling—he wanted to do that for her, for himself.

But, alas, he hadn't found a way to breach the wall of reserve Irene Obenchain maintained—holding him, and everyone else, at arm's length. He thought he'd made progress on New Year's Eve, but if anything, she'd retreated even further since the beginning of the new year.

At least she no longer apologized to him for the laundry or her early morning baking, of which he was grateful. The meals had improved. No longer did she serve him dishes heavy with potatoes and gravy.

He had to watch it, though, or grow fat and worthless—Irene Obenchain was a fantastic cook, her specialty...*pies*. She made pies out of almost everything, not only fruit and pudding pies but chicken, beef, pork, sausage—eggs, and he loved them all. And they were portable, he could take them with him on his rounds so he didn't have to miss a meal or cook for himself—not that he had to do much of that anyway. His patients, or their families, saw to it he had plenty of food—as a matter of fact, it was how he was paid for his services most of the time. As often as he could, he shared his bounty with Irene and her daughter. It was the least he could do.

The Meadow View streets were nearly devoid of any sign of life. He came into town, followed by the Kelseys in their wagon. He drove to the unmanned livery, unhitched the docile bay gelding from the shay, and led him to his stall as he usually did. He waved to the Kelseys and started to walk home. He was about to cross the street at the post office when Dora Melton, who'd stayed behind to man the telegraph and keep the post office open, stepped out the door and handed him a letter to deliver to Mrs. Obenchain.

Entering the house, he called out for Irene. When she didn't answer, he went to the back door and stopped for a moment to watch her run sheets through the wringer on the side of her wash tub. The front of her brown dress and white apron were soaking wet. Her long brown mane of hair, coming out of its pins, fell over one eyebrow and over one shoulder. She was red in the face, rumpled, and to his dismay, he found her disheveled state extraordinarily attractive.

This troubled him. It was a problem. Clearly, the woman didn't find him the least bit attractive. Oh, she knew he was a man, all right, and expected the worst of him for it. He'd deciphered that much. He supposed he shouldn't feel too bad. Her attitude was not reserved just

for him—it all had something to do with her husband—
he wasn't so dumb he hadn't figured that out.

Not very many people had anything good to say
about Abel Obenchain. Odessa had shown him a likeness
of her father. Elias thought Abel Obenchain a good-
looking man, a man with a roguish smile and twinkling
eyes.

From Meda-Belle, he'd learned Abel had been a
frequent customer at the boarding house. He could charm
the birds out of the trees, Meda-Belle had said. But that
seemed to be the extent of the man's talents. Abel had
tried going into business for himself building barns and
outhouses, but his enterprise didn't last long. He made a
stab at being a rancher, but the care and feeding of the
cattle fell to Irene. When she'd miscarried after a fall,
Abel gave up ranching and sold off his cattle.

Elias learned from Meda-Belle, Irene had lost two
children, one through a miscarriage and one, a six-
month-old baby girl, from pneumonia. Before Abel left
for the gold fields of Alaska, he worked most days up at
the Suncrest Mill. He wasn't a very reliable employee.
He had a habit of showing up late and some days not at
all. His job at the mill lasted for two years before he took
off to seek his fortune. Meda-Belle thought Abel had
kept the mill job the longest because of Barclay Russell's
fondness for Irene. Meda-Belle hinted Barclay would do
anything for her.

"Mrs. Obenchain, you have a letter," Elias said and
stepped off the back stoop. "Mrs. Melton handed it to me
as I passed the post office. The town's nearly deserted—
I guess everyone's gone to harvest the ice."

"How is Laura doing?" Irene asked, wiping her
hands on her dress and pushing the hair out of her eyes

with her wrist. "Odessa left with the Davises. They dropped by and picked her up. She could hardly wait to go. I promised her last night she could go if she finished up the sheets. She didn't, of course. So here I am." She pushed back the hair off her shoulder with a flip of her wet hand

Elias repeated what Laura had told him. "Laura says she feels like a waddling goose. I'm glad Tom decided not to go with the others to get ice. I have a feeling she could deliver any time. They followed me into town. Laura noticed the Emporium was open. She's gone to shop while no one's around to gawk at her. They'll come by in a while for her checkup. A little walk around town will do her good. I have a book on child care that might be of help—they've both told me they're a bit overwhelmed by the idea of twins."

Irene, he sensed, wasn't really paying attention. She was staring at her envelope. Head down, she said, "Sarah wouldn't want to close her doors. She might miss making a nickel. I wonder who she corralled into manning the store?"

"Well, I'm going inside," he said. "I need a drink of water; would you like a glass?"

"There's lemonade," she said and walked away, headed for the big pine tree to the side of the backyard and the shade it offered. He knew she liked to sit there and gaze at the mountains. He'd found her there a lot, sitting alone, in a daze, looking off into the distance. Once or twice he'd joined her, thinking they could sit and talk about things in general, but she always looked so uncomfortable, guilty, as if they were doing something illicit, so he stopped. Maybe, he thought, he should put a bench there, then maybe she'd feel better about his joining her.

****

The return address read *Verona, Virginia.* Irene opened the letter, fingers trembling. Unfolding the single sheet of paper, she glanced at the date at the top of the page, *March, 23, 1900.* The handwriting wasn't her father's or the childish printing and clumsy spelling of either of her brothers. It began in a clear and neat hand, *Dear Cousin Irene.* She stopped and turned the letter over to read the signature at the bottom of the letter. *Deepest Sympathy, Cousin Grace Pooley.*

"Papa, oh, Papa." Chest aching, throat tight, Irene held back the tears.

Taking a moment to prepare herself, she went back to the beginning of the letter. *Dear Cousin Irene, I regret to be the one to tell you your Pa, my Uncle Jackson Pooley, died peacefully in his sleep ten days ago. He suffered a series of heart attacks this past year that left him a shadow of his former self.*

Taking a deep, shuddering, breath, Irene put a hand over her mouth to hold back a sob of grief. *Your brothers have been taking care of his place. They asked me to write this letter. If you recall, they aren't much at reading or writing. I am happy to be put to use. A body don't know how to help in times like these.*

Irene smiled a sad smile. Poor cousin Grace.

Your letter arrived about two weeks before your Pa left us. He was very pleased to hear from you. He had your likeness beside his bed when he died. Also, the likeness of your little girl, Odessa Rose. I guess she must be almost growed now. My own daughter. Clementine, is fifteen, has a beau, and is thinking of marriage and babies. If I recollect, your girl was born about a month after my girl. It don't seem like that long ago, but I guess it is.

Irene turned the paper over. *Your Pa was upset Abel had not returned.* Irene checked herself, blinked and reread it. "Oh, God, no."

Last fall he asked me to write a letter for him to Dawson City, Yukon Territory, to find out if your husband filed a claim up there. He also had me write to the Port of Portland, Oregon, to see if that ship he was on got to its destination. Now your Pa is gone, I thought I should let you know what he was up to in the event you had done the same.

Irene closed her eyes, and shuddered with dread. "It couldn't be. No. No." The handwriting in the letter became a scrawl, going around the edges of the paper, and it was hard to follow—the words overlapped and ran in between the lines.

Your Pa was determined to find out what had become of the scoundrel. That's what he called him, "that damned scoundrel." You know how he talked. I promised him I would keep writing until I got an answer, and I will. I know mail is slow, but as soon as I get any word I will write to you.

Tears flooded Irene's eyes and spilled down her cheeks. The trees, the mountains, the sky—the colors ran together like watercolors in a painting, blending together in a watery pool. Rumbling up from deep in her chest, a sob escaped and clawed her throat. She started to shake. Then a pair of strong arms went around her, holding her—*Elias*. His scent enveloped her, warmed her— surrounded her. He smelled of rubbing alcohol, liniment and his own brand of masculine musk—she knew it was him even with her eyes closed.

Sobbing, drowning in her own tears, she gasped for breath. Panic had her clutching at his shirtfront. The floodgates were now open, and five long years of repressed grief, hurt, and anger set loose a torrent of emotions so strong Irene found it impossible to hold them back. The letter held fast in her tightly closed fingers, Irene clung to the only person who could save her from the riptide of emotions that threatened to suck her under into a dark abyss of despair.

Tugging the letter from her fingers, the doctor shook out the paper and read it. She was helpless to stop him, afraid to let go, afraid of what she might see in his eyes— to see censure in his wonderful brown eyes would be the worst. What must he think? Falling apart like this. Ugly and smelling of sweat and soap—a total wreck of a woman. So cold she hadn't even bothered to make inquiries as to her husband's fate. Of course she could've, should've tried to find out what had happened to Abel.

But in her heart, Irene was glad Abel was gone, out of her life. He'd lost interest in her, thank goodness. The heartbreak of losing two babies had stolen her desire for intimacy. She couldn't blame Abel. She was grief stricken. The sound of his laughter, his touch, had repulsed her rather than consoled.

Now she'd found out he'd regularly visited the ladies at the boarding house, she hoped he would never come back. Never. She didn't need or want him. It would hurt too much to think of him alive, living somewhere away from her, away from his daughter, his home, happy, laughing, and in some other woman's arms. She didn't want to know, she didn't, and that's why she hadn't pursued any inquiries.

"Oh, dear Irene, I'm so sorry," Elias said, his breath on her brow."

Swallowing down her sobs, she said, "No. No, it's not anything I hadn't expected. I've known…since New Year's, something…was wrong—that Papa might be gone. I knew I might not hear from him again. But why did he have to go and write—try to find Abel? He shouldn't have done that. Why did he do that? He had my cousin write letters. I didn't know—I didn't. I didn't want him to do that."

Pushing herself out of the doctor's embrace, she accepted his handkerchief.

"I…don't understand. I would think his inquiries would be helpful." The doctor tried to draw her back into his arms.

She shook him off. He kept talking, asking questions Irene didn't want to answer.

"Why do you sound angry? Your husband should be found. You and Odessa need to know what has happened to him."

Shaking her head, Irene sniffed back her tears and angrily wiped her eyes with her damp apron. "You don't understand…I don't want to know."

There, she'd said it aloud. Now he knew—knew what she was—she was a woman without a heart, with no soul. Defiance brought her chin up, and she looked him in the eye. "I don't want to know. I don't need to know. Abel left us, and that's all there is to it." Fighting for composure…fighting the urge to fall back into the doctor's arms, she took a deep breath and closed her eyes to tamp down her fury.

He held out his arms, tempting her to fall back into his embrace. "Come, Irene, explain to me, please? Settle yourself and talk to me."

"No. I can't...I don't want to," she said, rejecting his offer and the wonderful promise of safety. She did want to. She wanted to fall into his arms, unburden herself, never leave his side. But, after a moment to process what he'd said, she realized he wasn't talking about the embrace at all. He was referring to Abel.

The answer was still no. Shaking her head, she qualified her statement. "I don't want to know where he is, or what he's been doing. He left because—because of me. I drove him away."

Rising to her feet, she brushed the tears from her cheeks and returned to her wash, returned to the drudgery of the life she had to live—pinning sheet after sheet on her clothesline.

The doctor bowed to her, his eyes cool and shuttered. "Your letter, Mrs. Obenchain."

His cool formality, like a bucket of cold water, calmed her, doused her out-of-control emotions and latent desires. She let go of the clothesline and took the letter out of his fingers, never meeting his eyes. She should apologize, explain. But what could she say? She didn't understand herself.

A summons from the front of the house interrupted her self-recriminations.

****

Irene behind him, Elias opened the door to Tom's shouts for help. Laura, leaning against the house, face contorted in pain, held on to her swollen abdomen. A puddle of amniotic fluid soaked her shoes. Tom did his best to keep her upright, his arms around her swollen waist. Quickly, going around to Laura's other side, Elias aided Tom in getting his wife into his office. Irene closed the door behind them.

"Well, now, young lady, I believe your children have decided this is as good as any day to make their entrance. You're in town, the doctor is in." Elias said and with Irene's help, they got Laura onto his examination table.

Laura Kelsey was not a small girl, about five-foot-eight and all of one hundred eighty pounds, with dark hair and features very like her mother. But she had a gentle way about her and a kind heart. Elias knew Irene had a fondness for the girl and was worried for her.

"My water broke," Laura said, her gaze going to Irene, who straightened the skirt of her dress and helped her onto the examination table.

Elias held out his arm to Irene and drew her aside. "Get her shoes and those stockings off."

To Laura, he asked, "Would you allow Mrs. Obenchain to help you? She'll get you in a gown and make you comfortable?"

In the throes of another contraction, all Laura could do was nod.

Revealing nothing of the pain-riddled woman Elias had held in his arms only minutes before, eyes a little too bright, cheeks tinged with a slight redness, Irene nodded and took charge. "There's coffee, Doctor Rayburn. Perhaps Tom would like a cup," she said.

"Yes, yes, good idea. Come, Tom, we'll have a cup of something hot and brisk. We might be in for a long afternoon."

****

By the time Irene had removed Laura's wet shoes, stockings, and dress, and had her attired in an examination gown, the expectant mother was properly in

136

hard labor. Irene wanted to call Elias back into the room, but the girl wouldn't let go of her hand, and Irene didn't want to shout for fear it might sound like panic and frighten Tom.

"I'm so scared," Laura managed to say between clenched teeth. "I know Tom is, too. Nine months. It seemed far off…"

Irene leaned in to push the dark curls off the girl's perspiring forehead with a cool cloth. "Every woman about to give birth feels as you do, even your own mother. We're all frightened of the things we can't control. Think about all the women who've done what you're doing. Think about that, Laura. Think of all the children born healthy and happy."

Laura sucked air, arched a little, fighting the contraction.

"Holding your breath won't stop it. These babies are coming," Irene said. "The more you try to hold them back, the more pain you're going to have. Breathe, Laura, breathe. Relax your fingers and breathe. You can sit up if you like. I could rub your back."

Irene stuffed pillows behind Laura and began to massage her shoulders and neck. "Think of it this way, each contraction is like going uphill to reach a big door. You have to work your way up. The door is heavy, but once you're through, you glide for a minute or two until you go uphill again and through another door and another, each time opening the doors for your children, clearing the way for them to make it through, bringing them closer to the final door and into your arms. Turn your fears into excitement, anticipation, Laura, and all your hard work will get easier. They don't call this labor for nothing."

Laura laughed in spite of the contraction that gripped her. "Here's another door. A big green one."

Heartened, Irene laughed with her.

"Good girl. Breathe, keep moving forward through it, get to the other side, and glide."

Dr. Rayburn came into the room. "What's going on in here? You telling jokes to my patient, Mrs. Obenchain?" he asked, his voice stern, but his eyes were smiling.

"My babies are opening doors," Laura said. Striving to catch her breath, she giggled and struggled to see him over her mounded abdomen. Irene dabbed Laura's forehead with the damp towel.

Laura relaxed, lay back, and closed her eyes. "I'm a little out of breath trying to keep up. My babies are on their way to the next door."

"Aha. The rascals. Well, I'll try to make myself useful. I'll have to catch up to be there when they get there," he said and went to the pitcher of water next to the examination table to wash his hands.

"Tom's wearing a groove in your floor, Mrs. Obenchain. Maybe you could do your miracle with the expectant father."

"Just life," she said and exited the room.

Chapter Twelve

"Make yourself at home, Tom," Irene said. "There's coffee and pie here on the sideboard. In the backyard, there's a big tree. You could relax there if you like. I have to go back and help the doctor. I'll come out from time to time to give you reports on Laura's progress."

"Mrs. Obenchain," Tom said, "I can't sit around doing nothing. I want to be with Laura. She's so scared, and I'm scared for her."

"If you go in there, which I'm sure she would like, you mustn't transfer your fears to her. This might be a very long afternoon. She has a hard job ahead of her, and we have to leave her to it. She knows what she has to do. You have to believe in her and in a happy outcome. You're both excited. You've had nine long months to think about this, about the children, but not a lot about how they enter into this world. If you go in there, you must stand by and watch her work. There is nothing you can do to stop the pain. It is part of the process."

The young man blinked, nodded, and squared his shoulders. "I broke my leg when I was ten. It had to be reset, it hurt like hell, but it had to be done, and I knew it was going to hurt. My dad was there with me. I understand what you're saying. He made me feel safe and strong. I can do that for Laura—I can."

"All right. First, a piece of custard pie."

****

At five forty-seven in the afternoon, Laura Kelsey delivered her children. Still on the examination table, head propped up by two pillows, Tom at her side, she lay holding her children, one under each arm, a glowing smile of gratitude and pride on her face.

"Mr. and Mrs. Kelsey, you have one each, a boy and a girl," Elias said, at the wash basin scrubbing his hands. "They are healthy, of a good weight, of good color. I foresee no problems. You came through in flying colors, Laura. You are a true champion."

Irene tossed the pan of bloody water from the basin into the bucket to the side of the washstand and poured fresh water into the basin. Tears streamed down her cheeks unchecked. Elias draped his arm around her shoulders. "She's fine," he said, his voice barely above a whisper. "Easy birth really, especially for twins. I was afraid I would have to take them."

Alarmed by the very thought, Irene gave a start and turned to look into his eyes—the look they shared spoke volumes. Tom and Laura were truly blessed. Taking the babies would surely have posed a very high risk for the mother and the babies.

"I wish I knew what you said to her," he said and tugged her a little closer into his side. "She moved with the pain, following through. I really wasn't needed at all."

"You were wonderful," Irene said.

"We, Irene, *we* were wonderful. You anticipated my every move. I couldn't have done it without you. Thank you."

He squeezed her shoulder. "We'll let them have my bed tonight," he said and pulled back a little. "We'll see how everybody is in the morning and then decide if they can go home. I'll sleep on my sofa. She'll need your help with their first feeding. If her mother were here, I'm sure she would love to help. She's going to be sorry she missed this. I'd like to move Laura to the bed as soon as possible. She needs rest, and I'm sure Tom is ready to shut down for a while."

"I'll get her into a fresh gown," Irene said.

"Tom," Elias said, his arm around the new father's shoulders, "Let's give Laura a chance to change her gown. You and I will take these two little ones into the kitchen for a little bath, and you can get acquainted with your children.

"Mrs. Obenchain, you call us when you're ready to get her into bed.

"Laura, you let Mrs. Obenchain do the work. You've done quite enough."

Elias wrapped the babies in a couple of towels—unsure as to what he was going to use for diapers—and put one of the babies in Tom's arms. He was pleased the young man didn't appear to have any fear of the small bundle. He held his son close to his chest, examining the wee thing, awe and wonder shining in his eyes.

"Tom," Laura said and attempted to sit up, "the diapers and layette, Tom…?"

Rocking the infant in his arms, Tom gazed down at the wee mite and said to the baby, "You know, when we came down the lane, and your mama's water broke, I must'a dropped the parcel. Your daddy is a silly-willy, yes, he is."

"Well, Daddy, you better hope it's still there, or you'll have to go buy more," Laura said and sagged back to lie down.

"Good thing it's not raining," Tom said to the babe

in his arms.

Before leaving the room, he planted a kiss on his wife's forehead. "Don't worry, I'm pretty sure the parcel is outside the door. I love you. I love our children."

****

Odessa on her mind, Irene wondered what she was doing tonight. She shuddered to think—Silas and Trenton were up there, too, harvesting ice. Odessa, quite openly, had a crush on Silas, although it was clear to Irene, Trenton was the one who truly cared for Odessa. That was another thing—why did some girls, herself included, always want the fickle, flirty man, the one who couldn't love them in return, or *wouldn't* love them?

Her thoughts brought her around to Elias Rayburn— damn him—he was irresistible, kind, compassionate, attractive, a doctor, and utterly contemptible. It made no difference to anyone but herself he'd left his wife—left her as sure as Abel had left her. Everyone, the whole town, loved their doctor. And, yes, she loved him too, more to her sorrow.

She told herself, every long, lonely night, lying in her bed in the dark, she was a fool—asking for more misery. To want a man who would surely break her heart—undermine all her hard work to create and keep a respectable position for herself and her daughter within the community—her infatuation with the doctor was the height of lunacy. Elias Rayburn was a monster, Irene told herself. He was cruel—walking around, smiling at her, putting his arm around her, acting as if he wasn't married—what a bounder—he was an out-and-out cad.

She closed her bedroom door. The house was quiet. She'd helped Laura feed her babies. Now, babies clean and fed, new parents sound asleep for a while, Irene removed the pins from her hair and brushed out her tresses to lie over her shoulders in long, brown waves. After removing her dress and under-things, she rubbed her bare legs and feet, then slipped her cotton nightgown over her head. Hanging up her dress, she felt the rustle of paper in her dress pocket reminding her of the letter. Sitting on the edge of her bed, her lantern turned down to a soft glow, she read the letter again, very slowly reading the handwriting in the margins around the edges of the page, picking up some of what she'd missed

We buried your Pa on Dobb's Hill above the river. There is a fine view there. The wildflowers come up all around on that side.

Your brother Jerry is to marry a Lord girl from Wells Creek come Fourth of July. She's a fine young woman. They'll probably start a family right away. Jerry ain't getting any younger. They plan to live on your Pa's place.

You write back to me here at Verona: Grace Pooley, Beaver Creek Road. I'll be sure to pass the letters on to your kin. All my deepest sympathy. Your cousin, Grace Pooley.

Barely thirteen when she'd met the seventeen-year-old Abel Obenchain at a church social, Irene had been swept off her feet, literally. He picked her up and danced with her as if she were a rag doll, laughing, so full of fun, and so very sweet. He recited poetry to her, wrote poems to her hair, her eyes. At the time, Irene considered herself a woman—after all, she'd been working since the age of nine in a dressmaker's shop in Oregon City, earning her own way. Yes, Abel gave the impression he loved her—cared for her. But tonight, she had to admit he'd left her long before he'd left Meadow View.

She had to face it—Abel had fallen out of love with her—she'd denied it for years. He'd abandoned her many times, sometimes for weeks—off hunting, he'd said. Recalling all those nights alone—nights he didn't come home and, when he did, he smelled of strong drink and body sweat. So, the question she asked herself—did she ever have a marriage, or was it only lust? Yes, she'd married Abel at fourteen and pregnant. He'd promised to take care of her...of his child, and he had for a time. But after Odessa was born and their other babies passed, he lost interest in her, in their home. Looking back, Irene had to ask herself, did he leave her or did she leave him? Which was it? Abel never beat her—he never raised his voice to her. They barely talked. He shared what he earned—he bought this place, a fine house. He kept them sheltered and fed, like pets—a dog, or a cow. But there was no love—not for her, not for a very long time. He tried to love Odessa—he did try—Irene conceded.

Her conclusion—to look for Abel would mean giving up the illusion of her marriage. If he were alive, she'd have to accept it was his choice not to return. If he were dead, that would put an end to her disguise as the abandoned wife waiting for her beloved husband's return.

As a widow, she would be free to look for love again. She didn't want to try love again, not with her faulty judgment—she couldn't be trusted.

If she could keep her head, she'd be safe—protect herself from getting hurt. Abel's disappearance *had to* remain a mystery. She didn't want to know his fate. He certainly didn't care about hers or Odessa's. Her only hope lay in the hands of her cousin—maybe she would tire of the search.

Yes, she would pray for that.

****

Elias poured the dredges from the bottom of the coffee pot into his cup, added a generous dribble of whiskey, and thinned the brew with a little hot water. He made himself comfortable on the bench before the remaining embers in the hearth in the big room. Reflecting on the day, he smiled to himself, gratified it had a happy ending. He hadn't confessed, but he'd never delivered twins before. All had gone very well. Smiling down into the contents of his cup, he smacked his lips—the concoction really did taste terrible. The sound of a woman weeping brought him out of his reverie. The sound had come from Irene's room. He saw the light shining from beneath her door. No doubt it was the damned letter. Rising to his feet, he set his cup aside and took several steps toward her door—but caught himself. She should have someone to lean on. Irene Obenchain was a woman of enormous pride—he admired her for that, but pride was cold comfort. He couldn't go to her—offer her his shoulder to cry on—it might erode what little ground he'd gained today.

He knew his fascination with the woman was not healthy, nor was it honorable—they were both married. Regardless of her attempts to disguise herself, Irene Obenchain couldn't hide the fact she was damned attractive. If a man really looked, he couldn't help but notice her fine eyes and her soft, luminescent skin, and her engaging, infectious smile when she chose to use it. The woman did a good job of hiding her voluptuous figure. Working alongside her was a pleasure. Intuitive, quick and bright, in short, she was everything a doctor's wife should be—everything he'd wanted and hoped for.

As far as Marie, his actual wife, he didn't know what to do about her. Another month had passed, and still she hadn't responded to his request for a divorce, or an annulment.

Shaking his head, thinking to himself, Elias sat back down, the fire cast long shadows onto the log walls. He raised his cup of coffee and whispered a toast to the closed door, "Here's to now, Irene." He turned away from the warmth of the flames and promised, *someday*, before downing the contents of his cup and retiring to the narrow leather couch in front of the hearth that awaited him in his room.

Chapter Thirteen

July 4, 1900

Odessa skipped up the ramp of the livery stable, walked inside, and paused, giving her eyes a moment to adjust to the dim light within. She waved her hand in front of her nose and scrunched up her face, disgusted by the smell of musty hay and horse dung. Flies circled in a lazy dance in the air down the center aisle. She took a few more steps, hand over her nose. "Silas? Trenton?" Flakes of hay drifted down in front of her, and looking up, she spied Trenton's face, peering over the loft rail above her.

"We're up here. You got the stuff?"

Startled, she squeaked, jumped, hand to heart. Because she didn't want Silas or Trenton to think she was a dumb, scaredy-cat girl, she snapped her response. "I got it. I told you I could get it." She tucked the stuffed, cloth flour sack under her arm and started up the ladder.

"Have any trouble gettin' it outta the house?" Silas asked. One-handed, Odessa tossed the cloth bag at him.

Trenton squatted down and offered her a hand up. Hanging on to the ladder with one hand, Odessa tried to kick the skirt of her blue and white gingham dress out from under her feet. Trenton had her by the arm, pulling her up. She lost her footing on the smooth oak rungs. He dragged her up onto the loft floor. "Trenton Trask, you make me rip my dress, and I'll box your ears. Let go.

You're stepping on my hat."

Sprawled out on her stomach, dress up around her knees, she tried to rescue her wide-brimmed straw hat and managed to inflict pain on herself with her very own hat pin. She got to her feet thoroughly miffed and mussed.

Looking contrite, Trenton dipped down, avoiding the hat pin. He handed her the bonnet. "Sorry, Dessie, we don't have a lot of time. We gotta get ready for the race." He started to brush the straw off her backside. She slapped his hand away and snatched her bonnet from his fingers, delivering him a murderous glare.

Nobody saw you, did they?" Silas asked, ignoring her pique, and everything else, which fueled Odessa's ire even more. He pulled the dress, hat, petticoat, and tattered straw bonnet out of the flour sack, eyeing them with approval.

Teeth clenched, closing her eyes, Odessa took a deep breath to calm herself. "No, no one saw me. Mama's still helping with the pancake breakfast cleanup. I sorta forgot my hat, so I had to go home to get it. The rest of the stuff she'll never miss. She knows the old yellow thing doesn't fit anymore. The petticoat has so many holes in it she was going to use it for rags."

While talking, she took note Trenton looked older today—somehow—taller, shoulders broader, mature, manly. She thought it might be the way he was dressed today. He had on a cowboy shirt of fire-red and blue paisley, and around his neck, he wore the dark blue bandanna she'd given him for his birthday last year.

Silas, of course, was a dream. Looking at him gave her the shivers. Whenever she was around him, she had to fight off her tendency to giggle. His dark hair was combed close to his head, and the bright pink shirt and orange bandanna he had on brought out the bronze tone of his skin and the opaque gray of his eyes. The addition of his coal-black mustache offered a raffish air that put her in mind of a wicked Spanish conquistador. He looked dangerous—his smile hypnotizing, his eyes teasing and laughing at her—he set her senses on fire.

She stared at him and licked her lips. He grinned at her and winked. She dipped her head and blushed like an idiot.

"What about the bonnet?" Silas asked. "Where did it come from? She ain't gonna want it back, is she?"

Cheeks burning, Odessa pretended to care about the state of her mussed-up dress. Eyes downcast, she picked at the stay reeds of straw that, here and there, clung to her skirt. "That old thing, no. I found it in the same place I found the mannequin—behind the Emporium in the trash."

"You sure old lady Laidlaw ain't gonna want the mannequin back?" Trenton asked, worrying as usual.

Hands on hips, Odessa said, "I told you both. I didn't ask Mrs. Laidlaw. She's a witch and she doesn't like me or my mother. I asked Mr. Laidlaw—he flirts. He said I could have it. I told him I was going to use it as a dress form. He knows I've been sewing on some dresses—Mama buys material from him all the time. I asked him for the bonnet too. I told him perhaps I could mend it, weave in some flowers on the brim. He commended me on my ingenuity and imagination."

"Dessie, danged if you ain't a caution," Silas said. Chuckling, he shook his head. "Bat your pretty eyes, get a man all flummoxed in the head, you could steal the gold out of his teeth, and he'd think you a clever girl."

"Where is it?" Odessa asked, waving aside his backhanded compliment. There was a mound of straw in the corner but no trace of their prize. There were a couple of sawhorses with some boards laid over the top for a makeshift table set up in the middle of the loft but, other than that, the place looked bare.

"She's over here," Trenton said. Going over to the darkest corner of the loft, he kicked away the straw with the toe of his scuffed and well-worn riding boots. "Didn't think anyone would look for her over here."

"Early this mornin', we got some hair from the tail of one of them mustangs they brought in for the rodeo," Silas said. "Let's have a look."

Trenton retrieved a long hank of blondish hair from a spike sticking out from the low-hanging eves. Silas took Odessa by the arm and pulled her over to the open door of the loft. Trenton held up the length of horsehair against Odessa's soft, shiny locks. Both boys agreed in unison, "Close enough."

"We better get her dressed," Odessa said. "I mean— we should do it now, don't you think? You're both going to be in the race and the rodeo. Neither of you will have time. And I can't do it, because I told Junie and Susan I'd watch the race with them. If I disappear, they might follow me or tell Mama, and she might send someone to look for me. First place she would look would be here; she knows I come here to see you both. And if she found me here, she'd know we were up to something."

"She's right, Silas," Trenton said.

"Okay, we'll get her set up. We'll meet back here— let's see—probably about an hour or so before the sun goes down—that ought'a be about right. Barbecue will be over, and the dancin' will be almost ready to start."

"We'll meet back here, providin' you don't break your stupid neck," Trenton said under his breath. Turning his back on them, he started to pull the straw away from what at first Odessa thought looked like a naked body.

"Don't worry about me, little brother," Silas said. "Look out for yourself. You're the one who cut out that knot-headed buckskin for a saddle pony. She's too small to put up against Rob Morgan's black. My chestnut is the only horse that might have a chance."

"I was talkin' 'bout the rodeo," Trenton said. His arm around the mannequin's torso, he lugged it over to the sawhorse table. "I ain't worried about no black or your chestnut. My Curly Q is gonna leave you both in the dust. She don't like bein' behind nothin' or nobody."

Silas laughed. "She may not like it, but that's where she's gonna be."

"We'll see," Trenton said.

Wrinkling her nose, Odessa picked up her yellow dress with the lace flounce at the bottom of the skirt and eyed it with disdain. Setting aside the petticoat and the bonnet, she made room for the mannequin. She moved the boys out of the way to dress the oversized doll. The brothers continued to bicker and bite at one another.

"If you'd stop braggin' on yourself for a minute," Trenton said and handed Odessa the hank of hair. "I was talkin' 'bout you signin' up to ride broncs, you blockhead. That's where the broken neck comes in. Mama wasn't happy when she found out this mornin', and saw you'd put your name on the sign-up sheet."

"What was she doin' lookin' at the sign-up sheet? She don't usually pay any mind to who's doin' what," Silas said, and held the mannequin by the neck so

Trenton could slather glue over its pate.

"Here, let me do that." Odessa elbowed the brothers aside and proceeded to dribble the brownish yellow glue down the mannequin's temple and onto the shoulder. "You two don't know how a girl's hair should be—for Pete's-sake. There's stockings in the bag. See if you can manage to get those on."

Trenton nudged his brother. "Yeah, Silas, you got more experience than me 'bout that end of things."

"Shut up, pip-squeak."

Trenton dodged the swat Silas delivered. He stepped out of range, then moved back and held up the mannequin's shoulders and head while Odessa laid the hair so the bonnet would sit on the mannequin's head of long, strawberry-blonde hair just like hers.

Once they had the mannequin fully dressed, the boys stood her up and leaned her against the side of the table. "Get up there beside her, Dessie. Let's have a look." Odessa bounced over and stood shoulder to shoulder with the dummy.

The boys stood back and studied the ladies. "Whaddya think?" asked Trenton, his head tilted slightly toward his brother.

"Could be twins," Silas said, and both boys burst out in whoops of laughter.

Odessa did a little jig, unable to contain her anticipation. "This is going to be fun. Is the buckboard all set?" She couldn't resist giving the bonnet on the dummy a final adjustment.

"All set," Silas said and rushed ahead of her to be the first to climb down the loft ladder.

"Buckboard's out back. Got straw bales in the back you can hide behind," he said and grinned up at her.

Odessa blushed, aware he'd positioned himself perfectly to look up her skirt—it wasn't the first time. Offering her his hand, she leaped, bypassing the last few rungs, and tugged down her dress.

Laughing at her attempt at modesty, he said, "Got the jug under the seat. Trenton's gonna take the reins, and I'm gonna love up the dolly."

Silas kept her hand in his and pulled her up to his chest, his face close to her cheek. "Speakin' of lovin' up the dolly," Silas said, his breath soft and warm, so close to her cheek, "how 'bout a kiss for luck, Dessie? Trenton and me, we could use it today."

Heart in her throat, pulse pounding, Odessa gasped for breath and giggled. To her own ears, she sounded silly, unsophisticated—not at all mature. She desperately wanted to be womanly for Silas.

Her knees turned to water. She feared she might swoon—she definitely couldn't breathe. His smile was so warm and full of the devil, and he was looking at her, looking as if he really wanted her. The heat of her blush set her body to tingling all the way down to her toes. He held her so close she could feel the power in his arms and the solid muscle of his chest. Silas was a man now, and he was finally looking at her as if she were...a *woman,* not a little girl, not his playmate.

Impatient, Trenton, waiting above them on the ladder, cleared his throat.

Silas spared him a glance. Keeping Odessa in his arms, he moved out of the way. Trenton slid down the ladder to the ground.

"What'd you sign up for again, brother?" Silas asked. Grinning, he locked gazes with Odessa's.

"Calf ropin'," Trenton said, glaring at both of them.

"You know what I signed up for."

"Yeah," Silas said before he put his lips to hers. Too soon, the kiss ended. He gave her a playful swat on the behind and sent her off toward the open barn door.

Skipping out into the bright, warm July sun, Odessa stopped, bounced back, and planted a kiss on Trenton's lips. She turned and stuck her tongue out at Silas before she darted away.

Behind her, Silas burst out laughing. "You should see your face, brother—I ain't never seen that shade of pink before."

****

The breakfast tables were no longer shaded by the trees now the sun had risen directly overhead. Yellow jackets had started to gather in, feasting on spots of syrup and bits of sausage. Ida Bodeman, her daughter Helen, and Irene worked as quickly as they could to clear away the remains of the breakfast, fighting off the determined wasps.

Irene wasn't surprised she'd ended up serving and cleaning up after this community gathering. But she wasn't the only one this time. Ida and Helen also found themselves—volunteered.

Sarah had a knack for delegating, they all agreed.

Later the pile of unclaimed tablecloths, now neatly folded and stacked at the end of the table, would serve double duty for the barbecue later in the day. Irene put a stone on top of the pile to keep them from flying away in the breeze.

A cloud of dust blew down the street, bringing Barclay Russell around the corner of the Grange. "Mrs. Obenchain, the doc, is he back from Lower Bridge?"

"Good morning, Mr. Russell," Irene said. Smiling at

him, she dusted off her hands, thinking surely all must be done now—there couldn't be any more they needed to do. "Yes, yes, he's back," she answered. "He arrived late last night."

Brows knit together, he rubbed his hands together like an eager child. "Good, good, bound to be some broken bones whenever there's a rodeo. Good we got a medic here in town." He took his watch out of his vest pocket, flicked the silver cover open, glanced at the time, and snapped it shut. "Well, it's a fine day, ladies—a fine day. Got to get over to the startin' line It's almost twelve-thirty. Race starts right at one. See, you're about done here. That's good. All's good."

The top cloth on the stack of tablecloths flapped in the breeze. Irene held them down, and Ida found another rock to place on top of the pile.

Helen removed her apron. "We best be gettin' over there. We should leave before Sarah comes around again. She's sure to find something—she can be persnickety."

Ida took her daughter's arm. "I say, if Sarah Laidlaw wants whatever-it-is done so badly, she can do it herself. I saw her stuffing her face with pancakes. I haven't seen her since. And I don't want to miss the start of this race— not this year. Last year I was in bed with the croup. You know there's gonna be eight riders this year. Never been that many before. Some of those Shanico boys came over this year."

"I heard," Irene said, pleased to be included in the exchange. Sarah Laidlaw still tried to keep her in her place, but since she'd helped to deliver Laura's twins, Nathan and Nan, Ida Bodeman, and many of the other ladies of the town had begun giving Irene Obenchain the benefit of the doubt. "Fresh mustangs should give Rob

Morgan a run for his money," she said.

"Yes, indeed," agreed Helen. "They're small but used to running, Daddy says."

They crossed the street, going down to the post office. Junie, Susan, and Odessa skipped over to greet them. "We've got a good place over here, Mama," Odessa said and took her by the arm, dragging her along. "Junie's papa set up a bench and some bales of straw. We can all watch together. We can see the horses start and finish—they'll be right in front of us. We're right beside the box where Mr. Russell will be.

"Here they come. Oooh, oh, aren't they magnificent! There's Silas on Hector. And Trenton on Curly Q, and Rob Morgan on Midnight. And look at Tim Laidlaw—his horse is a beauty, isn't he?"

The horse was very impressive. He looked to be of Arabian stock. The smoky-colored horse pranced, neck arched, silver tail held proudly.

"Looks to be four hometown boys against four out-of-towners," said Wanda Davis. They all craned their necks to see the riders come and take their positions at the starting line.

Irene thought all of the horses and riders looked impressive. The Shanico boys looked mean to Irene, as did their mounts—they definitely had blood in their eyes.

Trenton, the smallest rider, was the youngest. His mount, Curly Q, a buckskin pony, was short, stocky, and broad of chest. She held herself in what appeared to be a relaxed, almost sleeping position, head slightly down. Trenton looked to be talking to her as they came up between Silas's chestnut and Tim's dancing Arabian. All eight riders lined up as best they could. The horses, excited and nervous, pranced and fidgeted. There were spectators everywhere Irene looked, all up and down the street, even perched up in the trees and on the rooftops of the businesses.

Irene spotted Meda-Belle among a half-dozen others who had pulled their carriages up under the trees between the stable and the post office. Meda-Belle waved, then tipped her parasol to her and smiled—no doubt she recognized the coral chintz fabric of Irene's blouse, the same fabric she'd given Irene a month ago.

Irene had made a blouse out of the bright, sunny fabric, and to tone down the color a bit, she'd bought fabric of dark brown for a skirt and decided to make a weskit of the brown to go over the blouse. She was pleased with the results. So pleased, she'd indulged and purchased a straw hat to wear for the summer. Even Odessa had noticed the new hat and remarked she looked smart. Irene took her daughter's comment as high praise indeed.

Odessa was coming along very nicely these days, thought Irene. She was learning to sew, helping with the mending. She seemed more thoughtful of late, and it was very gratifying.

Silas would be away for the rest of the summer—Irene was relieved. He was going up to Lost Lake to herd sheep. And Trenton would be fire-watching. So Irene thought, at least for the summer, she wouldn't have to worry about Odessa getting into trouble with the Trask boys.

Odessa, of an age now—*fifteen rushing on toward sixteen*—the age when it had happened to her. When romantic notions had gotten out of control. Irene prayed her daughter was smarter than her mother. It was nice today, to see Odessa being silly and giggly with Junie and Susie, as it should be.

Life was pretty good of late, which made Irene uneasy. Doom, surely, lurked somewhere close to hand. What form would it take? That was the question—where to look—and how could one brace oneself for the blow?

Chapter Fourteen

"This looks like front-row seats," Elias said and tipped his hat to Mrs. Davis, Mrs. Bodeman, and Mrs. Eberhard.

"Doctor Rayburn," Mrs. Davis said, "how lovely you made it back in time for the race. I think we can make room for you." She began to move down the bench, thereby shifting all of the other occupants down a notch.

Elias forestalled her. "Don't disturb yourself. I've been sitting too much lately. I'll go down here and stand by Mrs. Obenchain. Thank you."

Moving quickly down to Irene, he hoped to avoid any other invitations and cheerfully called out to Odessa over everyone's heads, "So Miss Odessa," he said. His gaze included the rest of the girls seated with her, "Who's going to win this horse race? Do we have a favorite?"

Odessa and her chums seemed unable to stop twittering. Elias really didn't expect Odessa to make a coherent reply, but she surprised him. "Silas says he'll win, but I think Trenton will take them all. He's lightweight, and his little mustang looks to have a lot of heart."

Her statement caused a number of spectators within earshot to mutter barely civil arguments. But Odessa's daring prediction, Elias proudly noted, was not squelched by the nay-sayers—instead, she put her nose in the air and dismissed them all.

Elias gave another look to the lineup of horses. All of them were restive, except Trenton's mustang. Elias didn't think much of the look of the animal; she was shaggy and tough looking. If the looks of the horses decided the winner, he would give the race to Rob Morgan or the Laidlaw boy. Rob's black was as showy as they come, and Tim's gray Arabian was spirited.

The riders from Shanico looked ruthless and determined. He foresaw trouble from this quarter—the winner's purse was twenty-five dollars and a pair of fancy spurs. He expected to be a busy man, what with the race, rodeo, and the celebrating and bragging afterward.

****

Sensing Elias was near, Irene recognized the set of his shoulders, the way he wore his fedora tipped slightly to the right, shading his brow, and the way he easily made his way through the crowd. She'd heard Mrs. Davis offer him a place on the bench. Feeling guilty, and mortified his nearness set her heart racing, Irene glanced around and caught Sarah Laidlaw's gimlet gaze focused on her.

"Upon which horse have you placed your bet?" Elias asked. His face so close to hers, his breath caressed Irene's cheek like a butterfly kiss.

Meda-Belle winked at her and laughed, obviously highly entertained watching the exchange.

Blushing, Irene shook her head and laughed off his question. "I don't have money to throw away on bets."

Barclay Russell's booming voice interrupted any further remarks.

If she were to guess, judging by the twinkle in the doctor's brown eyes, he had, once again, provoked her into taking him seriously. She should've known better. She'd finally realized, within the last month or two, he liked to tease, and she knew herself to be an easy target. The truth of the matter, he confused her, made her nervous and fluttery—only when they were working together did she instinctively know his wishes and his meaning.

"Riders," Mr. Russell bellowed again through his megaphone, more to the crowd than to the riders. "The course is east to the end of the street, turn right, continue around to the back of the Grange Hall and the boarding house, stay to the right, head west, go behind the post office, cross Main Street, go around behind the Emporium, head east all the way down to the school, swing back west up Main street to the finish line. The course is clearly marked with white flags all the way around. I hope all of you have had a chance to walk the course 'cause anyone that gets off course, for any reason, is disqualified. Any questions?"

All the riders hunkered down close to the heads of their mounts, all except Trenton, who simply stroked Curly Q's neck and said something into her ear that made her ears twitch and swivel from side to side.

Riders and horses fought to stay on the starting mark. Mr. Russell raised the starting pistol in the air, his gaze fixed on the second hand of his watch.

Bang!

The horses lurched—one of the Shanico riders lost his seat as his mount reared and screamed, eyes rolling to the back of his eye-sockets in fright. Tim Laidlaw managed to stay glued to his saddle even though his horse bucked and wheeled twice. Once Tim had him turned the right direction, the horse leaped forward and started to run and, once past the Emporium, drew up fourth in the pack.

Trenton's Curly Q, the only horse when spurred out of the gate, started out at a full run, nose pointed straight ahead. She looked as though she saw nothing but wide open spaces ahead. Trenton sat low and easy in the saddle, his legs hugging the mustang's sides, his knees pointed down to the ground and butt off the saddle, working as one with his horse. Like Curly Q, Trenton looked oblivious to the crowd, his gaze fixed straight ahead, right between Curly Q's ears.

A surge of spectators, including Odessa and her friends, moved forward to watch the horses and riders come up behind the boarding house, livery, and post office. The people in the carriages stood up, and some of the people in the trees tried to stand, almost falling off their precarious perches.

Doctor Rayburn and Irene waited where they stood, their view obstructed from time to time. "Oh, please God, don't let any of those boys be killed," Irene whispered, jaw clenched. Her fingers gripped and released the front of her skirt.

Elias put his arm around her shoulder and brought his lips down to her ear. "You know that's why they do it, to defy death, I mean."

"Is that why?" she said. Forgetting herself, she leaned back into his embrace quite naturally. "I don't think death enters their empty heads. I think they believe they're invincible, immortal," she said and sighed. "Trenton is only sixteen, and Silas is barely eighteen, and those other boys don't look much older. Rob is probably the oldest one out there; he's probably twenty. And the horses—I...I don't even want to think about those poor horses. They could fall and break a leg. Then what? Then those beautiful animals would be shot. Horse racing and rodeo are among the craziest, most wicked events devised by man."

Giving her shoulders a little shake, he said, "You worry too much about everybody else."

Irene turned to look up and met his steady gaze—he was serious. Suddenly aware of his body, his hips pressed against her backside, warm and solid—of his arms, his fingers on her shoulder—she pulled away from him. "It's a curse," she said, a rush of wanton, lustful thoughts raced through her mind. Her body throbbed with need—yes, most definitely, a curse.

****

He should've resisted the temptation, he knew, but Elias liked the feel of her body pressed against him—it felt right. And she'd been relaxed, hadn't even paid any attention to what she was doing—it was the natural thing to do. That pleased him no end. Now he moved a little in front of her and bent down so she could not ignore him and gave her delicate little nose a tap. "There. For today, I remove the curse."

She giggled, actually giggled…a girlish giggle, and shook her head, her cheeks rosy pink and her eyes dancing with light. "Doctors—you think you can cure everything," she said and looked away.

****

Cheers went up from the crowd behind them. The horses came around the post office and crossed the street. Irene scanned the crowd to see if anyone had seen—if anyone had guessed her heart. Her gaze first clashed with Meda-Belle's laughing, taunting smirk—the woman actually winked. And then Grace Wolfe's dark glare sent

163

a shiver of unease scampering down Irene's spine. Turning, looking the other way, she encountered Sarah Laidlaw's disapproving sneer.

Three riders—Silas, Rob, and a Shanico boy, who wore a black Spanish hat and rode a palomino pony—were all neck and neck as they disappeared from view beyond the trees, going behind the Emporium. Trenton came up fast, then Tim Laidlaw and the other three riders. A big cloud of dust wafted down Main Street, sifting over the onlookers. Shouts and cheers followed the racers. The volume of cheers went up as the riders reappeared, coming from the side of the schoolhouse.

Rob and his black were in the lead, and Silas had fallen back beside Tim Laidlaw. The palomino was riderless. Trenton was taking Silas, his mustang reaching out with leaping strides, the horse's intent clear, to get ahead of the pack.

Odessa screamed, "Trenton. Trenton. Go. Go, Trenton. Run, Curly Q. Run."

Jumping up and down, she flapped her arms as the racers came down the street. Irene noticed George Krauss had gotten down from Meda-Belle's carriage, the better to see, but now he'd come over to stand beside Odessa. Irene was grateful to him when he caught Odessa by the arm to keep her from falling off the straw bale. Irene caught his eye, and they shared a smile and a nod. Watching her daughter jump up and down was almost as exciting as the race.

Stretching, reaching out, Curly Q fought his way toward the front. At the saloon, Curly Q was on Midnight's flank. By the stable they were neck and neck, and as they passed Mr. Russell at the finish line, Curly Q was a good head in front of the black.

Irene, hearing Odessa's jubilant cries, feared she would run into the road, heedless of the rest of the racing horses. But George evidently had anticipated Odessa might attempt such a thing and picked her up, lifting her up high enough she could see above the crowd. He wore that big grin of his, blue eyes dancing with laughter and—something else—possibly infatuation. His undisguised delight set Irene to worrying George might have feelings for her daughter, feelings of a romantic nature. If that were so, then she could only feel sorry for the young man—he didn't stand a chance.

"He won. He won. He said he would," Odessa said, clinging to George, who lowered her to the ground, his arms around her. Irene stared, watching Odessa, in front of God and everybody, plant a kiss on George's strong cheek.

Poor George, stunned at first, laughed, picked her up again, and twirled her around. When he finally set her down, Odessa wobbled a little before leaping toward her and falling into Irene's embrace, breathless and beautiful. Her joy infectious, Irene laughed with her.

****

"Doctor Rayburn," Rupert Laidlaw shouted, running across the street in the wake of the last rider, "We have a man down behind the school. He's out cold."

Elias, who'd been laughing, also caught up in Odessa's elation, sobered and turned to Irene. He bent down and picked up the black doctor's bag at his feet. "Irene," he said but quickly amended, for the benefit of anyone who might be listening, "Mrs. Obenchain, come with me. I might need your help."

"Yes, yes, of course," she said and untangled herself from her daughter. Odessa skipped off, laughing her way through the throng of spectators. The last Irene saw of her, she was jumping all over Trenton, congratulating him.

Irene shook her head and happened to catch the look on George's face. Hands in his pockets, standing alone, he had eyes only for Odessa. The tenderness, the hurt Irene read on his face nearly brought her to tears.

George loved her daughter. She didn't know why she'd never seen it before. George was always around, coming by the house, helping with the chopping of the wood, teasing Odessa, making her laugh.

****

After a half-hour examination of the young rider, Elias said, "Nothing broken, a mild concussion. If he takes it easy, I think he'll be all right."

"Thank the Lord," Irene heard Ruby Trask say—eyes to the heavens.

Ruby, looking particularly festive today—her hair in a braid that circled her head like a coronet, a pair of gold hoop earrings dangling from her earlobes, decked out in a rainbow-hued skirt and yellow blouse, had reason to celebrate—Trenton had taken the cash prize and the spurs.

"Tino is my nephew," she said. "Did I tell you? I did, didn't I? If my sister's boy dies, while my boy won the race, she'll never forgive me. She'll never let me hear the last of it. I tell you, never—probably put a curse on me."

"Well, he's not even close to death. A tap on the head and the wind knocked out of him," Elias said. He rose and stood to give Irene room to dress the gash above the boy's right brow.

"Augustino, Tino," Irene said, prodding the boy to

rouse him a bit to clean the dust and blood from his face, "can you open your eyes? You need to open your eyes now."

Tino Atiah opened one eye and squinted the other one, winced, and squeezed his eyes shut. "Pegasus, Pegasus. Where's my horse?"

Irene shook her head, "Shhh, rest yourself. Your horse is fine. See, he's over there in the shade."

Unfortunately, the boy tried to look, rising up on his elbows. He groaned and slumped back, eyes closing.

Irene set to work to bring him around with smelling salts and bathed his face.

Speech slurred, he asked, "Did we win? Peg could beat 'em all…beat 'em all."

"I guess he's still a might confused," Ruby said. "Can we move him out of the sun?"

Elias helped Irene to her feet, then carefully helped the boy to stand. "Easy now, take a couple of deep breaths, and let's see if you can walk."

Irene, hand over her mouth, dubious, stood back and watched the boy stagger around in a circle. With the doctor's assistance, he made it over to his horse and the shade beneath the tree before promptly throwing up.

The boy's sky-blue shirt was torn, spotted with blood and ground-in dirt—his raven black hair, dull with thick dust. He was a tall boy, thin, too thin. Irene had assisted Elias in his examination. The doctor had made note of the boy's mended broken leg, his missing index finger on his left hand, the ear lobe that was half-gone, but with all of that, here he was talking about participating in the rodeo—it didn't make good sense to Irene.

****

"I don't know why you're pouting, Silas," Odessa said, walking with the brothers after the rodeo on their way to the barbecue. "Second place is nice. I love the gold and white ribbon—it's pretty."

"The Shanico kid, Tino, our cousin, he's a circuit bronc-rider," Trenton said. "He's got belt buckles and ribbons from all over. I've seen 'em. You almost beat 'im. You only lost by three seconds, Silas. I'd say you gave him something to worry about."

Silas stopped, ran his fingers through his black hair, and slapped his hat against his thigh. "Damn, I did, didn't I?"

"Damn right you did," Trenton said.

Silas draped his arm around his brother. "And you, little brother, you can't rope the broad side of a barn. What the heck were you tryin' to do out there?"

"Ah, Curly Q don't like chutes. She kinda lost her concentration."

"She lost it, all right, buckin' and snortin'. She passed the calf like he was standin' still. I near split a gut. The look on your face, Trent, God. I wish you could've seen your face."

Odessa quickly reminded him, saying, "Silas Trask, Trenton beat you all get-out in the horse race. Curly Q showed all of you. She loves to race."

Silas laughed, shrugged his shoulders. "She does love to race. You said she don't like to be behind nothin', I guess that means calves too. So, little brother, how you gonna spend your prize money? How 'bout you let me introduce you to some fine ladies I know over to the boarding house?"

The offer, delivered with a sly wink to Odessa, put Trenton to the blush.

Odessa sent Silas a sour look of pure disgust. And Trenton said, "Shut up, Silas. I don't think it's right, you talkin' like that in front of Dessie."

"Whoa, now, don't get your hackles up, little brother. I was funnin'. She knows about them ladies, don't you, Dessie? She don't mind me talkin' 'bout 'em. She's one of us," Silas said. He draped his other arm around her waist and tugged her closer to his side.

Odessa's heart skipped a couple of beats. She hated being one of the boys, but she could wait because she knew any day now, Silas Trask would see her, really look at her, and he'd realize he was in love with her, had been in love with her all of his life. She was all he would ever need. And when that day came, he'd also realize he didn't need those ladies at the boarding house, not for anything.

****

Buried in a deep pit over a bed of hot ash and sage coals for a full day and a half, the meat on the butchered-out, beef carcass was cooked to perfection and falling off the bone. Served up, and drenched in tangy barbecue sauce, it melted in the mouth. Sourdough rolls and potato salad rounded out a never-to-be-forgotten feast. Everyone was stuffed, Irene included, but not so full she couldn't make room for frozen custard, topped with fresh strawberries.

Together Irene and Elias found a shady spot under a tree to eat their dessert. "I need a nap," Irene said and scraped the last of the sweet frozen cream from her dish.

"We've had quite a day," Elias said. He sighed and set aside what was left of his second helping of dessert. Leaning against the tree, one arm behind his head, looking up into the limbs of the tree, he tallied the day's casualties. "Two concussions, three dislocated shoulders, a broken ankle, two sprained wrists, and so many cracked ribs I lost count, not to mention various cuts and abrasions, and—the day isn't over. I think we've more than earned our twenty-five dollar service fee."

"They're already passing the jug around," Irene said and set her empty bowl behind her. Near the BBQ pit, she'd observed a group of men shooting the breeze, smoking stogies, and supposedly putting out the fire. But they had a couple of jugs going around, and with each pass, their voices grew louder and louder, carried across the green.

"Yes, I noticed," Elias said and closed his eyes. "Mr. Borseth is very free with his brew. He offered me a swig. I was setting the ankle on the Shanico boy, the one who fell into the chute and almost got his brains stomped out by the crazy bull."

He turned his head and opened one eye. "He's a lucky boy. Did you hear him whining that now he wouldn't be able to dance with the girls tonight?"

Shifting his body toward her, he put his hand on her wrist, his gaze warm and full of tenderness. "Speaking of dancing with pretty girls, may I request the honor of soliciting a dance with you this evening, Mrs. Obenchain?"

Feeling more than a little giddy at the touch of his hand on hers and seeing the warm look in his eyes, Irene was momentarily struck speechless. Pressing her lips together, she managed to get her racing pulse under control, as well as her senses. "Doctor Rayburn, you know I don't dance."

"Don't or won't?" he asked, his gaze drilling deep

into her soul.

"Both," she said, feeling suddenly weak and pitiful—stupidly self-deprecating. Then lifting her chin, she said, "I can't, I should imagine. It's been a long time since I tried to dance. I would probably maim, should I choose to inflict myself on someone. You must count yourself lucky. I shall never consider being your partner. I wouldn't want to be the cause of your injury—the people of this town would never forgive me."

It was said as a joke, but she watched the light go out of his eyes, replaced by the old sadness—the sadness she'd seen the night he'd arrived. Usually, she would've turned away from that look, telling herself she didn't need to know the cause, but today had been fine and wonderful. To soften her rebuff, she said, "Anyway, thank you for asking. I shouldn't be surprised once the music starts, I will fall asleep with the rest of the babies."

Before he could protest, she went on to say, "I think I'll see if I can find Odessa. We should go home and freshen up before the dancing starts. Do you see her anywhere? She was sitting with the Davis family. I don't see her now. And...I don't see Silas or Trenton; that is never good. When all three of them are out of sight, I worry—seems I'm always trying to find that girl."

Elias heaved a heavy sigh and came to his feet. "You have a sensible turn of mind, Mrs. Obenchain. Usually, I find this characteristic of yours admirable, but at this moment—it's irritating and damned frustrating. But, yes, let's head for home—get away from here before Mrs. Laidlaw decides you need to pay for your supper by clearing away all of the feast like you did after breakfast. Maybe we'll find Odessa along the way."

"It's going to be a pretty evening to have a dance

outside," Irene said. Unable to think of anything else to say, she picked up their bowls and set them in her basket. He folded the blanket to fit under his arm, his face showing his disappointment. He didn't try to persuade her to relent. He took her hand and placed it in the crook of his arm, and they headed toward the road.

Chapter Fifteen

Trenton refused to help Odessa into the wagon.

She hitched up her dress above her ankles, found her footing, huffed, and proceeded to climb into the wagon bed unassisted. "I will not be left behind, Trenton Milo Trask. I helped put this together, remember. I am entitled to take part. Besides, this is the biggest, best prank we've pulled yet. This one is going to go down in history, and I intend to be in on it with or without your help." Tripping on a board, she nearly fell on her nose. Trenton grabbed her by the waist and roughly kept her on her feet.

Heaving a resigned sigh, he went around and climbed up to take up the reins. Leaning over the back of the buckboard, he asked, "You sure you really want to do this? I mean…Silas and me…we're…we're…well, it's okay if we cut up…but you're a girl…and folks think girls have to be…well… *ladies*…I guess."

"Trent," Silas said, climbing aboard, "you can be a real grandma sometimes. Leave her alone. Dessie said she's in, and she's in."

Silas settled the mannequin on his lap, one of her arms going up on his shoulder, the other arm limp, dangled down between his legs.

Odessa squatted and wedged her body between the straw bales to get comfortable.

"Could ya give me a little help here," Silas asked Trenton.

Cringing, Odessa removed a particularly long and sharp reed of straw from her thigh.

"I want the dolly's legs to be right. Maybe one bent up, spread apart, the other going across your knees, skirts up...you know...legs all akimbo...loose like."

"You'd know loose better'n me," Odessa heard Trenton say, although it was more of a growled response. Glancing up, she thought she could possibly help with the placement. Trent turned his shoulder and refused to give Silas any help whatsoever.

Coming to her knees, impatient with both of them, she leaned over the back of the seat rest. "Silas Trask, you'd think you were in love with this stupid doll. Get her on your lap, and let's go.

"And as for you, Trenton, stop worrying about me. I know what I'm doing. We aren't going to hurt anybody. We're having some fun. I found the mannequin. It was my idea, and I get to be part of this...this... whatever—drama—yes—our *drama*. We're doing a little vignette."

Pleased with herself, she ducked back down and stuffed herself back into position, her genius tickling her so much, she couldn't stop giggling.

"Okay, but your mama ain't gonna like it," Trenton said over his shoulder. "And I can see old lady Laidlaw's face now—it ain't pretty."

"Me, too," Odessa said back, still snickering to herself. "Mrs. Laidlaw is a persimmon, and Mama worries too much. Who cares? Come on, let's go before everybody leaves the grounds to go change or rest or...something."

"All right," Trenton said. "Hang on and start screamin'."

Once out of the livery, Trenton whipped the horses,

and the wagon rounded the corner of the post office, headed down the street at full speed. Silas let out a war whoop that could wake the dead. Odessa squealed with real fright, getting bounced around like a drop of water on a hot plate. Remembering her part, she screamed, then squealed because every time Silas let out a war whoop it startled her. In between her squeals of fright and screams, she heard herself laughing because she couldn't help it. Over the top of her squeals, screams, and laughter, Silas kept up a steady stream of whoops.

The wagon headed east down Main Street and made a beeline for the grounds around the Grange where everyone had gathered for the celebration.

****

Irene heard the war whoop, and her attention turned westward, as did several other heads, including Elias, who tightened his grip on her arm.

A runaway buckboard, coming right at them, barreled down the street. Two men wearing dark trail dusters, black hats pulled low over their eyes, sat on the seat. And sprawled across their laps was a female, her petticoats and limbs exposed, face obscured. She looked like she might be drunk, arms and legs loose.

The dress the woman had on looked very familiar to Irene—yellow with a white lace flounce at the hem. She'd added that flounce to accommodate a growing girl. The straw bonnet she wore on her head of strawberry blonde tresses was askew. Her legs, one bent, exposed thin cotton drawers and bare ankles, the other draped over the driver's knee, seemed at odd angles and stiff. The female's head and shoulders slipped off the passenger's knee when he passed a brown jug to the driver. After the passenger regained his grip on the woman, he proceeded to fondle the woman's breasts, then pressed a kiss to the woman's opened mouth.

The wagon drew near, and Irene felt the earth shake. She actually thought she could feel the ground tilt, rock side-to-side, as she, and those around her, gasped with horror.

From somewhere behind her, she heard Susan Laidlaw, or maybe it was Junie Davis, cry out, "Odessa? Mama, it's Odessa Obenchain. Drunk...she's drunk. Those men—who are they?"

In her state of shock, it didn't really matter to Irene *who* made the assumption the woman on the wagon seat with her dress blowing up around her hips, exposing her bare legs, and falling off her shoulders, was Odessa. What mattered was that anyone would even think it could possibly be true—although the woman did bear a very strong resemblance to her daughter.

If Irene had to make a guess, she would say the two men were none other than Silas and Trenton Trask. Which also increased the odds Odessa was in on this stunt, but Odessa most certainly was not the wanton hussy sprawled out on Silas's lap. It very well could be Odessa's dress, and her hat, but Irene couldn't believe the woman was Odessa.

Elias, holding Irene close to his side, lips warm against her ear, assured her, "That's not Odessa, Irene. Look at her. That's a mannequin. And Trenton Trask at the reins, see his red shirt there under his coat. Bet Silas is the other one."

"Yes, a mannequin—you're right, but...that's Odessa's scream...her squeal...I know it. I would know it anywhere." Turning her face into his chest, unable to watch, her voice constricted with mortification, Irene cried, "She's on that wagon. Odessa, dear God."

Everyone but Irene saw the wagon careen around the corner behind the school. And as it did, the man on the buckboard ripped the woman's head off and tossed it up into a tree, then an arm, then both legs—*still encased in snow white bloomers*—flew up into the air, then fell to land on a sage bush.

Loud, raucous, ribald comments and hoots of grotesque laughter rose up from the inebriated males near the barbecue pit. The screams of frightened children and ladies added to the din as a unified response of horror overwhelmed the throng. Children clung to their mamas, women fainted, men whooped and cheered—it was a mesmerizing, terrorizing, rip-snorting spectacle, and Irene knew her daughter was the genius behind it.

"Come, let's go," Elias said, urging her to move. She didn't have to be told to go—she wanted to run, but Elias held her to a fast walk. They passed the Emporium, and the wagon crossed the street in front of them. The occupants, laughing and congratulating themselves, pulled up in front of them. The three pranksters sobered.

Irene couldn't bring herself to make eye contact with any of them. If she did, she knew she'd go down on her knees and cry. Home. She wanted to get to her house and hide. Hide from the laughter, the soon-to-come ostracism, the rejection. It was coming. Odessa was going to feel it, experience it, as Irene had for these many years. All her work to protect Odessa was shattered in what amounted to a fifteen-minute childish trick.

****

Her mother's face, white as the doctor's shirt collar—looked positively stricken—it was wonderful. Odessa pressed her lips together to keep from doubling over with laughter. But the look she received from Doctor Rayburn sobered her. The look in his eyes gave her goosebumps. He'd never looked at her like that before—it was almost loathing, she thought.

All the way back to the stable, Silas kept up a steady stream of excited patter. "Did you hear 'em, Dessie? Did you hear 'em yell...and scream when I chucked her head into the tree? I didn't even think about it. I just chucked it. And the drawers, your drawers, they're back there in the bushes. Did ya see 'em? They landed right there in the bushes plain as day."

"Shut up, Silas," ordered Trenton once inside the stable.

Odessa, trembling, no longer laughing, very near tears, couldn't even see Silas. He was a pink blur. Suddenly she had a headache and wanted to go home.

"What's the matter with you two...we did it...we shocked 'em, and scared the hell outta the whole dad-blamed lot of 'em!" Silas said.

He hopped down off the wagon and stopped crowing long enough to take a swig from a full flask of brew he had tucked in his coat pocket. "I think I saw old lady Hazelton...you know, Junie's grandma. I think she actually swooned. Good-God-a-mighty, what a time...what a time."

"I said, shut up," Trenton said and helped Odessa out of the wagon and set her on her feet.

She started to sob and pulled away. Unable to look Silas in the eye, head down, Odessa started to run, run for home.

****

Elias remained silent, although he dearly wanted to give Odessa a good scolding and a whupping. Irene hardly spoke. Stoic and rigid, she ordered Odessa, as soon as she came through the door, to get cleaned up and ready for the dance.

"Are you sure you want to go? We could stay here. You must be tired," he said, trying to reason with her.

"We will return to the celebration," Irene said without meeting his eyes.

"I don't need to go, Mama. I'll stay here. Go to bed early," Odessa promised, almost pleading.

Her voice hard, unrelenting, Irene said, "You and I will go to the celebration."

Elias saw it as punishment. He couldn't say who Irene thought she was punishing, herself or her daughter. She was a proud woman, and he knew she would not retreat.

"You will hold your head up, Odessa, face your friends and neighbors, and give some thought to the consequences of your actions."

Against his better judgment, Elias kept his thoughts to himself and escorted Odessa and Irene back to the Grange where the music had started.

A sifting of dust rose up around the dancing couples. A ring of lanterns hung from posts and trees, illuminating the dance arena, softening their images. The couples drifted by as if in a dream to the strains of "Sweet Betsy From Pike."

Odessa pasted a smile on her lips and presented a brave face. She wore her favorite dress of white dotted Swiss over the green satin underskirt. She looked sweet, although tentative, and walked ahead of her mother.

Elias spotted Junie Davis—she stood next to her mother. She started to wave, but her mother stayed her hand and turned her around by her shoulders. Susan wasn't far away. She turned her head without prompting from her mother. Benny Davis and his brother Carl, their hands in their pockets, looked down to the ground as Odessa walked past them.

****

There was, of course, an area set up to keep the children, a small fortress of straw bales not far from the table of punch and cookies. But tonight, Mary Pritchard, the schoolmarm, was in charge of the nursery—that's when Irene knew for certain she'd lost what little status she'd gained over the years.

Elias found them a place to sit to the side of the dance floor, away from the main body of merrymakers. "I'll be right back. You both stay here. Don't worry, everything is going to be all right. I won't leave you alone for very long. I want to speak to the mayor."

"Elias…" Irene said, calling him back, her throat dry and constricted. She really didn't want to call attention to herself by talking at all. Reaching out for him, she drew him back, feeling all eyes upon her. "Doctor Rayburn, please don't…don't say anything," she said, her voice hushed and furtive. "You must stay away from us, don't you see. If you…if you try to…help, they will think… Oh, you know what they will think." Irene blushed to say it, but she had to make him see—she and Odessa were as pariahs—they carried misfortune around with them like the plague. To associate with them would only cause infection. "They will think what they have tried not to think all these months, that you and I…that we… Don't do it… Leave us alone. We'll go in a little while. We'll slip away. You stay. Don't give them any more fodder for the gossip-mill, please, Elias. Please listen to me."

****

Elias was at once elated and deflated—she'd used his first name and more than once. He'd waited a long time to hear his name on her lips. Not only had she spoken his name, she'd used it in a most intimate manner as if they were close friends. More than friends. Her eyes, she'd looked right into his eyes. They were so beautiful. How he wanted to take her in his arms and hold her, hold her until all her fears faded away. She placed her hand on his wrist, her eyes pleading. He could not commit to her request. He couldn't say he would, and he couldn't say he wouldn't. He felt his place to be at her side—he wanted to protect her, shield her from the barbs and insulting rebuffs. He was a doctor, trained to be objective, and he really was going to try to look at this ridiculous mess from all sides.

At least, that was his intent as he made his way to the punch table to get Irene and Odessa some refreshment.

"Doctor Rayburn, lovely evening isn't it?" said Sarah Laidlaw. Her demeanor syrupy sweet, Sarah sidled up beside him. He didn't much care for the saccharin smile on her face or the triumphant sparkle in her eyes.

"The atmosphere seems a bit oppressive, I think," he said, one eyebrow cocked. "Excuse me, I was fetching some refreshments for Mrs. Obenchain and her daughter."

He turned to walk away, but Sarah couldn't allow that. "They shouldn't have come. Irene Obenchain should've known how it would be."

He didn't doubt Sarah spoke for, and represented, the minds of many of the citizens present this evening.

Her imperious gaze swept the crowd. "The Trasks

aren't here, as you can see. Bet their pa is giving those boys a good thrashing for the stunt they pulled today. And, if you ask me, that's what that girl needs and has needed for a good long while."

Her voice had grown louder. Elias wasn't the only one listening to Sarah spout her opinion. "If her father were here, he would've dusted her saucy pants many times...I have no doubt. Her mama is too soft. A girl like that needs a firm hand. Her mama... Her...mother can't see the girl is no good and she won't ever be any good. Mark my words—Odessa Obenchain is destined for big trouble, has been since the day she was born—loose and full of herself to boot."

Elias drew himself up, took one step forward, and stared the woman down. Then he bellowed, "You've said quite enough, Mrs. Laidlaw."

He had to take a breath—he actually wanted to slap the woman. Clenching his teeth, he forced down his outrage. It was a futile exercise, he did realize, but Sarah Laidlaw had gone too far. There was very little hope of her actually feeling any remorse or shame, but he had to try.

"Glass houses, Mrs. Laidlaw, we should never forget that little homily. Righteousness comes easily to most of us—it is, after all, the shorter path, while the path to forgiveness takes more character and more effort. Ultimately, it is the more worthwhile of the two journeys, and the benefits are more far-reaching and rewarding. You see, one never knows, Mrs. Laidlaw, when one may have need of forgiveness, as no one, not even you, is perfect. To think so is, in my estimation, a sin, a very big sin."

****

In the end, Elias did as Irene requested. He left her and Odessa to sit, segregated and alone. Irene could feel his eyes on her. She didn't have to see him to know he was nearby, watching over her.

Poor Odessa, she was so obviously hurt and sorry, shoulders slumped, unable to look anyone in the eye. Irene's shoulders ached, but she refused to lower her chin or show any kind of shame, so she sat ramrod straight, hands clasped tightly in her lap, looking neither to the right nor to the left, trying to concentrate on the music, actually hearing nothing but the pounding of her heart in her ears.

Mr. Russell sat next to her for a few moments but didn't have much to say before he left her side to pay a visit to Miss Pritchard, obviously the new object of his affection. Elias caught Irene's eye, and she attempted to put on a brave face by offering him a nod and a smile.

Looking away from Mr. Russell and the beaming Miss Pritchard, Irene told herself she could now breathe easy—she no longer had to worry about hurting Barclay Russell's feelings—he was no longer smitten. From her brief observation, it would appear Mary Pritchard was responding favorably to Mr. Russell's attentions—Irene applauded the match.

After enduring an hour of isolation, Irene was sorry she'd forced Odessa to come. It was foolish of her to think they could bluff their way through the evening.

George Krauss came and asked Odessa if she wanted to dance. It broke Irene's heart. The crushed look on Odessa's face answered his request. She shook her head in refusal. "I don't feel much like dancing tonight. Too much sun today. Thank you, George."

Thankfully, George was there, handy, to rescue

Odessa when a drunk, a man neither Irene nor Odessa knew, asked to take her out on the floor. Odessa, afraid and appalled, backed up into Irene's arms. The man, drunk and insistent, tugged Odessa by the arm. Irene had her by the waist to keep him from dragging her away. George stepped in, took the man by the scruff of the neck, and told him to go cool off.

Irene looked around to see if anyone had witnessed the incident. Everyone, it seemed to her, watched and sniggered. She caught Grace Wolfe grinning from ear to ear and couldn't help but speculate if this was Grace's little joke—perhaps a little revenge.

That was all the humiliation Irene could endure. She had no trouble getting Odessa to agree to go home. She refused Elias when he offered to escort them. There was no need for him to leave, and besides, she didn't want to set tongues wagging any more than they already were.

Home safe, Odessa went to her room, and Irene went to hers. Feeling utterly powerless, Irene sat on her bed in the dark, listening to Odessa weep. She felt the old coldness creep in around her and the emptiness deep in her gut. Earlier today, she'd begun to think she'd left that feeling behind her, but now it was more acute than ever. It wasn't for herself. It was worse—it was for her child.

****

The following day, Odessa overheard Doctor Rayburn tell her mama Silas had been sent to the Owyhees to herd sheep with his Shanico cousins, and Trenton wasn't going to fire-watch for the Suncrest Logging Company after all, he was on his way to Lost Lake, also to herd sheep.

When her mother and the doctor glanced in her direction, Odessa didn't give them the satisfaction of seeing her react. She kept her head down and tended to her stitches on Mrs. Lamphere's chemise.

But inside, she seethed, raged against the injustice. Her head ached. She was sick from crying and wanted to scream at her mother.

Yell at me! Lock me in my room, say something, tell me what a fool I am. I can't stand this silent treatment. You too, Doctor Elias. Was it really so bad, what we did? It was supposed to be funny. That's all, funny. God, I hate this town, and I hate all of you!

Chapter Sixteen

May 4, 1901

Elias stood at the study window in Doctor Carter's house and looked out at the river. Canada geese and mallards swam in lazy circles in the icy cold water, the May sunshine warming their backs. He had a letter from Marie in his pocket and a yet-to-be-sent telegram in his hand.

"It's funny, in a way, this past year and a half has gone by at a snail's pace, and then again, the time has flown by so fast it's a blur in my mind's eye, so many new faces and places. I don't know how the days and weeks turned into months without my notice."

"When did you receive the letter, my boy?"

Elias turned and faced the doctor; he thought his mentor looked older, worn out—more so than when he'd visited in February.

"April," Elias answered. "She's married by now."

"I see," Doctor Carter said like a good doctor, his words, and his intonation, giving away nothing of his true thoughts.

The old man's eyes studied Elias' face, brows knit together. "When was the last time you asked your wife to consider joining you?"

Elias jerked to attention at the very idea. "I never asked Marie to come," he said, perfectly aware how heartless he sounded. "I asked her before she got on the train, but I never put the question to her again. That's why I find this so disturbing. I feel guilty I didn't do more, didn't try harder to bring her here."

"Well, then…I guess my question is why? Why did you not?" asked Doctor Carter. "Come, come, boy…you came here to talk about this. You know the answer. I can see how troubled you are. But you have to unload your craw, all of it. This has been festering for well over a year. I think you can let it go now."

Elias surrendered and sat down in the big leather chair in front of Doctor Carter's desk. He took a deep breath and handed Doctor Carter the letter.

Doctor Carter read to himself. Elias had memorized every word.

My Dearest Elias. It seems a long time ago we sat here in Mama's swing on the verandah, and you told me about your Oregon High Desert. You told me about crystal-clear rivers teeming with fish and waterfowl, and mountains covered with snow, their peaks so high and steep, very few men had ever reached the top. I was a simple, foolish child then. What I saw in my mind was a dream, a fantasy, but you required a woman, not a child. You needed a helpmate and partner

I was caught up in your dream, dear Elias. That High Desert country is your vision of paradise. I was not mature enough to realize your dream and my dream were not the same. Unfortunately, I woke up in Boise, Idaho. I shall forever be ashamed of my behavior and how I must have hurt you.

You said there is nothing to forgive, and you wish me nothing but happiness. I pray this is your true heart. Papa was able to achieve for us an annulment. It became final before the end of the year 1900.

Father has a new associate, a Doctor Stephen Howe. Doctor Howe and I have formed a close relationship. We find we are very much of the same mind, and we are to be married the second Sunday of April 1901.

What I most desire is happiness for you, dear Elias. I feel you helped me find my true life, the one I have always *wanted. I know I am going to be very happy, and that is what I pray for you, as well.*

Truest regards, always, Marie.

Doctor Carter sat for a moment, staring at the letter, and finally, he asked, keeping his old eyes on the paper in his hands, "This doesn't make you happy, I gather?" Looking up, he pinned a sharp bead on Elias. "Why is that? You hadn't asked her to join you. Did you expect she would remain unattached until you made up your mind what you wanted?"

"Certainly not," said Elias. The unexpected venom in his tone surprised him. He shrugged and took a breath to steady himself. "I'm very happy for her. She is far too lovely and intelligent to be left alone—a woman with no husband."

"Ah…ah," was all Doctor Carter said, "now I think I begin to understand and to see where all of this is leading. So, are we speaking of Marie or someone else?"

Elias looked into the old man's knowing eyes and smiled, then squirmed a little in his chair.

"Yes, well, I have hinted to you of my feelings for Mrs. Obenchain. They have not weakened. No. They grow stronger each day. There lies my guilt, you see. I couldn't ask Marie to join me because of my feelings, my growing feelings, for Mrs. Obenchain. There have been times, and I don't like to say it aloud because it makes me cringe with shame, but I was glad Marie wasn't with me, grateful she'd turned back—didn't want to come. I didn't ask her to come to Oregon again because I've been too much of a coward. I was afraid she might take me up on my offer, and I couldn't risk it. I've been hoping and praying she'd find someone else. You can't imagine how relieved…how horrible…how despicable I feel because of my initial elation over this," he said, and flicked his finger on the edge of the paper, "this news."

Doctor Carter cleared his throat, unable to hide his amusement, his old eyes dancing with light, he chuckled. "You keep referring to…*her*…as Mrs. Obenchain."

Elias couldn't sit still another second, so he popped up and began to pace before the window. "Well, yes…I try to remember," he said. "In my head, she has many names. None of which I could ever say out loud: My Dear, sweetheart, adorable Irene…" He shivered, thinking about the many times he'd almost slipped and called her by one of those endearments, and there had been several occasions and in front of other people. He knew Irene wouldn't have appreciated it.

"You have to understand Irene…Mrs. Obenchain…is an expert at reminding one…in so many, many ways…she is…and will ever be…*Mrs. Obenchain.*"

Clearing his throat, wiping the smile off his lips with the palm of his hand, the old man asked, "Has she ever given you any indication she has feelings for you?"

Elias laughed a self-deprecating laugh and plopped down in the chair. He had asked himself so many times this very question. The same answer kept popping up—*you are a fool, Elias Rayburn, a fool to ask, and a fool to hope.*

"We work well together," he said aloud, to himself mostly. Leaning forward toward the doctor's desk he said, "I don't know if I can explain—I've never tried to give my feelings, my intuition, words. We work well together; I said that, I know, but...I've never known anyone to have such a natural aptitude for nursing. I never expected to have my own nurse. I thought Marie would, would...perhaps at some point...want to join me in my practice—before we came west. But I...I never thought she would actually enjoy it...be interested. I don't think she would thirst for more information, or have the desire, like Irene has, to improve her skills...and on her own. Irene asks for books, for manuals, and charts.

"Did I tell you, I have convinced her to stop doing laundry for the logging camp? I've been giving her a share of my income...be it in produce...or chickens...or cordwood to compensate her for her assistance."

Doctor Carter cut in and asked the big question, "Elias, my boy, does she care for you...has she given you any sign?"

He sighed and slumped back into the soft leather. He looked down at his hands. His fingers worked the cuticles around his fingernails. "The only evidence I have gathered so far is hardly worth mentioning. Once, almost a year to date, she received a letter telling her of her father's death, and there was a brief moment when I thought she actually needed me. She allowed me to comfort her.

"She, of course, distanced herself from me after Odessa's escapade at the Fourth of July celebration last year. She had to soften a little as winter came on because we were stuck in the same house together for days at a time. Not that it's difficult to get along with her. No, on the contrary. There is nothing I would rather do than be caged up with that woman for the rest of my days if it were possible."

Elias looked up at the sound of his mentor's fingers drumming on his desk top, a sure sign of impatience.

"A few months back, Anna Davis—remember I told you—she was having severe, reoccurring abdominal cramps. Her appendix nearly burst. Irene assisted as I performed an appendectomy. Irene was fearless, steady, soothing Anna's parents, even though Mrs. Davis has been extraordinarily cruel and judgmental toward Odessa.

"It was a very near thing. The appendix was gangrenous, very large, and inflamed. As I closed the incision, Irene said something…at least I think it was something." He closed his eyes to recall her exact words. He repeated them to himself daily to keep them close to his heart. He clung to them. They were the threads of hope that kept him going.

"She said, 'Thank you, Elias. Thank you for giving me this. You make me feel worthwhile. You give me my pride back. No matter what happens between us, I will always love you for this.' "

"That's what she said. I now base my entire existence on those words. She has given me nothing more—no sign, no touching, no word. After she said that, she walked away. The barrier back in place. I'm Doctor Rayburn, and she is Mrs. Obenchain."

With probing frankness Doctor Carter asked, "Have you told Mrs. Obenchain how you feel about her? Does she know about this letter…about Marie remarrying?

Have you actually come out and stated your feelings?"

"Irene read Marie's letter, yes. She's the only person, besides you, I've shown it to. I wanted her to know. I thought it might change things between us."

"Well, what did she say?"

"She didn't understand. Then I told her what had happened in Boise. I've never told anyone, other than you, what happened. I think my pride was hurt more than I wanted to admit.

"She read the letter in front of the fire, tears in her eyes. I wanted to hold her. I tried to touch her. She pulled away and wiped her eyes and handed the letter back and said she was 'sorry, very, very sorry.' She got up and went to her room, and closed the door. I still feel very, very cold whenever I think of it. She didn't explain herself—why she was sorry. I don't understand women at all…and Irene Obenchain in particular.

****

Ignoring the fine bench Elias had made for her, Irene sat on the ground under her pine tree and drew the long, three-pronged pine needle between her fingers. Her thoughts were with Elias…no, Doctor Rayburn, she reminded herself. He was in Farewell Bend consulting with Doctor Carter. Ruby had breast cancer, but was there enough hope to justify an operation? He needed Doctor Carter's advice and assistance. The facilities in Farewell Bend at their new St. Charles Hospital were better equipped to perform this delicate procedure.

In a telegram, Doctor Rayburn recommended Irene go along on the expedition to harvest the ice. It was a very good thing she had made the trek. Oren Laidlaw fell off the scaffolding and tumbled down the throat of the ice cave on the fourth day they were there. He'd suffered a broken arm, head abrasions, and hypothermia.

Irene cringed, remembering Sarah's pitiful plea for her help. "Oh, Irene, save my little boy, don't let him die. I take back all the bad things I've ever said about you. Forgive me, please, take care of my boy. He's so small, don't hold his mama against him. Please?"

Sarah's pleading words sickened Irene to the core. She had nothing to say in the face of such shallow thoughts. Only Sarah could think someone would withhold aid out of spite. It was a very good thing Mr. Laidlaw removed his wife before Irene had a chance to gather her thoughts and tell Sarah she was the only person Irene knew of who would think to say such a thing.

However, the true reason Irene had decided to go to the caves was Odessa. She'd caught Odessa and Silas necking behind the cowshed. Irene didn't want her daughter to follow in her footsteps and marry foolishly, and she couldn't help but think marrying Silas Trask would be the height of foolishness.

Over this past year, Odessa had made her very proud. She'd studied hard, doing well in school. Miss Pritchard was grooming her to be a schoolteacher. The schoolmarm had spoken to Irene about the possibility of Odessa attending Oregon Normal School over in the valley next year. There she could get her teacher's certificate. Odessa was excited about the idea—it had been heartening. "I could go anywhere and teach and live on my own. Oh, Mama, think of it, I could travel like Papa. Maybe I could find him someday."

Irene sat thinking of those words. She'd started setting back money for Odessa's school. Nursing was slightly more lucrative than doing laundry and mending for the logging camp—and certainly less fatiguing. Irene had to admit she was sleeping better, she'd gained a couple of pounds, and she felt better. Actually, better than she had for years, even though she realized she was getting old. She would be thirty the middle of July.

She withdrew a folded piece of paper from her apron pocket. She kept it with her at all times for fear either Odessa or Elias would find it. It had never left her possession for the past eight months.

Dawson City, Assayers Office, Dept. of Claims and Deeds, Dawson City, Yukon Territory, August 14, 1900. Dear Mrs. Abel Obenchain: After an extensive investigation for the past three years, we have determined Abel James Obenchain died en route to Dawson City in the fall of 1896. A number of bodies were retrieved from several locations, but they were unidentifiable by the time the weather thawed, and search parties were safely dispatched. The number of John Does was in the hundreds. We are very sorry we have not been able to notify you sooner. These few personal items were still on the body."

The simple silver cross he wore around his neck upon a silver chain, his red paisley bandanna, his pocket knife with his initials carved on the buckhorn handle, and a scrap of the flannel shirt Irene had sewn for him were all that remained of her husband—all now safely buried within a cracker tin beneath the pine tree. She carefully placed a flat piece of slate over the spot, wiggling it back and forth to half bury it in the soft mulch of pine needles and pumice-rich dirt around the tree. Irene patted the earth beside her under the pine tree. Holding her hand there, she closed her eyes and prayed, "Rest in peace, Abel."

Irene looked up to the Three Sisters, dressed in their cold white robes of snow and ice, sensing their disapproval. *Forgive me*, she begged them. *Forgive me for not telling anyone, not even Odessa. I know she should be allowed to grieve for her Papa. But God, if I tell her, then Elias will surely find out. Odessa wouldn't understand if I asked her to tell no one else—she wouldn't. No one can know.*

Elias...Elias would have to leave. His living here has caused enough talk as it is. Mrs. Davis actually spoke to us last week when we were in the Emporium. And Sarah, she's been downright congenial. Odessa has a good mind. She could have so much more than I ever could have dreamed of having. I don't want her to have to depend on the likes of the Silas Trasks of this world. They take the parts they want and leave you heartbroken.

A tear seeped out of the corner of her eye, and she sniffed back the ache in her throat. *Elias. What to do about Elias? I can't let him leave me. I love him. He isn't anything like Abel. He's good and generous...someone I can count on. I need to know he calls this home, that I'm part of that. I would surely shrivel up into nothing but dust if I couldn't work beside him*

At least I have that...he's helped me find something...something I really know how to do...want to do. He's given me a whole new life. I can't risk losing any part of it now...not now. God not now. Forgive me. Forgive me for being a selfish, foolish liar.

Chapter Seventeen

"Mama. Mama."

Irene hurriedly wiped the tears from her cheeks and folded the letter to fit flat to the inside of her skirt pocket.

Odessa skipped out the back door, cheeks peachy pink, hair feathered around her pretty face, green eyes shining. "May I go with Anna and Junie? They've asked me to supper. Benny said he would bring me home."

Without thinking or reasoning, Irene answered, "Yes, go ahead," because it was easier to agree than fight or try to talk the girl out of anything. Besides, Irene really wanted to be alone. She certainly wasn't in the mood to endure her daughter's certain pout if she refused permission.

"Odessa," Irene said, bringing the girl back before she disappeared. "You've been to the Davises' a lot. We need to invite Anna and Junie here for supper some evening. Be sure to extend an invitation."

Odessa bit her lip and nodded, eyes downcast, a little smile playing on her lips. Irene experienced a moment of unease and wondered what her daughter was really up to. It was fine for her to have secrets with her friends. It was nice, actually, Odessa was once again being included.

"Yes, I'll do that," Odessa said and turned to go into the house.

"Anna must be busy these days," Irene said, following Odessa inside. "How are the plans for her wedding coming along? Have she and Rob decided for certain to build a house right away?"

Odessa brushed her questions aside with a wave of her hand. "I don't know."

"Are you and Junie still working on your report?"

Odessa picked up the mythology book she'd dropped on the kitchen table. "We're almost done."

"Well, don't stay too late—I know tomorrow is Saturday, but I should think Benny is expected to get up early since he's working for his father these days."

Going to the window, Irene asked, "Are Anna and Junie outside? You should've asked them in."

"Ah, no," Odessa said too quickly, and once again, Irene had the uneasy feeling her daughter wasn't telling her the whole story. "They...they're at the Emporium with Susan. I...I told them I'd meet Benny at the stable. He's getting a...a wheel repaired...or something."

Now Irene found that truly suspicious. She tried to read her daughter's devious little mind, but Odessa was good at hiding her thoughts and gave nothing away in her smile or the light in her eyes. "Hmmm, I thought his father had a forge out at their place. I should think he'd be able to fix a wheel himself."

****

"I don't know what Benny's doing. He said something about a wheel...that's all I know."

Odessa had to be careful not to give too much detail to her lie. Her mother was giving her that look. She had to be very careful not to smirk or chatter. She could show excitement, but not too much. That part was hard to maintain—she couldn't wait to get away from the house and her mother's sad eyes. She'd lived with that pitying look for a year now, and it was making her crazy. Odessa had one goal in mind—leave this house and her dour mother, leave her to rot in sorrow. She had a life to live, and she intended to let nothing stop her.

"Run along, don't keep them waiting. Give my regards to Mr. and Mrs. Davis."

Odessa didn't hesitate—the inquisition was apparently over. She gave a little hop and planted an affectionate kiss on her mother's cheek for good measure. "Okay. Are you alone tonight? Doctor Rayburn won't be back for the rest of the week, will he?"

Her gaze went to the medical journal on the table, obviously no longer interested in anything Odessa had to say, her mother shrugged and said, "Maybe longer. It depends if Mrs. Trask is to have an operation. Do you know if Silas's mother and father have gone to Farewell Bend yet?"

Trying not to hurry, Odessa went ahead and put on her coat and adjusted her black felt hat on her head. "They should've gotten there today. Trenton is watching the house and keeping the stock. Silas will go out and help when he can. When I spoke to Trenton, Doctor Carter had sent him a telegram saying they probably would operate the day after tomorrow."

Odessa started to walk out the door, but her mother stopped her and fussed with her hat, tipping it more to the side. "Well, when you see Trenton or Silas, you tell them my prayers are with their mother. She must be very frightened."

"I will. Bye."

Her mother followed her to the door and said, "You look very pretty today. You're growing up very fast. I'm proud of you, Odessa. This last year hasn't been easy for you. I know that."

Sudden tears welled up into her throat and Odessa swallowed hard. Closing the door behind her, she told herself, soon, soon she'd be away from here. Her mother's words of praise came too late. A year ago, she would've found them comforting, even encouraging, but now, they were empty words. They didn't mean anything to her. Now she just felt sorry for her mother; she would never understand, never see how she stifled and smothered all the joy out of life and the lives of everyone around her.

It was true her relations with the Davis family had improved over the last few months, but not to the point where she would receive an invitation to supper, and certainly not for the third time in less than a month. Her mother really was a fool if she believed that would happen. Susan Laidlaw was finally speaking to her. It no longer mattered to Odessa what Susan or Junie thought of her, or if they were her friends; she didn't care. She had Silas now.

It was too soon to tell her mama, but soon she'd tell everyone Silas had asked her to marry him. He hadn't, not yet, but Odessa was sure he would after tonight. He surely would. Then they'd get married, maybe by this summer—certainly before fall.

After tonight her life would never be the same. She'd been dreaming of this night. Tonight she'd give herself, all of herself, to Silas—give him what his kisses, his caresses begged for. It started last Fourth of July, the drive to become the only woman in Silas's life—forever.

Fourth of July, she'd found out who her true friends were. It wasn't Junie or Anna Davis, and certainly not Susan Laidlaw. Her true friends…the friends who loved her, were Silas and Trenton. Without them for support, she would've died of loneliness. She'd poured herself into her schoolwork simply because it was all she could do since no one would speak to her except Miss Pritchard.

It didn't help that her mama was so busy being the doctor's helper she didn't even notice her despair. As a matter of fact, she hardly spoke to her those first few weeks after the Fourth. There were no harsh words, no actions, and no punishments, only a sad look in her mother's eyes and the never-ending heavy sighs—God, how Odessa hated all the sighing and sniffing of silent tears.

She would've surely perished but for Silas and Trenton's continued friendship. When they came home in the fall, Odessa found ways to be with them, ways no one else would ever find out about, and she'd done a good job of deceiving and lying. Now Mrs. Davis was speaking to her mama again, and Mrs. Laidlaw was grateful her son hadn't died, so the pressure had eased up on Odessa to toe the line.

"Odessa, up here," Silas called down to her from the stable loft.

Looking up, she smiled a tentative smile, experiencing a momentary bout of butterflies in the pit of her stomach. But when Silas reached down to help her up the ladder, the warmth of his hands and the light in his eyes soothed away any doubts in her mind. "You're late. I thought maybe you couldn't get away, or maybe you changed your mind."

Putting her mythology book down at the head of the ladder so she wouldn't forget it, Odessa said, "You know I want to be with you, Silas, all the time. Sometimes it's hard for me to get away, is all. We have to be careful."

Silas pulled her up to the loft and into his arms. "Do I know that, Dessie? Do I? Are you gonna show me how much you want me tonight?" he asked, his voice husky, full of lust. He stroked her cheek with his fingertip, then her hair.

A shiver of desire spread and set her body tingling, vibrating to his touch. She closed her eyes and let all of her fears dissolve. She'd waited for so long, so very long to be held like this, to be loved like this. His question, *did she want him?* didn't even begin to explain the hunger, the need to feel, to forget everything, and be in his arms.

"Show me how much you love me, little Dessie. I want you to show me. Can you show me tonight?"

His tongue dove between her lips, and suddenly his hands were squeezing her tender breasts. He grabbed a handful of her bottom. She panicked and tried to pull away from him—she didn't like it when he got desperate, when he made her feel selfish for wanting more holding than groping, more tenderness than a rush to explore and conquer. She wanted to be all he needed, but it was hard when she didn't know what to do.

She shoved him away. "I don't think I like your tongue in my mouth," she said and wiped her lips with the back of her hand. "You've been smoking cigarillos. I can taste them."

Afraid she'd hurt his feelings, she said, "I'm scared, Silas. I don't know what you want I don't know how…I only know I love you, Silas. I love you, and only you, my whole life. Whatever it is I have that you want, take it, Silas, it's yours."

Words were lost in a storm of kisses. Her words of surrender were all Silas needed to take her. And it was just as well—she didn't want to be given any more time to think. It was time to let go of everything childish, and that meant her virginity. She'd give it to Silas—the man she would love for eternity.

Odessa didn't know what Silas was doing to her; he was touching her in places she'd never been touched before, kissing her as she'd never dreamed of being kissed. Some of it was painful, but it didn't matter. Nothing mattered except to give Silas pleasure.

Separating herself from what Silas was doing to her body, the memory of her father hugging her goodbye rose up into her mind, bringing with it a flood of tears.

Silas wasn't her father, but he was a man who would save her from the loneliness she felt. A tide of emotions: excitement, fear, guilt, and pure aching pleasure overwhelmed her. But she didn't try to slow Silas or stop his rush to have her. She didn't hesitate once the kissing and caressing began. She didn't hesitate to give her all and to trust Silas's eager hands.

It seemed to Odessa they'd been in the loft for hours, but it was still twilight when Silas rolled off her and lay face up, panting, sweating, a satisfied grin on his face. Left naked, exposed, with not even the security of his arms around her, Odessa, for a fleeting moment, feared she'd made another horrible mistake.

"Mmmm, Dessie, you are beautiful," Silas said, in a daze, a satisfied smile on his handsome face. Rolling back to her, one arm under his head, his free hand stroked her abdomen, her breasts. "You know what you've gone and done? You've ruined me, Dessie. That's what you've done. I ain't ever gonna want another woman, never again, only you."

Odessa stopped his traveling hands. "Good, Silas

Trask, you better not want any other girl. It's you and me…forever…you hear? You and me."

Silas laughed and rolled on top of her. He crushed her to the rough-hewn boards of the loft floor, and buried his face in her neck. Giving her no time to protest, he drove his knee between her legs. She felt his hands, warm and rough, search out the damp thatch of hair between her thighs and the key to her submission.

It was dark when next he released her. In the night sky, stars winked at them through the open door of the loft. Odessa was very cold, colder than she'd ever been. Shivering, feeling discarded, she lay watching Silas grope around him for his shirt and trousers.

"Will you meet me here again? Dessie, meet me here, again, Sunday…Sunday night?"

Trembling, angry, Odessa rose and began to dress. She didn't know if she was mad at Silas or mad with herself. She wanted to scream at him, scream, *leave me alone.* She felt dirty and sticky, acutely aware she should be home. She wanted to be home in her own bed, not in a cold loft rolling around in the hay like some animal, like some cheap whore, like one of those girls at the boarding house. Aloud she said, "I…I don't know, Silas, it doesn't seem right."

"Come on, we ain't hurtin' nobody. Nobody's gonna find out. I told you, I ain't gonna say nothin', not even to Trent. You gotta come. I gotta see you again, please?"

"I'll try," she said. Picking up her book, she hurried down the ladder.

"Wait," Silas said, "I need another kiss. Dessie, just one more."

On the verge of tears, she tried to smile at him. He

lay on his stomach, his torso draped over the ladder, lips puckered, eyes closed. He looked silly. He looked like her old playmate, her friend. She gave in and kissed him.

"Good night. I wish I could be there under the covers with you, all warm and sweet."

"So do I," she said, her voice a whisper, tears choking her words. "That would be wonderful. I want to spend every night with you, Silas," she said, lips quivering, arms weak. She hung on to the ladder. "I want to spend all my days with you."

Grateful for the dark, unable to hold back her emotions, she backed down the ladder.

Fearful someone would see her, she ran home. Consumed with guilt, Odessa scolded herself and shoved aside her childish fears. She would soon be Mrs. Silas Trask. She would have a life of respect, children of her own, and someone who would be hers. She was a woman now. But most of all, she was going to get away from her lifeless, loveless existence with her unfeeling mother and her sour disposition.

Chapter Eighteen

The heated rendezvous in the loft, two, sometimes three nights a week, had begun to lose their romantic appeal. Odessa found herself, during what should've been the blissful throes of passion, silently complaining to the cobweb-encrusted beams of the loft: *These darn, rough boards have splinters, and the straw is dirty, scratchy—probably full of bugs. I want a blanket to lie on. You don't have to be on the bottom, do you, Silas? Of course, the straw, the bugs, the splinters don't bother you.*

And lately, he was always in a hurry, especially if she tried to get him to talk about any kind of future for the two of them. "Ah, Dessie, let's not ruin this with a lot of talk," he would say. "Let's lay here a while and be together."

But he never stayed long. After a half-an-hour of rushed coupling, he was ready to get dressed and go. His excuse, he had to go out to the home place to help Trenton and his pa.

Odessa tried to understand—his mama was still very sick. From the conversation she'd overheard between Doctor Rayburn and her mama, the operation had resulted in the amputation of Silas's mother's right breast and muscles under her arm. The thought of it made Odessa queasy—she couldn't even imagine what that would feel like. Ruby was unable to move her right arm, but it was temporary. Doctor Rayburn said it was no less than a miracle she was alive. Ruby had survived, and if she could regain her strength before acquiring an infection, then she would have a chance to thrive a few more years.

Odessa didn't really mind that her sixteenth birthday passed quietly with only her mama and Doctor Rayburn. Her mama gave her a pair of new shoes and a lovely carpet bag for traveling. Doctor Elias gave her a dictionary of her very own. It had been his when he was in college.

She forgave Silas for forgetting her birthday, telling herself, of course, he hadn't remembered with his mama so ill. As for Trenton, she hadn't seen much of him. The few times she'd seen him, he looked hurt and worried. She thought it was because of his mama. Dressing in the darkness of the loft, she wondered about that.

"We'll go to Rob and Anna's wedding together, won't we, Silas?" she asked and buttoned her skirt, tucking her blouse in around the waistband.

"I don't know if I can pick you up at your door." He pulled up his trousers and buttoned the fly. "I'll be at the wedding party. Gonna send ol' Rob off in style. Got plans for a shivaree. Girls ain't invited to this one. Sorry," he said and reached out, found her face in the beam of moonlight coming through the open loft door, and tweaked her nose.

"I think Rob and Anna make a good couple. They even look alike in a way, both tall, dark hair. Anna said Rob is crazy to be married...he can't wait to start a family," Odessa said, trying to be subtle.

"He's crazy, all right," Silas said.

"Being married would be nice," she said and

combed her hair with her fingers, pulling the straw out of her curls.

"Who wants nice?" Silas said Impatient, he tapped his foot on the first rung of the ladder, ready to leave. "I got a hankerin' to see somethin' of whatever is somewhere else. Meadow View is nowhere. I'd like to get on one of them trains and go south, cross the border to Mexico."

"I'd like to see Mexico too," Odessa said.

"Yeah, well, you got to go to school, Dessie. You're smart."

His words stopped her, and she forgot to breathe, becoming lightheaded. She was sure she'd heard him right, and for some time now, she suspected Silas wasn't interested in getting married. What he'd said confirmed her suspicions. If he really meant it, then she was a fool.

Panic expanded into her chest and squeezed her heart. Her stomach did a little flip-flop. She thought she might throw up again—like she'd done this morning. Although she hadn't eaten very much supper, that was probably all it was, something she'd eaten. Descending the ladder, she started to get dizzy and stopped and hung on to the rungs for a second to let her world stop spinning.

On the way home, she wondered if there was any chicken left—she would have some of that when she got home. She hoped there was a breast. She liked breast meat, maybe with some of her mama's apple chutney.

****

"Good morning, Doctor Rayburn." Irene moved the basket of hot biscuits aside to make room for the platter of sausages and scrambled eggs. She poured a cup of coffee for herself and the doctor and sat down across from him.

"Good morning, Irene," he said without thinking. Irene blinked, but she didn't look offended or angry. He took that as encouragement. He rarely addressed her as Irene. She always, always, used his formal title of Doctor Rayburn. She was careful to do so. And he in turn addressed her as his helper and assistant, Mrs. Obenchain—it had become a habit, a habit he intended to break. It was time to get a few things straight between himself and Mrs. Obenchain—uh, Irene.

"I thought I'd visit Mrs. Trask this morning. Are you busy? Do you think you could come with me?"

"I would like that," she said.

Elias went on to say, "I think Ruby might be more forthcoming to another woman. The woman is stoic. She only says, 'I'm doin' fine, Doc,' when I try to find out how she's progressing."

Irene smiled. "I suppose she has to say that. She wouldn't want her family to worry about her and fuss."

"The woman has a right to have a fuss made over her," Elias said.

"Oh, she certainly does," Irene agreed, and as the jar of apple chutney was empty, she poured honey on her biscuit.

"I don't understand women," he said and helped himself to the sausages and eggs.

Irene smiled in sympathy. "You men do the same thing, only you're worse, but in Mrs. Task's instance, it's a matter of saving her nerves. There is nothing worse than having a man hover and try to wait on you. She knows how to take care of herself. She's given birth, she's nursed her babies, and her husband, and probably any number of sick critters."

"I see your point. But if you could come along, I would appreciate it."

"I am free to go with you. Odessa isn't up yet. She was late getting home again last night. She's making herself ill, trying to master Latin in these last few weeks before going off to school. I think she's suffering from a case of frayed nerves waiting for the letter from the admissions office. Poor girl can't eat, and she's sleeping too much."

"I noticed," Elias said. He didn't want to alarm Irene, but he'd seen Odessa leaving the stable three evenings ago. It was late, about ten-thirty. He'd been to Cloverdale to set a broken leg. He'd pulled into the stable to leave the carriage horse in her stall. While doing so, he encountered Silas saddling up. Then, on his walk home, he saw Odessa enter the house a few steps before he reached the lane.

He'd heard talk the loft in the stable was a favorite trysting place of the local Lotharios, Silas in particular. He hoped Odessa wasn't among those young girls who'd succumbed to youthful experimentation.

****

"Odessa," her mother said, attempting to rouse her out from under her covers. Odessa groaned, groggy. She burrowed deeper into her blankets.

"Odessa, it's time to get up. I'm going on a call to the Trasks with Doctor Rayburn. You'll have to wash sheets today. There's breakfast on the table—biscuits, sausage, gravy, and eggs."

The thought of food sent a wave of nausea sloshing up the sides of Odessa's stomach. Regurgitated chicken and chutney bubbled up into her throat. She swallowed and took a deep breath. Fist stuffed in her mouth, she closed her eyes tight against the spasm.

"Okay. Now, Odessa, get up, get dressed, or I'll call Doctor Rayburn in here to examine you." That worked. Odessa sat up and jerked her covers off in a fit of pique.

"Good," her mother declared without sympathy. "We might be back by noon, I'm not sure, but you've got plenty to do today. And eat something, Odessa. You look pale and thin. Even your hair looks starved. If you don't start eating again soon, I'll have the doctor look you over anyway. I won't send you off to the valley to school unless I know you're in good health. I don't want you being nursed by those folks. Doctor Carter's sister is expecting you to be able to do mending and ironing for your room and board.

"And no more late nights. You can do all the studying you have to do at home. I have a good mind to talk to Miss Pritchard. From now until September, you're going to sit up, eat at every meal, go to bed at a reasonable hour, and get plenty of fresh air. No arguments."

"I'm not sick," Odessa said. Denying her headache and her queasy stomach, she straightened, and the room tilted and gave a little spin. Irene didn't see her sit back down to wait out the ride. She was busy hanging up clothes.

"I think you need a new chemise and a couple pairs of bloomers. I wonder if we have time to make some?" her mother said.

Odessa tried again to stand. The dizziness was gone. When her mother turned around to face her before leaving the room, Odessa forced a smile and said, "There's plenty of time. I think there's some linen left over from the last pair of bloomers you made for Miss

O'Day.

"Why don't we get started on that today? You get them cut out, and I'll sew them up. And, Odessa, go outside today. I mean other than to hang up sheets. Fix yourself a nice lunch and go out and sit in the sun for a while."

Her mother reached out to touch the limp curl that hung over her brow. Odessa fought back her tears. "I'm really worried about you," her mother said. "You don't look like you feel very well."

Shrugging her shoulders, Odessa pulled herself together. "You'll have to stop worrying about me. I'm all grown up now. I'll be on my own soon."

Giving her a hard, narrow-eyed look, her mother said, "Hmmm, no, I don't think that's how it works. I think mothers always worry about their children, no matter how old they get. You wait, you'll see. You'll be a mother someday."

****

The Trask house, constructed of split logs and white caulk, a plain, small cabin with a shed roof covered with shakes, Irene likened the dwelling, the setting, to something out of a fairy tale—it had charm, whimsy—it appealed to her heart.

In the yard, chickens pecked at apple parings in the bare dirt. To the side of the flimsy-looking barn, Doctor Rayburn pointed to Sam Trask, who was repairing a holding pen. Irene waved at the man, but the vista from the front yard of the Trask house stole her attention. The house and barn were perched on the west side of a steep hill. From the front yard, one looked out upon a small, open glen where fat, white sheep grazed. Black Butte, Mount Jefferson, and the Three Sisters were among the peaks of the Cascades that made up the spectacular view from the Trask's front door.

Irene spotted Ruby sitting in a rocking chair on the front porch, apparently enjoying the fresh air and warm sun of mid-morning. Elias drew the one-horse shay up in front of the porch.

Irene smiled and waved, pleased to see Ruby up and dressed, wearing one of her colorful skirts, her hair simply dressed in long braids on either side of her head. Her right wing bound to her chest with a bright yellow scarf, she struggled to tuck a strand of hair back in place within her braid. The shirt she wore looked to be one of Sam's button-down, chambray shirts with one sleeve empty and a shawl of orange around her shoulders.

"Good mornin'," Sam said to the doctor. Hurrying toward them, he pulled a blue handkerchief out of his back pocket and wiped his hands.

"Sam," Elias said.

"Good morning, Mr. Trask, Ruby," Irene said.

"Good to see you getting some fresh air," Elias said to Ruby. He took Irene's hand in his to steady her as she stepped to the ground.

"Glad you come, Doc," Sam said. He took four long strides toward his wife and dabbed at the perspiration on his face and neck. "Tried to change the dressing on her last night, got all thumbs. I don't know…seems to me there's a lot of seepage. Is that what we should expect? She still can't move her arm, and she's in a lot of pain. She ain't eatin' much, either."

"That's 'cause you burn everything, and what you don't burn is still breathin'," Ruby said. "And I got a tongue in my head, Sam Trask. I can speak for my own damn self. I'll tell the doc if I'm hurtin'. You go back over there and tend to somethin' you know, like tendin' fence."

"She ain't feelin' so bad she can't bite at me, though. I figure she's on the mend, all right. You want some coffee? Still got apple pie I built yesterday."

Before Elias or Irene could reply, Ruby said, "Take my advice and have tea. The pie ain't bad, if you eat the apple part. Leave the crust. It's hard as brick."

Elias broke in, but Irene could see he had to work to hold back his amusement. "Maybe after I have a look at you," he said to Ruby.

To Sam, he said, "Tea sounds good."

"Well, I reckon my coffee is a little strong," Sam said.

"Ate three spoons, did that coffee," Ruby said, the expression on her face sober as a judge's.

"One spoon. It was an old spoon, had a crack in it 'cause I used it to chip ice," Sam said. Leaning down, he picked Ruby up and carried her inside.

"I can walk. My legs ain't broke," Ruby said.

"They ain't broke...yet...woman," Sam said and adjusted her weight in his arms. "I brought you out, and I'm takin' you in. All you have to do is shut your yap."

Shaking his head, Elias grinned at Irene and waved her to go ahead of him into the house.

Following Sam, Elias crossed the hard dirt floor of the large central room. He held back the curtain and followed Sam into the back rooms of the house.

Shaking his head, looking worried, Sam reappeared and said to Irene, "I'm glad to see you." He set a kettle of water on the cast-iron wood stove in the middle of the room. "She's in a lot of pain. She ain't sleepin' good.

"Trenton is a better cook than me," Sam said. He

handed Irene the tin of tea and nodded to her, giving her permission to do the measuring.

"Trenton's on fire-watch now. He tries to come every night to help out. I don't know what to do for her. She don't like me doin' housework. She says I got no notion of clean, and I tell you, sometimes, I come real close to turning her over my knee."

"Is she taking the laudanum?" Irene asked, measuring out the black tea from the tin into a brown ceramic teapot.

"She don't like to. She says she don't want to be a dope-fiend like her Aunt Esther."

"I'll let Doctor Rayburn know. Maybe he can help persuade her."

"Trenton has the best idea. He slips a few drops into her tea with some honey. But he can't be here, and I ain't no good at sneakin'. She always catches me. She don't trust me. The boy, he's kind of quiet like. Seems like I always spill somethin' or drop somethin' when I have to sneak.

"Silas, now, I'm glad he don't come 'round much. Ruby likes to wait on him, sew his buttons on—make special cakes, and such. He wears her out. Best thing he done for his ma is stay away while she gets back to herself—if she gets back."

"She'll be fine. She's doing better than anybody thought," Irene said. "This kind of operation is experimental, very risky, even under the best of conditions. Ruby has a lot of desire to live. You're doing a fine job, Sam."

"Will you show me how to get the gauze on her? I make a botch of it every time."

Irene looked around for a bowl or a pan. She spotted

a big, wooden, oblong bread bowl and set it down on the plank and barrel countertop. Using the inside of the bowl as Ruby's underarm and chest, Irene helped Sam form the gauze pads and stretch the gauze over the shoulder, or in this case around the bowl, with a minimum of tape and slippage.

When Elias came out of Ruby's bedroom, Irene glanced up and gave him a smile. For a few moments, he stood, watching Sam concentrate on his patient. Standing back, Sam proudly inspected his handiwork, turning the wooden bowl to one side then the other. He tugged at the neatly wrapped, inside and out, gauze pads and tape. "Doc, Mrs. Obenchain's been giving me some pointers on how to change them bandages."

"Good, your wife will be relieved. She's grateful we didn't have to resort to the maggots to help close the incision. And I don't think we'll have to leech her so long as there is no infection. There's good drainage, no redness, and no fever. I think you could leave the bandage off for a few minutes a couple times a day now. But she looks tired."

Irene lowered her voice and handed the doctor a hot cup of tea. "Sam says she won't take her laudanum."

"Hmm, well, I suspected as much. She didn't tell me very much during the examination. She winced a couple of times. That's about all the reaction I could get out of her. Your wife is a stubborn woman, Sam."

In his official doctor-to-nurse voice, Elias addressed Irene, "Mrs. Obenchain, remember those exercises we discussed. Maybe you could show Mrs. Trask how to do them today."

Picking up the tape and gauze, Irene smiled knowingly into his eyes. Passing him, she made her way to the bedroom.

Sitting in her bed, her shawl draped around her bare shoulders, Ruby lay with her right arm held across her bosom, eyes closed.

"Ruby," Irene said, almost whispering.

"Mrs. Obenchain," Ruby said and opened her eyes, and rolled her head to the side to see into Irene's face.

"I've come to show you some exercises and put on fresh gauze, but if you're too tired right now, I can show you the exercises some other day. I'll put the dressing on, then you can rest."

"I ain't resting. I can't." Ruby took a shuddering breath, and Irene saw a tear roll down her high-boned cheek.

Irene sat on the stool beside the bed and took Ruby's free hand.

It was several moments before Ruby spoke. "Going in…I didn't think I had a chance. I was going to die if I didn't have the operation, and I was going to die if I did, only I wouldn't have to wait. I could go and get it over with."

Ruby pulled her hand away from Irene's grasp and scrubbed away the tears from her cheeks. After a bit of a struggle, she removed a handkerchief from her shirt front and blew her nose. Irene didn't interrupt. "When I woke up…I was still here; I felt cheated. I was gonna have to stay and be…brave…I guess. I been mad as hell, until now."

Irene wanted to ask why but knew better and kept quiet.

"What I got is a second chance, you see. You might not have figured it out, but we waste a lot of time worrying about things that don't really amount to much in the end. Us women, I mean. We give a lot, but we don't know much about letting them that loves us give back."

Irene blinked in the face of this big truth. She wondered if Ruby could read her mind. She hoped not. Her mind had jumped to thoughts of Elias, warm thoughts, very warm thoughts.

"Now, now, not you," Ruby said and squeezed Irene's hand. "I was thinkin' of me biting at Sam when all he wants to do is help. He loves me, even though I ain't fit to look at."

Ruby stared hard at Irene, then rolled her head so her face was closer. "As for you, you got a man right out there. A man that thinks the stars and moon are in your eyes. Like my Sam. Sam thinks I'm some kind of gypsy temptress. Always has."

She sighed and tipped her head to the side. "I see you tryin' with all your might to hide your feelin's. I seen the doc try with all of his might to respect you. Well, it's a waste of time, Irene. I'm gonna call you Irene—a big waste.

"I know, I been pushin' Sam away for weeks, and he ain't gonna quit. He loves me. He's scared for me. Knowing what I know today, I ain't gonna waste another minute. Be damned what anybody else might say or think. Life is too short. Live it, drink it up, savor it, Irene Obenchain, or you'll have regrets when you get old. Me, I'd rather be able to say I got my share and then some, when my time comes around again."

Irene hated herself. She'd begun to tremble, and it was a dead giveaway. She wanted to deny it, but what came out sounded pathetic to her own ears. "It should be simple enough, but it isn't," she said, unable to look

Ruby in the eye. "I have a daughter, and I have to think of her."

"I ain't sayin' we don't make excuses. I got a big long list, myself. None of them will hold water. You know, the plain truth is, my boys and your girl, they got their lives to live, and we got ours."

Drawing herself up, Irene set aside the topic of life, time, and the waste thereof. Irene demonstrated to Ruby the series of grips and lifts Doctor Rayburn had recommended. She also replaced the bandage and gauze.

"I'm really tired now," Ruby said, speech slurred, eyelids drooping. "I think I can sleep. Would you tell Sam to come in here? I'll sleep better if he lies down with me. He's been leaving me alone, sleeping in the boys' room, way on the other side of the house. I suppose he thought he might bother me. But the truth is, I can't sleep without him next to me. I'll sleep, and I'll take the damned dope, but I want my Sam."

Sam came through the curtain. "I'm here, Ruby. I'm here."

"Yeah, well, you better not leave me alone in this bed ever again, Sam Trask."

Ruby patted the vacant pillow next to her head.

Irene withdrew. She turned to close the curtain. Sam lay down on the bed, careful not to rumple the covers or jostle the springs. Ruby let him put his arm under her head.

Irene closed the curtain behind her, a smile on her lips and tears sliding down her cheeks.

****

Irene sat beside him, very still—silent. After crossing Drift Creek, Elias encouraged the one-horse shay off the washboard, cinder road and onto the soft,

218

green grass beside the creek.

He tied off the reins on the dash and patted Irene's tightly folded hands. "Let's get down and sit a minute over there in the shade. Emily probably wouldn't mind a drink."

Looking a little startled, Irene glanced around her. "What? Oh, we've stopped. What a pretty meadow. Yes, yes, let's sit in the shade for a moment. I suppose you'd like to hear what I have to say about Ruby's progress."

Elias stepped out of the shay. Irene slid over and allowed him to take her by the waist, help her out of the conveyance. She stood for a moment, shading her eyes with her hand. "This is a beautiful spot, isn't it—the mountains, the creek, the glen, very restful." Closing her eyes, she took a deep breath.

He put his hand on her back to steady her as they crossed the uneven ground. "It is a really fine day, not too hot, not too cold," he said. She walked with him, right at his side, bodies touching.

Yes, this was a good idea. And for a second, Elias considered—tempted—gathering her in his arms and kissing her. Every instinct told him he wouldn't get a better opportunity than this. They reached the log, but she didn't sit. She stood beside him, he supposed enjoying the view. As he was bout to lower his head and take a chance, she stepped away from him and instead of sitting on the log, she sat down on the grass near the water beneath the shade of some willows.

Disappointed with himself for being a clumsy fool, Elias resigned himself to the fact he was not ever going to make any headway with Irene Obenchain, not today, not ever. Making himself comfortable beside her, he set aside his desire and asked about Ruby. "So, I guess Ruby finally said something of what's been going on."

Irene nodded, giving him a playful glance accompanied by a dreamy little smile. A smile he found very seductive, almost provocative, and he wondered if he was wrong—maybe there was hope after all.

"Hmmm, she did," Irene said. Quickly, she set her gaze on the creek and the glen beyond. "You see, she was certain she was going to die. She's been…disappointed, I guess you could say—angry she didn't die—now she's expected to continue to live."

Elias scoffed.

Irene held up her hand to stop whatever he was going to say. "She's angry she's going to have to learn to adjust to her deformity and give Sam credit for loving her even more because he almost lost her. Living, you see, is much harder than dying. At least to do it right, so Ruby says."

Holding his breath, Elias grew very still. This was important, something had changed, and he hoped it was for the good. He prayed it was very good. "I see. Well, I'm relieved she's come to grips with her mortality and her good fortune, as it will certainly make Sam's life easier. But what she said has somehow had an impact on you as well. So what's the matter? Don't you think you've been doing a good job of living?"

She waved her hand toward the view. "Oh, I've been breathing in and out. I've even been trying to live Odessa's life…pretending, trying to live through her—seems a silly thing to do at the moment. I would most certainly do it differently if I could do it all over again."

She made a little sound. It sounded like a giggle. She then leaned back to rest against his chest, her head nestled naturally on his shoulder.

Heart racing, he put his arm around her and savored the moment.

Sighing, Irene snuggled in, and Elias thought he must be dreaming.

"Ruby realized today she's got another chance to give it another shot, to do it right. She doesn't think I should have to almost die to live a full life. I think that's what she was trying to say."

"I wouldn't want that either," he said. His lips brushed her hair, his eyes closed, and he drank in the clean, chamomile and rosewater scent of her silky hair.

****

Irene looked off to the west. She wasn't sure she was brave enough to risk saying what had never been said, admit what had been her heart's desire…her dream. She closed her eyes and took a shuddering breath. "I've been dead, you know, for so very long."

He turned her by the shoulders to gaze deep into her eyes. "You're so beautiful—your wonderful brown eyes, so warm and full of light, your skin, right here, on your cheek—so fine. You're very much alive." His fingers brushed across her cheek and down the side of her jaw to her throat.

Irene could hardly breathe and dared not blink, or she would break the spell.

"You're so small and yet strong, so stubborn. I think you have a second chance coming, Irene. I think you deserve a second chance," he said and kissed her, gathered her into his arms, slowly, gently, his hands pressed her into his body.

The kiss, the embrace, was a dream come true. What a wonderful dream it was. Irene hoped never to awaken. This dream was a revelation. It was bright sunshine and a sweet, warm breeze. It made her light as a feather and gave her heart wings. Her lips, her body so long cold and dormant, coursed with hot blood. Her fingers daringly explored his neck, his face, his hair. She couldn't get enough.

After a time, giddy, she began to giggle. This was insanity, and it had to stop. She had to awaken. She pulled out of his embrace, got up, moved to the edge of the creek, shaky, breathing unevenly. She turned her face to the sky, up to God, and laughed.

God was teasing her—this wasn't real, it wasn't happening, it wouldn't last. It couldn't be hers. She had to remind herself her life was over. Now all there was, was hope for Odessa to have the chance she didn't take. Odessa was to have the dream, go to school, be a woman of independence, and if there should be love, then Odessa would love someone who was secure enough to allow her to be all she was capable of being.

"Irene," Elias said, coming to his feet to stand behind her. He took her by the hand.

"No," she said and placed her hands on his chest, "this is all there can ever be."

"This is the beginning, Irene," he said.

"And...the end," she said.

Shaking his head, he said, "I have no intention of stopping. I love you. I want the whole world to know."

"No," she said, shaking, her resolve thin as a cobweb.

"You can say no, but I tell you, we can't stop. I don't want to. I love you. You love me, don't you? You do love me, Irene?"

"God help me; I love you. But we don't count, and it isn't important what we want, what we desire. I love you. You gave me a chance to be more. You've made me believe I am more. I'm grateful. That has to be enough. It has to be enough, Elias, enough for both of us. I can't give any more than that."

"But it isn't…enough, Irene. At night, you in your bed and me in mine, I close my eyes and try to feel your body next to mine."

Irene stepped away from him. "This…this is terrible. I feel responsible. I should never have allowed this to happen. I knew the kiss was coming—I could feel it. God help me; I wanted it. We should never have gotten down from the carriage. We should go home right now, Elias. We can't do this."

"Damn it all, Irene. If you're worried about what people will think…what they will say, what more can they do…what more can those people in town say? They've shunned you, and they've made you a slave. They aren't going to hang you for living."

He didn't understand. How could he? "It's Odessa, Elias." There. She'd said it aloud. "You know it's Odessa I'm thinking of. We…can't be."

He'd gone red in the face, eyes blazing with pent-up fury. But she couldn't help it. When he came to her, pulled her into his chest, and began to stroke her back, she almost relented…almost.

"I'm stumped. I admit it, Irene. I don't know the future. All I know is you love me. I love you. I want you, and I'm tired of hiding my feelings. Now I know you want me too. Let's not hide anymore, Irene. Remember what Ruby said. Remember?"

In his arms, she felt safe, protected. For so long, she'd been alone, doing battle, and her thoughts came tumbling out. "Ruby knew how I felt about you, and she knows how you feel about me. I don't think we've been hiding anything from anyone, not anymore." This confession was said as much to herself as to Elias. Laughing, she said, "I've been a fool, and I guess I will never change. I'm sorry, Elias."

She laughed at herself, laughed at both of them. She couldn't bring herself to confess to Elias, but she realized now she'd been using the townspeople as an excuse, an excuse to keep him at arm's length. She wondered *why? What was she afraid of?*

And then it happened, and she said it out loud. Voice trembling, near hysteria she said, "If it all comes out...that we...we care for one another, then we can't live under the same roof. Don't you understand? I can't stand the thought of you living somewhere else, in another house. I want to see you, be near you, take care of you, work with you."

Elias held her tight. "We can, Irene. Marry me. Marry me, Irene. Don't say you can't. Don't say you're not free. He's not coming back. Abel, your husband, is not coming back."

Marriage. There it was, a word that hadn't entered her head as a possibility. *He wants to marry me. That's what he'd said. I am free.* She wanted to shout, *I am free, Elias.*

Oh, how she wanted to say it aloud for all the world to hear. How easy, how wonderful it would be to cave in, fall into his arms and never leave. She couldn't, not yet. It took everything she had to resist, to push away, and meet his pleading eyes to say, "Just for a little longer, Elias. Odessa will be off to school in the fall."

Taking her by the shoulders, he gave her a little shake, his voice husky, impatient. He growled. "She needs to know you have a life too, Irene. She needs to grow up and think about someone other than herself."

"We'll tell her before the summer is over," Irene said with more confidence than she felt.

Shaking his head no, he surrendered. "All right, but you are dancing with me at Rob and Anna's wedding. No more sitting on the sidelines, Irene."

That made her smile, and she had more hope than she'd had in a very long while. "Yes, I think it's time to dance again."

With a firm nod of his head, he said, "Good, then I can wait." The kiss, the embrace that followed, was not that of a man who would be content to wait, ever.

Chapter Nineteen

Anna Davis and Rob Morgan stood before Reverend Smalley at the altar of the Congregational Church and took their vows. The late morning sun streamed in from the arched, stained glass window.

Odessa fanned herself with the church-supplied woven-leaf fan, impatient with the heat, jealous of Anna in her snow-white gown. Fretting, worrying about where Silas had disappeared to, she paid little attention to the ceremony.

Refusing to look at Anna one more second, Odessa turned and scanned the gathering of friends and family of the bride and groom. But her gaze strayed back to the altar and found Trenton. As a groomsman, he stood straight and serious beside sweet, handsome, big George Kraus, giving his full attention to the proceedings.

Trenton did look wonderful—he looked like someone she could trust, had trusted, and who had trusted her. She tensed with shame. Looking away from her friend, so handsome and true, she straightened her shoulders. Lying to herself, she told herself she had nothing to be ashamed of. Oh, but how she wished she were home in bed. *Mama should have let me stay home in bed.*

****

Susan and Junie looked pretty, thought Irene. Anna had wisely chosen a soft shade of yellow as her theme color, and both girls looked lovely in yellow. She couldn't help but think Odessa would have looked lovely in yellow too. But Odessa had no part to play in Anna's wedding. It surprised her, after all the time Odessa had spent helping Anna with her wedding plans. Irene could see no sign of disappointment on her daughter's part. On the contrary, Odessa sat quietly, surprisingly disinterested. She looked a bit peaked; it was terribly hot, and the church was crowded. Irene was grateful for the fan she waved under her chin—it was a godsend.

Odessa's health, however, had started to really worry her. It was almost two months now since Irene had first become aware of Odessa's lack of appetite. She slept too late in the day and an uneasy silence clung to the normally talkative girl.

But then, in the last week, Odessa's appetite had improved some, and she'd been home more in the evenings, getting more rest. But there was a sad, worried look in Odessa's eyes that made Irene uneasy. It had something to do with Silas Trask, of course. He was conspicuously absent today, and clearly, Odessa was preoccupied with the fact. Irene hoped no one else would notice.

The day after their visit to the Trask home, Elias was called away to Prineville and had not been at all certain he would make it back for the wedding. The telegram she'd received last evening expressed regret at the possibility of missing the opportunity to dance with her. Irene couldn't decide if she was sorry or grateful for the emergency keeping him away.

Everyone in the church, except Odessa, sighed as Anna and Rob sealed their vows with a long, tender kiss. The couple walked back down the aisle together as man and wife, beaming, in love, so happy. A rousing cheer rose up from the congregation. Irene gave up a silent prayer that someday she would see her own daughter so deliriously happy.

****

The wedding reception took place on the lawn under the pines to the side of the church. Odessa avoided the crush of people who, like sheep, insisted on gathering in clumps in the narrow aisle and in the foyer of the church. She squeezed through the throng and made her way across the churchyard to the refreshment table. She found Trenton at the punch bowl, sharing a toast with George. Trenton had shed his coat and tie, looking inordinately mature, handsome, and wise—like the safe haven he'd always been.

Unconcerned with the formalities, Odessa pulled him away from everyone. "Where's Silas? He said he'd be here."

"Yeah, I know," Trenton said. "He was plannin' a big shivaree. Old man Bodeman and Milo Pederson caught on. Seems my brother forgot to ask if he could borrow Mr. Pederson's best team. So he decided to forgo the wedding for parts unknown, and he took the floozy, Grace Wolfe, with him."

"He's gone? When did he leave?"

The ground, these days, never very stable beneath Odessa's feet, began to slosh like pudding in a bowl. The trees started to swish and swing from side to side, and she feared she might throw up. "Why didn't he tell me?"

Trenton grabbed her by the shoulders and shoved her to the side of the lawn. Voice a low growl, he said, "Listen to me, you idiot. Silas was with Grace almost every night since the New Year's when we put paint on the outhouse seat."

He scanned the crowd. Odessa looked around too. They'd drawn some attention—George in particular. Trenton gave her a shake. "They was close, see. She knew he was doin' you in the loft, stringin' you along. She thought it real funny. I heard Grace talkin' in the saloon. She hates you and your ma—she's holding some kind of grudge against your pa. Your pa promised to take her with him when he left to find gold. She didn't have to say your name. The whole town knows it was you Silas had—you know—in the loft."

Odessa couldn't believe what he was saying. She shook her head and tried to shrug him off. But he got down in her face. "I love my brother, Dessie, but you got to get it through your head. He's like a tumbleweed or dust. He goes where the wind takes him. He gets in your eyes and your mouth, but he don't stay. He can't...he won't...ever."

Odessa squeaked and blinked back tears. "Grace Wolfe? Did you say Grace Wolfe?"

"Keep your voice down, will you. Everybody's lookin'."

Resisting, trying to pull away from him, Odessa balked. "Trenton Trask, you're lying. Silas wouldn't take that...that strumpet across the street. And he's borrowed the buckboard and Mr. Pederson's team of horses lots of times, and Mr. Pederson didn't do anything."

"Yeah, well, this was one time too many, and besides, this was for a dirty trick, a real dirty trick. Rob was kind of a regular, you might say, of Grace's. That is until Anna got hold of him. Silas sorta moved in and...took his place."

Odessa felt sick and faint and braced herself, her hands on Trenton's chest. She gazed up at him, her eyes swimming in tears. His face was a blur.

He turned his gaze heavenward. "Don't look at me like that."

Odessa shook her head at him. "I'm so confused and tired and sick. Nothing really matters. Silas is gone, and he didn't say anything to me about his plans. All right, he got caught stealing a team of horses—but he hasn't run off with that…that woman. He wouldn't. Of course he…he'd gone to the boarding house that one time on New Year's Eve, I knew that. But he certainly wouldn't want to run off with a woman like Grace Wolfe."

"I ain't ever gonna know why my brother does anything," Trenton said. "It's the devil in him, I guess. All I know is, last evening he come home mad as sin and started packing his gear. Mama was fit to be tied. She got the whole story out of him and started to help him pack. She was glad, I think, to see him go when she saw Grace was with him."

Odessa no longer heard anything he said. She watched his lips move, but her ears were buzzing, she was cold and clammy, and she knew she was on the edge of losing all control of her body, of her life, of everything. She wanted to scream and cry, and she wanted to hit something, pound, and pummel until her hands bled. Something was happening to her—her body was changing. She prayed every night and every day it wasn't happening, could not be happening.

"It can't be, Trenton, do you understand. Silas…Silas is supposed to be here—stand by me. He's supposed to be here. He's supposed to hold me and tell me everything is going to be wonderful. We'll be a family, and our child will be the most handsome, the smartest—God, he can't be gone, Trenton, he can't be gone."

"Dessie…Dessie?"

She heard his voice from far away. He was shaking her. She held onto him, clung to him as the world turned a somersault, and the trees in the sky and the ground swung up to one side then the other.

"Breathe, Dessie."

Trenton kept her from sinking to the ground, thank God—his arms around her.

"Come on over here. We can sit on this old shipping crate. You don't look so good."

Shaking, desperate, she whispered, "Take me somewhere, Trenton. Take me away from all these people," she said. Face turned into his neck, she grasped the front of his shirt.

"Yeah, sure," she heard him say. "I'm a man now. I can handle this." His statement offered hollow comfort. She wanted to giggle. *Oh, yes, we're all grown up— grown up stupid.*

"Nobody's at your place. We could go there. The doc's gone, ain't he?"

"Yes…take me home. Please, take me home?"

"Odessa, where are you going?" she heard her mother's voice say.

Trenton moved to her side, his arm around her waist. Odessa straightened and put on a smile. Speaking too fast, she rushed to say, "Trenton's going to walk home with me. I was feeling a little faint. I think it's the sun. This bonnet is too hot. I think I'll get the white straw one. I know it's old, but I don't seem to be able to stay cool today. Can we get you anything?"

"No, you go ahead, and thank you, Trenton. You two hurry back, though. You wouldn't want to miss the cutting of the cake and all the toasts. And the food, you need to eat something, Odessa. You'll be better once you have something solid in your stomach. Drink some water. You didn't eat enough breakfast. I told you, you would get weak in the knees before any real food would be offered."

"Yes, I know—we'll hurry back." Odessa took Trenton's hand and walked around the church out of sight of the gathering at the reception. Her legs turned to mush, her heart took a giant leap up into her throat, and all went black.

****

Elias pulled his carriage up beside the stump where the boy sat at the side of the lane. "Trenton, what's happened?" Odessa, cradled in the boy's arms, appeared limp and pale as a rag doll.

"She fainted, but she's come around a bit." Looking guilty, sweaty and pale, Trenton didn't appear much better off than Odessa. "It must've been the heat," he said.

Since the temperature today was quite comfortable, not even close to being what Elias would call hot, he doubted Trenton's diagnosis. "Maybe," he said and reached for his bag, opened it, withdrew a small vial, cracked it open, and waved it beneath Odessa's nose. Her eyes fluttered open, and she jerked her head aside. "Odessa, I'm going to get you to the house, and we'll have a look."

"I'm fine," Odessa said. She struggled to get off Trenton's lap and slumped forward. She would have gone to the ground if Trenton hadn't had a hold of her.

"Aha, yes, fine, I can see that. Trenton, hold her steady while I get aboard, then you lift her up here next to me."

Once Odessa was safely ensconced between himself and Trenton, Elias clicked his tongue, and they proceeded down the lane toward his office.

Odessa sagged against his shoulder. "I'm going to examine you, young lady. You sleep far too much, and your appetite is practically nonexistent—and I know about the vomiting, Odessa. No more evasion—I'm going to find out what's the matter with you. I think we both know, but we have to know for sure," he said.

Trenton helped him get Odessa inside and up on his examination table. "You can wait in the kitchen, Trenton," Elias said over his shoulder.

"I don't want to be examined," Odessa said.

Elias motioned for Trenton to leave. The boy hesitated for several seconds, wide-eyed and unmoving, holding Odessa's hand.

"I needed to get out of the sun for a little while and have a drink of water. I'll eat something; that'll help. I'll be fine, really. I don't need an examination. There's nothing wrong with me." Forehead damp, pale as a ghost, Odessa tried to sit up but fell back, eyes closed tight.

Ignoring her, Elias waved his hand and ushered Trenton out of the room. "I'm going to help you sit up. I'll unbutton your dress, take off your shoes and stockings, and get you in a gown."

Odessa stalled, "I'm fine, really," she said and propped herself up on one elbow to get to a sitting position. Elias moved quickly to keep her from sliding to the floor.

"You've been unwell for weeks, Odessa," he said and positioned her so her shoulders were leaning against his chest, while he unbuttoned her dress, took it down to her waist, and helped her get her arms out of the sleeves. "When was the date of your last menses?"

Irene—Elias couldn't help but think of how this would break her heart. She loved this girl so very much…wanted only the best for her…sacrificed for her.

Odessa turned her head to the side. He gave her shoulders a gentle shake. "Tell me, Odessa, tell me now."

The room went horribly quiet. She sobbed. He closed his eyes and wrapped his arms around her, hating his suspicions were no doubt a fact.

"April…the end of April, or the first…the first of May, I don't remember," she confessed, her words interrupted by sniffles and hiccups.

"Lie down. Let's get your feet up, and I'll get your shoes off. You're right. You're no doubt dehydrated." After he removed her shoes and stockings, he helped her sit up to take a few sips of water."

"I feel much better now," she said and started to sit up, a little more color to her cheeks.

"Uh, huh, good, have some more water," he said. He allowed her to drink half a glass full of water, then pushed her back down on his table.

Too weak to protest, she surrendered.

The examination didn't take long. It was obvious: breasts enlarged, her womb ripe with growing fruit— Elias sighed—it was as he'd feared.

****

Irene entered the house not at all surprised to find Trenton pacing around her kitchen table. "I saw Doctor

Rayburn go by in his buggy. Where is Odessa? She never drinks enough water."

Trenton, looking nervous and apprehensive, pointed to the doctor's office. A cold knot of fear wadded up, gathered volume, expanded, and pushed up under her rib cage, making it hard to breathe. Irene hesitated, her hand on the doorknob of the doctor's quarters. She closed her eyes and sent up a little prayer—even though she had very little faith it would do any good. She knocked, then stepped inside and quietly closed the door behind her, leaving Trenton to his pacing.

Her eyes went to the examination table and the rumpled white cloth that covered it. Of Odessa there was no sign, but her dress was draped over the privacy screen.

Head down, Elias continued his search, going through a cabinet, apparently looking for something in particular.

Taking a step toward him, Irene asked, "Elias?"

He turned to face her, and she recognized the look in his eyes. The expression on his face, it was the one he reserved for the most serious of cases—a furrowed brow, lips drawn tight into a thin line.

He started to put his hand to her cheek, but Odessa called out to her from behind the screen, "Mama, would you help me?"

Quickly, going behind the screen, Irene found Odessa. Her hands trembled, and tears streamed down her pale cheeks as she struggled to button the tiny pearl buttons down the back of her dress. Standing still like a scolded child, Odessa submitted to Irene's care, hands to her sides, head bowed. Her arm around her, Irene guided Odessa out from behind the screen to face the doctor.

"Here, I've found the booklet I was looking for,"

Elias said. He crossed the room and handed the pamphlet first to Odessa, then to Irene, as Odessa made no move to take it from his hand.

The Expectant Mothers Guide.
Odessa? God no, it couldn't be.

He put one hand on Odessa's shoulder and the other hand on Irene's. He directed his gaze to Irene. Looking deep into her eyes, he nodded his head. Then he put his finger under Odessa's chin and raised her face to meet his gaze. "I want both of you to listen to me. This isn't life or death, you two. A very wise woman once told me, 'It's just life.' "

He smiled at Irene and winked at Odessa. Irene felt the tears coming. There was no holding them back. Her throat was raw with them—it hurt to swallow them down.

"We can weather this together...we can," he assured them both. But Irene didn't want to acknowledge or even consider what he was hinting at and shook her head.

"Weather what? What is it? Is she sick? Is it cancer? What is it?"

"You know what I'm talking about, Irene. We've both seen the symptoms. We know Odessa is pregnant. She's about two and half months along, is our best estimate. Let me help. I can protect you both, you'll see. Everything is going to be all right."

Trenton burst into the room, and all eyes turned in his direction. Odessa broke away from Irene's embrace and practically skipped across the room to give Trenton an affectionate embrace.

Irene watched the scene with mixed emotions. It was perfectly obvious poor Trenton didn't have a clue as to why he was being lavished with her daughter's warm attentions. The boy stood like a statue, stiff, unblinking, frozen into immobility, unable to respond.

"Trenton," Odessa gushed, her teary green eyes too bright. "I know we said we were going to wait to be married, but…but we're going to have a baby."

Babbling, barely coherent, Odessa, shaking, very near hysteria, made her case to Irene and Elias. "We…we've been very silly. I know, but we love each other so. We wanted to tell you…really we did, but you wanted me to go to school…and we got carried away, I guess…didn't we, Trenton?"

Clawing at Trenton's chest, Odessa gave him a shake, then clung to him as if she were drowning. At last, he put an arm around her waist in a sad attempt to act the part of ardent lover.

"You know how it is when you're in love." Odessa gazed up at Trenton with far too much fervor.

The sight sickened Irene. She knew her daughter was self-centered, she knew how to lie and scheme, but she never would have thought her daughter cruel.

"Mama…sometimes you can't wait, but you know how it is. Trenton and me, we're like it was with you and Daddy. It seemed like we had so little time left…just this summer to be together. I'm sorry, Mama. I know I've disappointed you again."

****

Odessa knew the speech by heart. She'd lain in bed at night and practiced and practiced what she would say. She even imagined how her mother would look when she told her about Silas. It wasn't supposed to be like this. It wasn't supposed to be Trenton. It was supposed to be Silas. It was Silas she loved…Silas she wanted.

Trenton, she knew, had begun to grasp the

situation—Odessa could see it in his eyes. Some of what she'd said had finally sunk in. She didn't know if he would stand by her. But he'd always been her friend.

"Can Odessa and me have a little time to talk this over? We got plans to make, you see," Trenton said.

****

Elias tugged her arm to get her to quit the room, retreat to the kitchen, but she had to stop this. Irene opened her mouth and shut it. Trenton gave her a nod. She hesitated, took a breath, and allowed Elias to escort her from the room. He closed the door behind him and let loose of her arm. For a few moments, Irene stood staring at the closed door.

"I could use a cup of coffee," he said.

"We can't leave them alone in there," Irene said, her voice a hiss, her eyes never leaving the door.

Behind her, Elias huffed. "I think it's a little late to worry about that."

"Don't be ridiculous," Irene said. Disgusted, she retrieved the coffee pot from the warming shelf above the cook stove and slammed it down on the counter to make a fresh pot. "Trenton Trask is not the father of her baby. I know it, and you know it. I'd bet my best bonnet Silas is the father. And what's more, I can see by the flash of fire in your eyes you know it too."

"Weeks ago," he confessed. "I came home late and saw Silas leaving the stable for the boarding house. I'd heard rumors Silas was using the stable as a love nest."

Whirling around to face him, Irene had the overwhelming desire to throw the coffee pot at his head. Instead, she forgot about the coffee, yanked a chair back from the table, and made herself sit down before she exploded. Hands clenched tight in her lap, she glared at him. "Tell me, tell me what you suspected. Then tell me why you didn't say something to me."

He met her gaze and offered her a weak smile. She interpreted that smile as pity, which further infuriated her. When she huffed with impatience, he finally started to talk. "One night, about a month or so ago, I saw Odessa sneaking into the house when I came down the lane. She couldn't have been more than a few seconds ahead of me. I suspected something was afoot then. If she had been at the Laidlaws or with the Davis girls, I would have seen her on the road coming into town. I put two and two together, Silas at the stable and Odessa sneaking in late."

"And where I might ask, did you hear the rumors?" Holding up her hand, she didn't really need to ask. "The saloon, yes, of course, the saloon. Oh, I'm an idiot!" She put her face in her hands and groaned.

Hands back in her lap, she said, "For weeks, every time I went to the boarding house, Grace made sure she handed me the laundry, a knowing smirk on her face. And Paulette, she always looked like she wanted to tell me something. You know, she would open her mouth then press her lips tight together."

Irene shook her head and sprang to her feet, and went back to making the coffee. Working by rote, she measured out the beans, ground the beans, poured the water, and set the pot on the wood cook stove. She couldn't face him, couldn't stand to see the concern in his eyes…see the pity.

"And Meda-Belle," she said, head bowed, palms on the countertop, her back to Elias, who sat still and quiet. "Meda-Belle, my friend…what a laugh. She did try to warn me. I remember now. It was after the Fourth of July incident, she said, 'Little girls, Mrs. O, they can get into a peck of trouble, you know. They need talkin' to, just like little boys.' Yes, she was so right, but I waved her off."

Turning at last, Irene met Elias's worried gaze. "I thought I had explained, you know, given Odessa the little talk. Evidently, I didn't make it clear enough…use the right words to get through to her."

Elias stayed where he was, but she longed for him to come and take her, hold her, and tell her it was all a bad dream and that it wasn't really happening. Closing her eyes, Irene wished she could turn back the clock, turn back time. She had so many regrets eating away at her heart—she could feel them gnawing away, the pain almost unbearable.

Then Elias was there, his arms going around her. He drew her into his chest, and his hand stroked her hair. "I know what you're thinking," he said. His lips brushed her ear, his breath warm…so warm and soothing. "You're thinking this is your fault, that you should've said something, done something, to prevent this. But I tell you, there was nothing you or I could do. There was nothing we could have said that would have stopped Odessa. She knew what she was doing. I'm sure she knew the consequences of lying with Silas. She's been obsessed with him for years. She knew she was pregnant before I told her."

"Tell me what you've heard. What has everyone been saying? What does everyone, but me, know about all of this?"

Drawing her back to the table, Elias sat her down and went back for the coffee. He poured them both a cupful, sat, and reached for her knotted hands. "Grace

Wolfe, of course, was the first one to give me the hint."
He snorted, "I say hint. Grace, as we know, is about as
subtle as an avalanche."

"Her exact words, Elias," Irene demanded, cold with
dread. She had to know what the gossips were saying.

"I'm quoting Grace now—*Silas is quite a cherry-
plucker.*"

Elias blushed. He actually blushed. Irene closed her
eyes. "Grace Wolfe is disgusting," she muttered.

"She also said Silas had a private harvesting room at
the livery."

Groaning with mortification, Irene said, "Oh, I can
hear her cackle."

"Well, I wish now I'd done or said something to stop
her foul tongue from wagging," Elias said and let go of
her hands to take a sip of his coffee. It was cold. He made
a face and set the cup aside. "All I really heard was Silas
was using the stable to…to…meet up with a girl. Most
everyone in town knows Odessa is…was…crazy about
Silas. No one ever came out and said to my face it was
Odessa he was seeing there."

"Oh, God, Elias, I could die." Irene whimpered, her
voice dropping to a groan. "She's been lying to me for
months. She hasn't been going out to the Davis place.
She's been meeting Silas. I knew…I knew. No, I didn't
actually know, but I suspected, and I didn't stop her. I
closed my mind to it and chose to believe what she
wanted me to believe. I really am a fool, a blind, stupid
fool."

Taking her hands in his again, Elias told her, "I wish
with all my heart I could take away your pain. I can't do
that, but I can stand with you, Irene. I can and I will. You
can count on me. I'm not going to desert you."

Coming to a conclusion, Irene squared her shoulders. "I can't allow Odessa to trap Trenton into marriage...*fatherhood*. Trenton doesn't deserve that. You saw her. She ambushed him."

In response, Elias answered, "Odessa has been paddling in fast water for a while now. She almost drowned. She's latched onto the nearest limb to save herself. I say she got herself into this. Let her find her own way out."

Irene nodded, fully aware of her daughter's flawed character. "She's been thoughtless before, careless, but this...this is terrible. Poor Trenton—and Ruby and Sam, they've been through so much. I heard someone say today, after the wedding, that Silas had left home."

"Grace Wolfe went with him," Elias said.

"Oh, dear God, this is too much," Irene said, head in her hands.

Reality hit her. Panic surged up into her chest. Her heart thumped and skipped several beats. Eyes to the ceiling, she said, "She's going to have a baby, Elias. Odessa can't be a mother. She's supposed to go to school. She can't go now. She won't be able to go. We'll have to let Doctor Carter's sister know...all the arrangements...this is impossible!"

****

"Trenton, you are my anchor, thank you," Odessa whispered. Tears welled up anew and made speaking nearly impossible. They stood in the middle of the room, Trenton still hanging on to her.

Odessa couldn't stop shaking. She had so much to do, so many thoughts raced through her head, but Trenton would help her—he would help.

"Well, I'll marry you, Dessie. It don't matter to me

242

I ain't the father. Least this explains why you ain't been feelin' so good. A baby, Dessie, you're gonna be a mama."

She pushed out of his embrace and began to pace the room. "Trenton Trask, don't be a clunk...I'm going after Silas. I wasn't sure I was going to have a baby. I hoped...maybe, but now I know, I'm going to find Silas and tell him. You have to tell me where he is, which way he went? You can help me get a horse, and I'll be gone."

At first, Trenton stood, mouth open, then he reached out and grabbed her and roughly spun her around to face him. "You're daft! Maybe it's the heat, whatever—you can't go after Silas, Dessie. He's not alone. Remember, Grace is with him. I don't know which way they went. He wanted to go to Mexico, but he said they might go to San Francisco, and then again, he said something about Canada, too. You can't be ridin' off on a horse in your condition."

He shook his head. "No, I ain't gonna help you get a horse. We'll get hitched. Let folks think it's my kid. Best thing to do is get back to the wedding and find the reverend, and marry on the QT. I bet Pa would be glad to help me get up a cabin on the farm. Ma's going to be a grandma. She's going to like that. She sure is fond of babies."

Repulsed by the thought of motherhood, Odessa listened to him spout. She jerked away and resumed her march up and down the room, pulse pounding, mind hatching plan after plan and discarding them as soon as they took shape. She had to think.

Eyes blazing, she stopped directly in front of Trenton and poked him in the chest. "If you think for one minute I'm going to be stuck on some sheep farm,

Trenton Trask, you have another think coming. No! The baby isn't due until January. You're crazy if you think I'm going to stay here and let everyone talk about me behind my back. When Silas knows I'm going to have his baby, we'll be married, and he and I will go to Mexico or San Francisco. We talked about going somewhere. I want to go somewhere. I don't want to stay here. I can't...I won't."

Trenton hauled her into his chest, his eyes gone hard and unrelenting. Odessa, for a second, was frightened—this wasn't the Trenton of her childhood—this was a man pushed to the edge. He took a breath, his grip relaxed, and his voice, when he spoke, was gentle and kind—her friend Trenton again, "You ain't gonna be talked about. You'll be my wife. We'll be fine. You'll see. Let me take care of you. I want to take care of you. I been staying out of your way 'cause I knowed you was sweet on Silas. But he didn't love you. I love you. He's been going over to the boarding house after bein' with you—lyin' with the hellcat. He bragged to her about what he done to you. Don't you get that?"

Odessa didn't want to hear this, and she tried to break free, but Trenton had grown strong, strong in more ways than she wanted to know.

Digging his fingers into her shoulders, he gave her a good shake. "Dessie, I don't mean to hurt you, but you got to get the notion of my brother bein' any kind of father or husband out of your head. He don't care about you. I care, Dessie. I care, and I'm glad to be here for you. I will always be here for you, and now I'm gonna be here for your baby. I'm gonna be his daddy."

Chapter Twenty

Sitting on the church steps, sulking, Odessa tried to convince herself she didn't care. As far as she was concerned, they could all go to blazes. Silas was gone, and he'd taken that woman with him.

"You vant some punch?" George asked, appearing out of nowhere, towering above her. "Two cups I got here. Mrs. Trask, she tinks you vas lookin' like sometin' good you need to vet yer vhistle."

Looking up, the sun directly overhead, Odessa winced in real pain. A sharp jab like that of an ice pick poked her right behind the temples. George stood there like a giant. He shifted to the left and completely blocked the sun's glare. Odessa couldn't really make out his face, but she did see his big, white toothy smile.

George had a big face. He was handsome, she supposed, in a Nordic sort of way. A lot of the girls, Susan Laidlaw in particular, found his powerful, woodsman-type build extremely attractive. Odessa did find George's accent interesting, but right now she wasn't in the mood to talk to anyone. She certainly didn't want company, so she nodded and took the cup of punch from him, hoping he would take the hint and go away.

Shading her eyes, Odessa glanced over and caught Mrs. Trask watching her. She delivered the lady a half-hearted smile.

"Thank you, George." To her dismay, George sat

down on the step below her. The only good thing about it, he did provide some shade.

"Someting I got to say. I guess you vant to be left alone, but I tink maybe I should speak."

Odessa gritted her teeth. To get up and leave would be rude. She was caught. Eventually, he'd leave.

"Silas, sad he makes you. I know dis."

Holding her breath, Odessa cast a furtive glance around her and wondered if everyone knew… Was it written on her forehead Silas had left her pregnant…run off with Grace Wolfe?

George, ignoring her sour expression and her squirm of discomfort, went right on talking. "Dat Silas and my papa alike, I tink. Vhen I vas little, home he vas, den Mama, a baby she vould have, and go again he vould. Five children, Mama had. Two sisters and me helped raise dem, you know? Den, vone-day Mama says going home she is to Nort Dakota to live vit her sister, taking my sisters and da babies too. From dat time on my own, I am."

George turned toward her and took her hand in his big paw, warm and strong. The second he took her hand, her headache subsided, no longer pounding against her temples. She gazed into his blue eyes and almost forgot her anger.

"Mama said, tired she vas of looking at Papa's back," George told her in a voice so low and private Odessa forgot where they were. "I tink maybe dat Silas is like my papa. Don't let him break yer heart, Miss Odessa. It's a pretty girl you are," George said. His knuckles brushed her cheek, light as a feather.

"George," Trenton called out as he came out of the church.

"Trenton," George said. His hand fell to his side, and he rose to his feet. "Dat music sounds pretty good. It's not so good vitout Rob, but it's pretty good. Tink I go find some toes to step on," he said. A big grin on his face, he winked at Odessa and started off toward the music and the couples gathered in front of the church.

He turned back around, unsmiling, his eyes only for Odessa. "Miss Odessa, maybe you dance vit me, yah?"

Without even giving it a moment's hesitation, Odessa answered, "Yes. Thank you, George. Let me drink my punch first."

Trenton sat down beside her, "What did he want?"

"He didn't want anything," Odessa said, irritated, unwilling to share what George had told her. She wanted to keep his story to herself, pull it out later and think about it. "Your mother sent him over with a cup of punch."

"Oh," Trenton said. He followed George's retreat with a jaundiced eye. He continued to watch him until George asked the Laidlaw girl to dance, then he shrugged him off.

"So, what did Reverend Smalley say?" Odessa asked, to turn his attention back to her.

"He has to go out of town tomorrow, but he said he'd be back day after tomorrow to perform the ceremony. "He wanted to know why we were in such a hurry. I…I kind of had to tell him."

"No, Trenton, you told him? Oh, no, why? Why did you do that?"

"He won't tell anyone. He's a reverend, for Pete's sake. He can't," Trenton said.

"A lot you know," Odessa said. She popped up and began to look around for an escape route.

Trenton stepped down and stood in front of her, which put them nose to nose.

He looked fierce again. He looked like he wanted to slap her.

She tried to get around him.

He put his hands on her shoulders, leaned in, and told her, "I know this, Dessie. I got to get to Farewell Bend, get a license, and get back here by day after tomorrow. That's what I know. I got to take time off of work, and I don't think that's gonna go over very big with the boss. That's what I know. And I know you got to get a new face on you, girl. Anybody lookin' at you don't need no words. They can read the whole dumb story right there," he said and gave her nose a hard poke with his finger. "That's what I know."

Nose stinging, eyes blinking with surprise, Odessa glanced toward the dancers and hoped they hadn't drawn any unwanted attention.

"Mama and Doctor Rayburn are coming this way. Smile," she said and took him by the hand and pulled him along behind her.

****

Irene couldn't miss the forced smile on Odessa's face and felt sorry for Trenton, who looked positively haggard. As much as she hated it, her daughter was the villain in this mess—as well as the victim. Trenton didn't deserve any of this. He was such a good boy—no, he was a good young man.

"Trenton spoke with Reverend Smalley. He's going to marry us day after tomorrow," Odessa informed them, her eyes challenging Irene to gainsay her.

"That doesn't leave us much time, Odessa," Irene said. She hoped to make the best of it, putting a proper face on this rush to the altar. "You'll need a dress, and we'll need flowers."

Odessa cast Trenton's hand aside like a dirty stick. Red in the face, eyes blazing with fury, she took a menacing step toward Irene.

Elias moved closer to Irene's side, his arm going around her shoulders.

Spitting the words out, Odessa informed her, "This isn't going to be a celebration, Mother—not like Anna's wedding. We'll say some dumb words and sign a piece of stupid paper. We don't need flowers. And I don't need a...*special*...dress—there's nothing special about this farce."

Her body started to tremble. Desperate, Irene had to find normal. Undaunted by Odessa's irrational outburst, she pressed on. She knew better. She knew where it would lead. "Odessa, you'll need a dress," she said and tried to touch the girl, get her to calm down and see reason. "Every girl needs a dress for her wedding. I still have my wedding dress; you could wear that. We'd have to let down the hem, but I think it would fit."

Odessa smirked, then began to snicker, but not in a nice way. "Funny, I can't picture you as a blushing bride, mother. Young and virginal." Laughing too loud, Odessa snorted. "No, no, you weren't virginal at all, were you, Mother? Well, like mother, like daughter. I'd nearly forgotten. Daddy had to marry you, didn't he? I can't wait to see what you call a wedding dress. I wonder, will it bring me any better luck than what you had?"

Beside her, Irene heard Elias suck in his breath. He stiffened, and Irene squeezed his hand, hoping he would hold his tongue. A long, drawn-out moment of tense silence yawned between mother and daughter.

Trenton broke the silence. "Let's dance, Dessie."

"I don't feel like it," Odessa said.

Trenton took her by the shoulders and turned her toward the dancing couples out on the lawn. "Come on, you always was good at playactin'."

Odessa shook her shoulders free. "All right, all right, but first, I want something to eat and some cake before it's all gone."

"That sounds fine to me," Trenton agreed.

Irene, left to watch them walk away as if the whole world had not slipped off its axis, simply stared, open-mouthed, wounded to the core of her being.

"How about you? Cake first, or do we have our dance now?" she heard Elias ask her. His lips brushed her ear, his breath soft and warm. "She didn't know what she was saying, Irene. She was striking out. You're the easy target."

Odessa and Trenton had joined in the celebration. Irene found it hard, nearly impossible to look away. "She is very good at pretending—and lying—isn't she? From all appearances, no one would suspect she's set herself—and Trenton too—down the path to disaster. They appear to one and all what they have always been—good friends. Good friends, having a good time at their friends' wedding. But I don't think I can do it. I can't pretend nothing is wrong, Elias. Everything is wrong. Everything."

"Cake it is, then we dance," he said. He ignored her little mew of protest and propelled her forward and into the throng of guests.

"Elias, no. I can't dance today, not with all of this going on, I can't. And I certainly couldn't swallow any cake. I couldn't. I'll congratulate the bride and groom, then go sit in the shade."

He shook his head and opened his mouth, but she stopped him. "Before you start working on me to dance, I know I said I would…and I want to, but not today. Not after all…*everything*…I wouldn't enjoy it."

He pulled in his chin, and sucked in his breath. He exhaled and said, "Very well, but first I think we should sample the cake to be polite."

"Fine, yes, to be polite," she said and started forward again. He moved her along, giving her no opportunity to stop. His actual phrasing began to register, and she squeaked in protest and came to a sudden halt. "First? What do you mean…first? Elias?"

****

Waylaid by an unexpected funeral at Crooked River, Reverend Smalley didn't return to Meadow View for fourteen days. When he did return, he came down with influenza. Elias put the man in quarantine. At the end of July, the reverend began to rally, but Elias told Irene he didn't think it likely he'd recover sufficiently to perform the marriage ceremony for Mr. Russell and Miss Pritchard next week. Which meant Odessa and Trenton had to postpone their nuptials until the second week of August.

After Anna and Rob's wedding, Odessa sank deeper and deeper into depression. Irene was at a loss for how to help her. Deep in thought, she didn't hear the knock on the front door; the second tattoo got her attention. Opening the door, she found Trenton and hoped he had news that would entice Odessa out of her room.

"Mrs. Obenchain, I come to see Dessie."

Irene glanced toward Odessa's closed door and wondered if her daughter knew she had a visitor. "Of course, but…she's resting."

"Oh, well, you can tell her when she wakes up I got us a preacher."

"Trenton, that's wonderful. Is Reverend Smalley up?"

"No, but he's on the mend. I talked to Mr. Russell, and he told me he found a way to get a preacher over here from Eugene. He'll be here end of the week to do Mr. Russell's weddin', and stay and get the knot tied for Dessie and me the next mornin'.

"I'm in town this mornin' helpin' build a perch in one of them tall pines in the middle of town so's we can fire-watch. I've set up a watch sight on Rooster Rock where I can see for miles. We tested the signal with mirrors this morning. The guys at the mill saw the flashes plain."

Irene ushered him inside.

"I can't stay. I got to go on duty here pretty quick. I been takin' on as much as I can so I could get some extra pay and time off for a little trip into Farewell Bend. I thought Odessa and me could have a night in a fancy hotel—a honeymoon."

"Hotel?" Odessa cried from her doorway, definitely interested, Irene observed.

"Dessie, I got us enough cash we can have a room at the Timber Inn for our honeymoon night," Trenton said.

Drawn to Odessa, he crossed the room to be near her. Irene didn't think Odessa would ever understand how much Trenton cared for her.

Leaving Trenton to take care of Odessa, Irene slipped away to the backyard. Drawn to the slate stone that covered Abel's box of possessions, she sat on the ground next to it, closed her eyes, and prayed very hard.

****

The first Saturday in August, the skies overhead clear, a mild breeze cooling their cheeks, everyone, the whole town, gathered to celebrate Mr. Russell's and Miss Pritchard's long-awaited wedding day.

Irene had hoped Odessa would want to get out and have a bit of fun. But she wouldn t budge. "Nobody's going to notice I'm not there, and if they ask, tell them I have the influenza, or the pip—bunch of rosy gossips anyway. Trenton's on watch up on Rooster Rock. It's too hot to be stuck in a stuffy little church. I don't want anyone to see me like this. I look awful. My fingers are puffy, and I hate my hair. Go, leave me alone. Bring me some cake or something—I'm hungry."

"Well, good," Irene said, "at least that's something, I guess. There's ham in the pantry, and cheese; have some of that to keep you until we get back."

Odessa made a face. "I don t want ham. I like chicken. You know what I really would like— watermelon...a big, juicy watermelon. When will you be back? There's nothing to do here all by myself."

For a moment, Irene considered staying home— maybe coax Odessa to eat something. Maybe she could help her with her hair.

Elias took her firmly by the arm and propelled her out the door. Over his shoulder, he said, "You know how these things go, Odessa. We'll be back in a couple of hours."

Incensed, and resisting his high-handed treatment of her, Irene dragged her feet. "Why did you say that? We won't be gone that long. I don't think we should leave her alone for more than an hour."

In response, Elias growled and rushed her away from the house. "I'm getting pretty fed up, you know—with both of you."

"Well, I'm sorry," she said and would have pulled her arm free of his grasp, but he wouldn't allow it.

"For the past few weeks, Odessa has done nothing but whine, complain, complain, complain, and you...you're obsessed with catering to her every whim. You have to stop, Irene. Stop. There's nothing you can do or say that will please her...nothing. She's a grown woman, not a child. Although her behavior would suggest otherwise. She can feed herself, dress herself—even entertain herself. You spend far too much of your time trying to make things right for her, and you don't get enough rest. She's getting married, Irene. She's going to be a wife...and a mother."

Biting her tongue, Irene listened to him. She wanted to take umbrage but, to her dismay, she couldn't argue—he was right. "I'm aware Odessa is behaving like a spoiled brat. Her behavior is nothing new. But I also know a lot of her bad attitude has to do with her condition, and that's why I don't want to leave her alone for very long. She's unhappy. I'm her mother, and I don't want her to be unhappy."

Stopping at the end of the lane, Elias pulled her around to face him. "Okay, but I'm worried about you." His hand brushed her cheek. "I've been worried about you for a couple of years now. You aren't happy, and I want you to be happy, Irene. You can't do anything to make Odessa happy...unless you bring Silas back. And we both know that might make her happy, but it would also be certain disaster, which would most assuredly make her miserable."

His eyes smiled down on her, and he lowered his head. Irene stretched up on her toes to meet his lips, at first gently. Then pressing more insistently, as his tongue found the crease between her lips, she opened for him, reveling in all the wondrous sensations that coursed through her body.

Coming back to her senses, her hands on his chest, she pushed away, her gaze darting first one way then the other, afraid someone might have witnessed them kissing, afraid someone might guess she was on fire— pulse racing.

Impatient, he pulled her back into his chest, taking her chin and lifting it so she had to look into his eyes. "Don't you realize, Irene Obenchain, I'm what you need? I can make you happy. I'm a doctor, I'm all the medicine you need, and you're not taking full advantage of me."

Staring up at him, her breath caught in her throat. Irene blinked, then blinked again, one hand on her heart and the other on his chest. "Elias, my God. I'm going to be a grandmother."

Throwing his head back, Elias laughed, nodded, and to her chagrin, laughed all the way down the street to the church.

****

A bright flash, and the sound of distant thunder, brought Odessa to stand in the open doorway. The sky had gone a strange color, a dark orange. She wandered up the lane and looked toward town. The school bell was ringing, someone was clanging the flat steel tire at the livery, and people were running across the street shouting and waving their arms toward the southeast. On the lower slope of the mountains, flames shot straight up

255

in the air like fiery swords. The wind, heavy with smoke, soot, and ash coming from the east, stung her eyes. A lightning bolt flashed, and thunder rolled over the town almost immediately, letting her know the storm was directly overhead.

She closed the door on the approaching disaster, and after a moment or two of sheer panic, she began to fill baskets with bread, fruit, anything people taking refuge might need to take to the church, where she was sure the townspeople would gather. She had come to a standstill to think of what else she should take with her, when she heard George shouting at her to open the door.

She opened the door, and before George could speak, she said, "I'm ready to go. Could they use blankets? Seems too hot, but…"

"Miss Odessa, a stand we're making here 'cause a vell you got. To the church you should get."

Looking into his face, his cheeks bright red, blue eyes red-rimmed, blonde hair plastered to his head with sweat, Odessa felt a strange need to gather him to her bosom and hold him for a few moments to drive the fear from his eyes. His good clothes, ridiculously small for his big frame, were covered with dust and soot, and all she could think was, *good, now maybe you'll have to get some new ones.*

Glancing out the door, past his broad shoulders, she saw the men running to the side of the house, shouting orders to one another. "You're going to be here, George?"

"Yes, ma'am. Fires, dis vay coming. Mr. Russell's got da boys digging da trench behind dis house. If da fire heads for da big meadow ve got a chance. My yob it is to keep it avay from town. You best get going. Your mama, vorried she is about you."

Muttering to herself, thinking about the food she'd gathered and the blankets and everything else, Odessa said, "I shouldn't leave then. I'll stay right here and try to help, George. Do what I can. I can bring water and coffee." Alert, more engaged than she'd been for weeks and weeks—at last, Odessa had something she could do. "I can dig dirt as good as anyone."

"Time I don't got to argue, Miss Odessa. You yust stay out of da vay. No time I got to look out for you. Dat fire is comin'. It's comin' real fast."

Nodding her head, invigorated, challenged, Odessa said, "I'll stay out of the way, George. Go. Go do what you have to do. I'll get set in here."

Odessa stood at the opened door and watched a wagonload of loggers leap to the ground and set off on the run to the side of the house, where they started to throw dirt. "George?" Odessa called out to his back. He stopped and turned, "have you seen Trenton?"

"No, miss," he said and hurried off toward the smoke.

****

Inside the church, Irene took charge of the battle-scarred and weary. Elias, after a long drink of cool water, ventured outside to see if he could be of any use. Curly Q, dazed and wheezing, covered with a layer of soot and lather, wandered across the churchyard, coming toward him. He approached her, talking low, soothing words of sympathy.

He reached for the reins that dangled from her bit. "Curly Q, you look like you've been through the fires of hell. Where's your friend, Trenton, huh?"

His face close to the horse's neck, Elias didn't see

Sam Trask come up on the horse's flank. "Trenton inside?" Sam asked.

"Trenton? No, Sam, I haven't seen Trenton. I was asking Curly Q where he might be."

"I think we better keep her walking," Sam said to no one in particular.

"Yes, if she goes down, the smoke will stay in her lungs. I'll get young Oren Laidlaw. He was sulking inside because he's too little to help fight fire and too big to be left with the women, but I think he could handle Curly Q—walk her a bit and let her have some water, not a lot, just some."

"Right," said Sam, distracted, his gaze to the mountains and the billowing black plume of smoke. "Doctor Rayburn?"

"Yes, Sam."

"Don't let on to Ruby about this. Trenton could be down in the creek bed waitin' it out. That's what he'd do if he was able. Curly Q might'a spooked with the storm and all."

Elias nodded in agreement.

****

The Suncrest Mill burned to the ground. It was a miracle, Elias thought, that with the help of a downpour of alternating rain and hail, the trench around the town held throughout the afternoon. He and the rest of the men of Meadow View chased the fire out into the open to the east of town and beat it down in the grass and sage. Spot fires sprouted up throughout the night, they had to be dealt with, but Mother Nature was with them and the rain was steady right up to daybreak.

He and Irene slept shoulder to shoulder on one of the church pews. All the church's pews remained occupied with exhausted, oxygen-starved victims. Children and babies slept on the altar. Some of the wives and mothers had fallen asleep on the floor beside their spouses or children. It was quiet for the most part.

When George came staggering in with Barclay Russell slung over his shoulder, it was Meda-Belle who offered the boarding house as a makeshift hospital. Sara Laidlaw overheard the suggestion and opened her mouth to give a protest, but Barclay's new bride, Mary, readily took Mrs. Lamphere up on her generous offer.

George slumped down on a bench. Elias saw to Barclay and assessed his hurts. Irene set to reviving George.

"George?' Irene said and handed him a cup of coffee.

"She's fine," he mumbled, before she could ask. "All day, your girl makes da coffee and brings da vater." He told her, his words slurred and interrupted by the occasional need to cough, "She fixed up burns and kept us going. Trench, she dig for a time. I put a stop to dat pretty quick. She sure kept us going, dat girl did. Vhen I come down here, she vas asleep at da table, to bed I put her. A blanket I put around her. You got a good girl dare. I see Curly Q at da livery. Trenton, he's back den?"

Irene looked startled. "My God, no, I haven't seen or heard of Trenton all day. I haven't had time." Looking around, Irene's eyes found Ruby and Sam—they were in an alcove, wrapped in each other's arms.

"We haven't seen him, George," Irene said. Her mind swamped with fear and dread, she imagined Trenton's fate. "There's still food up front on the altar if you would like some."

"No tank you, Ma'am, I got to get back. Dis fire, she

ain't over yet. It's going to be a veek or better, I tink, maybe, before we get it out. That Trenton, up dare on Rooster Rock, he saw the lightning strike right avay. They saw his signal at the mill, and the mill relayed to da town ust like planned. Dat vas a good ting. Ve vas lucky dis time."

Chapter Twenty-One

At dawn, Elias, along with Sam Trask, George Krauss, and Rob Morgan formed a search party to look for Trenton. The rain had stopped Low clouds held the remnants of smoke and ash close to the damp earth. Spot fires burned near Tam Rim. Hot-shot crews of ten chased the fires around the side of the mountain to the lava fields.

Sam on Curly Q, and Elias on a hack from the livery, separated from George and Rob, rode along the creek bed going southwest. Rob and George continued up Three Creeks Road, their destination Rooster Rock, where Trenton had set up his signal post.

Sam clung to his belief that Trenton was alive, hunkered down in the creek bed. He kept repeating Trenton may be hurt, but he wasn't dead—he couldn't be dead.

Sam's mantra echoed in Elias's head, and he willed it to be true for Sam's sake. They'd gone a few hundred yards away from the road when Sam jumped down from Curly Q's back and slid down the bank into the creek. Elias followed as fast as he could, but he was unused to riding a horse, and it took him a moment to find his legs.

It wasn't Trenton's body lying half in the water; it was a deer carcass. Sam, overcome with relief and filled with dread, crumpled up and wept "I thought, I thought it was my boy," he sobbed. "Trenton would've pulled a tarp over his head like I showed him. But this poor creature," Sam cried, his hand waving toward the charred remains of the deer, "could've been, it could've been..."

"We should get it out of the water," Elias said. "Water supply is probably ruined as it is; no need to leave this to rot and make it worse."

The two of them struggled up the rocky wall of the creek bed and dragged the carcass between them. Elias didn't feel like he was of much use. He kept sliding back down into the water. Sam, on the other hand, possessed the strength of two men. Elias suspected fear and frustration empowered the man.

Once the dead animal was up and out of the creek, they sat near the creek under what had been a stately pine. The ground was black, scorched all around them, still hot, spirals of smoke here and there curled up from the earth. They sat in silence to catch their breath.

Two shots echoed across the hillside behind them. Sam was on his feet and reaching for Curly Q before Elias had time to determine from which direction the shots had come. He didn't know how old Sam was, but he sure as hell had more stamina and strength than Elias did at this point. Groaning, his backside cramping, Elias made himself get on his horse and follow Sam back to the road.

They galloped for a mile or more until they spotted George sitting on a boulder to the side of the road with his head in his hands. George must've heard the horses and came to his feet. Elias could see him, see the despair on his face. The man squared his big shoulders and swiped tears from his jaw.

"Did you find him?" Sam asked, calling out, barely waiting for Curly Q to stop.

"He's over dare 'bout thirty feet, but...Mr. Trask, he's...he ain't...Rob is vit him—I couldn't..." George said and hung his head.

He turned to Elias. "Doctor Rayburn, he's dead. Burnt almost beyond recognition. Trenton ve knew it vas 'cause he vore dose boots vit dah Spanish heels, and dah spurs he von at da Fourt of July roceo. But his head is all busted up."

Elias looked down the road the way they'd come; Trenton had almost made it. They were only a couple of miles from town and even closer to the mill. Elias and George walked through the charred, burnt-out woods where Rob stood over Trenton's remains. Sam, on his knees, wept.

Elias contemplated God's plan.

Ruby, with cancer and death standing over her bed had, the way Elias saw it, dared death to take her. She was disappointed the Grim Reaper rejected her.

Trenton, a boy on the brink of becoming a man, a married man with a family, no thought of death or of the...*what ifs*...in life, had been taken with a callous, random disregard. He found it incomprehensible. He couldn't imagine Sam's despair. It must be overwhelming.

****

Her mother and Doctor Rayburn beside her, Odessa walked home from the graveyard in a trance, numb and unseeing, yet moving, breathing. Trenton was gone. He'd left her, like Silas, like her father. He was gone, no word of goodbye.

"Well, I'm grateful to everyone for all their kindness," Odessa heard her mother say as they headed down the lane toward the house. 'Even Sarah managed to say some kind words about Trenton. I think I saw genuine sorrow on her face."

All Odessa felt, all she could see was desolation—the burnt woods to the south of town, the blackened earth, the smoke hanging low to the mountains, and she had to wonder if anything would ever be the same. Even the big meadow, always so green and expansive, had lost its charm, now appearing as nothing more than a barren wasteland. The fire had taken more than trees. It had taken some of the heart of Meadow View—it had taken Trenton, her dearest friend in all the world. She didn't see how the scarred land or her heart could ever heal.

As soon as they got home, her mother started to fix something to eat—that's all her mother ever thought about, that and sleep and rest. Odessa didn't think she would ever eat again. Why should she? What was the point?

The doctor started to read his telegrams. He'd put them aside that morning to be certain he'd be present for the funeral.

One of the telegrams was from Doctor Carter. Odessa listened to him read it aloud. "Fires burning north, near Juniper Butte, and south of Farewell Bend along Deschutes River." Looking up from the paper, the doctor told them, "Doctor Carter has sent out a call for help. The fires north didn't involve very many people. It was expected to burn out once it hit the Crooked River Gorge, but the fire has hit in the midst of an influenza epidemic, and there are victims of fire and influenza who are fighting for their lives—too many for Doctor Carter to handle."

He turned and put his hand on her mother's shoulder, turning her to face him. "I have to leave as soon as we've eaten."

Odessa couldn't bear to watch them standing there as if they were the only two people in the room. She was a ghost in this house—*a problem*—well, she wasn't going to stay and fade into the woodwork like a good little girl. Silas was out there, and she would find him or die trying.

****

The slam-bang of drawers and doors opening and closing didn't register with Irene, not right away. Her mind on Elias and his announcement that he had to leave, go out again to care for victims of influenza renewed her fear he'd contract the disease, disappear from her life.

A loud thud startled her, and Elias, out of their preoccupation with the fires and the virus. "Odessa, are you all right? What in the world are you doing?" She moved the stew pot away from the flame, and a crash sent her rushing to Odessa's door. "What are you doing?"

On the bed was the new valise Irene had bought for Odessa to take to school. It overflowed with clothes. A leather traveling case sat on the floor with books, toilet items, and more clothes carelessly stuffed inside. Odessa pushed Irene aside and reached to toss a nightgown that had been on a hook on the back of her door onto the bed.

"What does it look like?" Odessa asked in a nasty tone that left Irene to wonder if her daughter had lost her mind. "I'm getting out of here. Silas ran away, Papa ran away...men leave...I'm leaving."

"Odessa, don't be ridiculous. Come eat. Sit down. Calm yourself. This isn't good for the baby, and it isn't good for you."

"You can't tell me what to do any more." Odessa

said and stuffed her clothes into the bag.

"Odessa…"

"Don't *Odessa* me. I'm leaving. Trenton was going to get me out of here. Get me away from you. I was willing to live in a sheepherder's shack, for Pete's sake, to get out of here. Well, I don't need him. I don't need anybody."

"You're being really foolish, Odessa. Where do you think you're going?"

Odessa stopped, stabbed her with a sharp glare, and in that second, Irene recognized the raw fear, the panic, and more, a loathing—directed at her.

Her voice gone cunningly quiet, Odessa asked, "Do you really give a damn?"

Irene was speechless. She opened her mouth to rebut, but there were so many retorts on the tip of her tongue it was hard to pick just one, so she didn't say anything. Odessa misunderstood her inability to speak and held up her hand. "Don't bother trying to convince me. I don't accept false coin."

"What are you talking about?" Irene asked, shaking, afraid of where this silly argument would lead. "You have always been…and will continue to be, my main concern, Odessa. I give a damn. Everything I've ever done has been with your best interests in mind."

Odessa laughed in her face. "You, *Mother*…are incapable of any warmth or feeling. You have kept me fed and clothed, but you've starved me of warmth and affection. Ask Doctor Rayburn. I think he knows what I'm talking about. He won't stay. He'll get tired of your cold heart. He won't stay, and I won't stay. We won't stay and wait for you to thaw. Papa left because he got tired of getting left out in the cold. I'm full-grown. I'm getting away from you, just like Papa. Wherever I end up, it will be a lot warmer than here, in this house, with you."

Elias, behind her, in the doorway—Irene could feel him there, solid and steadfast. But she wished him gone. She flinched when his hands went to her shoulders. Trembling, hand clutched to her abdomen as if Odessa had served her a blow with her fist, one thing Irene knew for certain was she was through taking the blame for all the tragedy in Odessa's life. No, no more.

"I've worked until my fingers bled. I've gone without food, shoes, clothes, and sleep to give you some of the things other girls have. How can you accuse me of...of not caring? You're confused and hurt, Odessa, I can understand that, but you can't say I haven't cared for you...loved you."

"Confused?" Odessa spat back at her. "No. No more...I'm not."

"Well, you can't leave. You don't have anywhere to go. You don't have any money," Irene said and started to remove items from her satchel.

"I have the money for my school. You owe me that. I worked for that." She snatched the nightgown out of Irene's grasp. "I'm going to the Yukon to find Daddy...or maybe I'll go to Mexico and find Silas."

"The baby, Odessa?" Irene pleaded. "You're going to have a baby. You can't think of yourself now. And don't bother your head about finding your father...he's dead."

Irene clamped her lips shut, slapped her hand over her mouth, and cursed her tongue. Odessa stilled, eyes opened wide, staring at her. Behind her, Irene heard Elias suck in his breath. Closing her eyes, she prayed for the earth to open up and swallow her.

A horrible silence hung upon the air. Nothing dared to make a sound.

"Dead...Papa is dead? How do you know?" Odessa shook her head. "No," she said, eyes narrowed and suspicious. "How do you know that? You can't know." She moved forward to get in Irene's face. "You're making that up. You're making that up to keep me from running off."

Irene reached into her apron pocket and withdrew the folded piece of paper she'd kept there. Creased, stained, the ink faded. She hesitated a moment, then handed it to Odessa.

Odessa stared at the paper, hands shaking. After reading the letter, she folded it, closed her valise and her traveling case, picked them up, and, on her way out, passed the letter to Elias.

"I'm going to stay with the Trasks," she said, in that other voice, the voice of a cold heart. "Maybe they'll know where I can find Silas."

Headed for the front door, Irene trotted alongside Odessa. Her hand on the valise, she said. "You can't walk all the way out there carrying these heavy cases."

"I'll get a ride. I'll find George."

"Odessa...don't do this." Irene stopped on the threshold and slumped against the doorjamb, "Odessa, please." Her plea fell on deaf ears. She watched until Odessa turned onto the main road and went out of sight.

It took a moment for Irene to remember—Elias, Elias had the letter. Letter in hand, he stood at the hearth, gazing into the cold grate.

"You have to let me explain."

"Do I?"

"I was waiting to tell you. I was going to."

"The date on this is August last year. You've had twelve months, Irene. I don't think you wanted me to know. I don't think you wanted anyone to know. Hell, you said you didn't want to know. Was it your cousin? She sent the letters of inquiry, not you. Oh, no, not you. She gave them your address, didn't she? You didn't want to know, did you?"

Lips pressed tightly together, head tilted to the side, her guilty tears, hot and wet, dribbled down her cheek.

She looked into his eyes, hard and unforgiving, and drew herself up to face the truth. She had to make him understand—somehow, she had to. "You're right. I didn't want to know."

"I guess there's no more to be said then," he said, anger gone, replaced by a shrug. "I want to marry you. I want a life with you. I love you. And clearly, you don't love me, or at least not enough—first Marie and now you. I wonder, is it me? Is my judgment flawed? Why can't you love me as much as I love you?"

Tired of being misunderstood, her feelings discounted, Irene shouted at him, "You're so wrong." Hands balled into fists, she snarled. "You are wrong. Odessa is wrong. I love you. I love you both. Whatever I've done, I've done for you, to protect you, Doctor Rayburn...your reputation in this town. If this town knew I was a widow, you would have to leave this house, don't you see that?"

"No, I don't see that at all," he said and waved the letter in her face. "You worry too much about everybody else, what they think.

"Odessa wanted to feel loved; she didn't really care about a new dress. She didn't really care about food; she wanted to be held, cherished, loved, and made to feel special…Irene, that's all. It should be simple for a mother to give, but did you give it, or did you think *appearances* mattered more?"

Irene couldn't believe her ears. She screamed at him. "Odessa wanted dresses and pretty things. That's all she could think about. She never gave a thought to how much it cost me, how hard I had to work. I wanted things. I wanted shoes without holes. I wanted more than two dresses to my name. I want to be loved. Odessa never tried to help me or help herself. Odessa doesn't know what she wants, not really."

There was no going back now. Irene knew she was out of control.

Tears washed down her cheeks, unchecked emotions bubbled out in great heaving sobs. There was nothing for it but to rail against her own insanity. "You want—Odessa wants—what about me? I wanted a husband. I wanted my babies and a home. I wanted a family, friends, and kind neighbors. I've had to work for what little I've got…what we needed…what I thought Odessa needed. And I did what I had to do. You…Odessa, you know nothing about me or what I want. Go on, get out of here. Leave me alone. I don't need you. And contrary to what Odessa thinks, what you think, I sure as hell don't need an ungrateful woman-child on my hands."

She couldn't bear to look at him, read the hurt in his eyes. Shaking, teeth chattering, she brought up her chin. "Odessa is right about one thing—*men* leave. You're free to leave. You have no strings. Find another place to set up your office." Chin up, shoulders back, she said, "I can't leave. This is all I have. All I have—all I had—is—

was—this house and Odessa. Then you came along. I started to think I could have more—be more. You're wrong, and Odessa's wrong. You think I don't love you enough, but the truth is I love you both too much. I love you more than myself—more than my petty needs. I've put you and Odessa before everything I ever wanted…needed…craved, or dreamed of. I put Odessa's standing in the community before my own. I tried to protect your reputation. And both of you accuse me of not loving, of being cold. Go…you want to go. If you can't understand, then go. Whatever this is between us— it will never work…never. I was a fool to think it ever could."

To Irene's dismay, he turned away from her without a word and laid the letter on the table, and went to his room. Fifteen minutes later, she heard him leave. She sat down at the table and cried. Her hand found the letter, and she crushed it into a tight ball.

Chapter Twenty-Two

It was already October, and winter was coming. No new cases of influenza had come up for two weeks, and Elias hoped it was an end to the epidemic. He had concluded, weeks ago, he couldn't let go of Irene. He needed her, and in his heart, he knew she needed him. They both needed to stop wasting time.

He reached the house noting the days getting shorter and already dark. Aware, in his absence, Irene had tended to the sick and had continued to enforce his orders of limiting social functions, even church service, during this time of widespread illness. If she was as exhausted as he was, she was in bed asleep.

The house was dark inside as well as out. He tried to be quiet as he raided the pantry to ferret out something to eat. He found the biscuits, honey, and butter, then discovered some fried chicken on the shelf above. Arms full, he snuck everything off to his room, where he had water heating for tea.

After making short work of his meal, he washed his face and climbed into his downy-soft bed. Taking a deep breath, grateful to be home, he smelled the fresh linen and closed his eyes, and sent up a prayer of thanks for Irene Obenchain and her excellent housewifery.

****

Elias had returned. Irene lay very still and guessed he was in her pantry. Smiling to herself, she hoped he'd find the chicken she'd purposefully left for him, and the biscuits. She'd tried to leave food every night in the faint hope he would come home. It was all she could do.

It took everything she had not to get up and take care of him. Turning onto her side, she faced her door, yearning to go to him…feed him…touch him, perhaps rub his shoulders as she'd done a hundred times after a long day, or days, without good rest.

She felt so very empty. The house echoed with angry voices. Watching the light from under her door fade to darkness, she closed her eyes and pictured him seated before his fire, dark circles under his eyes, eating his cold meal. Her body ached, longed to hold him…lie with him, feel his strength.

One thing had become very clear, she couldn't spend another night not knowing if he meant to leave her for good. Tiptoeing across the sitting room and the kitchen, she reached his door, her hand hovering above the door latch. Undecided, full of indecision, she lowered her hand to her side, stood for a long moment, staring at the door, then turned back to her room. After taking two steps, she turned back, reached for his door, and opened it.

The time for wondering…*what if*…was over. She had nothing more to lose.

"Elias," she whispered into the dark, torn between hoping he was awake and praying he was not. She stood for a few moments listening for movement, or maybe snoring.

"Irene…what is it? Are you all right?" she heard him ask. He sounded groggy, half asleep.

Quietly, she closed the door behind her and stepped into the room. Coming closer to the warmth of the fire, she shivered. Teeth chattering, she peered through the darkness to see him. The bed was in a dark corner of the room. The fire in the grate was weak, giving off very little light and hardly any heat.

In a voice tentative, above a whisper, not sounding at all like herself, Irene said, "I don't know why I kept the letter from you. I thought I knew, but I don't. Please…can we talk? I've missed you. I don't expect you to…to understand…but…well, I'm sorry," she said and turned to go.

"I've missed you too," she heard him say to her back. His words stopped her. Trembling, she didn't dare turn around, or she'd go to him, beg him to touch her, hold her…make love to her.

"Don't go, Irene."

Unbelievable, his words, so simple, were like an angel's chorus to her ears.

"Come to bed. Sleep with me. I'll sleep better if you're here beside me…please."

Closing her eyes, she thanked God and asked Him once again to forgive her foolish pride.

****

"I'm too tired to talk," Elias said. "So lonely, Irene—lonesome for you—God, how I've missed you." He watched her come across the room, her hair down around her shoulders, shadows across her face. She looked like a beautiful apparition, a dream come true. Her body was in silhouette, the firelight behind her, and he wondered if he was so very tired, after all.

Drawing back the covers, he waited for her. As she drew near, her eyes grew wide. He saw her raise a hand to her throat, then fold her other arm across her waist. She stepped back into the shadows.

"Aww, Irene, no, I don't wear a nightshirt," he said in answer to her retreat. "I haven't since I was thirteen and my mother stopped tucking me in."

Staring at him, fingers over her lips, she whimpered and came closer to the bed and said, "In Virginia, Mama, Papa, my two brothers and I, all slept, ate, and bathed in our one-room shack. Mama died when I was five. Papa sent me west to live with a cousin when I was seven because he and my brothers had to go to work in the coal mines. Mama's cousin was poorly. Because I could read and write, she found work for me in a seamstress shop when I was nine. I slept in the attic above the seamstress shop. I've always dressed and undressed under the covers. No one ever tucked me in.

"I met Abel at a street dance when I was thirteen. I got pregnant, and he married me.

"I guess I don't know how to be affectionate, at least how you and Odessa want. It's no excuse, I know. No one ever consoled me, held me, comforted me. I did what I had to do with no sass, and no whining, or I wouldn't eat."

Heart in his throat, he watched her undo the buttons at the throat of her nightgown. She tugged it down one shoulder, then the other. The garment slipped to the floor. She stood before him in all her glory—naked and so beautiful. In awe of her courage, he gazed upon the curves and planes of her body. Her shoulders were straight and strong. Her breasts stood full and round, firm yet appearing as smooth as butter in the firelight. Her nipples, dark and hard, protruded. Her waist was small, and her hips beautifully curved, perfectly formed down to her thighs. He marveled at the body she'd managed to hide from everyone all these years. He dared not blink for fear he would awaken from this dream.

****

Irene lay down beside him. She wanted to tell him she knew what she'd done was wrong, but he wouldn't allow her to talk.

"Shhh, we don't need to say anything. I heard every word you said. Thank you for allowing me to see into your past. But right now, I don't want words. You and I have waited so long, Irene. Shhh," he said and kissed her.

Irene willed herself to set aside all her doubts, at least for tonight. So many years had passed without touching, so many cold days without feeling. Irene was lost to his kisses—he didn't have to ask her not to talk. There were no words, just sensations.

In all her memories of making love with Abel, Irene couldn't recall anything like she experienced now. Her entire body throbbed with desire. Wantonly, her hands, eager to feel her own skin, her breasts, the folds of her womanhood, begged Elias to give himself to her, fill the heretofore sleeping void.

The first wave of climax came swift and hard. Neither of them had time to fully comprehend what was about to happen. Giddy like children, tears in their eyes, in each other's arms, they took a moment to ponder their spontaneity. Then, with slow deliberation, they savored each other's bodies, testing each other to see how and where the most pleasure could be derived, then they tried it again, just because they could, and after that, they fell asleep at last. All cares and worries set aside.

****

Elias awoke to bright sunshine and the smell of bacon, fried onions, and potatoes. He lay, eyes closed for a few moments, wondering if he'd dreamed he'd made love to Irene Obenchain, not once but three times, during the night—had she really come to him, given herself wholeheartedly, or had it been the most sensual…fantastic dream he'd ever had?

Alone in his bed, he rolled over and pulled the vacant pillow into his face. Inhaling, he smiled; there was her scent—soap, lavender, and something very like honey.

Knowing it was not a dream, he couldn't dress fast enough. He could hear her in the kitchen, setting the table, cooking. What was she doing cooking when what he wanted was to hold her, look into her eyes, and rekindle their desire?

****

Irene turned the bacon with fearless efficiency. She heard him moving around in his room, awake, dressing, she supposed. She was ready—she'd been rehearsing what she wanted to say.

It was a mistake—last night.

Did she regret what had happened? No, she wasn't silly enough to think she could have stopped herself. No, she'd wanted Elias, all right, wanted and needed him for a long time. She loved him, God help her. But he really did have to leave now. She had to evict him. If he stayed, she knew they would bed together every night. It could only become an addiction. To give him up, now they'd made love, wouldn't be easy, but it was the right thing for both of them. She had to make him understand.

His arm came around her waist, and she stiffened. Eyes closed to steady herself, her decision to evict faded with the ripple of desire that skittered down and settled into a delectable flutter at the apex between her thighs.

"Good morning," he murmured. "I'm hungry, but to

277

be honest, I'd give up food if you'd come back to bed."

Elias turned her around and forced her chin up so he could see her face. "Your cheeks are rosy red, and you have yet to look me in the eye. You're not embarrassed, are you? You were...*are* wonderful. Last night was wonderful. Let's do it again. We could start now."

It took great effort and resolve, but Irene pushed herself out of his embrace, picked up the hot skillet, and put it between them. "We're going to talk now," she said.

In response, Elias grinned and put up his hands. "Okay, let's make plans. You are right. We have to be practical, I suppose. We'll talk, eat to keep up our strength, and go back to bed."

Irene lowered the pan and shook her head at him.

"You're not smiling. So you've found a dark cloud in this blue sky of ours," he said and took a chair at the table and waited for her to pour his coffee and place food on the table. "You look sad. Obviously, I'm ignorant of the problem. I refuse to eat until you get it off your chest," he said and sat back in his chair. "Sit down, and let's hash this out, no pun intended."

She stood beside his chair for a moment, looking into his eyes, so brown and warm. She gathered all her willpower. She must resist the desire to melt into his arms. "You have to go," she said and sat down, proud of herself, her gaze unwavering from his.

"I just got home," he said. "Where am I going?"

"I mean it, Elias. You have to get out—today, not tomorrow—your office...everything."

The twinkle went out of his eyes, replaced by hurt, then rekindled to shine as a stubborn gleam. Rocking back in his chair, then forward, he pounded his fist on the table. "No! You've been running scared for years. No more…get your bonnet. We're going to Farewell Bend."

"Why?"

"Just get your bonnet, woman!" He rose to his feet. "After last night—after you used me, drove me wild with your caresses and kisses, you have the temerity to kick me out into the cold, bleak world. No, sir. You will make an honest man of me…*today*!"

Towering over her, very serious, he put her on notice. "You are mine, Irene Obenchain, and I am yours. There is no going back. You've been calling the shots long enough."

Irene set her jaw. "Elias Rayburn, you tell me why first. I've got work to do today. I can't be going off on a jaunt."

"Get up," he ordered and came around the table and tugged her out of her chair. "This is no idle jaunt, my good woman. This is your wedding day."

"Elias?"

"I said get your bonnet. And wear a good coat. It's cold."

"I'll need more than that. I can't go to Farewell Bend looking like this," she said by way of protest.

Holding her at arm's length, he looked her over. "You're right. Let your hair down. I want to see it like you wore it last night." He gave her coiffure a few tugs here and there, releasing hairpins and combs, and her hair came down across her shoulders and down her back. He fluffed it out with his fingers. "There, that's better. You look at least five years younger. No more mud hen. My wife is a stunner. She's full of fire and light. She's exciting. *You* are exciting…you are alive and sensual, Irene—I had guessed as much, but now I know it for certain."

"I can't go out looking...looking like I just got out of bed," she said. Her fingers fumbled to put her hair back into place. She reached out to retrieve her hairpins from him. He pulled her hand behind his back, bringing her body up against his, with nowhere to look but into his intense gaze.

He shook his head and warned her, "I don't know what you're going to do with your hair or what you're going to wear, but you better be ready to go in half an hour, 'cause we are leaving for Farewell Bend. We're getting married. You cannot trifle with my affections. You will do the right thing by me, Irene Obenchain." He snatched a sausage patty off the plate and a biscuit and started to leave the house, stuffing the biscuit and patty in his coat pocket.

"Where are you going?" she asked.

"I've got to send a telegram or two. I've got arrangements to make. Get to it," he ordered and closed the door on her, leaving her blinking in a state of shock.

Her knees buckled, and she grabbed hold of her chair and plunked down. She'd lost control of the conversation. Somehow she was going to Farewell Bend—to get married. She realized, of course, he hadn't asked—she was told. She put her hand to her mouth to stifle a giggle.

Twenty minutes later, her reflection told her, *too severe*. She pulled a few wisps of hair out from the snood and let them fan about her ears, forehead, and temple.

Her reflection nodded in approval. *Yes, that's better, perfect for traveling.*

Considering her reflection, she looked like a woman who'd spent the night making love. There was a softness...a dreamy look on her face. She smiled at herself. Her cheeks glowed.

"Hey, let's go," Elias hollered from the other side of her door.

Irene jumped into action, donned her violet dress, tucked a creamy lace fichu in the neckline, and pulled her blue cape with the fur collar out of her wardrobe. She would take her brown skirt and coral blouse for a change of clothes.

The ceremony? She wondered if they would recite their vows to a judge or minister?

She dumped the yarn out of her knitting bag on her bed and stuffed it with extra underclothes and stockings, opened her door, and stood framed in the doorway, her bulging, battered knitting bag clutched in her hand.

"You are a beautiful woman, Irene," Elias declared, his voice husky, his eyes full of desire—desire for her. "Did I mention I love you?" He crossed the room and took the bag from her, then pulled her into his chest with his free arm. Their gazes locked, intense, full of heat and need.

"This is crazy, Elias," she said, finding it hard to swallow and forgetting to breathe. "Kids run off and get married. We're old, old enough to control ourselves— way past the age where we lose our heads."

"Hmmm, I didn't know there was an age limit on this sort of thing," he said and attacked her earlobe.

"Enough," he said and pushed himself away, "we better get going. I told Doctor Carter to set up the ceremony for five o'clock."

"Elias, it's already nine-thirty."

Taking out his pocket watch, he corrected, "Nine thirty-seven, to be precise."

"We should get going then," Irene said and headed

for the door.

"Not so fast." His hand snagged her by her skirt and tugged her back.

"What?"

"Well, my dear, I won't haul a woman off to the altar unless I'm certain of her heart. You know I love you, but I'm not at all certain of your feelings. I know you lust after my body."

Irene gave him a punch in the shoulder, giggled, and shook her head at him and his silly smirk. She sobered and made herself look him in the eye. Trying hard to keep a straight face, she said, "Elias Rayburn, I'll spend the rest of my life loving you. I admire you. I trust you, and I love everything about you, your mind, your heart, and yes, I do love your body. So much so I've endured many a sleepless night because you were so close and yet out of reach."

"Have you, now?" he said, drawing her close, about to start kissing her again.

"No. No, now, Elias, remember the time. We have to go, right?"

Frustrated, he growled, straightened, and took her by the elbow, guiding her outside to his waiting buggy.

Chapter Twenty-Three

"Married? Mama and Doctor Rayburn? No, he wouldn't want to marry her. Why would he want to marry her?" Odessa closed her eyes and swayed. George stepped forward, ready to catch her.

In a fit of pique, she wadded up the telegram and threw it on the ground, and with the heel of her shoe, she ground it into the dust.

"My wedding! Should've been me getting married, me and Silas," she said. Fighting to keep her balance, she swatted George out of her way. "Mama's too old to have feelings…too old to be getting married again. She's never wanted me to have anything."

"For a valk, ve should go down to da creek, Miss Odessa? Maybe stick our toes in da vater?"

Odessa blinked and came back to the real world. George was there. He was always there. She heaved a resigned sigh. He'd said something. What, she couldn't say. It was hard to remember to breathe with the baby kicking at her all the time.

Looking at him, she marveled—God—he was a big man. If only he didn't dress so funny. She supposed it was hard to find clothes to fit him. He had good eyes. She couldn't resist his smile; it was almost childlike in its innocence.

Nothing seemed to touch George. He'd never succumb to rage or frustration. She didn't think a simple

283

man like George would ever know what it was like to want something so bad it was a physical ache—she envied him.

All the proof the world needed as to the extent of her stupidity was this…this *child*…the living evidence of her folly. This child would forever be her albatross.

The final slap in her face was the telegram. Her mother had married Doctor Rayburn. Her mother, at last happy now she, her no-good daughter, was gone from the house, out of the way.

"Down to the creek, I thought maybe a valk, Miss Odessa. Vould you like dat?" George repeated.

"Yes," Odessa agreed. Blinking back her tears, she swallowed the cold hard lump in her throat. "I'm too hot, and the creek would be nice."

"Good, den," George said, his smile back in place and his blue eyes twinkling with good humor.

He turned and waved to Sam and Ruby, "Okay, down to da creek ve go for a little vhile."

****

Blue skirt hiked up to her calves, Odessa watched George gingerly put his big, bare feet in the stream one toe at a time. She hid her smirk behind her hand. The water was colder than one would expect, and the day was hot for October. There was fresh snow on the mountains, which reminded her of the seconds, the hours, the days, and the weeks ahead that propelled her, against her will, closer and closer to motherhood. Her joy in the moment paled at the thought.

George hissed. Up to his ankles in the mountain stream, he began to move about a little. "You know I got big ears."

"What?" she asked.

"Big ears for listening—you could talk, I could listen."

"Oh." Looking at him, Odessa thought his ears were nice, not too big, not too small—manly ears—handsome ears, she would have to say. While she studied his face and his hair, George bent down and fished out a rock crystal. Holding it up to the sun, he examined it, then handed it to her.

For a moment, gazing at the beauty of the rock, feeling its sharp planes and turning it to see into its facets, Odessa forgot her troubles. When she looked up, George stood watching her, warmth in his eyes. His admiration reminded her of who and what she was—she was fat, she was used goods, and George was a fool. Bitterness consumed her. Feeling particularly vengeful, she tossed the beautiful rock back into the stream. She turned her back on him and climbed the bank to sit in the shade of a willow.

George stayed in the water, peering down, looking for the crystal. Finding it, he put it in his pocket and sat next to her on the bank. Legs bare up to her thighs, Odessa gave no thought to George being a threat to her virtue. No, George was like the trees or the stones in the creek—he was just there.

"I don't understand it, George. Why would Doctor Rayburn want to marry my mother? Why would she want to marry Doctor Rayburn? She doesn't like men. She doesn't trust them. We're alike, you know. We don't have any luck with men. Mama doesn't like anybody, really."

"You don't tink your mama should be married lady again?"

"I don't care if she is or isn't," Odessa said, her chin

out, nose in the air. "What she does doesn't concern me, not anymore. I don't care," Odessa said, drawing circles in the dirt with her toe.

"Yah, vell, maybe dis is a good ting. You like the doctor, I tink. Maybe he vill be a good ting for your mama. She's had a load, vorkin' and keepin' food on da table and clothes on your back. Sometimes vin a body has to vorry about dat, dey don't have so much time for fun. Now she von't have so much vorry vit da doctor dare. So all dah time she don't have to vork. And maybe you von't have so much vorry if da doctor is dare for you too."

Drawing her legs up to her chest, Odessa folded her arms around her knees and put her head down. "I don't know what to think. I haven't gotten anything right for years."

George's hand hovered above her bowed head. Odessa leaned in and burrowed her face into his broad chest. George folded his arms about her, and for a few moments in time, Odessa allowed herself to be held, consoled.

****

After spending a week in Farewell Bend, Irene and Elias arrived home and found a bottle of wine and a note on their doorstep.

Doc, you took your sweet time, but I knew I wasn't wrong when I sent you back out in the snow that night. The note was signed, *Meda-Belle.*

Irene insisted Elias tell her what, exactly, had transpired at the boarding house upon his first night in Meadow View, and how was it he'd gone to the boarding house in the first place?

Blushing, he recounted every detail, including

descriptions of the costumes the ladies wore and at what point it had dawned on him he'd stepped into a bordello. By the time he was through, Irene was gasping for air, laughing so hard her sides ached.

When she could breathe again, Irene recounted her initial interview with Meda-Belle, and how she'd barely escaped becoming one of Mrs. Lamphere's new recruits.

Every day, their first week home, they entertained well-wishers—the Laidlaws, the Bodemans, Laura and Tom Kelsey, the Meltons, and, of course, Barclay Russell and Mary. The whole town was pleased with their union. Every single one of them wanted to know why it had taken them so long to get the deed done, which made Irene feel more than a little ashamed for being so blind-stubborn.

She lay in her husband's arms, under the warm down coverlet in her big bed, in the room she swore she'd never sleep in again, and marveled at how sweet her life had become. The only dark spot was Odessa.

"I thought she would have come home by now."

"You heard what George said. She doesn't know what to think. That's a good sign she hasn't closed her mind entirely," Elias said. He ran his finger over her temple, to her jaw and down her throat to her collarbone.

Eyes closed to savor his touch, gooseflesh bloomed, and a wave of delight rippled through her body, yet Irene managed a reply, "Well, she should be home. She should be here. She's going to need you...and...I hope she will need me."

He found her breast, and his fingers toyed with her nipple. Irene put her hand over his to stop him. "I want to be with her when she has the baby, Elias. I'm going to go see her."

****

"We'll both go. Tomorrow, but don't expect too much." He drew her closer. He couldn't believe it was really true—they were married. This last week, Irene had surprised him every day—she was funny, warm, and passionate, and every night he'd gone to sleep believing he couldn't possibly be any happier than he was at that moment. He thought it idiotic, but he wanted to touch her all the time, hold her. She was like a magnet; he couldn't stay away from her for more than a few minutes.

As for Odessa, Elias was doubtful she would come home anytime soon. To do so would mean facing her mistakes…facing the truth of her situation as a woman alone with a child. He didn't think Odessa was ready for that, and to say the truth, he didn't know if she ever would be.

****

Ruby and Odessa were gathering eggs and feeding the chickens when Elias and Irene pulled into the yard. Heavy clouds scudded across the sky, and a cold wind tickled the pine branches and made the skin tingle.

The Trask farm, situated in a draw along Drift Creek, had escaped the fires, the meadow grass, still green, the pines tall, untouched, stately. The willows and golden aspen had started to lose their leaves—signs fall had arrived.

Irene waved at Ruby, who'd put down the pan of feed on a nearby stump to come out to greet them. Odessa, Irene saw, stood in the doorway of the chicken coop, looking mulish. Irene couldn't take her eyes off of her daughter and her rounding figure. Tears welled up in her eyes, and she tried to smile. Quickly, she hopped down from the buggy, greeted Ruby with a hug, and rushed past her to the chicken pen.

"Hello," she said through the chicken wire.

****

"Hello," Odessa said. Apprehensive, on the defensive, Odessa hid her mixed emotions of shame, blame, fear, and sorrow behind an outwardly bland façade. Inside she was startled, surprised by the transformation. Irene was beautiful. Odessa had to look down at the dirt to keep from staring. Her mother looked so young. Her hair, her complexion, the expression on her face, the twinkle in her eyes made her look so young. Gone was the weary look of disappointment. This was not the pained, tight-lipped woman Odessa held in her mind's-eye.

Why? How? Could it be Doctor Rayburn's doing—was it love?

The idea sickened her…she wanted to scream, run, hit, and hurt.

"How are you feeling?" her mother asked, her brown eyes swimming in tears.

"Okay, I guess," Odessa answered, her throat constricted with emotion.

"You look well," she said, a little smile hovering on her lips.

Unable to stand it any longer, Odessa snorted and remembered her mother didn't give a damn about her. Why should she? She approached the chicken-pen gate, pushed it open, forcing her mother to step aside. Locking the gate behind her, she faced her mother. "What do you care how I feel?"

It pleased Odessa to see the stricken look in her mother's eyes. Good. She wanted to lash out, hurt someone, her mother most of all.

"Odessa, of course I care."

Odessa didn't wait to hear more—she didn't want to hear anything her mother had to say—didn't want to hear the excuses, the lies. Quickly, she marched into the house, aware her mother and Doctor Rayburn followed on her heels.

"Sit down, Irene," Ruby invited, "have some tea. Would you like some, Doctor Rayburn?"

"In a bit—first, I'd like to check on you, Odessa," he said, following Odessa across the room. "I want to see how you and the baby are doing."

"We're doing fine," Odessa said. Arms folded protectively over her abdomen, she backed into a shadow-filled corner.

"I think you are, but I'd like to check on you and the baby all the same, to be sure," he said and moved closer to her. Holding her in his gaze, he put out his hand. "Wouldn't you like to hear the baby's heartbeat?"

"God, no!" she said, shaking her head. Appalled by the very notion, Odessa found the fact of the life growing inside her frightening, terrifying.

The walls closed in on her. There wasn't enough air in the room. The doctor went on to say, "You don't have to. I thought you might be interested. He or she's got all their fingers and toes. And if you'd allow me to listen for a minute, I can tell you approximately how big the baby is."

Odessa closed her eyes and gulped for air. She felt Doctor Elias's hand go to her shoulder, then move to her back to stroke her in lazy circles. His voice soothed her, encouraged her to take deep, slow breaths. Some of her panic began to ebb. His hand on her back went away and came under her chin, forcing her to look into his eyes.

"How's your appetite? Are you drinking lots of water? Is there any swelling?"

"Just my belly," she said, resisting the temptation to stick her tongue out at him.

He smiled down at her, placed his stethoscope around his neck. There didn't seem to be anyone else in the room now, just the doctor and herself. She no longer felt threatened or cornered, only defenseless, like a leaf in a gale, unable to help herself—going with the wind.

Forgetting to be surly, she offered him a weak little smile and confessed, "I've got sour belches, especially at night when I lie down and he starts doing a jig."

****

Overhearing, Irene tilted her head to the side to see around Elias. "I had the same problem when I was carrying you. Every night I was bilious something awful."

Elias said, "He's starting to get big enough that he's pushing on your stomach and esophagus, and when you lie down there's more room for him to stretch. I think I have something for the sour stomach. Be sure you stop eating a couple of hours before bed; that will help. And cut back on the high acid foods. Now…will you allow me to examine you?"

Automatically, Odessa nodded before she found the words to object.

"In your room would be best."

****

Irene watched them disappear behind the curtain beyond the kitchen. She wanted to go too. She wanted to hear what Elias had to say, but instead she sat at the rough-hewn dining table and accepted a cup of Ruby's tea.

Ruby put her hand on Irene's arm. "Don't you fret. She's eatin' and sleepin' fine. And if my guess is right, we're gonna be grandparents of a fine healthy boy."

"A boy? You really think so?"

"I know," Ruby stated emphatically.

"No one can really know," Irene said, amusement in her voice.

"Well, I know. It's a boy."

"How could you know that?"

"I tied my wedding ring on a string…"

"Ruby, not that old wives' tale?"

"It works. I've been right thirteen times. Twice with my boys and four times with my sister's children—two boys and two girls—Doris Melton's two children.

"Doris? You did that for Doris?"

Ruby nodded proudly. "Yup, a boy and a girl, and my cousin Wanda had three babies—a boy and two girls. My sister's neighbor's girl had two girls. If Mary Russell has a girl, like I predict, and Odessa has a boy, I'll be up fifteen straight."

"Mary Russell is expecting?" Irene asked. Her giggle bubbled out of her like an artesian well, and she covered her mouth. "Oh, I am sorry, but how wonderful is life, anyway?"

Ruby laughed with her. "Barclay and Mary were out here last week. Sam sold them some laying hens and a couple weaner pigs. Mary and I talked; she was bustin' to tell someone. I guess she won't be teachin' school, after all." The news set Irene off again, and Ruby joined her.

When Ruby could finally catch her breath, she said, "Nope, Mary won't be teachin' school, I don't think, not if Sarah Laidlaw gets wind she's in a family way. Poor

Mary, she'll never hear the end of it from that quarter. I can hear Sarah now."

Her nose wrinkled up and her lips pursed, Ruby gave her impersonation of Sarah Laidlaw, and a very good one it was. "*It's against the rules for married ladies to teach school…and for this very reason.*"

Irene, giggling, didn't comment. She was distracted as Elias came out of the back room and sat down across from her.

"Did you talk to her about coming home?" Irene asked.

He laid his hand over hers and shook his head.

Irene sighed and huffed with impatience.

"I couldn't, Irene. She's too frightened. Right now, it's more important to get her prepared to give birth," he said.

"Odessa should be home with us. Once there, *we*…you and I could help her."

"Is that why you came out here, to drag me home?"

Irene looked up, and there was Odessa a couple feet from the table, the familiar hate-filled gleam in her eyes. Irene drew herself up from the waist, calmed her instinct to go on the defensive. "I don't want to *drag* you anywhere, and certainly not home if you don't want to come. I want you to *want* to come home."

"I can take care of myself," Odessa said, her jaw set.

"You have family, me, and now Elias, we want to help you, support you. You need us. You need all of us, Ruby and Sam too. You're not alone, Odessa."

Ruby interjected, "And George."

Irene, taken aback, pivoted her head, an unspoken question to Ruby.

"George," Ruby said and nodded to Irene's silent

question.

Her gaze once again on her daughter, Irene added, "And George too. We all care about you, and we will all stand by you and the baby."

Irene could see it wasn't enough to convince her, so she added, "I'm sorry I kept your papa's death from you. I was wrong. I can't take back what I did, and I won't try to explain why I did it."

Odessa stuck out her stubborn chin. "You did it because you think I'm a child."

"No, I know you're not a child. I was being selfish. I am selfish. I'm working on myself." Sensing this was no time to hold back, she further confessed to everyone present, "I was afraid of losing Elias."

Odessa blinked, her gaze darted first to Elias, then back to Irene. "Afraid of losing…you were afraid of losing a man, a man you love?" Odessa laughed mirthlessly. "That explains everything, yes. The question is, can you understand what I did, Mother? Can you?"

Interrupting, no doubt hoping to derail the direction the conversation had taken, Elias interceded, "Odessa, we would like you to come home. If not today, then soon, before the baby gets here."

Irene came to Odessa and reached for her hand to look straight into her beautiful sad eyes. "We've both done and said things we regret, Odessa. I know there are things I…I haven't done that I should have. It's not too late, Odessa. I'd like another chance to be the mother you need. Elias is right. Maybe today isn't the right time, but soon, Odessa, please."

Chapter Twenty-Four

Elias reluctantly left Irene to go to Redmond on his rounds the first week of January. He'd begun to think Odessa wouldn't be home before the baby was born. Ruby was a competent midwife, and Odessa was in good hands should he be gone when her labor started.

He said as much to Irene, but she wasn't having any of it, wearing herself out arranging and rearranging Odessa's room. After emptying out one of her bureaus, she had him move it into Odessa's room, then she brought in the old cradle that her babies had used into Odessa's room and set it beside the bed. The cradle that George had made went into the sitting room...then she exchanged it for the old cradle. One thing Elias knew for sure, in Irene's mind there was no doubt Odessa and her baby would come home and soon. He prayed she was right.

****

A telegram for Irene arrived three days after Elias left, informing her he'd be home late the next evening, God willing.

They'd been in a deep, dry, sub-zero freeze, but today it had warmed ten degrees and started to snow. The wind had picked up. Irene worried there was a blizzard coming, which could delay Elias's homecoming. At two o'clock in the afternoon, dark clouds gathered to the north, the sky incredibly dark. She had three lanterns lit, two fireplaces going, the new cook stove stoked to the maximum, and still she felt chilled to the bone. By four o'clock a full-force gale was blowing. The pines were whipped by the will of the elements, and the wind pushed a draft down the chimney throats. The house filled with a light haze of smoke.

The front door blew open, a plume of white snow billowed in, and there stood George Krauss, looming large, covered in snow, his face hidden behind a wool muffler, stocking cap down low on his forehead and over his ears. In his arms was her daughter, well protected in three wool blankets and a down comforter.

"George, my God!" Irene cried and rushed to close the door behind him. "Get in here and get to the fire."

Odessa poked her head out of the comforter, snow plopping to the floor. "I wanted to come home today," she said.

Alarmed, Irene asked, "Are you having labor pains, Odessa?"

Teeth chattering with cold, Odessa shook her head to reply, "No."

But once Irene had the comforter away from her face the better to see into her eyes, Odessa wavered. "I don't know, maybe. I hurt all the time. I can't tell anymore. I can't stand up straight, but I've been like that for a week."

George set Odessa down on her feet and swayed back on his heels. Eyes closing for a second, he braced himself against the closed door.

Irene extended her hand. "George, you get over to the fire. There's hot coffee on the side arm. Help yourself."

Irene began to divest Odessa of the layers of

insulation she had around her. "Where does it hurt?" Irene asked.

"Down low, in front," Odessa said. Irene picked up the blankets and draped them over the back of a kitchen chair.

Breathing a sigh of relief, keeping her thoughts to herself—*no, not labor, but a prelude of things to come.*

George rubbed his hands together over the fire.

"Take your coat off, George. I'll get you a cup," Irene said and guided Odessa to the settee in front of the hearth.

George shook his head and put back on his gloves. "A valise I got to bring in. Better I see to da horse, ma'am. Can't leave him standing out in da storm. To da livery, I'll take him. Mr. Pederson, he'll let me bed down dare. I'll come back dis evening."

Hands on her hips, Irene said, "Don't be daft. You can't go back out there, George. You will have some coffee and a hot meal. You certainly can't stay in a barn tonight. You'd freeze. It's bad enough the animals have to. There's room for the horse in the shed, and feed. We have lots of room here. I'd feel better if you stayed."

Looking to Odessa, Irene expected to find her ready to back her up, but she sat warming herself, unconcerned, before the fire. Looking back at George, Irene caught him smiling. He hunched his shoulders and left before she could thank him. Irene stood seething, appalled at her daughter's total disregard.

"Odessa, whatever possessed you to make George bring you home today, of all days? It's so miserable outside."

"Well, it's good to be home, thank you," Odessa snapped.

Irene took a moment to breathe and check the rebuke she wanted to give. "Yes, it is very good to have you home. I've been waiting for you, expecting you every day." Irene wrapped her arms around her daughter and held her tenderly. The girl tipped her head away to the side, unyielding. Irene sighed and let her go. "If I'd known you were out in this weather, I would've been so very worried. You both could have frozen to death, Odessa—poor George."

"I had to get out of there," Odessa said and stood up to put her backside to the fire. "Sam and Ruby are sweet, and they're generous and kind, but as the weather closed in, they started bickering and fussing—if it hadn't been for George coming out the last few weeks to play checkers or just talk, I would've walked home weeks ago."

Irene sank down beside Odessa. She had to laugh. *Weeks ago.* Odessa would've been home weeks ago if George hadn't kept her such good company.

"I almost walked home one day," Odessa confessed and stretched her toes out to the fire. "George came out, and we went for a walk in the snow, so I could get out of the house and away for a little while. He came out this morning to help Sam slaughter hogs. I packed up, and by the time he was ready to leave, I'd said my thanks to Ruby and Sam, and here I am."

Irene shook her head to dislodge the chastisements she wanted very much to give her daughter. Relaxing the tension in her neck, she decided to take the more political approach. "It's wonderful you're home, but Odessa, you should tell George thank you for delivering you safely. At least tell him he must stay here tonight.. he can't go back out there."

Her gaze going to the door, Odessa seemed to at last take note George was no longer in the room. "Yes, I suppose, but I don't think George minds the weather or the cold," she said and sat by Irene, holding out her hands, rubbing them together. "He said it's much colder in North Dakota where he was born. He's always doing stuff for everybody. He was out to help Sam at least two, three times a week."

Irene, about to suggest George didn't come out to do...*stuff*...for Sam, but came out to see her when the object of their discussion returned with his bedroll under one arm and Odessa's things under the other. He looked more like a walking snowdrift than a human being.

Jumping to her feet, Irene took command of the situation. "Odessa, get George some coffee. Put those things anywhere, George. There's a bottle of rum in the larder behind the cracker box tin. Odessa, put some in George's coffee."

Pushing the man toward the fire, Irene said, "I'm going to help you get out of these things. We need blankets, Odessa. Can you feel your toes, George—your fingers?"

Irene looked to Odessa, who was taking her time pouring the rum into the coffee mug. "The extra bedroom has blankets in the chiffonier. Bring them here." She turned her attention back to George. "We have to get these boots off, George." His pant legs and the laces on his boots were caked with snow and ice. It was not easy to remove his boots. "I'm going to get you some dry clothes, George. I'll be right back."

Odessa returned with the blankets. "Help George with his buttons. I bet his fingers aren't working too well. We need to warm them up slowly. We'll try a pan of tepid water for his feet."

****

Odessa set the blankets on the kitchen table and pulled one out of the stack to bring over to him. "She's as bossy as ever," she said. George grinned at her and tried to unbutton his mackinaw, but it was no use. His fingers wouldn't bend.

"Here, I'll do that," she said and pushed his hands away and shoved the blanket into his chest.

"You take after your mama," George said, a pleased smirk on his face.

"I do, do I? Then you mind me and get this coffee cup in your hands, then maybe you can thaw out and do your own darn buttons," she said and tugged on one sleeve, then the other, to divest him of his coat. She was about to unbutton his trousers, but George's ice-cold hand stopped her.

"I tink maybe I better do for myself now."

Odessa giggled. "Are you blushing, George, or are your cheeks just red from cold?"

He scowled at her, unusual for George. Odessa knew she wasn't helping matters by laughing at him.

"You like to tease me, but you shouldn't take off a man's trousers. It yust ain't proper."

"Quite right, George," her mother confirmed, coming from her big bedroom with a dry pair of socks and a big flannel shirt. "Odessa, you and I will make up the bed in the spare room for George while he gets out of his snowy trousers."

To George, her mother said, "You wrap one of those blankets around your middle until your trousers get dry. Sing out when you're ready."

"Tank you, Mrs. Doctor."

Odessa fought back the urge to stick her tongue out at him for being so darned polite to her overbearing mother.

****

"Your room is ready for you…and the baby," Irene said as they spread the flannel sheets on what would be George's bed. "But it's so cold. Why don't you sleep with me tonight? Elias is on rounds and won't be back until later tomorrow. George could probably take this bed out to the living room and set it up before the fire. Remember when we used to sleep out there? No wood, no sawdust under the rug. I was so scared, full of fear, beside myself with worry."

Odessa stopped and straightened to rub her back. "I remember our beds out there. But I didn't know you were afraid."

Irene plumped the feather pillow, then put her hands on her hips. "Well, I was scared to death all the time. We were almost out of food, only a handful of raisins left. I didn't know what to do. I hated sleeping in the big room in the cold bed without your father. Even when our food got low, and we were down to a couple of sticks, I felt better sleeping out there on our little cots before a cold fire with you next to me. You were my reason to keep going. When I was in the big room alone, it was too easy to cry and feel sorry for myself."

Irene had her daughter's attention now, and Odessa asked, "You cried?"

"I liked to never stop crying,' Irene said and shook out the comforter and smoothed out the wrinkles. "Any little thing could set me off. I found one of your daddy's buttons from one of his shirts one afternoon while you were at school, and I didn't think I was going to stop. I

301

think I used to tell you I had a cold."

"You always had a cold," Odessa said and sat down on the bed. "Why didn't you let me see you cry? I cried all the time too. We could have cried together."

Sitting on the other side of the bed to face her, Irene disclosed her regrets, "Yes, yes, I know that now. I was being selfish again. I thought I was protecting you. I thought I had to keep my fears a secret, put on a brave front, and keep things as normal as possible. We—I—didn't give you a chance to grieve for the loss of your father. We could have done that together. I'm sorry. Parents make a lot of mistakes, for the right reasons, but mistakes all the same."

"You sure you want me to sleep with you? I'm so big," Odessa said, her face all scrunched up into a frown.

Irene smiled at her and said, "You're not so big. You just feel big."

"I don't sleep very well. It's hard to get comfortable, and I always have to go, you know what I mean?"

"I do indeed. It's awful, isn't it? I'll fix you a cup of chamomile tea. That used to help you sleep, and we'll keep the thunder mug close to your side of the bed so you won't have to go far. We'll warm our bed with hot bricks, and we'll be snug. I venture we'll both get a good night's sleep tonight."

Odessa's eyes were wide, a far-off look in them, and she said more to herself than to Irene, "I remember your tea. Funny, I hadn't thought of it for a long time. It's nice to be home."

Irene smiled. Tears welled up in her eyes, and she threw her arms around Odessa and drew her close, holding her tight. At first, Odessa remained rigid in her embrace, then she relaxed her shoulders, and Irene began to think there might be a glimmer of hope for them after all.

Chapter Twenty-Five

After breakfast, young Hubert Laidlaw delivered a telegram to Irene from Elias. Due to weather conditions, his arrival home would be delayed at least one more day. Two feet of snow covered the ground between Meadow View and Redmond in some places, according to the stage driver, Puffer Clark, who'd told Mr. Laidlaw, who'd told his son Hubert, who was running all over town spreading the word like the town crier. In short, the roads were impassable. Everyone had holed up where they were, and—God willing—that was somewhere warm and dry.

Thanks to George, the wood box was full, the water barrel was full, the cow was milked and fed, and the morning wasn't even half over. When George offered to take the boarding house laundry over to Meda-Belle, Irene was grateful and glad to see him go. He filled up a room with his restlessness.

Odessa sat before the fire, giving the appearance of being busy, but Irene suspected the sock she was mending wasn't getting very many stitches. From time to time, Irene heard her sigh and noticed with each sigh, she shifted positions and rubbed her back. Her face puckered up into a scowl, and Irene couldn't tell if she was impatient with her mending or with her discomfort. Probably both, Irene decided.

When George returned, he did what he could to coax

Odessa into a better frame of mind. He joked with her and sang to her, and recited bawdy poetry to her. Irene blushed at his poetry, but the sight of Odessa smiling and giggling caused Irene to be more tolerant than she might have been otherwise.

While George kept Odessa entertained, Irene read Elias's notes in her daughter's file. Odessa was due to deliver the second week in January. It was January 12. Looking out the bedroom window, Irene saw nothing but ice and snow. Elias could not possibly get home in weather like this.

She had to face the facts. It could very well be she would have to deliver her own daughter's baby. Delivering babies was something she'd done several times, but not on her own. Elias had been there to guide and assist. And there was the added fact of George Krauss. Irene couldn't help but think he should be elsewhere. He wasn't the father. And, then again, George might be better than no assistance at all.

A warm wind began to blow in the early hours before dawn of the following day. She lay listening to the steady drip, drip of the snow melting off the roof. Closing her eyes, she thanked God for the sudden thaw. Elias would start for home today.

Shortly after noon, news arrived in Meadow View of the flash flood at Tumalo. George reported, after a visit to the livery, that Drift Creek had turned into a roaring rapid, overflowing its banks, the water the color of creamed coffee. The sun came up warm and bright, shooting the temperature up to nearly seventy degrees by mid-morning.

No word came from Elias.

George left them to help the men of the town place

sandbags at the edge of the creek at the school. He checked in at noon to let them know Sam and Ruby were sitting on an island at their place, but they were doing all right.

****

The sensation of warm sticky fluid running down her legs gave Odessa cause to panic. Irene tried to explain what was happening, but Odessa couldn't hear her own screams and curses.

"I have to go somewhere...get out of here," Odessa said. "I can't do this...I won't do it. I don't want to. I don't want to."

Using considerable force, Irene stopped her from putting on her coat and walking out the door. Odessa shook her off and whirled around. "You don't understand. I can't do it. I can't do it. I don't want it. Without Silas...I don't want it," she said and slumped down in the nearest chair, shaking with rage and fear.

"It wasn't supposed to happen this way." Odessa sobbed into her hands. "I was going to get out of here, get away from this town. Silas was supposed to love me."

Kneeling before her, her mother took her in her arms. "I know the dream, sweetheart. I know the dream. Listen to me," her mother asked, giving her a little shake, "listen carefully...Odessa...listen now. The baby...*your* baby is coming today. It wouldn't matter where you went, you can't run away from it...or ignore it...the baby is on his way."

Odessa tried to look anywhere but into her mother's eyes. She didn't want to hear it, didn't want to believe it. With hands on either side of Odessa's face, Irene forced her to look into her eyes and see the truth.

Her mother smiled, and Odessa fought the urge to

306

slap her.

Then her mother asked the question that drove away all her panic, "We haven't had a chance to talk about it, but do you have a name for the baby?"

Odessa squeezed her eyes shut and gulped as two huge tears dribbled down her cheeks and off her chin. She swiped at her runny nose with the back of her hand. "Ruby wanted to name him Carlo after her papa, and Sam wanted to name him Jacob after his daddy. But I don't like those names."

"You're pretty certain it's a boy?" her mother asked, a gentle, coaxing smile on her lips and in her eyes. She helped Odessa to her feet, and they started to move toward her bedroom.

"Ruby said it was a boy. You don't think it could be a girl, do you?"

"It could be a girl," her mother said and laughed. "But Ruby's wedding ring on a string has a reputation for accuracy. We'll soon find out, I think. If it's a girl, we'll have to put some lace on all those blue gowns you and Ruby made. Are you feeling any twinges yet?"

"No, I feel fine…ugh…oh…" Holding tight, Odessa clutched at her mother's hand. Her other hand reached out and clawed at the kitchen table. Holding on to her mother, it was all Odessa could do to remember to breathe through the onslaught of the contraction that crested, then ebbed away.

"That was more than a twinge," her mother said. "You walk around if you feel like it. Sometimes it feels better to move around between contractions. And you can use the table or a chair to hold onto when the contractions come. You need to change your clothes. Put on one of your nightgowns and warm stockings. I think it'll be a while yet, so do what feels right." Odessa nodded and started for her bedroom and fresh clothes.

****

Irene watched the girl stand for a few moments in her doorway, feet apart, one hand braced on the door jamb and the other on her back as another contraction plowed into her body. As soon as it was over, she disappeared.

In her nightdress, a wool shawl around her shoulders, Odessa made it to the settee before another contraction sucked the wind out of her.

"You're doing great, honey. Really good. I'm going into the doctor's office now to get things set up in there."

Irene, heating the water, heard Odessa moan. She turned around and found Odessa bent over, going down on her knees. Irene came to her side and rubbed her back while the contraction ripped through Odessa's body.

"Maybe it won't be so long after all," Irene said, trying not to show her panic. She needed to do an examination to check the degree of dilation. They were both going to have to overcome their awkwardness with one another, and Odessa had to trust her. Irene had to trust herself before she could convince Odessa, and it was important to do so quickly.

The examination table was ready. For the past thirty minutes, she'd surreptitiously timed the contractions. The labor had progressed rapidly. Irene remembered being in labor with Odessa, and this was almost a repeat of that experience. Once the water broke, not more than three hours passed before she delivered.

"I need to examine you," Irene said and helped her up from the chair before the fire.

"Examine me? Why? Why would you examine me?

Doctor Rayburn, I mean Doctor Elias, will examine me. The doctor will do that."

"Elias isn't here, and I don't think he'll get here before you deliver. You're well along now. Together we'll deliver your baby, Odessa."

"You can't deliver my baby."

Trying to sound confident and not on the defensive, Irene stated, "I can and I will. I've helped deliver several babies…I know how it's done."

"But Doctor Rayburn was there with you. He isn't here yet. We have to wait until he gets here."

"We can only wait as long as the baby waits," Irene pointed out. "When it's time…it's time. This baby won't wait any longer than nature allows, and there is nothing to stop him. Now come over here and get up on the table and let me see how far along you are."

Irene could feel the baby's head and knew things would move quickly now the baby was in place. Odessa, in the throes of a pushing contraction, probably didn't hear a word. But Irene, speaking softly, placed her hand on Odessa's abdomen. "Don't try to stop it or control the feeling…the need to push, you push…breathe and push. Good, you're doing very well."

The hour went by in a rush of concentration and agony. Odessa screamed and wailed against the pain and injustice of her plight. And Irene, sweat dripping into her eyes, prayed she was doing it right.

The baby boy entered the world at 6:35 p.m., on January 13, 1902. Irene cut the cord and wept. He weighed in at seven pounds, four and a half ounces.

Odessa, grateful to have expelled the cause of her torment, began to laugh hysterically.

"Look who come in on a freight wagon?" George

bellowed, bursting through the front door of the house with Elias in tow.

"Elias," Irene called out. "In here. Odessa…help her, Elias. I've got the baby." In Irene's mind, it would never be clear what George said to calm Odessa. She was simply grateful he was there, and Odessa listened to him.

While she cleaned the baby, Elias helped Odessa expel the afterbirth. George moved Odessa to her own bed in her room, and Irene dazed and humbled, followed with the baby cradled in her arms.

Alone, with the baby lying next to Odessa, Irene bathed her and helped her into a clean gown. "He's pretty, isn't he?" Odessa said, her head turned to the side, gazing at her child through weary eyes.

Irene pulled the covers up around her and the baby and smiled down at the newborn. He had a peach complexion, his skin smooth and delicate. He had a shock of black hair that lay close to his perfectly shaped head. He was a long baby, a string bean, Irene thought, long legs and torso, even his hands and fingers were long. Irene guessed he would grow up to be tall. "He's very pretty," she agreed, wonder revealed in her voice and a bit of reverence. "I don't suppose he would appreciate us saying so. He looks to be all *boy* to me."

The baby stretched in Odessa's arms, his face scrunched up, his lips formed a perfect pout, and he let out a lusty wail. "Maybe he would like to nurse?" Irene suggested. "Let's see if you have something for him."

Irene started to help Odessa bare her breast, but Odessa stopped her and pushed herself away from the baby. Irene paid no attention and began to unbutton her nightgown.

"I don't want to, Mama. Can't I try it later?"

"I don't think he's going to let you wait. It's very simple and extremely convenient. You'll see. You let him do the work, and you relax. He already knows what to do. I should imagine he's been sucking on his thumb for a couple of months, practicing."

Irene stood back and watched Odessa try to get the baby to suckle, but mother and baby soon became very frustrated. He was screaming and, Irene thought, Odessa was on the verge of screaming too. She showed Odessa how to get him to latch onto her nipple, and the baby settled down contentedly, but Irene could tell by the disgusted expression on her face, Odessa was not comfortable with the arrangement.

"You don't need to do it too long on one side. Switch him over in a few minutes. Keep tickling his cheek to keep him awake. That's right, now you've got it. You are very good at this. Breathe, sweetheart, and enjoy it. They don't stay this tiny for very long. Soon enough, he'll be crawling around, and you won't be able to cuddle him like this."

"I can't nurse him and tickle him at the same time," Odessa complained. "How can he breathe? I'll smother him. I'm going to fall asleep on him. I hate it when he cries…he's so loud."

Irene felt herself getting impatient. Sorry for her tone, she said, "He's going to cry, Odessa. He can't talk. It's his way of letting you know he needs your attention." She took a breath and schooled her irritation. "You'll learn to read his wants by his cry, and you'll soon know when he's serious and when he's fussing for no good cause."

Thinking to distract her from this foreign task, Irene said, "We can't keep calling him *he* or *the baby*. What is his name? Did you think of one?"

She was relieved to see Odessa relax a little. Awkwardly, she tickled her son's cheek. Odessa beamed, and Irene sniffed back a tear of pride as the child began to suck more vigorously. After a few moments, they changed him to the other breast, and Irene stood back as Odessa successfully placed him on the nipple.

Odessa drew the child in closer to her bosom, her gaze full of wonder. "I think he'll be Beau Morran Obenchain," she said. "Silas's middle name was Morran. It's a family name on Sam's side."

"I like that very much. Beau Morran, it suits him," Irene whispered and leaned over the two of them to stroke the child's forehead. He stopped sucking, smiled, then went back to work.

His suckling stopped, the nipple in his mouth, a film of opaque, blue milk between his lips, Beau fell fast asleep. Odessa couldn't coax him to suckle more. She leaned back and heaved a sigh of relief.

"You should sleep now," Irene said. "For now, you sleep when he sleeps."

Odessa snuggled down into her covers and said, after a yawn, "I'm hungry."

"You rest, and I'll fix you something." Irene smiled, and before she could close the door, Odessa was asleep...like a baby.

Chapter Twenty-six

"You're wearing yourself out," Elias said while Irene served him breakfast. "At least let me hold Beau while you do that."

Irene, Beau cradled in her arms, stirred the pot of oatmeal. "I can handle the baby and serve you breakfast. Besides, it's done now," she said, closed her eyes, and took a breath. "I'm sorry. I didn't mean to snap at you." She set the bowl of cereal on the table.

Tired, yes, worn to the nub, yes. It wasn't Elias's fault. It didn't help that it was no one's fault but her own. Beau would be a month old tomorrow. Irene didn't know where the time had gone or how she'd gotten herself into this predicament.

At first, she thought to be available to help Odessa with the baby—show her how. However, once she demonstrated a procedure, such as burping, diapering, bathing, etc., Odessa proclaimed herself incompetent, begged Irene to do it rather than upset the baby.

The time for demonstrating long over, Irene had charge of everything, right down to catering Odessa's meals at all hours of the day and night to taking care of the extra laundry and housekeeping that goes along with an infant.

All the while, she, in her naïveté, kept right on believing any day Odessa would want to take over. Odessa, Irene presumed, would eventually want to claim her right to her creation.

But, so far, no sign of reclamation was forthcoming. As a matter of fact, day by day, more and more, as Irene took up the slack, Odessa distanced herself—sliding right back into her carefree, pre-motherhood life. It was awful, it was quicksand, and Irene was sinking deeper and deeper with no way out.

Each night after Elias fell asleep, Irene got up and opened their bedroom door a crack. She was alert to any sound and attuned to the baby's rhythm. If Beau woke up, she wanted to hear him. Usually, he would cry for a moment or two before Odessa came awake to nurse him and change him if needed.

Tonight Irene had fallen asleep right away but woke up to Beau's unanswered cries. Lying there, she listened and waited and soon became alarmed. Something was wrong with Odessa. Something had happened. Or…worse…something was horribly wrong with Beau.

"Elias," Irene whispered and poked him in the ribs. "Elias…the baby…something is wrong with Beau." She swung her feet over the edge of the bed.

Beside her, Elias wrapped his arms around her waist and pulled her down. "If Odessa needs your help…*our help*…I'm sure we'll hear about it shortly. Leave them alone."

Tense, alert, Irene made herself stay in his embrace. She forced herself to relax and concentrated on the stars outside her bedroom window. A milky-blue beam of moonlight fanned across the room—and the baby cried.

"All right," Elias finally said. "You better go see if you can help, but don't take over. If you're gone for more than twenty minutes, I'm coming in there to get you."

Irene had her robe and slippers on in a flash and

skipped out their bedroom door before he'd finished his warning.

Odessa wasn't in her bed. Beau was in his cradle, his blankets kicked off, his face red, his little nightdress bunched up under his arms, and he was wet with drool and spit-up. He smelled sour, and he was mad. Irene picked him up and spoke assurances to him while she changed his gown and diaper. "There now, shall we go find Mommy? Maybe she went outside to the privy. Let's bundle you up, and we'll go have a look."

They went to the edge of the back porch. There was no lantern light coming from the outhouse. Irene, with Beau wrapped up warm and snug in a blanket, stepped off the porch and went up the path, the ground beneath her feet frozen, covered with frost. No one was in the outhouse. She hurried back to the house, and Beau began to cry.

"Elias," she called over the baby's wail. "She's not here. Odessa is gone. She's not in the house, and she's not outside."

Irene heard Elias groan, and a beam of light shone into the living room from their opened bedroom door. "What? What do you mean she's not here? Where else would she be? She has to be around here somewhere," he said and tied his dressing gown around his bare body.

"I don't know, but she's not here. Beau's hungry. What should we do?"

"Feed him," he suggested, deliberately being obtuse.

"Well, yes, I would do that," she agreed. "What do you recommend, Doctor Rayburn? I have the proper equipment, but I'm out of his favorite flavor."

Elias shook his head and muttered an oath under his

breath. "He'll have to take sugar water. We don't have a choice."

"Will he get an upset tummy?"

"He might—I don't know," he said and scrubbed his head. "Let me get my trousers on."

Irene paced the living room with the wailing child in her arms. Elias reappeared in his stocking feet, trousers on and robe tied about his waist. "We won't give him very much, just enough to take the edge off his hunger. Do you know how long he's been asleep? I know you get up and open the door so you can hear what's going on in her room. I also know even though you're in another room, even asleep, you know more about his habits than anyone else in this house. So, how long has he been asleep?"

Irene, embarrassed, took her lower lip between her teeth, hesitated, then confessed, "Yes, I know. I know to the minute, exactly, how long he's been asleep when he burped, had a bowel movement." Irene straightened and looked him in the eye. "In answer to your question, well, it must be almost one o'clock, so I would say almost four hours. He's a good sleeper. He's a very good baby," she said, on the defensive.

"And well he should be. You're there the moment he begins to whimper. I'm sure he has very little to complain about," said Elias, pulling the collar of his robe up around his jowls.

Irene handed over the squalling child to him and rushed back into their room and his office. "The other day, I saw a baby bottle. I think it was here on a lower shelf in this old medicine cabinet. I thought then I should wash it. I don't think we've had to use it more than once or twice. I'll wash it with soap and water and see if I can find the nipple for it. I know it's down here somewhere," she said, setting miscellaneous tincture bottles and vials up on the shelf to get them out of the way.

In no time, she had the bottle clean and a tepid solution of sugar water prepared.

Elias handed her a small brown bottle. "Put a drop of this in the water. It's oil of peppermint. It might soothe his tummy.

She reclaimed Beau and sat with him in the rocking chair by the hearth. "You don't have to sit up with us," she told him, alternately rocking and cooing to the baby, who took the offered sugar water with a scrunched-up face, and a moment of hesitation. "As soon as he goes to sleep, I'll put him back in his bed, and I'll join you."

Elias hovered nearby, a disapproving scowl on his face. Making her feel extremely self-conscious and guilty.

****

Feeling utterly useless, Elias started to go back to bed, but he stopped and turned to look at her. Her shoulders were slumped, her hair tousled. She looked rumpled, warm, adorable, and he knew the real problem—he was jealous of Beau.

"You aren't going to come to bed after he goes to sleep, and you know it."

Without looking at him, Irene answered, "No."

"You're going to wait up for Odessa, aren't you?"

Very near tears, she said, "Did it occur to you maybe she's run off, Elias? She might not be coming back."

Coming to attention, he disappeared into Odessa's room and poked his head into her wardrobe. Almost sorry to find nothing missing, he returned to the living room. "She hasn't. Her things are here."

"Where could she be?" Irene asked.

There really was no way of answering that without getting into trouble, so he tried to fudge—make up something that sounded good. "I don't know. Maybe she went out for a walk." He sat down on the settee and tried to think of some reasonable excuse for Odessa, but it was damn near impossible. "Maybe she couldn't sleep. You've had those nights, so have I, when sleep won't come."

"But Beau...she left him alone without telling me. That's unforgivable," Irene said to the baby in her arms, her eyes brimming with tears.

For a moment or two, all that could be heard was the baby trying to satisfy himself with sugar water. He grunted and squirmed, obviously not fooled by the substitution.

"Yes, yes, it is unforgivable," Elias said. "What are you going to say to her?"

Irene shrugged her shoulders. "I don't know. I'm going to sit here and think about it."

"Right. Well, I'm going to bed. I'm supposed to go out to the mill tomorrow and make a well check on some broken ribs," he said, not feeling very charitable toward his wife or Odessa at the moment.

"I love you, Elias. I know you think I'm a fool to do what I do. I appreciate your patience with me—with everything."

Coming back, he went down on his knees in front of her, one hand to her cheek and the other to the baby's head. "I love you. I love this little guy. I love Odessa. We are a family. Good night."

"Good night," Irene said and sniffed back her tears.

****

Odessa stealthily opened the back door of the house. She removed Trenton's mackinaw and hung it up on the hook on the back stoop. Ruby said she could have it, and she was pleased to give it to her. On tip-toe, Odessa picked her way around the kitchen table and crossed the living room.

Her bedroom door was open, as she'd left it. She unbuttoned her flannel shirt, took it off, and stuffed it into her hat. Inside her door, she came to a standstill. Her mother lay stretched on top of her bed; she could see her form by the moonlight that shone through her window.

Biting her lower lip, she backed up. She needed to find her nightgown and fast. If she could get out of the trousers before her mother woke up, she might have a chance.

Slipping behind her door, she shed Trenton's trousers, which had fit her perfectly. It had been a stroke of luck yesterday when George had taken her and the baby for a visit to the Trask's, finding some of Trenton's clothes in the little room where she'd changed Beau's diaper and fashioned him a bed in Trenton's old bureau. No one had questioned the extra bulge in the bundle of Beau's diapers. Then, as George had driven them past the saloon, the music and laughter drifting on the frosty night air, the germ of a plan began to sprout in Odessa's mind.

She hadn't intended to be gone so long. The saloon had been busy, so busy hardly anyone noticed the young man in the droopy, water-stained, leather hat and tattered mackinaw come in and take a seat near the door in the corner—her disguise had worked perfectly.

Mrs. Lamphere dropped by the table to serve the boy a drink. That was a tense moment; Odessa declined with a vigorous shake of her head, expecting Mrs. Lamphere to call her out. Instead, Mrs. Lamphere suggested sarsaparilla or coffee. In a raspy voice, hoping to sound like a callow youth, Odessa told her coffee would do. Then Paulette O'Day came over and begged Odessa to dance. She even sat on her lap. Petrified and having to work very hard to stay in character, Odessa didn't betray herself by giggling or squealing. She simply pulled her hat down lower over her flaming cheeks, shook her head, and refused to move from her spot in the corner.

The music was lively. Odessa, in the guise of a young boy, sat unmolested and watched the men play cards, and the girls flirt and entice and incite lust and high passion—it all seemed so exciting and forbidden, it stirred her blood. Odessa vowed to do it again. Maybe she'd have to toe the line for a while, but she would think of a way to do it again. She didn't need George.

Studying Paulette, Meda-Belle, and the new one whose name Odessa didn't know, she saw how they toyed with the men, cozying up to them to buy them drinks and slip them money for the price of a kiss or a tickle. If she had to be a woman, then it was time to turn the tables and learn to get what she wanted instead of the one being used and left alone.

"Mama," Odessa said and approached the bed and tapped her on the shoulder. "Mama, I'm sorry."

"Where have you been?" her mother whispered, sitting up and rubbing her eyes.

"I couldn't sleep," Odessa said. "I lost track of time. I…I was thinking about Silas and Trenton. Going out to see Sam and Ruby, I guess, brought back a lot of memories for me. I walked down to the school and sat on the steps, and I fell asleep."

"You must be frozen," her mother said and took Odessa's hands in her own.

Odessa shrugged and searched for a plausible reason why she wasn't cold at all, not even her hands. "Not really," she said. "I put on a pair of long johns before I left, and I had on my wool skirt and sweater under my coat."

To get her mother off her appearance, Odessa asked, "Did Beau wake up?"

"Yes, he did," her mother said. "We had to give him sugar water. He might have an upset tummy. And he won't be asleep for long. You should have come and told me you were going out. I would've helped you express some milk for him."

In the dark, Odessa turned her eyes away and sneered. She shivered at the thought of milking herself like a cow…it was disgusting. When she turned her eyes back to her mother, she managed to say in all sincerity, "I'm sorry. I shouldn't have been gone so long. I didn't mean to. Poor little guy. I wasn't here. I'll apologize to him, too."

Her mother started to get up from the bed. "Well, I'm glad you're all right. We were very worried. I'm going to bed for a little while. It must be almost one thirty."

The saloon closed at one o'clock; Odessa knew what time it was. "Is it really?" she asked. "I didn't realize it was so late. Oh, dear, I really am sorry."

Odessa crawled in under her covers. "I wanted to talk to you. I've been wondering, how long do I have to nurse Beau?"

****

Irene couldn't believe this. She stood over her

daughter and stared.

"I mean, I know some women enjoy it and manage to do it until the baby is walking and talking, but I don't want to. Could we get a goat? I understand their milk is very good for babies. Ruby said so. She even said we could borrow one of theirs when the time came."

Irene swallowed her outrage, too tired to get into this now. She needed her bed. She needed to lie next to her husband, close her eyes, and her mind to Odessa, her unbelievable ignorance, and her callous heart.

Chapter Twenty-Seven

For two weeks, Irene slept with one ear cocked, attuned to every creak and squeak the house made, but there were no more late-night wanderings, as far as she knew.

Beau thrived. However, as Odessa's milk began to dry up, he grew more and more discontent and vocal. Irene couldn't decide if it was Beau's hearty appetite or Odessa's lack of enthusiasm that was the cause of this circumstance, but by March, it was decided they take Ruby and Sam's offer of a goat.

As was their usual habit before going to sleep, Irene and Elias lay talking. "Now she's not breastfeeding, she's more attentive," he said, one arm behind his head and the other hand stroking her cheek. "She was down on the floor with him, playing, and I heard her singing him to sleep after supper. One thing's for certain, Beau is happier on the bottle."

"Yes," Irene said and turned her face to kiss his fingers. "He's growing, and he's much happier, I'll grant you. Most nights, he sleeps almost six hours. I'm not convinced it's because he's no longer hungry. I think part of it has to do with Odessa. She's finally relaxed with him—she's actually started to enjoy him."

She draped her bare leg over Elias's thigh, snuggled close and rested her head on his bare chest, and heaved a weighty sigh, unable to let go of a sense of unease. "Beau is happier, and Odessa is coming around…but I don't know…something is wrong. I don't trust Odessa when she starts to behave—when she's not complaining all the time."

She paused, unsure if she should confess her latest sin. "I eavesdropped on her and George today. They were in the backyard with Beau, sitting under the tree. I was hanging up sheets. Odessa appeared almost, I don't know, flirty. It wasn't real. I could see that. She batted her eyes, giggled, and teased him with little kisses, playing a part. To be brutally frank, she was acting like a tart. I felt sorry for George; he doesn't deserve Odessa's taunts. He's been so good to her and to Beau."

Pausing, Irene deliberated whether she should go ahead and reveal the rest of the conversation she'd heard between George and Odessa. It was none of her business, and yet she was worried. George could get hurt. He was a true friend to her daughter. There didn't seem any way she could warn George. He was a grown man, old enough to make his own decisions.

"Out with it," Elias said and gave her shoulder a little jiggle. "What else? There's more to this."

She rolled off him onto her back and stared up at the ceiling. "George asked Odessa to marry him." She turned back to Elias, her hand going to his neck, her cheek resting on his chest. "He's making big plans, Elias. He wants Odessa to be part of those plans. He's bringing his sister out here, all the way from North Dakota, to take care of his house and…Beau, should Odessa accept his offer. His sister will be here sometime in May, Elias. That's only a couple of months from now.

"His house, at Black Butte, is finished, and tomorrow he's going to Powell Butte to buy cattle—he plans on being gone for a week. I guess Rob Morgan is going with him. I don't know if Rob intends to purchase cattle too. I didn't get details.

"But the thing is, George wants Odessa to think about marrying him…be his wife."

The idea of Odessa leaving, taking Beau with her, was too painful for Irene to contemplate. She wanted her daughter to be happy, to have a home of her own, and yet the house would be so very empty without her and the baby. And it was too painful to think of another woman caring for Beau, a stranger.

She held back the rest of what she'd overheard.

George promised they would travel. Lena would take care of the house and the children. He also promised Odessa his love and devotion. And he said he knew she didn't return his regards.

Irene didn't know how to reach Odessa, to get her to see the cruelty of leading George on.

Shamelessly, Irene had listened to George pour his heart out. Her daughter sat there unmoved by the gift she was receiving. She did finally relent, unbend, to say she would think about it.

Irene's heart ached for George. And she was more than disappointed in her daughter. She was mortified.

****

George's proposal left Odessa restless, feeling caged. She had to escape. Impatient, dressed once again in Trenton's old trousers, shirt, and her scratched and worn boots, she stayed quietly reading in her room. Her door opened a crack, she heard Elias start to snore, and she set her plan in motion. She kissed her sleeping Beau on his cheek and promised she'd be gone only an hour, then climbed out her bedroom window.

Seated in her corner at the saloon, she sipped her sarsaparilla. George showed up. It was all she could do to sit and watch Paulette apply her considerable womanly charms on George to tempt him to go to the boarding house for a little fun. George resisted, begging the woman to excuse him. He'd come in to try his luck at a few hands of faro. Odessa slipped away undetected as soon as he took his chair.

Seeing George with Paulette, watching him, hearing him laugh and flirt aroused something in Odessa. She didn't like to think it jealousy, but by heaven, if that tart had sat on his lap, she'd have wanted to scratch her eyes out.

****

The rain, cold on her face, turned to big, sloppy flakes of snow—Odessa didn't care. The excitement burning inside her kept her warm. Her hands and feet could freeze and fall off. It didn't matter—Silas was home. He'd come back, and he wanted to see her.

Her mother didn't argue when Odessa suggested she leave Beau behind, which was a relief. Silas, of course, would want to see his son, spend time with him, but they needed to make plans and to do that, they needed time alone.

Her mother stood back as Sam helped Odessa onto the buckboard seat. Before he climbed up to sit next to her, Sam said to her mother, "We'll see to her. Silas brought the tart with him. She's over to the boarding house. Probably wants her old job back. He's itchin' to be off to God knows where. Before he takes off again, I told him he needed to make things right with Odessa, at least see her. I don't think this is gonna go how our girl wants it."

In that know-it-all way her mother had, she answered, "I know, Sam. But we'll never convince her any other way."

Throwing back her shoulders, Odessa set her spine and pinned her eyes on the road ahead. Chin up, she told herself her mother and Sam, they didn't, couldn't possibly understand. Of course, Silas had to throw off the traces. He was scared, scared of his love for her. And, to say the truth, she was scared too. But together, they could do it, make a home, be good parents for Beau—together, it would be heaven. She would make him see how it could be—Silas would never leave her behind again.

The ride to the Trask place seemed to take forever, the road muddy and rutted. The wind blowing hard pelted them with rain mixed with snow.

"Let me down, Sam," Odessa said before Sam could pull the team up to the barn.

"You let me help you down—them boards is slick," he shouted and held her back, arm thrust across her chest. "He's in the shed there."

"Why is he in the shed? Is he sleeping out here, too?" she asked. Sam picked her up by the waist and set her on her feet.

"You go find out for yourself. We all tried, but I guess you got to hear it from the horse's mouth. So, go on, you'll find him in there, such as he is."

Inside, the shed was dry, but that was about all one could say. Too dark to see properly, Odessa headed for the faint light at the back and to the side of the small cribs on either side of the narrow aisle. She rushed forward and stepped into the golden light cast by a lone lantern. She felt a momentary sense of foreboding, but brushed it aside, thinking it to be excitement, and skipped toward him.

"As pretty as a frisky colt, the same old Dessie," Silas said on a laugh. "Always up for a lark."

Odessa giggled and hiked up her skirt to pick her way across the crusty, dirty shed floor. Silas shook his head and grinned, ogling her exposed ankles. She tugged her rain-soaked bonnet from her head and set her curls free.

"By God, you are beautiful. You purt' near suck the wind right out of me. I'm weak in the knees. Welcome to my parlor. I got a little fire going over here in the corner. You look like you could use some heat."

The sound of his voice, so familiar, stopped her. The lantern light behind him obscured his face and gave a dark outline to his body. Uncertain, suddenly shy, Odessa reminded herself *he wanted to see me...he asked to see me.*

"Come closer, girl. Let me have a look at you." He took her cold hand in his and pulled her into what appeared to be his quarters. It was Spartan to a degree— a dry mound of hay for his bedroll, a milking stool and barrel upon which to eat his meals, and the main and most important feature, of course, the camp stove in the corner.

"Take off your wet coat. I'll give you a dry blanket for your shoulders. You always wanted me to get you a blanket, didn't you? I got one like you always wanted," he said, his voice low, warm, seductive, his breath close to her ear.

Odessa allowed him to unbutton her coat, her fingers numb and shaking so badly she would've made a botch of it herself.

It was nice to have Silas fuss over her, although he

didn't exactly present the romantic figure she'd held in her mind's eye. He needed a shave, and his clothes, dirty, sweat-stained, reeked of manure. And his hair, usually black and glossy, looked greasy and flat and hung ragged about his forehead, ears, and dirty neck.

He started to drape the blanket around her shoulders and stopped and whistled.

Odessa followed his gaze and folded her arms across her chest. Her breasts were full, not as full as they'd been while nursing, but they were round and firm. She'd come to terms with the fact she now had a woman's body. Silas looked her over as if she were a prize cow. Ashamed of the shape her body had taken, she snagged the blanket to hide herself.

"No, no, now, let me look at you." His boyish grin in place, his eyes glittered in the lantern's light.

She'd decided on wearing her blue dress today. It was of warm wool and fit close to her skin. It buttoned up the front in a simple, comfortable style to accommodate nursing a baby. It was one of her better dresses, and she'd worn it because she remembered Silas liked the color blue.

"My, my," Silas said. Circling, he looked her up and down. "What a difference a few months can make. Why, Dessie, you've come into full bloom. You look fine…better than fine…you look good enough to eat."

Eyes downcast, Odessa caught sight of the bulge in his trousers and realized his manhood had become erect. Her cheeks burst into flame, and she raised her eyes to find him grinning at her.

"How about a kiss? We're old friends…a friend should kiss a friend hello after a long spell apart."

Recognizing the hunger in his eyes, hearing warmth

in his voice sent a shiver of anticipation and desire down low in her belly. Tilting her head and lifting her chin, she met his lips. They kissed a soft, fluttering kiss, but he tasted of tobacco and something else—maybe whiskey. Odessa tried to pull away, but he stopped her. His hand against her back, his other hand slid around her waist. He crushed her into his body. Soon the kiss grew hungry, desperate. His tongue, hot and sour tasting, plundered her mouth.

Fear returned her to her senses. The stubble of his unshaven face scraped her cheek and burned her lips. The smell of his unwashed body made her sick to her stomach.

Although repulsed, she went down to the mound of hay with him and let him kiss her neck and undo the buttons on her dress, all the while telling herself, *Silas, Silas wants me, he wants me. He's home, and he still wants me.*

Then alarm bells started to peal a warning in the far recesses of her reasoning brain. It was his fingers; they pulled at her still-tender nipples and forced themselves into the moist valley between her legs, and she could no longer ignore her panic.

Here she was again, her legs spread, giving herself to him without the benefit of one word of tenderness.

An accusation screamed in her head—*fool!*

She was worse than a whore. She was a mindless wanton giving of her whole body and soul for what? A kiss.

Without thinking, Odessa brought up her knee like George had shown her. Her delivery came hard and swift.

Silas flopped on his back. Doubled up in pain, he

freed her. Once on her feet, Odessa hurriedly buttoned her dress and pulled up her drawers.

"I want to hear words, Silas Trask," she said, her voice to her ears an unnatural snarl. Empowered, she shook with rage and silently blessed George for showing her how to defend herself. "You come home after gallivanting around the country with that whore and expect me to open my legs and welcome you back free and easy. No! You're the father of a baby boy. His name is Beau Morran, and he needs a last name. He needs his papa's name. Then and only then do I ever give you my body. And you stink," she added for good measure.

Holding his crotch, Silas huffed and puffed and struggled to his feet. Hands on his knees, he retched before coming up to his full height. "Goddamn you, that hurt. You like to kill me."

Shoulders humped, he buttoned his fly and tucked in his shirt.

Odessa stood, waiting, arms folded across her bosom, furious. "Me, me, I *should* kill *you*. You left me. You didn't even bother to say goodbye. I gave birth to your child, Silas. It felt like *I* had died. No one would speak to me. Everyone shunned me. So no, you don't get to *damn* me. You're the one going to hell if you don't do the right thing. Step up, be a man."

"A man?" Shoulders back, he sucked in his gut. "What do you know about being a man? The only man you ever knew was your pa. Admit it, that's why you take a shine to me. I'm like your pa. Me and your pa we're the flash-in-the-pan kind of men. Neither of us is the kind of man to stay around and become a whipped-dog husband and a pa to a passel of brats."

He might as well have slapped her. His words hit her

hard. She stumbled back.

Silas came forward and got in her face, his eyes full of fire. "And you, you can't tell me you want to be a *mama*. I know you don't. You want what I want. You want excitement and, yeah, danger. You always did. We're a lot alike."

It was Odessa's turn to feel as if she'd taken a knee hard to the groin. Nearly doubling up with the blow, she turned away from his sneering aspect. Tears blurred the darkness of the shed.

"Don't you love me at all, Silas?" she asked. Arms wrapped about her waist, her voice sounded small and pitiful to her own ears.

"There you go with the love crap," he said and threw up his arms. "Women. It's always love with you. I don't want no part of it, never did…never said I did."

She whirled around and pounced on that statement. "You said you loved me. You said it when we were up in the loft, and I let you…let you use me. That's all it was for you, magic words to get what you wanted, that's all. God, I'm an idiot!"

"Hell, yes, I said a lot of things I didn't mean, 'cause I wanted to be your first. And you wanted me to take you. You were prime for the taking, Dessie. Don't stand there and tell me you weren't burnin' to have me in you. I know better. I didn't have to force you. You was all hot and juicy."

His snort of disdain sickened her. Her throat clogged with tears and shame—he was right. If she had a gun or a knife, she'd kill him, then kill herself.

"Love. Forget that stuff. It ain't for the likes of you and me, Dessie," Silas said and took her once again by the shoulders. He placed one dirty finger under her quivering chin and forced her to look into his eyes. "We ain't got it in us to love nobody. We got bigger things to do, don't you see?" He gave her a rough shake. "Jesus, I can't believe it's taken you all this time to figure out I don't love you. I don't love nobody. Sure I said the words, but they didn't mean nothin' to me."

"You lied to me, Silas. I believed you when you said you loved me," she said, tears rolling down her cheeks.

"Ah, hell, you lie all the time to get what you want, Dessie. I seen you turn your mother sweet hundreds of times with your lyin' mouth."

Odessa hated herself, hated her tears. She was weak and pitiful, pathetic and, yes…stupid. And what was worse, everything he said was true—they were alike. Trembling, she shook her head. "I wanted to go with you, Silas…see things and do things with you…no one else. I do love you. I gave myself to you," she said, fighting against the urge to hit him, beat him about the head and shoulders until he stopped talking, stopped spouting home truths.

He took her hand. "Oh, come on. You got lots of time to go see things," he said and tried to pull her into his arms. She shoved him away.

Arms to his side, he moved in front of her. "Hell, with your looks and the body you got, you could make a lot of money right here in Meadow View. If you was to take yourself to Portland, why, the sky would be the limit. You could set yourself up real smart. Be your own boss, get a clientele, you know. Shoot, I'd come, and I'd pay for it."

She put her hands over her ears. She couldn't stand to listen to him. His words were so in line with what she'd been thinking. It was more than she could bear to hear him give her thoughts a voice. Her fantasies sounded sordid and dirty, the way he put it.

She grabbed her coat and ran outside. The rain had turned to snow, and it was starting to stick. Blinded by tears, she started down the lane, running for home.

Chapter Twenty-Eight

Sam caught up with her, and somehow he got her up on the wagon seat. After riding in silence, deep in her own thoughts for over two miles. Sam gave a little jump when Odessa put her hand on his arm. "You can drop me off at the Mercantile. I need to get Beau some ointment. He's teething, and he has a rash on his bottom. Thank you," she said. "Don't bother helping me down. I can do it. You better get back home; it'll be full dark soon. Ruby will be worried about you. Looks like it might snow all night. It's getting colder too."

"You sure you're all right?" he asked.

"Oh, yes, I'll be fine," she said and even managed a smile to reassure him.

"Give my love to Ruby. Tell her I'm sorry I left before seeing her. I'll see her soon, and I'll bring Beau," Odessa said. Carefully, she made her way off the side of the buckboard and waved to Sam as he turned the team around and headed back the way they had come.

The sound of the piano and men's voices drifted into the street from the opened doors of the saloon across the street. The tune, "Buffalo Gal," in ragtime teased her. Like a moth to a flame, Odessa headed for the warmth and light.

*****

"I'm sorry, George," Irene said to him and waved him inside. "Odessa left with Sam a little before noon to

335

go out to the Trask place."

Elias took his coat. "Come in, warm yourself…have some coffee, George."

George handed his coat to Elias and asked, "Odessa's gone to da Trask place?"

"Have you eaten, George? We were about to have some chili," Irene asked, her hands clasped tight to her waist.

"Yah, I'll have some chili. Miss Odessa, why out to da Trask place? Why did she go on a day like today?"

Beau began to cry. George walked over and squatted down beside him. "So little fella, you come avake to say hello to big George?" Gazing down at the child, George said to the child in a voice so low Irene could barely hear. "Odessa—your mama, she's a wild ting. Nobody tames a wild ting. If they stay, they stay because they want to, not because anyone else wants them to."

Irene dished up the chili and set the bowls on the table with the cornbread. She sat down with a bottle of warm milk ready for Beau and reached for the baby. George picked him up and reluctantly handed the child to her, then sat down. He didn't eat—he sat watching the baby eat.

Irene looked up and, after taking a deep breath, she said, "According to Sam, Silas arrived home a day or so ago. Sam looked terrible. Something is wrong, but Odessa needs to hear it from Silas, whatever it is. She won't believe anyone else where that boy is concerned."

George offered Beau his finger, and the baby hung on to it. "I guess dat's true. Nobody can keep her from da hurt of it."

"No, I guess not," Elias said.

"She should be home any minute. It's almost dark.

Surely, Sam will want to be back home by supper time," Irene said.

"Okay if I vait here?" George asked.

"Sure, George. Eat up," Elias said. "Tell us how the cattle drive went? Must have gone well. You made the trip in record time."

"Yah, ve got all dah cattle settled in at da ranch. The drovers, I follow into town."

****

Odessa entered the saloon. Furtively, she kept close to the wall and made for the table in the corner by the door. She swayed and braced herself, hands to the back of the chair. Once in the chair, she lowered her head and cradled it in her arms.

She didn't think anyone had noticed her, not yet. Head down, she removed her bonnet and combed her hair back from her tear-stained face. Giving the room a quick glance, she took inventory. A half-dozen mangy, boisterous drovers took up the tables in the back of the room, partaking of platters of meat and potatoes. Dolly, the new girl Odessa had observed upon her last visit to the saloon, and Paulette worked the table, waiting on them. She didn't see Mrs. Lamphere at the bar or at any of the tables and breathed a shallow sigh of relief. And then she saw Grace Wolfe heading her way.

"Well, honey," Grace said, her voice quiet and easy, her manner reeking genuine concern. "You look cold and hungry." Grace pulled up a chair and sat with her back to the room. "You know this ain't a safe place for you, sweetie." She leaned across the table and positioned herself in front of Odessa, blocking the view from the party at the back of the room. "I got a room at the boarding house. You could get dry and warm up there.

385

Maybe you'd like something to eat? Mrs. Lamphere is a real good cook."

"No, I couldn't impose," Odessa said, assailed by fatigue, exhaustion so great she prayed she would die from it.

I'm a mess. George shouldn't want me. I'm silly, soiled, and selfish.

I make everybody miserable, even Beau. Silas is right. I need to give up thinking there's love somewhere with someone. Everywhere I go, I'm there. I ruin everything.

"Come on, sweetie," Grace said and took her gently by the arm, getting her out of the corner. "You look like you need a place to think for a while. Some time alone will do you good. Grace will get you some food, then if you want to talk, maybe I can help."

"I came in to listen to the music," Odessa said.

"Oh, sweetie, I got a music box, we can listen to music in my room. You ain't safe in here. Come on with Grace. Let me take care of you."

That sounded wonderful—if only the offer had come from anyone but Grace Wolfe. But she was so very tired, and going somewhere, *anywhere* but home, sounded good. Odessa allowed herself to be led out the front door and around the corner. Once Grace had her inside the boarding house, they went up the stairs.

Odessa stood inside Grace's room and took in her surroundings. It smelled nice, like sandalwood and lilies. The room was clean and tidy. Somehow Odessa hadn't expected Grace Wolfe to be neat. Taking her by the hand, Grace pulled her farther into the room. "Now, you got to be quiet, see, 'cause you wouldn't want Mrs. Lamphere to know you was here. She'd tell your mama. But you can trust me, I ain't gonna tell a soul," Grace said and unbuttoned Odessa's coat for her. and motioned for her to put her feet up and lie down on the bed.

"I bet I can guess what, or should I say…who's got you so down in the mouth," Grace said and stoked the fire in her little stove. "I bet it's that rascal, Silas. He sure does have a way with the ladies…not a good way, mind…but a way, if you get my drift."

Odessa threw her arm over her eyes and started to sob great heart-wrenching sobs.

Sitting on the edge of the bed, Grace wrapped her arm around Odessa's shoulder. "There now, you let Grace take care of you. I bet before the night's over, you'll be laughin' and havin' a good time. You wait and see if you ain't. How 'bout a glass of somethin' warm and fizzy to take away the cold?"

After a couple of warm brandies, Odessa, light-headed, no longer cared about anything or anybody. She hadn't giggled with a chum in a long time—Grace Wolfe, grant you, was not exactly Odessa's idea of the ideal chum, but she was the first female in a long time that had tried to be her friend.

At first, Odessa thought Grace outrageous to suggest she try on one of her flamboyant, skimpy costumes for the sheer fun of it. But as she tried on one, then another, and another, it felt so darn good to giggle and be silly that she lost track of where she was and how much she was drinking. The costume of the moment was a leather dress with a low V-neck, beaded down to the belly and split up the sides to the thigh. Odessa stood before Grace's mirror while Grace tied a beaded leather thong around her forehead. Catching a glimpse of herself in the mirror, Odessa burst out laughing. then they both laughed to see a titian-haired Indian maiden looking wide-eyed and ridiculous grinning back at them.

"Well now, I do believe I like this one best of all," Grace said, a teasing grin on her grotesquely painted face. "We could be sisters. You sure are a pretty girl. It don't matter what you put on, you look good, girl. You want to try some of my rouge...maybe a little color on your lips?"

"Grace," Mrs. Lamphere called from outside Grace's door, "Grace, you got a client in there?"

"Uh, yeah," Grace answered and put her finger to her lips to warn Odessa to stifle her giggles. "I'm gonna get him somethin' to eat in a minute."

Silence. Then Mrs. Lamphere said, "Good...see you at the saloon in a while."

"Sure thing," Grace said. She held her finger to her lips. The sound of the woman's heels clicking down the stairs faded away.

"Hey, that was close," Grace said.

Odessa put her hand over her mouth to stifle her mirth.

Grace pressed her painted lips together, laughter in her eyes. "I better get you some food. Help yourself to the brandy, and I'll be right back."

****

After an hour and a half, George began to pace. Irene and Elias had run out of conversation. Every once in a while, George stopped and opened the door to look outside—it was dark, and the snow had stopped, freezing into a crust of ice that coated the trees and road.

He closed the door and stood for a moment staring at the floor. "I got to do somethin'."

Elias nodded. "Could be, because of the weather,

Sam didn't want to risk bringing her home. She's safe enough with Sam and Ruby."

Irene understood Elias's reasoning, but it didn't relieve her or George of their worry. Irene couldn't blame the man for his agitation, his impatience. Here he was, waiting for Odessa to come home, give him an answer to his marriage proposal, and she was off seeing another man. Of course, George didn't know Irene knew he was waiting for an answer. She was not at all comfortable with the knowledge.

"Yah, I guess so. I don't like it—something is wrong somewhere. I can feel it. I tink maybe to the saloon I go over for a little vhile. I don't get drunk. I just got to do someting."

"I'll go with you, George," Elias said. "Could be Sam stopped in for a shot of whiskey before he headed home."

George put on his coat.

"You come back here tonight and stay the night," Irene said to George and handed him his hat. "You can't go home. In the morning, you can go out to the Trask place."

George nodded, and Elias headed out the door.

Irene went over to the cradle where Beau played with a ring of leather George had made him while he waited. The baby lay chewing on the knots and tugged his toes. Irene smiled down at him and wondered where her daughter could be.

Chapter Twenty-Nine

Elias followed George into the saloon. George waved to the drovers in the back corner. Elias didn't see Sam anywhere, but he spied Miss Wolfe. She was busy applying her wiles on two of the six men at the faro table.

Paulette threw her arms around George.

Meda-Belle, at the bar, gave Elias a nod and answered his unasked question. "Yeah, Grace is back. I'm keepin' an eye on her," she said.

George disentangled himself from Paulette's embrace and ordered a beer for himself and Elias.

Paulette sneered and took a sip from her glass of whiskey. "She's back all right, and she's makin' it hard on the rest of us. Dolly's worried there won't be enough business to go 'round."

"It is good to see you, George," Meda-Belle said. "We've all missed you. Good of you to bring the doc along with you tonight. The drovers say you got your cows all tucked in at your place."

George nodded and saluted with his beer. "We vas lucky. Made good time. Had a good crew."

Glancing back to the faro table, Elias kept his eye on Miss Wolfe, as did Meda-Belle. She raised her eyebrows and was about to comment when a new girl, a girl Elias hadn't met, came up to the bar and pinched Meda-Belle on the shoulder, apparently upset about something.

"What kind of place is this?" the girl said, then

stepped around Meda-Belle and approached George with a sly gleam in her brown eyes and a smile on her painted lips. "So, who's this big hunk a'meat? And I haven't had the pleasure of meeting this prime piece?" she said, her sights set on Elias. "These two your private stock, Meda-Belle, like the ones Grace hustled outta here? I don't know how you expect me to make a livin' if your girls can take 'em on two at a time. I don't think I can compete."

"I beg your pardon?" Meda-Belle said, her feathers definitely ruffled. "What the hell are you talking about, Dolly?"

The girl, Dolly, spun around to face Meda-Belle. "What do I mean? I mean that Grace woman marching away with a man on each arm...that's what I mean. Probably gonna take one of 'em up to the new girl you took on earlier. What is Grace anyway...a pimp for the sweet little dab? The kid too good to come down here and do her own work—Grace got to pick and choose for her?" Dolly shifted her ample hips and said with a shake of her blonde head, "I don't see how the three of us are gonna get any business at all workin' it like this."

"Dolly, will you explain to me what you're talking about?" Meda-Belle asked.

Impatient, Dolly said, "You don't know what I'm talking about. Oh, that's rich. You don't know anything about a sweet-lookin' little piece of prime goods, angel face and hair the color of honey?"

Elias heard Paulette suck air, then hiss a curse, "Balls-o-Friday."

"Maybe I better go up and see what's goin' on around here," Meda-Belle said. "Dolly, I don't know anything about a young girl workin' here. I took Grace back, that's all. Go back to the table and get to work. Those boys are lookin' mighty lonesome."

Quietly, she said, her hand going to Elias's arm. "You and George, come with me? If there are two men up there with some kid Grace has shanghaied, I might need some help convincing them to get out. If it's Grace making up for lost time, then that's her lookout."

Elias didn't protest or hesitate until they were outside, then he came to an abrupt halt. "Okay, now, you tell me what you think is going on, Meda-Belle."

She grabbed him by the coat front and practically dragged him down the alley. "Come on, I think we better hurry. I'll fill you in on the way. Odessa's been coming in from time to time."

He stopped dead in his tracks.

"Don't look at me like that," she said and gave him a tug to set him back in motion. "She's been dressed in boy's clothes, wearing a hat and coat. I recognized her right off. No one else but Paulette got a close look at her. Grace hasn't been around, so she couldn't know."

"But you think Grace has got Odessa up there in her room?" George held the door of the boarding house open for them.

Meda-Belle nodded. "Yes, yes, I do. I don't know why…or how, but I know Grace Wolfe, and this would be the perfect revenge."

"Revenge for what?" Elias asked, following her up the stairs.

"How the hell should I know? Grace lives to take revenge. Odessa is young and pretty. That's enough in Grace's book," said Meda-Belle. Picking up her skirts, she rushed up the stairs.

****

Odessa awoke to a fully lit room, her head hurt, and she was sweating. It wasn't her room. Her room didn't have a bearskin throw on the bed or green satin drapes at the window. And her room didn't smell like sandalwood and crushed tiger lilies. She didn't have any golden candles to burn in crystal candle holders at her bedside. And there had never been two dirty, grimy men in her room before—her mother wouldn't allow it.

"Beau, where's Beau?" she asked and wondered why she was dressed in leather—however, not enough leather to cover her naked thighs and arms.

"There. See, boys, she's askin' for you to be her beau. I told you she'd be waitin' with open arms."

Odessa heard Grace say, from somewhere near her head, "Now, sweetie," she said in a soothing and gentle manner that temporarily gave Odessa a false sense of security. "These two boys is gonna cuddle you and love you up until you're silly with it. You're gonna forget all about nasty old Silas."

Turning her head, Grace addressed the men, "You boys are gonna see she don't remember why she was so sad, aren't you, boys?"

To Odessa, Grace said, "You don't got to worry, they aren't mean, and they know how to share and take turns. Why, these two gents are gonna make this a night to remember for you. And when they're done, I'll get you two more. Hell, you can do it until you're so wet you slide off the bed."

Grace laughed in Odessa's face as if she'd painted a delightful picture for her enjoyment, and the boys laughed too.

"You relax, feel good all over, and let the boys do the work," Grace advised, a grin on her face and a nasty gleam in her dark eyes. "They got two twenty-dollar gold pieces for you, so be a good girl. Remember, don't scream or make a lot of noise. You wouldn't want Mrs. Lamphere to find out what you been doin'—she'd tell your mama.

"Okay, boys, she's all yours," said Grace. She backed away from the bed to make room for the men.

Odessa pulled the leather dress down over her knees, but that pulled the top down, and her breasts spilled out, almost completely exposed. One of the men sat down on the bed while the other one removed his coat and hat and started to loosen his belt.

Odessa turned her head to see Grace, a big smile on her face, back out of the room.

She felt sick, belched, and swallowed down the bile.

One of the men, the one with the thinning hair and mustache, reached for her breasts. The other one, she couldn't see his face, crawled between her legs and started kissing her thighs.

A rough hand dug into her womanhood. A scream erupted without her permission.

Following the scream came the vomit. Both men leaped off the bed and cursed her while brushing the filth out of their hair and off their skin.

Odessa slid to the floor and hid between the bed and nightstand. The door burst open. Peeking over the edge of the bed, she saw George. His shoulders filled the doorway, his head nearly touching the header.

Without warning, he grabbed the balding man with the mustache by the seat of his pants and the back of his shirt and tossed him into the hall. She heard the man scream and the thud and bang of his body as he tumbled down the stairwell. The younger of the two men grabbed his coat and hat and leaped across the bed. George lurched around the end of the bed and kicked him in the butt. The man howled. Odessa heard him cursing as he stumbled down the stairs.

Closing her eyes, she wished herself small and invisible. Knuckles in her mouth, her body tucked into a ball, paralyzed with fear and shame, she prayed she would go undetected.

"Odessa…Odessa, it's all right now," Doctor Rayburn said. "We'll get you home. I'll get your coat and your clothes. George will carry you. You're safe, Odessa. Can you hear me?"

Pulling in tighter, she hid her face in the scarf on the table and prayed for death, mortified Doctor Rayburn should find her here like this. The room had gone quiet. Unable to resist, she took a peek, and there he was, George, on his hands and knees, not more than a few inches from her.

****

Elias gathered up Odessa's clothes. Curious, he followed Meda-Belle into the hall and came to a halt. She stood before a closed door at the end of the hall. Without making a sound, Meda-Belle took the handle with both hands, and with a turn of the knob, and the full force of her hip and shoulder, she rammed the door, sending the person on the other side of the door to the floor.

The person on the floor was Grace. Meda-Belle placed the spiked heel of her shoe lightly over the prone woman's throat. "So…you want to play games. Well, here's a game. You pack up and get out. I'll let you keep what you made last night, and I don't kill you. And you don't ever show your face here again."

Plainly, Grace wanted to fight back. Face red, she

squealed curses like the pig she was. Elias considered intervening, then thought better of it. Meda-Belle had the situation under control.

"You better think hard, Grace, before you take me on. I got a couple of pounds on you," said Meda-Belle.

"Get your goddamn, stinkin' foot off my neck, you old bat. I'll leave."

Grace gave Meda-Bell's ankle a good swat and rolled over to get on her feet. "I've had my fun. I got back at the little twat for the paint trick, and I got back at her mama for taking the doc out of my reach. And, it feels like I got a little back for all the snubs I've suffered from the likes of the Laidlaw bitch and all the other snotty women in this town. Maybe them sheepherders over in Shanico could use some excitement."

****

"Come on, Odessa," George said and reached to touch her hand.

Odessa looked into his eyes and blinked. She reached out to him. "George. Oh, George, take me home? I want to go home. I'm so sick."

"You bet you, I take you home, Miss Odessa."

He wrapped her up in the coverlet on the bed and scooped her up with no more effort than it took for him to pick up Beau. "Here, all dis time, I was tinking you vas with Silas, maybe run off wit him. Instead you vas yust in trouble. Hell, I been vatching over you long time. You rest and don't you vorry. You're a little worse for drink. You'll sober quick enough, have a big head for a vhile. I get drunk plenty times, and my head don't fall off."

"Ouch. Oh, George, don't make me laugh." She whimpered and giggled anyway. "I feel so awful. I smell awful, and I can't even imagine what I look like."

"You look pretty silly, like doll in costume. It don't matter to me. You always look pretty like picture to me, Miss Odessa."

Groaning, overcome with shame, she averted her gaze as they passed Doctor Rayburn at the head of the stairs. "No, George, I don't want to be pretty like picture. I think I want to be plain. I never want to be pretty again."

"We got to be what ve are," he said and headed down the stairs.

Meda-Belle had her hat and coat on. She followed them down the stairs and out the door.

Chapter Thirty

Irene sat by the fire, unable to concentrate on her mending. Beau, nearby in his cradle, slept peacefully. When the front door flew open, Irene came to her feet. George, with Odessa in his arms, her daughter's cheeks painted with a circle of orange and her lips dark, ruby-red, the color at odds with the pallor of her skin, struck Irene almost funny in a grotesque, nightmarish way. Hand over her mouth, holding back a sob, Irene swallowed down her rising hysteria.

George moved farther into the room, and the pungent odor of vomit—vomit and alcohol, wafted into every corner. Which brought Irene to the conclusion her daughter was drunk. The question was, where and how had she gotten herself into this state? Elias, looking grim, ushered Meda-Belle inside and closed the door. He handed Irene Odessa's coat, shoes, and clothes.

Her arms full of Odessa's things, Irene followed George into Odessa's room and stood by as he laid Odessa down on her bed.

Irene tried to take solace in the fact Odessa was alive, not hurt, bleeding, or dead somewhere between the Trask house and town, as she'd feared. Or gone, gone with Silas to God knows where—only drunk.

"Irene, now, she ain't hurt," Meda-Belle told her from the doorway. "She's had too much of Grace Wolfe's special peach brandy. That stuff would make a dog sick."

Her mind was in a scattered state. The one thing Irene knew for sure—she didn't want to hear anything Meda-Belle Lamphere had to say.

Recognizing the problem, Meda-Belle backed up. "You go ahead, take care of your girl. I'll wait for you out here and then give you what I know," she said before retreating to the living room.

****

Elias put his hand on Meda-Belle's shoulder. "Come over by the fire. It was good of you to come along."

Meda-Belle reluctantly went with him. "Well, we'll see about that. I sure hope this don't drive a wedge between Irene and me. She's about the only friend I ever had. I can't afford to lose her."

His arm around her, Elias could feel Meda-Belle trembling. He settled her by the fire.

"I'm in a lot of trouble, Doc," Meda-Belle said. She shook her head, her gaze directed toward the flames in the grate. "Almost as much trouble as that girl in there," she said without looking up at him.

"I'm sure you had good intentions. You have a good heart, Meda-Belle," Elias said.

"I don't know…I'd like to blame it on the she-devil, Grace, but I don't think I should let her take all the blame. I should've told Irene right away what was going on. I was watchin' Odessa, and knew what she was doin', keepin' an eye on her these last few weeks. But tonight…tonight I didn't see her come in…I didn't know."

"Before you go beating yourself up too badly, put some of the blame on Odessa. I don't know what happened or what you think you could've done to stop her, but we both know Odessa Obenchain has a way of creating her own catastrophes."

Meda-Belle smiled a weak, lifeless smile. "Yeah, I know. Reminds me of myself when I was a kid. But I didn't have nobody who cared. I didn't have a mama like Irene. You know, I admire that woman more than anyone I ever met. I'd sure hate to lose her as my friend."

Elias shook his head, "Oh, now, I don't think it will come to that," he said. His gaze locked on the door to Odessa's room. He patted Meda-Belle on the back, and speculated as to what, exactly, the girl had been up to.

****

Irene, finding her voice at last, her tone curt and dry, said, "George, thank you." She dropped Odessa's coat, clothes, and shoes on the floor and started to remove the blanket and instantly recognized the costume. It belonged to Grace Wolfe.

"Let's get you cleaned up," she said to Odessa. Adopting the tone she used when nursing patients, Irene could remain detached, efficient, and stop the chaos from taking over her mind.

Accepting his dismissal, George started to leave, but Odessa stopped him. "Are you mad at me?"

Irene saw him squeeze her hand. His blue eyes shifted to meet hers, silently asking her for mercy on Odessa's behalf, then he returned his gaze to Odessa's upturned face. "Aw, I don't tink ve should talk about any of dis now. You sleep. I'm going to stay here. Too far, and too bad da veather is for me to go home."

"I'm sorry," she said.

Breaking Irene's heart, a single tear slid down her daughter's rouged cheek. George's Adam's apple bobbed up and down. He swallowed, nodded, and backed out of the room, closing the door behind him.

Irene handed Odessa a washcloth. Obediently, Odessa scrubbed her face. Irene took the cloth and rinsed it while Odessa got out of the ridiculous leather costume. Irene kept her mouth shut. If she tried to speak, she'd scream.

Odessa thoroughly washed her arms and body before donning her nightdress. Irene took the cloth, said nothing, and tucked Odessa's blankets up to her chin.

"Mama?"

"Don't say anything. I can't stand it." Irene said.

Odessa sank down in her covers and closed her eyes. "Everybody is mad at me—Silas, Sam, Doctor Rayburn, George…and you. Sweet George."

Irene watched the tears run freely down her daughter's white cheeks. It was all she could do not to gather her up in her arms and promise her everything would be all right. But she couldn't do that—she didn't know if anything would ever be all right ever again.

"George asked me to marry him," Odessa said. "I don't think he'll want me now. I'm stupid, I know. I've ruined everything. You don't have to tell me. I can see what you think. I've always known what you thought of me. I could see it in your eyes. You don't say anything, but your eyes say a lot. Did you know that, Mama? Silas said I was dumb, and he's right All this time, I thought I was so smart, smarter than everyone…fooling everyone."

The need to scream and slap the daylights out of her daughter shocked her. Irene had never felt like this before. To strike out went against her nature to nurture and protect.

When she swooped down and grabbed Odessa by

the shoulders and pinned her down to the mattress, her rage frightened her. Shaking, shocked by her own lack of control, she shook Odessa until her eyes began to bulge.

Through gritted teeth, Irene gulped down huge sobs. "I'm sick to death of your inability to see or feel anything for anyone but yourself. Get this through your head, Odessa, I am not, and I have never been *mad* at you. I'm *frightened* for you. I'm frightened by your need to self-destruct. George isn't *mad*. You scared him. You scared everybody. And sometimes I think that's what you want. You want everyone to be scared for you. It's your way of testing us, testing our love for you.

"I don't know the details." Irene shook her head and closed her eyes. "I don't need to know," she said, her gaze locked with Odessa's startled countenance. "I know whatever you've done, George saw the danger, even if you didn't. I love you. I've always loved you. I will continue to love you and care what happens to you, as will George, poor man, and Elias, and Sam and Ruby. We all care what happens to you.

"You have a son who depends on you to take care of yourself so that you can take care of him. You don't have any guarantee he'll love you the way you want.

"What puzzles me, what makes me want to shake some sense in you, is why…why can't you accept our love? Why isn't it enough? Why do you challenge us all the time? I don't know why you feel as if you're all alone.

"Maybe it's you, Odessa, who doesn't love. Maybe it's you who withholds love, keeps it locked away inside. Stop it! Stop it right now. Stop being so damn stubborn. I'm afraid if you don't, you could end up all alone, blaming everyone for the loss of your son, for the loss of a man who wants nothing more than to make you the center of his universe.

"Start loving yourself, Odessa," Irene begged. Tears blurred her vision and choked her words. "You are worth it…you are. Wake up before you do something so…*despicable*…unforgivable that not even you will be able to live with it."

Irene pushed herself away. She had to save herself from slapping the girl. She had to get away from her before she did something, said something she would never be able to forgive or forget.

****

Elias and Irene sat at the table with Meda-Belle. Meda-Belle took a deep breath and gave them a rundown of the evening's events and Odessa's previous visits to the saloon. George stood at the fireplace, his hands in his pockets. Silent and sober, he sipped a toddy of rum and coffee.

Meda-Belle gathered her coat and rose to leave. Irene came to her feet and wrapped her arms around her. "You've always been a good friend to me and now to Odessa. We owe you our gratitude. It was lucky for Odessa you saw through her disguise, and tonight…well…she was lucky, that's all."

"It sure don't feel like I did nothin'. I wish now I'd done it differently. Maybe I could've talked some sense into her or scared her off somehow."

Irene laughed and swiped a tear from her cheek. "Oh, Meda-Belle, you will never know how many times I've said that to myself. I don't think there's much anyone could've said to reach her. Odessa had to find out for herself. I hope she's finally learned her lesson. I don't know how many more times I can stand picking up the pieces and putting Odessa back together."

****

In their bed, with Beau in his cradle on her side of the bed, Irene and Elias lay in each other's arms, talking. The room, as usual, was enveloped in darkness, with a few coals glowing in the fireplace.

"George didn't have much to say," Elias said into the darkness.

"I noticed that too," Irene said, positioning her body to get closer to him.

"Did Odessa tell you what happened between her and Silas?"

"No, well, she said he told her she was stupid."

"Good old Silas, how very helpful of him. I hope to hell he goes away and stays away," Elias said and folded his arm across her bosom to draw her close.

"Yes...I do too," Irene said, keeping her true thoughts to herself. In her heart, she wished Silas Trask to the devil, along with Grace Wolfe, but that wasn't very Christian of her. Finding they had very little else to say on the subject, they kissed, closed their eyes and eventually fell asleep.

****

Irene opened her eyes and sat up in bed. The room was dark but for the soft sliver of light coming from the other side of their bedroom door. She glanced toward the baby's cradle and swung her feet over the side of the bed to be sure he was all right. The cradle was empty. Beau was gone.

Chapter Thirty-One

"He's been really fussy lately. Mama says he's teething."

Bedroom door opened a crack, Irene couldn't see Odessa or George. She presumed Odessa was talking to George. For a few tense seconds, silence ensued, and she waited to hear more.

"Yesterday, I would've said he didn't like me," Odessa said.

Irene sucked in her breath and closed her eyes—she knew the feeling.

"Too little he is to tink like dat," George said.

And to herself, Irene blessed George.

"I know," Odessa said.

"I didn't want him, you know," Odessa said, her voice so quiet it was almost a whisper. Irene had to strain to hear. Opening their bedroom door a little more, the better to see and hear. Irene held her breath; she wanted to hear this. She didn't want to miss a word.

"I blamed the baby for keeping me from finding Silas. Then the baby was here, and I felt like he was using me, taking advantage of me. So I stopped nursing him. I thought that would be better, but it wasn't, because…because he liked Mama better than me. He cried when I held him, and he was quiet and sweet with her."

"Odessa," George interrupted, "I don't need to hear

all dis, not really. I already suspected how you vere feeling. It isn't all dat uncommon for a young motter to feel overvhelmed, I don't tink."

"No, George, don't make excuses for me. I want to tell you these things. You saved me…I need to tell you these things…I need you to understand who I really am.

"Silas said he loved me, but that was because he wanted…well, you know what he wanted. I was silly enough to let him because I thought he would help me run away. I can't explain why I wanted to run away. I guess I've always wanted to run away. I thought my papa left to get away from my mama. Now I think he just wanted to go somewhere else.

"Like my papa, I thought there had to be a better somewhere else. But I wanted to be somewhere else with Silas. Silas said we were alike, and I think we are. We think about ourselves, and we don't care what anyone else might need…or how they might feel. I know my papa was like that. I know that now."

Her voice had drifted away. Irene chanced a glance through the crack in the door. Odessa had turned her head away from the fire. She swiped her cheeks with the back of her hand. George offered her his kerchief.

Irene choked back a sob and clamped her hand over her mouth.

George put his arm around Odessa's shoulder.

Irene tried to remember to breathe.

Odessa finally said, "Mama says you aren't mad at me."

"No, I ain't mad at you."

"She says I scared you."

"You sure did," George said. He leaned forward and set his chin gently against her brow.

"I didn't…I wasn't…thinking…about anyone but myself," Odessa said, her hand going to his jaw.

Drawing away, she dropped her hand to her lap.

George squared his shoulders, but his arm remained about her shoulders.

"I feel dirty and stupid and worthless. The things Silas said…I guess, they made me kind of crazy."

She paused, took a deep breath, set her spine straight, and faced George. "I went into the saloon to listen to the music. Like I'd done before. The music always made me feel better. I never thought…I didn't think anyone would even notice me."

Irene heard the sob and ached to hold her.

"You probably don't want to marry me now."

His eyes to the fire, George removed his arm, braced his elbows on his thighs, and set his chin in the palms of his hands.

Irene felt guilty for eavesdropping, which increased twofold when Elias sneaked up behind her and put a hand on her shoulder. Instead of pulling her away from the door, he cocked his head to one side of her head to hear better.

Irene sniffed back her tears and patted his hand.

George sat back, long legs stretched toward the fire, arms folded across his broad chest, eyes to the hearth. "Vhile I vas driving dem cows, I thought about you and how you don't love me so much. I tink maybe you laugh at me sometimes because I'm big and slow. I don't know if you could ever tink wary much of me. I vondered maybe you vould soon get tired of me…run off with Silas, or some otter fella. I thought maybe dat's vhat you done ven I come here to see you for answer to question."

Irene held her breath.

"If you vas to do dat, I don't tink I could live no more. I got a big love for you," George said to Odessa's face.

Irene couldn't see his profile, but she'd heard him just fine.

"The voman I take to wife, a strong voman she vill have to be, a voman who can vork at my side is vhat I need, vhat I vant. Cattle I got now. Driving dem to market I vill, and my wife she vill go vit me. My little sister is coming to help vit da house, and she vould be good with Beau. I want lots of children. I like dem. My wife, she's got to vant dem too.

"I don't know if you can do all dat. I tink you got it in you to do dat. You're a strong girl, and you ain't afraid, but I don't know if you got big enough heart?"

Odessa removed the bottle from the sleepy baby's mouth and put Beau across her lap on his stomach. As Irene had shown her, Odessa patted Beau gently on his back until he burped.

Irene heard him mew a little protest when Odessa placed him in his cradle. But he quieted, and Irene smiled. Her lips began to tremble. Feeling something akin to pride, tears welled up in her eyes.

Odessa turned and fastened her gaze on George. Hands in her lap, she said, "I don't know if I know how to do all of what is needed to be a rancher's wife. But I know I want to try. I liked helping Sam with his farm. I know your ranch is big. I also know you have big plans to make it even bigger. I can learn. I would want to be included in everything. I don't want to be left behind ever again. If you still want me...I'm going to love you as much as you love me."

Odessa paused and put her hand to George's jaw.

"You're right about my laughing at you. But I think I know what to do about that. It's the way you dress. Your pants are too short, George. I could make you a new suit. Mama would probably help me."

"You vould do dat for me?"

"I would love to do that for you," Odessa said.

"Love?" George asked.

"Love…George," Odessa said.

They embraced and kissed.

Irene, weeping quietly, closed her door and turned into her husband's arms.

****

"They look happy, don't they?" Irene asked, locked in Elias's arms, waltzing to "Moonlight on the Water." The late afternoon sun warmed the big meadow beyond the trees of the church.

"She looks radiant. All brides look radiant," Elias said, his lips close to her forehead.

"I know…but Odessa…we know she's… Well, not so long ago, her heart wasn't exactly engaged."

"Will you stop—I believe she's really happy now. George looks handsome. I heard her tell him."

Irene pulled back to gaze into his eyes. "She told him he looked handsome?"

"She did. When I gave her to him at the altar, I heard her whisper."

"Well, she did a very nice job on his new suit. He does look very imposing in dark blue. It brings out the color of his blond hair and his sky-blue eyes," Irene said. "Did you see, he bought her a big music box as a wedding present, with lots of disks…some of them rag-time."

"I did see," Elias said. "I also took note how they

laughed together, enjoying the private joke. I think there's hope for this marriage. I really do."

They circled around the green to the music, accepting congratulations from everyone. When the music stopped, Elias started to guide Irene over to where George's sister Lena sat in the shade with Beau, but Irene stopped him. "Take me somewhere quiet for a minute. I'm feeling a little giddy with it all. Maybe some water."

Elias smiled and veered off to a more secluded spot behind the church. They sat for a moment in silence on the steps at the back door of the church. He waited for her to tell him why she looked so worried. Her daughter was happily married today to a kind, caring man. Her grandchild had fallen into the cream with the arrival of Lena. It seemed to Elias their worries had dwindled down to practically nothing.

"Here you are," said Sarah Laidlaw, a cup of punch in each hand. "I thought I saw you two sneak away. It is warm this afternoon. I thought you both could use a little something to quench your thirst."

Sarah held up her hand. "I won't bother you but for a moment. I wanted to say I'm very happy how things have turned out. I suppose your big old house will seem very empty now."

Before Irene could think of anything to say, Elias spoke up, "Hmmm, no, not for long."

Sarah's mouth dropped open, her eyes darted from Irene's blushing countenance, then to Elias's grinning aspect.

"Elias…" Irene hissed.

"Are you…Irene…are you expecting?" Sarah asked.

"Ah, now…now, Sarah," Elias said, giving her a

wink and a warning smile, "You'll have to wait and see."

"Oh, you two—well, congratulations." Giggling to herself, Sarah rushed off, no doubt, to spread the word.

Irene heaved a sigh of exasperation. After a restorative sip of her punch, she said, "Whatever were you thinking? You practically told her I'm going to have a baby."

"I did, didn't I? Well...we are, aren't we?"

Irene's mouth dropped open. She squirmed to avoid his eyes. Cheeks warm and upper lip dewy, she blushed.

Oh, Elias did love to make her blush. Irene did blush easily these days. "Yes...we are," she said, forcing herself to look him square in the eye. "I was going to tell you. I wanted to tell you. How long have you known?"

"Oh, Odessa and I speculated about it weeks ago."

"Odessa?"

"Yes, she noticed you falling asleep in the middle of the day. And your lack of appetite in the morning and your sudden craving for pickle relish on everything from baked potatoes to corn muffins, which I have to say is disgusting."

"Odessa knows?"

"Yes, she knows," he said. A sly smile twitched at his lips.

"Is she all right with this? I mean, it is a little strange. I'm a grandmother. Elias, are you all right with this? I can get a little obsessive with babies. I'll try not to, but I can't promise. I'm very frightened, you know. I lost a baby, as you know...and Jessie died of influenza. I didn't want to say anything until I was really certain."

"My dear Irene, I don't think it strange you are with child—on the contrary, it's perfectly natural. And as for me, I am absolutely beside myself with glee. You will never know how difficult it's been for me to hold my tongue until you decided to let me in on your condition. Odessa has been very good about disguising her glee as well, so have no fear there.

"As for your obsession with babies, I think we'll have a contest to see who's the more obsessive, you or me. And as to your fears—I am going to take good care of you. This baby is going to be born healthy with all his fingers and toes and right on time…Christmas…I think." He enfolded her in his arms and proceeded to convince her of his happiness for a few moments.

"I think I knew your condition before you," he said, his voice husky with desire.

"Oh, did you, now?" Irene challenged, taking a moment to catch her breath.

"Hmmm, your lovely breasts…they gave the game away." His fingers traced her nipples over the bodice of her new, green satin dress. Instantly, they came to attention. She blushed and squirmed with desire.

"Meda-Belle guessed too," he said, and held her a little tighter, anticipating her reaction, a playful grin on his face.

"What? Does the whole town know?"

"Meda-Belle doesn't think you should be taking in her laundry anymore, and I quite agree."

"Oh…you two decided that, did you?" Irene challenged and pushed herself out of his too-close embrace.

"Yes, that's what we decided. You may continue to do custom sewing," he conceded, "but only if you want to."

"Oh, well, thank you very much," she said and popped up and began to sputter and pace in front of the steps. "Everybody knows I'm pregnant. That's wonderful," she said to the treetops.

"Yes, it does make it easier, you know. And Ruby is waiting to do the wedding-ring-on-the-string-thing over your tummy. She's sixteen and zero so far. She's anxious to make twenty. So we have to help her all we can. She has a reputation to think of now."

Irene stopped and turned her furious gaze upon her husband, then both of them began to laugh. They laughed until they cried, and they would love until they died.

A word about the author...

Born in Burlington, Iowa, the youngest of six children, all of us spaced three to four years apart, which meant that I had an older brother who was twenty when I was born. Moved with my parents, and an older sister, to Oregon when I was ten years old. Grew up in the Willamette Valley, attended a vocational school, clerk stenographer course, which was enlightening but not useful. Married my high-school sweetheart. Had two children.

I've worn many hats—store clerk, meat wrapper, kite factory production line, pumped gas, then I discovered water exercise because of debilitating arthritis and became an instructor. I enjoyed that for eighteen satisfying years. I still do water exercise for my own enjoyment and wellbeing but no longer instruct. I began writing my own stories about the time my husband went on swing shift. I was a big fan of the Georgian period, Georgette Heyer being my favorite author. Back then you had to type the manuscript on paper and send it off through the post. Came close to being published a couple of times. Then the years passed and I started to write Oregon historical fiction. I create characters who become my family. I'm home when I tell their stories, I laugh, I cry, I fume and fuss, I cheer for them, and I'm proud to be near them.

We've moved a lot, lived in California, Idaho, Washington, Oregon Coast, Central Oregon, but we always return to the Willamette Valley. Every time we've moved, we roam and learn the history and the past around us, including the geographical past, as well as discovering the impact of the human occupants. Those details I strive to add to my stories. I want the reader to see, smell, be immersed in the time and place, and join the community in which my characters live. I write stories I love to read.

Thank you for purchasing
this publication of The Wild Rose Press, Inc.

For questions or more information
contact us at
info@thewildrosepress.com.

The Wild Rose Press, Inc.
www.thewildrosepress.com